THE KITCHEN MAID

When Jenny secures a job as a kitchen maid in a grand house in Beverley, she gains the attention of Christy, the young master of the house, but their love culminates in a scandal which forces Jenny to leave Beverley and everything she knows. Cast aside by her own family, Jenny has to rely on her ailing aunt Agnes and her husband Stephen St John Laslett, who have been disowned by his wealthy family. As Agnes grows weaker she asks Stephen to make her an unusual promise – one which makes Jenny the mistress of Laslett Hall...

THE KITCHEN MAID

THE KITCHEN MAID

by

Valerie Wood

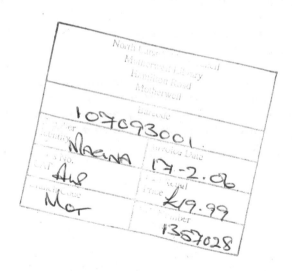

Magna Large Print Books
Long Preston, North Yorkshire,
BD23 4ND, England.

British Library Cataloguing in Publication Data.

Wood, Valerie
        The kitchen maid.

        A catalogue record of this book is
        available from the British Library

        ISBN   0-7505-2425-1

First published in Great Britain in 2004 by Bantam Press
a division of Transworld Publishers

Copyright © Valerie Wood 2004

Cover illustration © Gordon Crabb

The right of Valerie Wood to be identified as the author of this work
has been asserted in accordance with sections 77 and 78 of the
Copyright, Designs and Patents Act, 1988

Published in Large Print 2005 by arrangement with
Transworld Publishers

Magna Large Print is an imprint of Library Magna Books Ltd.

Printed and bound in Great Britain by
T.J. (International) Ltd., Cornwall, PL28 8RW

To my family with love

ACKNOWLEDGEMENTS

My special thanks and appreciation to my editor Linda Evans and all the Transworld team who have shown that they believe in me.

My thanks and love as always to Peter, Ruth, Catherine and Alex for their constant support and encouragement.

Books for general reading:

Old Beverley by Philip Brown. East Yorkshire Local History Society in association with Humberside Leisure Services, 1983 (reprinted 1987).
Historic Beverley by Ivan and Elisabeth Hall. Sponsored by Beverley Borough Council, 1973.
A Time to Reap by Stephen Harrison. The Driffield Agricultural Society, 2000.
An Historical Atlas of East Yorkshire, edited by Susan Neave and Stephen Ellis. The University of Hull Press, 1996.

CHAPTER ONE

The door clanged behind her, heavy, solid and final. Jenny grasped the bars at the top, standing on tiptoe to see through them. 'Fetch me paper and pencil, will you?' Her voice broke into a dry sob as she shouted to the retreating warder. 'Please.'

'Want to write a confession, do you?' his muffled voice called back.

She sank down onto the wooden bench and put her head in her hands, her shoulders shaking. How have I come to this? Christy! What have we done?

At midday the door was unlocked and she was handed several sheets of thin paper and a stub of pencil, and a tin bowl of lukewarm soup that she tasted and then poured away into a metal pail, which stank of other people's urine. She gazed at the blank paper, scribbled on a corner of it with the blunt pencil then scraped the tip against the brick wall to sharpen it. There's not a great deal to write, she pondered. But I must write everything down just as I've always done, in case I forget; or I'm sent on elsewhere and don't ever come out, which is more than likely, as it seems as if everything and everyone is against me. So this is for me, not for them.

She put the tip of her tongue between her teeth and began.

'They said that I'd killed him. They stared at me and pointed an accusing finger. They wanted me to say, yes, I did. It would have made it easier for them. But I didn't say it. I said, why would I do that? I loved him.

He laughed, the constable, I mean. Christy's mother didn't laugh. She screamed at me that I was a whore. A jezebel. The sort of language that I never expected to hear from a lady's lips. Well of course she was upset, who wouldn't be, seeing your only son lying in a pool of blood with a great hole in his chest?

It looks bad for me, I realize that. I was holding the gun. It was in my hand when the master rushed in. He had to prise it from my fingers to take it from me. I didn't speak at first. Couldn't speak. All I could do was stare at Christy, with his neck stretched back and his handsome face so still. I hardly remember what happened next, only that they brought me here and locked me up, even though I swore that I hadn't done it. But of course I can't tell them everything. I'll have to give them a story and stick to it.

I saw him for the first time at the kitchen door. I was new. It was my very first place of work and everything was confusing. Everybody was above me, of course. I was the lowest of the low. But my ma told me that I was very lucky to get such a position, especially coming from Hull when usually Beverley folk would normally only employ Beverley girls. I don't know how my ma knew that, seeing as she had never in her whole life set foot outside the town of Hull, but that was what she said. She was a bit jealous, I suspect, because I was leaving to go somewhere fresh and somewhere she had never been.

I was dead set on working in Beverley. I wanted to get out of Hull. Not because I didn't like it, but because I wanted to see other places and I'd heard about Beverley with its racecourse and a pleasant bit of countryside round about. So I set off one day; I was thirteen and I'd found sixpence in the Market Place and instead of giving it to Ma as I should have done, to help out with the groceries, I kept it, and as soon as I was able to get away I cadged a lift from the carrier who was going to Beverley. I'd like to have travelled on the train but I didn't have enough money and I would have had to wait a long time before I found another sixpence. I didn't tell Ma where I was going and I knew I would get a leathering when I got home, because she had sent me out on an errand and expected me back within the hour.

It was grand travelling with the carrier. He was a real friendly fellow and when I told him that I only had sixpence and was going to look for a place of work, he said he would take me there and back for that price, as long as I wasn't late for the pick up near the King's Head. I sat up at the front with him and he told me what he knew about Beverley, about the big houses in New Walk and about the Beverley beck where the barges were and which ran through to the river Hull; and about the tannery, which stank something rotten sometimes. No worse than the blubber yards or the oil mills in Hull, I bet, I said to him and he agreed that it wasn't. He told me

15

there was even a place called Paradise, and I laughed and didn't believe him, but I found out later that it was true.

We passed through some lovely country, proper country, I mean, with open fields and cows and sheep in them and bushes and trees. Real pretty it was, and I got a good feeling inside me and thought how much I'd like to live here. When we arrived in Beverley, I fell silent. I was overwhelmed. I could see the big church, which the carrier told me was called the Minster, and I could hear the bells ringing, a right din they were making, and then we drove through one market place which he said was called Wednesday Market and had an obelisk in the middle of it, and then into another, which he said was called Saturday Market. There was a great hustle and bustle there with waggons and carriers and men on horseback and folks milling about on their business. It wasn't quite square, and it had cobbles underfoot, and around it old buildings and shops still with the little glass windows, which hadn't yet been gutted and improved like they have been in Hull. There were inns and shops and a fish shambles, and a splendid monument with columns and the Beverley coat of arms above it, which the carrier told me was the Market Cross and was used for proclamations.

He dropped me off and said I should be back in good time because he wouldn't be able to wait, and then he pointed up the road and said I should go up to New Walk and take a chance that somebody there might take me on, even though I didn't have a reference which he said they would ask for. I didn't know what a reference was, but I reckoned that I could manage to do a job of work without one.

It didn't take me long to walk up there; it was only a small town and I passed another lovely church called St Mary's, and some more shops and inns and alehouses, and several pumps where I took a drink of good water, and I reckoned that Beverley folk were as well catered for in their bodily and spiritual needs as they were in the town of Hull.

As I went out of the town I went through an archway which when I looked up I saw had a house on either side of it. I'd never seen anything like it before and haven't since, but I learnt later that it was called North Bar and the inside of it is called Within and the outside of it Without. It has a gate and is one of the ancient entrances to the town. I've often wondered since what the people living upstairs thought about folks coming and going underneath their house.

I felt as if I was in the countryside as I went up New Walk. It was very pretty and lined with shady trees and hedges and there were wooden seats for folks to sit on, so I could only guess that it was a place where those who had the time and leisure used to walk. The houses were only few and what I would call substantial. Most of them had gardens and some had stables and paddocks where horses were grazing. Well, Jenny, I thought. Nothing venture, nothing gain, so I smoothed down my hair and went down the first path to a house of three storeys and made my way round to the back.

My mother calls me a plain girl. You weren't in

17

the front row when they were giving out beauty, she was always reminding me, but then nobody will ever think you're flighty for you look very sensible, even though you're not. I'm not very tall, my nose is small and straight, and my mouth is quite wide; my father says my smile fills my face. My eyes are good, though, hazel-coloured with long lashes, but my hair is straight and dark brown and I generally wear it in a plait as I am doing now and did on that day. So I thought that my plain looks might stand me in good stead at gaining employment and that beauty would possibly be a disadvantage.

It was not to be, however, for the first kitchen door was simply closed in my face as I made my request, and when I knocked at the second one the girl who answered it said I couldn't be seen without a reference. When I owned that I hadn't one, she shook her head and said it was of no use even asking. She did, though, as if taking pity on me, suggest I walked on a little further to try a house owned by Mr Ingram, who was a gentleman. I supposed her to mean by that that he didn't have to work for a living, which must be a very nice position to be in. The girl said that she had heard that their kitchen maid had just left, so I might be lucky if they weren't too particular. I hoped that the significance of her remark was that I didn't possess a reference and not anything to do with my character or appearance, and I decided to try my luck there.

It was an imposing dwelling and I thought that I would be very lucky indeed if I were able to work there. I knocked boldly on the kitchen door and asked the girl who opened it if Mrs Ingram was requiring any kitchen staff. I thought it wouldn't do any harm to use her name, as if I had heard of her. I was asked in and the girl called out for the cook.

I gave her a neat bob of my knee, because I guessed that she was quite important in the household, and immediately informed her, in my best manner, that I didn't have a reference and hoped that it didn't matter.

"I'm a good worker," I told her. "Clean and honest." I thought it best not to mention that I had come to Beverley with a found sixpence, though that hardly qualifies as dishonesty.

"Where have you worked before?" she demanded quite fiercely. "Are you from Beverley? Cos I can soon find out about you."

I confessed that I was a stranger to the town and that my birthplace was Hull and that I had only worked at home for my mother who had taught me about housekeeping. That was the real reason for my wanting to come to Beverley, though I didn't tell her that. I'm one of ten children, you see, fourth from youngest with three boys below me. Of the six others, three boys and three girls, one boy and one girl had left to get married, the others were employed but still lived at home, and being the only girl left without a job of work I knew that I would never get away, because I was too useful.

My father has always had a steady job – he's a foreman down at the docks – and my mother works three days a week at the washhouse. She took our dirty washing every fortnight and had it done for free, and sometimes boiled a suet pudding there, so she wasn't keen to give up work and stay at home to do the jobs that she said I could do.

I could quite see that my life was planned out. I would look after the younger boys until they were old enough to work, and I would do the cooking, shopping and cleaning for the others, and I didn't care for the prospect. Not one bit.

"How old are you?" the cook asked.

"Nearly fourteen," I replied and reckoned that eight months off my birthday was near enough.

"And never worked?"

She sounded scandalized and I hastily explained that my mother preferred me to be at home to help her, but that I wanted to be independent and earn my own living.

"Well," she said. "It just so happens that I need a kitchen maid." She ran her fingers over one of her chins as she gazed at me. "I prefer a country girl really. They know how to work. And I've never taken anybody on without a reference before."

"Where would I get one?" I asked, seeing the job slipping away from me and thinking that if it meant buying one, I could ask my father who was much more generous than my mother.

She frowned from under her eyebrows, which were grey and shaggy, and said, "Well, from anybody who knows you to be of good character."

"That's all right then," I said. "I can get that all right. When can I start?"

She told me that I could start straight away as long as I brought the reference with me. I was to get ten pounds a year, but could have an advance of two shillings when I had been there a month and proved satisfactory. I would get two sets of clothing, plain dresses and aprons, and four caps, the price of which would be taken out of my wages, and which I must keep clean, washed and ironed at all times.

Now all I had to do was go home and face my mother and obtain a reference.

I told the carrier about it on the way home. "I'll give you a reference," he said. "You seem a bright cheerful girl to me," and so he did. When we arrived back in Hull, he pulled out a sheet of paper from a box under the seat. "What's your name?" he asked, and when I told him it was Jenny Graham, he wrote it down, *Jenny Graham is a bright cheerful girl*, then he signed it. The paper had his name on it. I suppose he used it for his customers as a receipt like our grocer did for his better-off customers.

I passed the grocer on my way home so I popped in and asked him if he could give me a reference and he did, which said I was sharp with figures and knew a bargain when I saw one.

By the time I arrived home, I had another from the butcher, one from the apothecary, one from a friend of mine who said if I wrote it as I was better at spelling and had a better hand than she had, then she would sign it, and by a stroke of luck I had met Miss Smithers who had taught me for the short time I was at school, and remembered me, and said she would write one that evening if I would care to call round at her lodgings to collect it.

Another stroke of luck was that my da was at

home when I got back, but not my mother, who, he said, had gone out looking for me. "You've been gone all day," he said. "She was beginning to think you'd run off."

"I didn't run off, Da," I told him. "I've been out to get a job. And I've got one, as a kitchen maid in a big house in Beverley. Will Ma be mad at me, do you think?"

"She might." He pondered. "Is it what you want, our Jenny? Do you want to leave home?"

I nodded. Yes, I did. My sisters worked at the mills and they all came home after work too worn out to help with anything like housework, but not too tired to brush their hair and go out to meet the lads at the inns in town.

"All right," he said. "I'll speak up for you."

He'd always had a soft spot for me, had Da. He never leathered me as Ma did if I did something wrong, and I knew I'd miss him.

This will be the last time I ever get the strap, I thought, wincing with pain, and when Ma put her arm back to give another blow I put my hand behind my back. "I'll not be able to work tomorrow if my hands are swollen, Ma, and I shan't want to tell Cook why."

"That's enough," my father said. "She deserves 'strap for not telling where she was going, but she doesn't merit a leathering for getting a job. She's done well there, going all 'way to Beverley by herself."

Ma was silenced then, for although my da was a quiet man, once he had made a stand he always stuck to it, and that was when she said how lucky I was. I gave a bit of a smile inside then, for I knew that my mother would boast to all the folk she knew about her youngest daughter who had obtained a position of work in Beverley.

CHAPTER TWO

'Da gave me sixpence for the journey the following day, but it wasn't the same carrier as previously and he was rather morose and not inclined to talk. It was raining hard, so by the time we arrived in Beverley and I had walked to Mr Ingram's house, I was cold, wet and hungry and beginning to think that perhaps I might have acted hastily in leaving a comfortable home. We were not rich by any means but neither were we poor. My older brothers and sisters, those who were still at home, made a contribution to the household pot and so we were able to pay our rent, buy coal and have at least one good meal on the table every day as well as gruel for breakfast. We were better off by far than a lot of people.

When I arrived at the house it was well past dinnertime, but the servants were just sitting down to their meal. Mary, who answered the door to me as she had done the day before, asked me in, told me to drop down my bag and wash my hands, then come and eat. "We eat after we've fed them upstairs," she said, "so if they've not finished off all the meat, then we can have it."

I dipped my knee to all of those sitting down at table for they all turned to look at me, and then they shuffled up on the bench to make room. "This is Jenny Graham, Mrs Judson," said Cook to a grim-faced woman dressed in black who was sitting opposite her. "If she's brought a satisfactory reference, she'll replace 'girl who's left."

Mrs Judson looked at me without smiling, as did a bald-headed elderly man who was sitting at the head of the table. I wondered what he did for he seemed too old to work, and I discovered later that he didn't do very much except look after the wine cellar and the silver, and wait on table, and that he had been with the family so long that he couldn't be replaced. He was the butler and his name was Thompson, but we always called him Sir.

"Is she a Beverley girl?" Mrs Judson asked, and I was about to open my mouth to answer when I caught sight of Mary who shook her head and put her finger to her lips.

"No, Mrs Judson, she is not," Cook replied. "But then I didn't want a Beverley girl. If you have local girls they're always wanting to run home on some errand or other, or else they attract followers, and I won't have that. That's why I prefer country girls, like Mary. They're much more sensible, but then," she gave a deep sigh, "beggars can't be choosers."

"And where are you from, girl?" Mr Thompson asked me directly, looking at me over his spectacles and down his mottled red nose.

"I'm from Hull, sir," I said. "Born and bred." I was going to give him my history, but on glancing at Mary again I decided against it. There was silence then whilst we ate and I had never in my life seen such a good dinner on the table. A leg of pork which was less than half eaten, a big dish of floury potatoes and a bowl of peas which were very sweet and tasty. When we'd finished all of that, we had a steamed treacle pudding with a hot sauce.

I would have liked to have a lie down after such a feast, but the cook called me to her as she sat in a comfortable chair and Mary and another girl cleared away the dirty dishes. I stood in front of her as she looked over my references and then she said, "Do all these people know you?"

"Yes, mum." Well they did, all but the carrier. "They know me to be of good character," I said, remembering that good character was what she had wanted.

"But they don't say if you are any good around a kitchen," she grumbled. "And call me Cook, if you please, or Mrs Feather."

I decided that I couldn't possibly call her Mrs Feather for she looked so unlike one, being very portly and solid in figure. "They wouldn't know about that, Cook," I replied. "You'd have to ask my ma."

She humphed a bit and pondered, and then said, "I'll try you out. See how you shape. Start with washing 'pans and dishes and then I'll get Mary to tell you your duties and show you where you'll sleep."

We slept, Mary and I and a parlour maid called Polly who was a good deal older than us, in a room at the top of the house that was reached by narrow back stairs. There was a small window in the roof and if we stood on a chair we could see for miles. I loved to do that for there was a view of trees and meadows and birds flying about, and several times I saw a fox slinking alongside a hedge. In the far distance there were some hills that Mary said were the Wolds, which was where she came from. Oh, yes, and up there I could hear the church bells ringing, both the Minster's and St Mary's. The room had three small beds, a chest of drawers where we each had one drawer, and a washstand with a jug and bowl. There was a chamber pot under each bed and I was glad of that, for I wouldn't have wanted to share with strangers. It's different with family. At home we had one for the girls and one for the boys, but Ma and Da had their own.

So I looked around and thought that this was to be my home from now on, and I made myself as comfortable as possible.

The next morning I was to set to work proper. I was to rise first and rake the kitchen fire which was kept in all night. Then I had to set the table for the servants' breakfast. Mary said she would get up with me on the first day and tell me what to do, but after that I must muddle along as best I could and she would have an extra half-hour in bed.

It wasn't hard work, though I didn't like scrubbing the floors. Cook never seemed to be satisfied and would poke about in all the corners looking for dirt. At home I only ever swept our floor with a besom, for my mother said it was a waste of water to wash it when there were always feet tramping in and out. What I did miss about home, though, was slipping out of the house when the work was done and the dinner prepared, and going to have a wander around the Market Place or a stroll down to the pier. I had had a sort of freedom, which I didn't have at the Ingrams' house. When one job was done there was another one waiting, and because I was the lowest of the low, I was at everyone's beck and call.

I'd been there a month before I saw anybody from upstairs and that was because Mrs Judson, who had come down to the kitchen to have a glass of ale with Cook, realized that she had left a pair of Mrs Ingram's gloves, which she was bringing down for cleaning, on the hall table.

"Slip up and get them, Jenny," she said. "But don't let anyone see you."

Mary and Polly were elsewhere, otherwise she wouldn't have asked me. I straightened my cap and smoothed down my apron. I was wearing my afternoon white one, not my morning grey, and hurried upstairs into the hall. I'd picked up the gloves and was just having a quick look round and admiring the polished floor and the perfume of the flowers, and the gilt mirror on the wall, for I hadn't been up here before, when the front door suddenly opened. I hadn't realized that Mr Ingram had his own key. I thought he rang the doorbell like everyone else and had it opened for him by Mary or Polly when they saw or heard the indicator jangling in the box in the kitchen.

"Door," someone would shout and off they would dash up the stairs. Anyway, there he was and there I was, and I dipped my knee, murmured 'sir', and backed away to the kitchen stairs. I needn't have worried though, for although he looked at me he didn't see me, and it was then I realized that I was invisible. We all were, even Mary and Polly, who cleaned the rooms and laid

27

the fires and changed the bed and table linen, and helped at table. Only Cook and Mrs Judson and Mr Thompson were seen by those upstairs.

Then one afternoon I heard the kitchen door sneck rattle and I went to open it. The door sticks sometimes. Polly was upstairs serving tea to Mrs Ingram and some of her friends who had called. Mary was out on an errand and Cook was having a nap.

"Just a minute," I called out, thinking it was Jem, the general lad who brings in the coal and does odd jobs. Him and me are about on a par for status, though he's been there longer than me and takes delight in telling me so. "Hold your hat on, I'm coming."

Imagine my surprise when I pulled the door open and a stranger stood there. He gave me a grin and said hello in a very familiar way and started to come in.

I put my hand up to stop him. "Hold on," I said, though not impolitely. "Who are you? What's your business?"

He stared at me for a moment, then he laughed. "And who are you? I haven't seen you before."

I lowered my hand then, for by his accent he wasn't a servant, but I couldn't understand why he was using the kitchen door. "I'm Jenny," I said. "Kitchen maid."

"Well, how de do, Jenny kitchen-maid." He made a mock bow and took hold of my hand. "I am extremely pleased to meet you."

I was quite nonplussed. He was older than me, tall and rather thin. He was handsome in an intense kind of way with dark eyes and curly hair, though I've always preferred fair males, being dark myself. But his eyes and manner were merry and he had a very winning smile.

"Where's Cook," he asked, "and Mrs Judson?" He peered over my shoulder and with that I moved on one side to let him in, realizing that he wasn't a stranger to the house.

"Cook's asleep," I said. "I think Mrs Judson's upstairs."

"Good," he said. "So I can sneak in."

"Sneak in?" I was quite perturbed. "Sneak in upstairs?"

He nodded and started to take off his jacket, which I noticed had green marks on the sleeves. "I've been on the Westwood, larking around with some of the local lads. I've got rather muddy and Mama will not be very pleased if she sees me like this. Is there anything to eat, Jenny kitchen-maid?"

"But – who are you – sir?" I added. "Do you live here?"

He nodded. "I'm mostly away at school, but now I'm home for the holidays. Christopher Ingram – Christy, everybody calls me, except my father, of course. He always calls me Christopher."

"I beg your pardon, Mr Christopher," I apologized. "I didn't know. Nobody said anything about a son." But then, I thought, why would they? I wasn't supposed to know about anything that went on upstairs, though I did know that there was a daughter, Julia, and she had a governess, Miss James, who never came downstairs.

Just then Polly came into the kitchen with an empty tray in her hand. She nodded to him and murmured, "Afternoon, Master Christy." It was

29

more of a mutter than a murmur, for she was rather a sour puss was Polly and rarely smiled.

"Good afternoon to you too, Polly. I was just asking Jenny kitchen-maid if there was anything to eat, cake or something." He looked at the cake that Polly was taking out of a tin. "That looks scrumptious."

"It's for upstairs, Master Christy," she said grumpily. "But I'll cut you a slice." Which she did, then put the rest onto a china plate with a pretty linen doily underneath. She cut up a slab of ginger parkin and put that on another plate, made a fresh pot of tea, put them all on the tray and went back upstairs.

"Very jolly our Polly, isn't she?" Master Christy spoke with his mouth full of cake. "Jolly Polly."

I smiled, for that was one thing that Polly was not. She was as dour as could be and I reckoned that one day she would end up being a housekeeper just like Mrs Judson, for they were both stamped from the same mould.

He asked me where I was from and how long I had been working there and expressed surprise that I had come all the way from Hull to work in Beverley. "Beverley's a fine town," he said. "I shall set up here when I have finished school. I have friends here already, but not the kind that my parents would approve of if they knew. Butchers' sons, innkeepers' sons, farriers' lads, you know. Young fellows who live on barges down at the beck."

They sounded very respectable to me, and I told him so, forgetting that I wasn't supposed to have an opinion and should speak only when

30

spoken to.

"Not suitable for me, according to my parents," he said, licking his fingers and dabbing them on the plate to catch the last of the cake crumbs. "Only gentry, or bankers and lawyers. They don't know that I come down here either." He gave me a wink. "They didn't mind when I was little, but they don't know I still come to be spoiled by Cook." He then gave a wicked grin. "Will you spoil me, Jenny kitchen-maid?"

I gazed at him very solemnly as I considered, but I knew immediately what the answer would be. Yes, of course I would.

CHAPTER THREE

'I saw Christy quite often during that summer. He would come into the kitchen unannounced and Cook would feed him with whatever she had. A piece of apple pie or a slice of cake; he liked his sweet things, did Master Christy. He was always asking me to take a walk on the Westwood. But of course I couldn't. For one thing I wasn't due for any free time, and for another if we had been seen together I would have lost my job. I kept telling him this but he only answered, "But no-one knows you, Jenny kitchen-maid, and it wouldn't do any harm."

I came to the conclusion that he was lonely when he was at home. His sister Julia was too young for his company and the young working lads of his own age he was friendly with were not able to take time off. But there came a day when I was sent on an errand to the shops in Saturday Market. It was sunny and warm and I must admit that I was dawdling, enjoying the sheer pleasure of being outdoors and not confined to the heat of the kitchen. I'd stopped to look in a draper's window to admire a length of muslin, when I became aware of a reflection in the glass of someone standing behind me.

"Good day, Jenny kitchen-maid," came a whispered voice. "That colour would suit you very well."

I turned and looked up to see the smiling face of Master Christy. "Good afternoon, sir." I dipped my knee. "Yes, that colour green is a favourite of mine."

"I'd buy it for you if I had any money," he said. "But alas, my father keeps me very short of allowance."

"It wouldn't be proper, anyway, Master Christy," I said very primly, though I couldn't help but smile at the notion. "My ma would be very shocked and so would yours."

"Then if I can't buy you a pretty thing, come for a walk with me."

"I can't do that," I said, though I felt I would dearly like to.

"Yes, you can." He pulled on my arm. "Please do, Jenny. I'm so very bored."

Well it just so happened that I hadn't been able to make the purchase for Mrs Judson. She required a set of buttons in a particular size and colour. I had tried several haberdashers where I had drawn a blank and was about to enquire at the draper's, and I reckoned that if I went for a very short walk, then I could say that I had spent the time trailing all round Beverley in the quest for the buttons.

"All right," I said. "But no more than half an hour."

His face lit up at my words and I thought that even if I got into trouble, it would be worth it just to see the look of pleasure on his face. We sped off, cutting down a passageway at the side of the Green Dragon inn across Lairgate and up New-begin which was said to be one of the oldest streets in Beverley, and headed for the pastureland of the Westwood.

I hadn't been there before and I was delighted with the rolling dips and valleys, the lush green grass, the trees and bushes, and we ran up and down those little valleys as if we were children, although of course we were not; but for a short time we could pretend that childhood had returned and that I was not a servant girl and he my master's son.

"This is where I come to meet my friends," he said, lying down on the grass and putting his arms behind his head. "The friends I can't take home to meet my parents."

I sat down beside him and took off my bonnet, which had become askew as we had chased about. I shook my hair free, smoothed it and started to pin it back again.

"What pretty hair, Jenny kitchen-maid." He fingered my straight brown locks. "So thick and glossy."

I shrugged away from him and bent my head as I felt a flush coming to my cheeks. I pinned up my hair and put on my bonnet, my eyes averted, yet I saw the slow smile on his lips. "I must get back," I murmured. "I shall be missed."

"Yes." He jumped to his feet. "Come on then. I'll walk you back. I'm so glad you came."

I looked up at him. "So am I, Master Christy, but I mustn't do it again."

"Why not? Where's the harm in it?"

I knew the harm of it. I would become too fond of him and that just wouldn't do. And besides, his parents might forgive him for having local lads for friends, but they wouldn't tolerate a friendship with a servant girl.

"I'll get into trouble," I said evasively. "If anyone found out, I mean."

He sighed and nodded. "I wouldn't want that, Jenny. But it's a pity. I would like us to be friends."

"We can still be friends," I said. "We must just make sure that no-one else knows."

And so that is how it was over the next two years. We would exchange conversation in the kitchen when others were there, for he still came down whenever he was home from school, and sometimes we would accidentally meet when I was on my afternoon off. Except that it wasn't an accident, for if I wasn't in the kitchen he would enquire where I was and maybe where Mary was too, just to deflect suspicion. This he told me, for he would come and look for me. He knew where I went in Beverley for I followed the same route on my time off and walked to the Westwood in the area of Fishwick's mill.

"Hello, Jenny kitchen-maid," he would call and I would smile and greet him in return. "Hello, Mr Christy," for he was now too grown to be called Master Christy. At nearly eighteen he was tall, and already had a neat beard and sideburns, for as I said before he was quite dark, and it must have been a chore for him to use the blade every day. Sometimes our hands would touch involuntarily as we acknowledged one another. Well, that is what friends do, isn't it? Men shake hands and ladies extend theirs. I've seen them do it when I've been upstairs. Yes, I do go upstairs now; at least I did before being locked up in here. I joined Polly as an upstairs maid when Mary was promoted to Mrs Ingram's personal maid.

Christy introduced me to some of his friends. There was William Brown, whom he always called Billy Brown butcher boy – Billy's a handsome lad, broad-shouldered with thick brown hair, and blue eyes with long lashes – and Henry Johnson the farrier's son, whom he named Harry Farrier. I realized then that he had nicknames for all of us, for I was always Jenny kitchen-maid.

There were times when he was away, and I was out doing errands or on my afternoon off, that I would bump into Billy or Harry and we would exchange the time of day, and Billy in particular, if he was free from his father's shop, would ask me to go for a walk, and sometimes I would and sometimes I wouldn't. It would depend. There were occasions when I thought I could smell the blood of the animals on him and see a dark red stain on his hands, and then I would shake my head and say that I had to get back to the house.

He would gaze at me from his deep blue eyes and look rather sad as if he knew the reason why, so I would make a point of waving to him the next time I passed the butcher's shop.

Harry never asked me to go for a walk: he was much too shy, which was a pity for I might have done. He was small, not much taller than me, wiry like the terrier that was always at his feet. I liked the smell of him, of leather and horse and hot singeing iron. He didn't talk much but when he did, he spoke solely of horses who were his one and only love. He even looked a bit like a horse, I thought, with his long thin nose and dark eyes.

Christy's parents decided to give a party for his eighteenth birthday. Lots of wealthy young men and many pretty marriageable young ladies would be specially invited, for although Christy was too young to be married I overheard his mother say that the time had come for him to assess who was eligible and who was not. "It's never too early to start looking and planning," she said. "We must discover if any of these young women will make a suitable wife and mother to future Ingrams."

I had been standing against the wall waiting whilst Mr and Mrs Ingram, Christy and his sister were having luncheon, and at her words I felt myself grow hot and then almost immediately turn cold and shivery. I hadn't ever thought of his getting married, and as my eyes looked towards Christy his turned to mine and I was struck by how soulful and lost he seemed. I straightened my back, for I was very aware of Polly standing at the other side of the room where she could see my face, and she never missed a trick didn't Polly.

"I'll not get married for years, Mama," Christy exclaimed and I was surprised by the anger in his voice. "I'm much too young. Another ten at least."

His father agreed, barking out, "He must decide on a career first. Banking, perhaps, or the law."

Again Christy glanced at me as if looking for support, but of course I couldn't give it. I wasn't even supposed to be listening, but I heard him say clearly enough, "Neither of those things, Father. I haven't yet decided what to do. I might even travel abroad for a while."

"But you might meet a foreign lady and bring her home." His mother was all of a twitter at the notion. "We couldn't have that, Christy. Not here!"

They finished their luncheon then, and Polly and I moved to clear away and as I reached for Christy's plate, he brushed his fingers against my wrist as if reassuring me, and I knew that he would come downstairs to the kitchen as soon as he was able.

He came down later in the afternoon and sat on the edge of Cook's table swinging his leg and munching on an apple. "What do you think, Clara Cook?" he asked. "Have you heard?"

"Heard? I never hear anything, Master Christy. I'm as deaf as can be." Cook was the only one who still referred to him as Master.

"Mama wants me to think on marriage. I'm too young, don't you think? What say you, Jenny kitchen-maid?"

"I'm no longer a kitchen maid, sir," I said. "I'm upstairs now. Tilly is 'kitchen maid."

He got up from the table and grabbing hold of

me, whirled me around. "You'll always be Jenny kitchen-maid to me." He had a big grin on his face and I thought how merry he was now, even though he had been so cross over luncheon. "Jenny upstairs maid doesn't have the same ring!"

"Put her down, Master Christy." Cook was severe with him. "It doesn't do to be so frivolous with servants. You'll give the girl ideas above her station."

Polly sniffed and looked down her long nose. "I'd guess she has them already," and I knew that she had somehow seen that look or sensed the mood between Christy and me.

Later in the day when Polly was serving tea and Cook and I were in the kitchen, Cook humphed and cleared her throat and said, "I've something to say to you, Jenny." She waved a finger at me. "Don't think because Master Christy is so friendly like, that he's just 'same as us. Because he isn't."

"I know that, Cook." I kept my eyes on the pile of napkins that I had been folding. "Why would you want to remind me? Just because he was larking about!"

"Well sometimes you young lasses get ideas – aye, and sometimes, young gentlemen do as well, even nice young men like Master Christy." Again she shook a finger. "But I'm telling you that no good ever came of it. Servants and gentry just don't mix."

Of course I knew that she was wrong, but I couldn't say so and the moment passed with my resolve to be extra careful, for now Christy was home we saw each other most days.

We prepared for the party, which was to be in

three weeks' time. The house was given an extra cleaning, though it always seemed very clean to me. The marble mantelshelf in the drawing room was washed with soapy water and polished, and the iron grate black-leaded until it shone. The hall floor was given an extra waxing; the Indian rugs were put out on the hedge in the garden and given a beating, which brought the colours up beautifully, and I wondered if the country they came from was as rich and vibrant as they were. The cushions too were taken outside to be shaken. The feathers flew up into the air, and the sparrows and thrushes twittered and sang as they waited up on the tree branches for them to drift down, so they could collect them to line their nests.

Mrs Ingram discussed the menu with Cook, and with Mrs Judson and Mr Thompson she spoke of the desirability of taking on temporary staff: two more maids to help in the kitchen, one more for upstairs to serve food, and an under butler to help Mr Thompson serve the wine and fruit cup. It was amazing to me that so many people would be needed, but I suppose they wanted to make a good impression on the people attending.

"Of course," said Christy as we sat beneath a tree on the Westwood, "Father also wants me to meet the parents of these young women. There may be some association I could take up. He's inviting lawyers and landowners as well as people in industry. Though not trade, you know."

"So not Billy Brown's father?" I smiled at the thought of seeing Billy's father drinking wine and eating fancy pastries whilst still dressed in his bloodstained apron.

"Of course not," he said. "Certainly not trade." He turned to look at me and clasped my hand. "But I wish that you could be there, Jenny."

"I will be there," I said, very quietly. "I shall be Jenny upstairs maid, won't I?"

He nodded and squeezed my hand. "But I meant as my friend, Jenny, so that you could come and talk to me, or join in the dancing."

"Dancing," I breathed. "Is there to be dancing?"

Nobody downstairs had mentioned dancing and I wondered if they knew. I couldn't mention it of course, because they would want to know how I had heard of it. I had to be so careful.

Mrs Judson was the first to tell of it the next day. "There's to be dancing," she said.

"Shall we be able to listen to the music?" Mary asked. "Or watch?"

Mrs Judson put on a prim face, but then she relaxed. "Well, I suppose there'd be no harm, as long as no-one saw us."

So that is what we did. After we had served supper in the dining room and the guests had adjourned to the drawing room, we, that is Mary, who had come down to help, Polly, the temporary maid and I, rushed to clear away, leaving Tilly and the two other kitchen maids to wash the dishes. Then we hid at the top of the kitchen stairs and listened to the music from a piano and a fiddle, and tapped our feet and wished that we could have a dance too.

From where we stood we caught glimpses of swirling gowns, pretty flowered muslins and shiny satins, and tailcoats flying, for some of the younger guests danced their formation into the hall.

There was much whispered speculation from Mary and Polly, with an occasional curt remark from Mrs Judson, as to which young lady would eventually be chosen for Mr Christy. I didn't join in this debate, because I knew with an absolute certainty that it would be none of them.

CHAPTER FOUR

'Nothing came of the introductions to the young ladies, as I knew it wouldn't, though Christy did obtain a position within a bank. His father had shares in it, so I believe, but Christy spent little time there, and if I'm perfectly honest, if I had had any money I wouldn't have entrusted it to him for he didn't have a head for figures.

But it was an occupation of sorts and his mother was overheard to say that it would suffice until he married. The assumption being, as Mrs Judson sniffed, that he would marry someone very rich. I never thought of marriage for myself, but if I had wanted it, I think that Billy would have asked me. We met frequently. He rose very early in a morning and by teatime he was free. He would hang around the Ingrams' house or sometimes knock on the back door. Cook didn't discourage him for he often brought a string of sausages or a ham shank, or maybe a piece of offal, and these would be eaten in the kitchen and not find their way upstairs.

"You could do worse, girl," Cook used to say.

"You'd never go hungry and you'd have some standing in 'town as a butcher's wife."

"Couldn't stomach 'stench of blood, Cook," I would answer. "Nor the sound of slaughter."

But there are worse smells I've discovered since being in here. There's an odour of unwashed bodies for a start, for there are no washing facilities to speak of, and a stale stink of mutton fat which they serve under the guise of food; but worst of all there's an unwholesome smell of fear and that is coming directly from me.

Christy had a huge argument with his father when he was twenty. Mr Ingram said that he wasn't learning anything about banking and so must choose another career. The army had been suggested, but Christy had refused, and quite rightly. He was far too gentle to be amongst rough soldiers, even though he would be placed as an officer. And besides, he would never be able to make a decision about anything important, for I have to say he was quite negligent in the matter of resolutions, preferring to put them off for another day. At least, that is what I thought then.

I was returning from a visit to Hull during October. My father had been ill and I'd persuaded Mrs Judson to give me some time off to see him. I'd gone there and back in the day and I'd like to have stayed longer as it was Hull Fair week. I always used to enjoy that, but Mrs Judson insisted that I came back on the last train. It had been a dank wet day and when I arrived at Beverley station it was dark and gloomy. Imagine my shock when a figure loomed up in front of me. I was very startled.

"Hello, Jenny kitchen-maid." A voice I recognized greeted mine. "May I walk you home?"

"Mr Christy!" I said in relief, and was very pleased to see him for I didn't really fancy walking along New Walk in the dark, for although I knew that there were villains locked up in the Correction House, I also knew that there were some who had their freedom and were quite able to pounce on a young maid if they should see her alone and without an escort. "What are you doing out here this evening?" We were familiar enough for me to question him in this manner, you see, even though he was my employer's son. "Have you been meeting friends?"

"What friends have I, Jenny?" he asked glumly. "You are my only friend and that is why I am here. I asked Tilly where you were and the time of your arrival." He tucked my arm into his. "And she told me."

That girl hasn't learnt sense, I thought to myself. She should have said she didn't know, though I was very glad indeed that she hadn't.

We walked quite slowly, chatting of this and that. I told him of my father who was much better, and of my mother who was still as short-tempered as ever, and then of my two sisters who were still at home and wanting me to go back so that they didn't have to do so many chores and housework.

"But you'll not do that, Jenny?" Christy sounded quite anxious.

"No fear," I said. "Indeed I won't!"

"Because I'd miss you, Jenny kitchen-maid," he said softly, and bent his head towards me. We were entering New Walk. It's a tree-lined road with many shady places, and, so as not to be seen, we found that quite naturally we eased into one of those places where the branches hung low and we could lean against the broad tree trunk.

It was as if I had been waiting all those long years for him to put his arms round me and kiss me gently on the mouth. We had grown up together; we had shared our childhood in a way, although we were in different circumstances. Him upstairs and me down. But that had never really seemed to matter. We were meant to be together, we were both sure of that. And that was what Christy said that night. That we should be together always and for ever, come what may.

I couldn't begin to explain the lightness of spirit, the joy unfurling inside me when he said those words, even though I knew that our future wouldn't be easy; that there would be objections from every quarter.

"I'll always love you, Jenny kitchen-maid," he whispered into my ear that night. "There will never be anyone else for me."

"And I will love you too," I said in return.

"For ever!" he insisted. "You must say for ever."

I smiled at him in the darkness and he touched my cheek with his fingertips. "For ever," I whispered back. "For ever and ever. Amen."

He seemed satisfied then and with a little more kissing to seal our promise, we went on our way. We parted company just before we reached the house and I went through the kitchen door and he through the front, and I remember thinking that it wouldn't always be so, that one day we should enter a door together.

"Have you got a young man?" Lillian asked me one day about six months later. She was a new maid, come to replace Polly, who had obtained a place as a housekeeper, as I always knew she would. "I often see that butcher lad hanging about."

I was about to deny it, when I thought to myself that perhaps a hint that I had a young man would throw people off the scent when I went on my afternoon walks to meet Christy. "Billy?" I said innocently and lowered my eyelids. "He's quite sweet on me."

"So you go to meet him, do you?" She gave a knowing look. "Mind what you get up to! Don't get in 'family way."

I decided that I didn't like Lillian much. She was too nosy by far and forever giving the other maids the benefit of her advice, which I would never take as she was younger than me.

"Know all about that, do you?" I said rather sharply. "Then you must watch yourself too," and she had the grace to blush.

Nevertheless, it was a worry that had been bothering me, for Christy and I were, by now, lovers in the full sense of the word; but it wasn't as if he had forced me. Oh dear no. I was very willing to show how much I loved him. What I wanted, what we both wanted, was to show everyone else how much we cared for one another.

"When I am twenty-one, Jenny," Christy said, "I will come into my grandfather's legacy. Then we can go away and be free to marry. We can be man and wife, which is what I want more than anything else in the world."

I couldn't believe that anyone could love me so much. Me. The plain girl. Jenny kitchen-maid. I went around doing my daily tasks and hoping that no-one would be able to tell from my face that I was bursting with happiness. It didn't occur to me to wonder why he loved me. I just knew that he did. But as I think about it now, I think I know the reason why. It was because I accepted him as he was. I never asked him to do what he didn't want to do, as his parents did. Always badgering him to choose a career, or find a wife out of the available and eligible young ladies who were paraded before him at parties and balls. And I never thought to wonder why it was so important that he should make the right choice when he was so young. But now I know why.

The trouble started when he reached his majority, which means when he became of age. It meant that he no longer had to do what his parents said and that he could make decisions for himself, and so he told his parents that he was going away with the woman he loved, though he didn't name me, and that he didn't want to meet any other wishy-washy young women, no matter how rich they were.

Well, the rumpus that ensued. His mother went to bed for a week, his sister had hysterics and his father said that he was going to see his lawyer to find out if he could rescind Christy's grandfather's legacy.

"How can he do that?" I asked Christy when we were at last alone. It had been very difficult lately to find a spare ten minutes to meet; the evenings were light and we were very afraid of being seen.

"Father said he will get a doctor to say I am of unsound mind and not able to govern my own affairs." His eyes glittered when he spoke and it did seem as if he had a kind of madness on him.

"But why would he want to do that? Surely your happiness is of the most importance to your parents?"

"No," he said bitterly. "The most important thing to my family is that I marry someone rich and do it soon." He looked at me with anguish in his eyes. "Father is nearly bankrupt. His shares have been falling for years. If I don't marry well and save them, then they'll lose everything. Julia won't have a dowry and Father's cousin from Worcester will inherit the house if Father can't maintain it. What am I to do, Jenny?" He was almost in tears. "What am I to do? I can't give you up. Won't give you up."

I was heartbroken. All my dreams were shattered, but I knew what was to be done, even though it was very hard. "You'll have to find a wife as your parents say, and after a little while when things have settled down, we can become lovers again. If you have a separate house then I could come and work for you, perhaps be the housekeeper?"

I was beginning to warm to the idea. Being housekeeper would be a big step up for me, and if the new wife was very rich and they lived in a grand house, my status would improve immensely. I never imagined that there would be a difficulty in his finding such a wife, for he was very presentable and charming, though I knew nothing of the dealings in the marriage market.

He was staring at me with a strange light in his eyes. "You don't love me! You can't love me if you can suggest such a thing!" His voice was hoarse and strangled.

"Christy!" I exclaimed. "Of course I love you. I'm only trying to think of a way out of this dilemma! If your father succeeds in his plan, we can't marry. And if we run away, what would we live on?"

He looked at me and his mouth dropped open, and I knew that this hadn't occurred to him. He'd never had to think about where money came from before. "Well," he said. "You will be able to find work. There's always an opening for a respectable servant, and I will do whatever I can to obtain a position, although of course," he sighed, "I'm not trained for anything."

As gently as possible, I explained that I would no longer be considered respectable if I had run away with my employer's son. "Besides, I wouldn't have a reference." And I remembered how I hadn't known what a reference was when I first came to the Ingrams' house.

He was very moody and tense then, and before we parted company he made me vow again that until death did us part, we would always love one another. "I shall think of something, Jenny." His mouth was set in a tight line. "I will think of a plan. We shall not be separated. I am determined on that."

I realized that he had always been rather spoiled by his parents, particularly his mother. They had

48

pandered to his whims and allowed him to do mainly what he wanted, with, I supposed, the view that he would in turn look after them when they needed him. What they hadn't seemed to realize, and this I found surprising, was that Christy had a very stubborn streak and if he was told he couldn't have something, then he wanted it all the more.

They asked him time and again who was the woman he wanted to marry, but he refused to be drawn, and spent many hours locked in his room, unwilling to see anyone. His sister Julia proclaimed he was ruining her life, for no-one would want to marry her if her father became bankrupt. Christy flung open his door, for she had been hammering on it, and shouted at her. I was in the room next door and heard him. He bellowed that it wasn't his fault if his father had made poor dealings, and he didn't see why he should ruin his own life just for her. Which, I must admit, I considered was rather a cruel thing to say, and I thought he should have shown more sensitivity to Miss Julia's feelings.

Mrs Ingram ventured down the back stairs into the kitchen a few days later, something she never did as a rule, and beckoned to me. "Quickly! You're Jenny, aren't you?"

I was amazed. I'd been in her service for five years, yet she hesitated over my name. But I dipped my knee and said that I was.

"Mr Christy will take some food in his room," she said. "But he insists that only you must take it up."

I was extremely relieved as I knew that he

hadn't eaten anything for almost three days, nor allowed anyone in his room to clean or change the linen or even bring fresh water for washing.

"He'll have a little beef and chicken," Mrs Ingram continued, "and perhaps put a slice of bread there too, oh and a glass of red wine. He particularly asked for that. It will bring his strength back, I expect," she added vaguely.

I prepared a tray and put on it a plate of sweet cake as well as the other food he had asked for. I knew that he wouldn't refuse to eat that, even if he only picked at the meat. Mrs Ingram was waiting in the hall when I came up the stairs. She put her hand towards me in a pathetic, imploring way. "Do take note of how he seems, Jenny," she said. "What state of mind he is in. And come to tell me when you come down."

I said that I would and felt her eyes follow me upstairs. I was rather sorry for her. She must have been most anxious, not only for Christy but for all of them, and it crossed my mind that if the worst came to the worst, it would be pretty bad for all of us downstairs too, for we would find ourselves without work. It wouldn't matter too much for Mrs Judson, Mary, Tilly or Lillian. They would find other positions, but Cook was old and Mr Thompson even older. He would never find another place and I found myself wondering if he had managed to save enough money to keep him from the workhouse.

If this was my house, I pondered, I would do things differently. If I was married to Christy and lived here, I would make sure he went to the office or the bank every day and not leave it to other people to look after my fortune. I daydreamed a little on this and wondered if I could find a solution, but of course I knew that I would never be accepted. The Ingrams would die of shame if their son were to marry a servant girl, particularly one whose name they couldn't remember.

I tapped on Christy's door. "Who is it?" His voice was very sharp.

"It's Jenny, Mr Christy," I replied, mindful of anyone listening. "I've brought some food as you asked."

He opened the door a crack and on seeing that it was only me he opened it and grabbed hold of me, pulling me inside and then locking the door. "Christy," I whispered urgently. "You must eat." I put the tray down on a table and went to open a window. It was extremely stuffy in the room and smelled very stale. But he followed me and taking hold of my shoulders he turned me round.

"Jenny. I've thought what to do!" His eyes were red. They flashed and moved from side to side, and if I'm honest I felt a little scared of him. He seemed very agitated and I wondered if it was because he had been without food or drink.

"I've thought what to do," he repeated. "My parents can have my money and you and I can be together for ever."

"Yes. Yes," I said. "Why don't you eat and then we'll talk about it?"

"I'm too excited to eat." He began pacing about the room and I saw that he hadn't even dressed properly. His shirt buttons were undone at the neck and his hair hadn't been brushed, and he was barefoot. "We've got to do it, Jenny. We've got to do it together."

"Do what?" I tried to speak softly and patiently for he really was in quite a state. "What must we do, Christy?"

He turned his head quickly and looked at me with a sly expression. "Shan't tell you yet. Not until I have thought it through properly. Besides." He lowered his voice to a whisper and I had to strain to hear him. "If I tell you before I'm ready and anyone suspects us, they may try to worm it out of you."

I smiled then. "Christy! No-one suspects anything. We've been very discreet." But even as I said it, I felt uneasy. I didn't know why. Just a feeling that came over me.

"Do you love me?" He came very close. "As much as before?"

"Even more," I vowed and wondered if I might have even more reason for making a pledge.

"Promise me then." He held me close and I was beginning to worry that his mother waiting downstairs might become suspicious. "Till death us do part."

"Till death us do part," I repeated. "Now, please eat, Christy. To please me."

"Very well." He smiled with his lips but his eyes were still startled and wide and I was sure that he wasn't well. "I'll do it for you, Jenny kitchen-maid. Then I will make the plan. The final plan."

CHAPTER FIVE

'It's so cold in here.' Jenny stopped writing and rubbed her hands together, squeezing her fingers to bring back the circulation. Then she moistened the tip of the pencil with her tongue and began again. 'I swear I've never felt such cold. Though our bedroom window in the attic at the Ingrams' house often had ice on it during winter, it was never like this place where the water runs down the walls and the one and only blanket is damp. My nose is constantly dripping and I shake all the time, though I expect that's with fear. I'm afraid. Very afraid, for if they don't believe me and accept what I say as the truth, then I know the outcome. They'll send me to York and it'll be the gallows for sure. The Ingrams were, still are, a respected family in Beverley and they'll want justice. Even now when rumours abound about a possible bankruptcy and Christy's death, they are considered to be respectable. That's what Billy told me, anyway.

Billy, yes. Billy's been in to see me. He's the only one who has. Not my mother or father, sisters or brothers, not one of them, even though they must have read about Christy's death and my remand in the newspaper. Billy said he'd bribed the warder with a joint of meat. He also said that the hearing was to be next week.

When Christy told me that he was making his

53

final plan, the worry about it and not knowing what his intentions were was making me feel sick and unwell, and I thought that if we were to run away somewhere, then I would like to know about it in advance, so that I could prepare myself. But no. He wasn't going to tell me until he was ready, he said.

Then he came out of his room and it appeared that everything was back to normal. He joined his father in the library and I often heard the sound of their murmurings and sometimes their laughter. But I knew that there was something not quite right. Christy had an odd look on his face, though his father seemed relieved that he was at last talking to him and his mother again, though when I was waiting on table, I saw and heard them making conversation which seemed very stilted. Mr Thompson commented on it too when we were having dinner in the kitchen. "I tell you there's something not quite right," he said, rubbing his chin in a worried manner. "That young man is too restrained. I feel very uneasy about him."

"I'm nearly ready, Jenny," Christy said one morning. "Another couple of days and we shall be together for always."

I was relieved. I would be glad to get away, and without anyone noticing, I washed my clothes and aired them and put them tidily in my drawer, ready to pack when Christy said the word for us to leave the house. Except, that wasn't his intention. At least, not in the way I had foreseen.

The library was always Mr Ingram's private domain. Mrs Ingram or Miss Julia never went in there, but Christy did at his father's invitation, and as I said, they had both been in there lately with the door firmly closed. When I went in to clean early one morning before the family were up, I noticed that some of the furniture had been moved. The leather chair that was normally kept behind the desk had been put near to the gun cabinet and another chair drawn up next to it. I could only assume that Mr Ingram and Christy had been examining the guns together. As far as I knew, Christy had never before expressed any interest in the guns.

I looked at the cabinet, which had glass doors, and could see the guns behind them. I'd always thought it dangerous to have them on show like that and that it would be safer to have them behind wooden doors, but Mr Ingram liked to look at them. Some of them had belonged to his father and grandfather who had both been soldiers, so I supposed they were antique and valuable. Once or twice when I had taken tea or coffee in to him, I would find him handling or cleaning the weapons. Once, in an absent-minded kind of way, Mr Ingram spoke to me about them. One was a double-barrelled gun, he said, but that didn't mean anything to me. Another was a fowling piece, and he had several pistols and revolvers. There were also boxes of cartridges stacked neatly on the top shelf. The doors were always kept locked, of course, but whenever I polished the glass, I couldn't help but feel uneasy.

That day I rubbed my duster over one of the doors to remove the finger marks, and felt a slight movement as if the glass was loose. I can't say I had noticed it before, but it definitely rattled as I rubbed. I heard the library door open and turned round expecting to see Lillian with her brush and ash bucket to clean out the grate. Only it wasn't Lillian. It was Christy. He was wearing his dressing robe and slippers and as he came in he put his finger to his lips, then locked the door.

"What are you doing?" I dropped my voice to a whisper. "You'll get me into trouble." Though as I said it, I rather feared I was in trouble anyway.

"Ssh," he said. "Listen. Tomorrow morning be ready for our journey. Say your prayers, then come down here to me at half past five."

"What? In here, do you mean?" I was quite disturbed for once again he seemed wild, with his eyes moving from side to side. Which was unusual for that time in a morning. Most people are half asleep and their eyes are bleary. But not Christy. He was very much awake and his eyes glistened.

"Of course in here." He rebuked me as if I should have known, but of course I didn't. How could I? He hadn't told me anything about his plan. But then he kissed me on my cheek so I excused him for his sharpness. He'd been under a lot of strain and I knew that once we were gone from here, I'd be able to soothe away his worries.

I felt guilty though. I would be letting Cook and Mrs Judson down by just going off without giving notice, and I tried to soften the oncoming blow by discussing with Cook what were the chances of a young woman getting a job without references as I had done five years ago. And by asking Mrs Judson how she would manage upstairs if ever either Lillian or myself were taken ill and were unable to work.

The reply from Cook was that no girl would be taken on these days without a reference. "You were lucky," she said. "You caught me when I was desperate for somebody. But I could tell that you wouldn't let us down. You were a plain girl, not at all flighty as some of these young madams are who don't stop in a job longer than five minutes. You've been a good worker and you deserved to go out of 'kitchen and upstairs."

I felt worse after this reply. Not because she thought me plain, but because she was wrong in her judgement of me, and I would indeed be letting her down. I didn't mind so much about Mrs Judson, for she was as sour now as she had been when I first came here, but she surprised me by saying darkly that she could see the day coming when none of us would be needed. "If things don't change soon," she muttered, "we shall all be looking for other situations."

So you can imagine how I felt. I didn't know what Christy was scheming, or if he would have any money for us to take on our journey, for he had said before that his plan would mean that his parents would have his inheritance and we would be together. It was a worry that I couldn't shake off.

The next morning I rose at five o'clock. Mary had a different room now, nearer to Mrs Ingram. It was much nicer than the one I shared with Lillian, though we had more space now that there were just the two of us. Lillian turned over as I tiptoed out of the room, but I don't think she heard me. I crept downstairs with my few belongings in a small bag and wearing my thickest shawl, for it was a cold morning. Through the attic window I'd seen a mist hovering over the rooftops and I hoped that it would clear quickly for our journey, wherever that journey was taking us.

The library door creaked slightly as I entered and I gave a little gasp when I saw that Christy was already there. I was early and I thought I would be the first down, but there he was sitting in his father's leather chair that was once more placed by the gun cupboard. I wondered who had moved it because Lillian and I had put it back in its proper place only the day before.

Christy smiled when he saw me and put out his hand to greet me. "Come here, Jenny kitchen-maid," he said very softly. I put down my bag and moved towards him, putting my hand into his and sitting on his knee.

"Christy," I whispered. "Why–"

"Ssh." He kissed my fingertips. "I'll tell you everything now. Now that I'm ready. I wasn't ready before, you see. I had to gain my father's trust." He smiled again. A smug, satisfied kind of smile, as if he had won something to which he wasn't entitled.

"Are we not going then, after all?" I couldn't help but ask.

"Of course we're going. We're ready at last. Did you say your prayers this morning, Jenny kitchen-maid?"

I had to confess that I hadn't. I say them at night, when I remember, but morning prayers, well, there never seems to be any time, what with washing and dressing and everything. Besides, I've never been very religious, though I went regularly

58

to church with the Ingram family when it was my turn.

But Christy insisted that I should kneel down right there and then, and he knelt with me and we said a little prayer that we were sorry for what we were about to do, and asked for forgiveness. I really wanted to just get going and I'd have been happier to say a prayer of thanks once we were out of the house. I knew that if we were found there, then Mr Ingram wouldn't be very forgiving. I would be sent off at a moment's notice, and I don't know what would have happened to Christy if– Well, it doesn't matter now. That situation didn't arise, so it's of no use talking or even thinking about it.

I got up off my knees and brushed down my skirt and I vaguely wondered if Lillian would brush the carpet as well as clean out the fire. She wouldn't be very pleased about it, I knew that for sure.

"So, Christy," I whispered. "Are you going upstairs to get ready? Folks will be about soon."

"I am ready," he said, and took a small key out of his dressing robe pocket. That was what was bothering me, you see. The fact that Christy was still in his night attire whereas I was fully dressed for a journey.

He lifted his hand with the key in it and gave it a little shake. "Here it is." He grinned as if he had been really clever, and slipped it in the gun cupboard lock. "I've been waiting and watching Father to see where he kept it hidden, and at last I found out."

I didn't understand what that had to do with anything, but if Christy had asked me, I would

59

have been able to tell him where the key was kept. I'd seen Mr Ingram take it out of a desk drawer many times whenever he wanted to look at or clean his guns. The desk drawer was kept locked, of course, but the key for that was always in his waistcoat pocket.

Christy opened the door of the cabinet. "I tried to loosen the glass," he said, "in case I couldn't find out where the key was kept," and I thought that when we were man and wife, I would have to take care of all practicalities, because Christy wouldn't be very good at it. But I didn't mind that. He was charming and merry and handsome and I loved him.

"What are you doing? You must be quick, Christy, and get ready. Why do we need a gun?"

"I've just told you, Jenny kitchen-maid. I *am* ready." He nodded his head very solemnly. "*We* are ready. We're going on an unknown journey and we are going together."

He put his hand into the cabinet and drew out a pistol. I'd seen it before. On that day when Mr Ingram had spoken to me, he'd taken it from the cupboard and told me that it was a lady's pistol and that it was silver. I remember thinking, the time I first saw it, that you would never guess that it could be lethal, for it was so pretty and dainty.

"Are we taking it with us?" I asked. "Won't your father be angry?" I was sure that he would be, unless Christy had written him a note to say he had only borrowed it.

He turned to me and smiled again and once more took hold of my hand. "We're not taking it with us, Jenny. We're leaving it behind. We're leaving everything behind." He patted my hand and I felt the cold weight of the pistol on my knuckles as he did so.

"I don't understand you, Christy," I said, and my words caught in my throat, for I was just beginning to. "Put the gun away, Christy dear, and go and get changed."

"No." He stared at me. "We said we should be together always. Didn't we? We promised!" His voice was low and I was afraid.

"We are going to be together. But we must be quick. Lillian and the others will be down soon."

He looked at the little silver pistol and turned it over in his hand. "We shall be gone by then," he said softly. "It's ready. I came in last night after everyone had gone to bed and loaded it."

My voice failed me and so did my understanding. Surely he didn't mean what I thought he meant? But he did.

"We can't have a life together, Jenny kitchen-maid," he said in a sad voice. "They won't allow us. The only thing we can have is a death together and a life afterwards in heaven. That's why I wanted you to say your prayers, so that we could be sure of us both being in the same place."

I was horror-struck. I loved him; of that there was no doubt. But to die with him? A feeling of nausea swept over me and I was reminded of something else. I shook my head. "No, Christy. We have much to live for. Besides, it would be a sin. A suicide and a murder."

He hesitated then as if it was something he hadn't thought of. "A suicide and a murder?" he whispered. "I don't want that. I want the bullet to

61

go through both of us. I want us both to sit in this chair. That's why it's here. I've worked it out. I shall sit here with you on my knee and we shall die together."

I gave a shudder and thought I was going to be sick. "It wouldn't work, Christy. One of us would be horribly injured. Please don't," I begged. "Let's just run away and take whatever life has to offer."

"No!" I saw the stubbornness on his face. "I've taken weeks to plan this. I'm not going to be put off now." He sat down in the chair and pulled me down onto his lap. "It will be all right. We won't feel anything. We'll just put our heads together and—"

"No, Christy! I can't." I took hold of his hand and eased his finger away from the trigger. The metal felt cold and smooth to my touch.

"You don't love me," he accused, and wrapped his hand over the pistol once more.

"But I do," I whispered. "That's why I want to save you. We can have a life together."

He put his other hand over mine and I'll never know if he was agreeing with me after all, for as he clasped my hand our fingers entwined, there was a resounding crack, and that's why I'm here in this cold miserable place, waiting for judgement on my life.'

CHAPTER SIX

'All rise.'

Feet shuffled on the floorboards and there was muted nervous coughing and clearing of throats as the magistrates, the mayor, and two aldermen of the town of Beverley entered the Guildhall. Mr King appeared for the prisoner. The public turned their eyes to the bowed figure in the dock as the charge was read out that Jenny Graham, the prisoner held on remand, had wilfully and with intent caused the death of Mr Christopher Ingram of New Walk, Beverley.

'The prisoner was found with the weapon in her hand,' Sergeant Hopkins told the Bench, 'and the inquest on the body of the young man found that he had died of gunshot wounds to his heart.'

Mr Ingram, father of Christopher Ingram, was the first witness. His face was grey and lined as he told how he had rushed downstairs in his night attire on hearing the sound of a gunshot.

'And what did you find, Mr Ingram?' Mr King asked. 'Please tell us, even though it will be painful for you.'

'I found,' Mr Ingram said in a low voice, 'my son slumped in a chair and Jenny Graham standing over him with the gun in her hand.'

'And did she say anything?'

'She said, "Send for help. Quickly." That's what she said. "Send for help. Quickly."'

'And did you, Mr Ingram?'

Mr Ingram shook his head and, bringing out a large white handkerchief, blew his nose very loudly. 'No. Not immediately. There was no point. I could see that my son was dead. I sent for the night watch and he ran for the constable.'

'And what did the prisoner say, when you said you were sending for the authorities?' Mr King looked over his spectacles at Mr Ingram and then at Jenny Graham.

'She didn't say anything,' Mr Ingram replied. 'I took the gun from her and she started to weep.'

'Was she weeping from fear or sorrow?' Mr Dibnah, one of the magistrates, asked severely.

The mayor interrupted. 'That is neither here nor there, Mr Dibnah, and not for us to question at this hearing. And anyhow, how would Mr Ingram know?'

Mr Ingram glanced at Jenny. 'I don't know, of course, but she seemed to be very shocked.'

'Why was the prisoner in the library with your son at that time in the morning?' the mayor asked.

Again Mr Ingram shook his head. 'I don't know,' he said. 'That's the strange thing. My son was still in his night robes, but she–' He nodded towards Jenny. 'She was dressed for outdoors.'

What am I to say? Jenny thought as she stared back at him. Do I tell them that Christy wanted us to go on a journey from which we couldn't return? If they decide he's committed suicide then that's a sin, and he'll be denied a Christian burial. But if they decide I killed him then that's murder and I shall hang.

They were speaking to her. What did they say?

64

I'm so confused. 'Beg your pardon, sir. Could you repeat the question?'

'I asked,' Mr Dibnah said, 'why were you in the library, dressed as if to go out and with some baggage with you which contained your belongings? Were you leaving the Ingram household?'

'In a manner of speaking, sir. Yes, I was.'

'Had you given notice to your employers that you were leaving? Were they aware of your intentions?'

Her words stuck in her throat as she spoke. 'Only Mr Christy knew, sir.'

'Speak up, please,' Mr Dibnah said sharply. 'Let the Bench hear you.'

'Mr Christy knew sir,' she said, in a louder, trembling voice. 'I'd discussed it with him.'

'I find that hard to believe,' Mr Dibnah began, but was again interrupted by the mayor, who said, 'This is a hearing, Mr Dibnah. We wish to know only the facts so that we can ascertain whether or not to send this young woman for trial.'

Mr King turned to Jenny. 'Tell us why you should inform Mr Christopher Ingram that you were leaving, but hadn't told his parents, who were your employers?'

She took a deep breath. 'He was kind to me, sir, and we used to talk when I first came to 'Ingram household as a kitchen maid. He was always very merry.'

'Were you fond of him?' Mr King asked.

'Oh, indeed I was, sir. We all were, down in 'kitchen. He was such a jolly fellow.' *Jenny kitchen-maid.* She heard Christy's voice in her head and stifled a sob. She blinked her eyes and lowered

65

them. 'Everyone will feel his loss.'

'But why was it,' Mr Dibnah questioned, 'why was it that you were in Mr Ingram's library that morning if you were about to leave? What business did you have in there? And why were you holding the pistol which according to Mr Ingram was normally kept in the gun cupboard?' He spoke quickly and sharply.

I need now to lie, Jenny thought. If I don't, we are both damned. Me and Christy.

'I was going to write a note, sir. To say I was sorry for leaving so suddenly.'

'To Mr Ingram?' another magistrate asked. 'Why not to Mrs Ingram?'

'I knew there'd be paper on the desk, and besides, Mr Ingram paid our wages, sir. I thought it would be only right.'

'Why were you leaving in such a hurry?' the mayor asked. 'Surely you could have given a week's notice?'

'I'd rather not say, sir.' I could tell them I'd heard rumours of bankruptcy, she thought, that even Mrs Judson had said we'd all be looking for other work, but that would put Mr Ingram in a very embarrassing position, though I suppose now that Christy has gone they'll get his inheritance. 'It's a private matter,' she added.

'Ah!' The magistrates nodded sagely as if they now understood. 'And so you went into the library and found Mr Christopher Ingram unexpectedly there?' Mr King said. 'Did you explain your presence and what did he say to you?'

Oh, Christy! What am I to say? What will they believe? 'He said he hadn't been able to sleep, sir,

66

so he'd come downstairs. He hadn't been very well, as Mr Ingram will tell you. He hadn't slept properly in weeks. He said to me that to pass the time he'd been looking at his father's gun collection. I told him that I was leaving and wanted to leave a note to his parents, and – and he asked me not to go.'

'Yes,' said Mr King kindly, 'and then can you explain what happened? Did you write the note?'

'No, sir. I didn't, because Christy – Mr Christy showed me the gun. He said it was silver, which I already knew. Mr Ingram had shown it to me before. He said it was a very fine piece.'

'Who said that?' Mr Dibnah asked sharply. 'Mr Ingram or his son?'

'Mr Ingram, sir.' I feel very faint, Jenny thought. If I let myself fall will they stop the questions? 'Could I have a cup of water, please?'

'We'll adjourn for fifteen minutes.' The mayor rose to his feet and so therefore did everyone else. 'Give the prisoner some water and let her sit down.'

Jenny sipped the water, then sat with her head on her knees as the fifteen minutes ticked by. Then she stood up as she was bid, clutching with white knuckles at the rail in front of her as she waited for the magistrates to file back in.

'So?' The mayor looked down at his notes. 'Mr Christopher Ingram was showing you the pistol. Did he seem at all agitated or disturbed?'

Jenny's breath quickened as she remembered Christy's wild eyes. 'No, sir. Not at all. He was quite tired, I do believe, and of course he would be, as he hadn't slept. He said to me, "Look how

67

beautifully it's made. It's a work of art." Then, as he was putting the pistol into my hand' – she gave a slight sob and the mayor gave a sympathetic shake of his head – 'it went off.' She looked directly at the mayor. 'We could both have been killed, sir. Then think how bad it would have looked.'

'Indeed it would,' the mayor said crisply. 'But we are not here to speculate how things might have been, but to deliberate on what happened that morning, and it seems to me that there has been too much familiarity between employers and servants. When servants can slip into libraries to write notes or discuss the merits of guns and pistols with their masters!'

He glanced across at Mr Ingram, whose mouth turned down at the rebuke. 'In those circumstances,' the mayor went on, 'respect is diminished. There should be a barrier at all times. And from what I understand from the constable who has made considerable inquiries, Mr Christopher Ingram was a frequent visitor to the kitchen and on friendly terms with the cook and other maids.'

Jenny glanced around the courtroom. Mrs Ingram was there. Her face was partly covered by the veil on her hat, but she bowed her head as the mayor spoke. Mrs Judson was sitting at the back with a sombre expression and not looking at anyone but the magistrates on the Bench.

'What I can't understand,' the mayor continued, 'is why the pistol was loaded. And who loaded it? Mr Ingram has already given a statement to the effect that he never left the guns actioned for use. It couldn't have been the prisoner for she's only a girl.' He looked across at Jenny. 'Unless you're a country girl and used to your father or brother handling firearms?'

'No, sir. I'm from 'town of Hull. I've never known guns.'

The magistrates seemed visibly relieved. 'Not a Beverley resident, then?' said one. 'There can be much mischief when employing people from out of town.'

Jenny spoke up. 'Cook said that she didn't like to employ Beverley girls because they were always slipping home or had followers.'

'And I understand that you did not have followers, Miss Graham?' Mr King said.

Jenny glanced across to where Billy was sitting. He was leaning forward with his hands clasped between his knees and his head bent. 'Only one, sir.'

'Was there any possibility of jealousy between your young man and Mr Christopher Ingram?' one of the other magistrates asked. 'Had the deceased propositioned you in any way?'

There was a slight gasp from the public and muttering as people whispered into each other's ears.

'Certainly not, sir. He was always a gentleman, though as I said, he was a very merry fellow. Always friendly.'

'Well, I think that's enough on that subject,' the mayor interceded and gave a scathing glance at his colleague. 'Conjecture adds nothing to this unfortunate young man's character, or to his family's reputation, which has suffered already because of this calamitous incident.'

The magistrates put their heads together and had a whispered conversation from behind their hands. 'We shall adjourn for an hour.' The mayor rose again. 'And then come to a conclusion.'

As she was taken back to the cell, Jenny felt sick and asked for more water. It was tepid and tasted stale when she took a sip. The warder took the cup from her when she had finished. 'I reckon you'll get off,' he said. 'They'll see there was no reason for you to shoot him. If you'd been carrying on with him, that would've made a difference.' He glanced down at her as she huddled in a corner. 'But anybody can see you're not the type.'

'Because I'm a plain girl?' she murmured, remembering that Christy had said she was beautiful.

'Aye,' he said. 'His sort marries plain women, rich of course,' he grinned, 'and carries on with pretty ones.'

'Of course they do,' she lied. 'I'm sure you're right.'

'I reckon,' he said chattily, as if, now that he was convinced she was innocent, he could have a conversation with her, whereas previously he had only given her instructions. 'I reckon he was going to top himself and you interrupted him.' He nodded his head sagely. 'Otherwise why would the gun have been loaded? They won't say so of course; they'll want to keep it hushed up. It wouldn't do for that sort of thing to get out.'

A bell rang and she stood up. 'I think you're wrong,' she said, wanting to quash any rumours that might circulate. 'Christy wouldn't have done that.'

70

The warder raised his eyebrows as she used the familiar name.

'I happen to know that he loved someone,' she said, as he unlocked the door. 'So why would he want to kill himself?'

'You should have told them,' he told her. 'You'd definitely be off the hook if you had!'

'I would have been giving away a secret,' she said softly. 'And I couldn't do that.'

'All rise,' the clerk to the court called and they stood again as the mayor and fellow magistrates filed back in. Mr King gave her a discreet nod.

The mayor addressed the public. 'We have discussed this matter during adjournment and are all of the opinion that the death of this young gentleman was an unfortunate accident. It behoves me to state that anyone keeping fire-arms should ensure that they are kept secure. Mr Christopher Ingram was obviously inexperienced in weaponry. He may have loaded it himself just to see if he could, with disastrous consequences.'

He turned to Jenny. 'It seems to me that you are a sensible young woman, and I hope that the present difficulties which made you give up your employment with the Ingram family will be satisfactorily resolved.' He gazed from over his spectacles, which were perched halfway down his nose. 'But you would be advised to leave Beverley until such time as this unfortunate incident is erased from present memory. You are free to go and without a stain on your character.'

'Thank you, sir,' Jenny whispered. Her legs felt

weak and she trembled. Free to go. But where shall I go now that there is no Christy to come with me?

CHAPTER SEVEN

Jenny was taken to collect her belongings and then she waited until everyone but the porter had gone from the Guildhall before she stepped outside. She wanted to avoid curious eyes staring at her, but as the door closed behind her she saw that Mrs Judson was waiting. It was raining and she was huddled in a doorway. Her long black coat trailed around her ankles and she held a black umbrella. She signalled to Jenny to come across.

'I waited for you,' she said. 'I've brought your wages up to the day you left.' She gazed severely at Jenny. 'You should have told somebody you were leaving, Jenny. Cook or me. It would have been only right.'

Jenny was grateful for the money, which Mrs Judson handed over. She hadn't expected it. 'I'm sorry, Mrs Judson. I know that I should, but–' she shrugged. How could she possibly explain?

Mrs Judson nodded and her small eyes pierced into Jenny's face. 'There'll be things you can't tell, I expect,' she said in a low voice. 'And I don't suppose it was all your doing. He was always a bit odd. Even when he was a child he had strange ideas. About life, and death.'

Jenny stared at her, then said, 'It was kind of

you to think about my wages, Mrs Judson. I'm surprised they were willing to pay me.'

'They weren't,' Mrs Judson said. 'At least, Mrs Ingram wasn't. She's convinced that you killed him. It was Mr Ingram who agreed when I asked him. I pointed out that it would be churlish not to. If you got off, that is. You'd not have got them if you'd gone to trial.'

'No,' Jenny hastily agreed. 'Of course not. But,' she added impulsively, 'it was an accident, Mrs Judson.'

'Yes. I expect it was.' The housekeeper took a deep breath and looked away from Jenny and down Register Square as if she was only interested in the people passing by. 'But he'd sucked you into one of his mad schemes, I expect,' she muttered. 'I'd seen that gun cabinet had been opened before, and not by Mr Ingram either. I was feared that there might be an accident sooner or later.'

She shook her umbrella open. 'You're well out of it anyway. You'd be best leaving Beverley for a bit, like 'magistrate said. Just till folks have forgotten about it, which they will. Though the Ingrams won't. Specially not her.'

'Well, he was her son after all,' Jenny said. 'I do understand.'

'And she heard you say that you loved him,' Mrs Judson said. 'When the constable came and accused you. She wouldn't have liked that, not after all her plans for him.'

Jenny lifted her eyes to Mrs Judson's face and, to her surprise, saw compassion, which she had never expected from her. She had always been so dour.

73

'We all heard you say that,' Mrs Judson said. 'We were gathered on the stairs, listening. All of us. We'd heard the shot.' She gave a deep sigh. 'We were all prepared to say that we loved him, Jenny. Cook, me, everybody. If you'd gone to trial, that is.' She stepped out of the doorway and raised her umbrella. 'But you didn't. Truth will out in the end.' She gave what might have passed for a smile and a nod and walked briskly down the street. Jenny stared after her until she turned the corner.

Did they know? Jenny pondered. Did they know that I really did love him? And that he loved me? She felt a lump in her throat. She had barely been able to grieve, yet she grieved now and was overwhelmed that the other servants had been prepared to stand up for her and say that they had all cared for Christy, that they had all loved him.

Did they think that my love for him would have appeared less than it was, if they had told that? If that was what they thought, then they didn't understand. I loved him right from the start. Since I was thirteen years old. And now he's gone. The loss, fear and grief, which had held her fast, and now the relief at her liberty, overcame her and swamped her dull mind. She put her head down, her shoulders shook uncontrollably and the tears poured unchecked. She stepped back into the doorway that Mrs Judson had vacated and slid down onto her heels.

Someone stood over her. 'You all right, Jenny?' It was Billy.

'Hello, Billy,' she choked. 'Billy Brown, butcher boy.'

74

He looked solemnly at her. 'Jenny kitchen-maid,' he said in a low voice and she shuddered.

'My father's making me a partner,' he said slowly. 'We're going to open another shop.'

His blue eyes held hers and it seemed as if he was asking her something, rather than making a statement, but she didn't want to enquire what the question was. I've enough to think about for the moment, she thought. 'I'm going away, Billy,' she told him. 'I'm leaving Beverley for a bit. 'Magistrates want me to, anyway.'

'Yes.' He nodded. 'Where to?'

'Don't know.' She blew her nose. She didn't know. Where could she go? 'Back to Hull, I suppose. Back to Ma and Da, if they'll have me.'

He opened his mouth to say something and she said quickly before he could find his voice, 'I don't want to stay here in Beverley. Everybody'll be pointing a finger and talking about me.'

'Aye. That's what my father said.' He lowered his eyes and spoke quickly, but didn't look at her. 'But I'd have you, Jenny.'

'Yes, Billy,' she whispered. 'But I can't.'

'It's too soon, I know that. He wouldn't have made you happy though,' he said, lifting his eyes to her face. 'He was a bit – you know, different.'

'Yes,' she agreed. 'He was.' But I would have made *him* happy, she thought. 'Will you walk me to 'railway station? I'm going to try and get a train into Hull.'

'Do you want some money for the fare?' he asked. 'I'll give you some.'

She shook her head and stood up. 'Thank you, but I'd rather not. I've enough for third class.

Single.' She blinked away her tears as she gazed at him. 'You've been a good friend, Billy. I'll not forget that.'

They walked without further conversation towards the railway station where Billy waited as she purchased a ticket and then saw her onto the train. 'Hold on tight, won't you, Jenny?' he said solemnly. 'I heard of somebody falling out of a train and breaking his head.'

'I'll be careful,' she assured him. 'It's not far.' She cringed as a shrill whistle blew and the engine got up a head of steam and a cloud of black smoke enveloped them. 'I'll be in Hull in half an hour,' she shouted. 'Goodbye, Billy.'

He raised his hand. 'Goodbye, Jenny. Good luck.'

'I knew you'd be back!' As Jenny opened the door, her mother glanced up and put a clenched fist against her bony hip. 'Said to your father, I did. Mark my words, I said, she'll be back when it's all over. Where else would she go? I said.'

'Can I stop?' Jenny asked, and thought that her mother looked even thinner and more wrinkled than when she had last seen her. 'What did Da say?'

'He said she's nowhere else to go. She'll have to come here.' Her mother sniffed and lifted the kettle onto the fire. Then she turned to Jenny and appraised her. 'You'll be expecting, I suppose?'

'To stay?' Jenny said. 'I don't know. It's up to you.'

'No, I meant expecting, as in expecting a babby. That's what I meant.'

'Oh.' Jenny heaved a deep sigh. 'Yes, I think so.'

'I knew it,' her mother said. 'I said, she'll be expecting and will want to come back here.' She folded her arms across her thin chest. 'But I don't think so. We've no room for a babby and besides, you'll not be able to work. Nobody would employ you, not now.'

'I could look after 'house like I did before I went to Beverley,' Jenny said. 'Can't I?'

'No.' Her mother busied herself making tea. 'You can go to your aunt Aggie. She'll have you. She needs some help.' She sat down at the table, poured two cups of tea and sipped hers before saying, 'I've written to her already to tell her you might be coming.'

'What do you mean?' Jenny said. 'Who is Aunt Aggie?' Jenny was amazed that her mother would make arrangements for her, without knowing the outcome of the hearing. 'And anyway,' she said, 'you can't write!'

'I can make out all right,' her mother protested. 'She'll understand what I wrote.'

'Who is she? I've never heard you mention her before. And how do you know she'll have me?'

'She's my youngest sister. She left her husband when you were only a little bairn, and went off with a young swell. Nobody mentioned her name in years. Then after her husband died, she wrote to say she'd married this fellow.' Her mouth turned down disparagingly. 'Made it legal, she said. He's a countryman; they live 'other side of Beverley.'

'So how do you know she'll have me?' Jenny asked again. 'She doesn't know me!'

'She sent a letter some weeks ago – just after

you were locked up. She asked if I had a spare daughter who could come. She'd got none of her own. She's sick. Won't get better, she says. She wants someone to do for her, clean 'house and that, and look after her husband.'

'I don't want to go.' Jenny didn't like the idea of looking after a dying old woman or her husband.

'You've no choice,' her mother said calmly. 'I've just told you. You can't stop here.'

When her father came home, he said she didn't have to go to Aunt Aggie's, that she could stay with them if she wanted to, but then her sister Emma came in from work and later two of her brothers, and Jenny saw how crowded it would be when everyone was at home. She also noticed the hostile glare from her sister.

'Is it his babby?' Emma asked. 'Him that was shot, I mean?'

'It's nothing to do with anybody else whose child it is,' Jenny said sharply.

Her sister shrugged. 'I only thought you might claim some money from his folks, that's all. They'll have plenty, I expect?'

Jenny didn't answer, and thought that at one time she would have assumed that the Ingrams were rich. But that was before Christy had told her about the possibility of his father's bankruptcy. They wouldn't have been destitute, of course. Someone, friends or family, would have helped them out. Still, all the same, she thought, it would have been a disgrace for people such as them.

Another brother came into the house. He was carrying a young child. A heavily pregnant woman, unknown to Jenny, followed him and sat down unbidden on the only unoccupied chair. She sighed deeply and looked across at Jenny. 'Are you that lass that was in 'papers?'

'Probably.' Jenny shrugged. 'I don't know. I haven't seen any newspapers.'

'Don't they let you read 'em when you're locked up?' the woman asked.

'Who are you?' Jenny asked.

'Hey.' Her brother, who hadn't acknowledged her presence, suddenly spoke up. 'This is Nance. She's wi' me. If you'd stopped at home you'd know who she was.'

'Well, I didn't, did I?' she replied. 'I found work and left.'

'Aye and it went wrong and now you're back wi' your tail between your legs.' He stared hard at her.

'Had summat else there as well by 'look of her,' Nance said coarsely.

Jenny turned to her mother. 'I'll leave in 'morning. Where did you say Aunt Aggie lived?'

CHAPTER EIGHT

'You've to go to Beverley on Saturday, day after tomorrow,' her mother said later after Jenny's brother and Nance had left. 'Get 'carrier from 'Green Dragon and ask to be dropped off at a place called Etton.'

'I can't!' Jenny said. ''Magistrates said I should leave Beverley.'

'You can pass through,' her mother argued. 'They can't stop you from doing that!'

'Besides, it's market day,' Jenny insisted. 'I might see somebody I know.'

'Well, that's what she said.' Her mother pushed Emma out of the way whilst she put more coal on the fire. 'She said it was 'onny day he could pick you up.'

'Who?' Jenny asked.

'Him. Aggie's husband. He'll collect you and take you up to their place.'

'Does he have a name?' Jenny said tartly. 'Or do I just hang around waiting for 'first fellow to suggest I go with him?'

'You should be grateful there's somebody willing to take you on,' Emma interrupted. 'Specially when you're in 'pudding club.'

'Ah, well–' Her mother hesitated. 'They don't know about that yet. Well I didn't know, did I?' she retaliated at Jenny's groan. 'I didn't even know if you'd get off 'charge and come home, let alone know what state you were in!'

'So when did you write to say I would go? How many Saturdays has he been waiting?'

'Two,' her mother answered. 'That's why you'll have to go this Saturday. He might not wait much longer.'

Jenny spent the following day wandering around Hull. She'd hardly been back since going to work in Beverley, as she only came home for the occasional visit. She walked the length of Whitefriargate and looked in the shops, then crossed over and cut down the old streets towards the river. She stood pondering for a moment as she watched the barges. Some of them will be going to Beverley, I bet, she thought. I could mebbe have gone by barge. I'd have liked that, sailing along the river and going through the lock into the beck.

She continued her walk along the waterway, cutting through the narrow staithes when her way was blocked by merchandise, until at last she came to where the river Hull flowed into the Humber estuary. She crossed over towards the pier now named Victoria Pier, in honour of the Queen who had graced the town by a visit in 1854. Jenny vividly remembered the celebrations, which had been in October, the year before she had taken the daring step towards independence and gone to Beverley.

She glanced about her. She had been only one in a crowd of thousands who had gathered here to see Her Majesty and Prince Albert, the Prince of Wales, the Princess Royal and the other members of the royal family and their entourage. There had been grumbling from some people over the great expense entailed by the visit, but the majority of the public were thrilled and excited to be seeing the Queen for the first time.

Jenny had lost sight of her father and mother in the crush of people who had gathered on the pier to see the Queen depart on the royal yacht, the *Fairy*. Many thousands more had waited at the station the day before to watch the Queen's arrival and hear the singing of the choirs which greeted her. There had been flags and bunting from every private window and corporation building and it was said that the playing of the national anthem couldn't be heard for the cheering of the crowds.

She remembered trudging home alone that evening, thrilled to have seen the Queen in person, knighting the mayor of the town, right here on the pier. Jenny had pushed her way through the mass, bending down and crawling between legs until she got to the front and was rewarded by seeing the Queen beckon the mayor to kneel. Taking the sword from her officer, she had laid it upon the mayor's left and right shoulders, then commanded him to rise as Sir Henry Cooper.

Still on her knees, Jenny had stared open-mouthed at the ceremony and her ears were deafened by the cheers of the crowd. Glancing from the Queen to the rest of the royal party, she saw that the young Prince of Wales was looking down at her with a droll smile and raised eyebrows. She'd grinned back and thought that he would find it amusing to see someone's head poking out from between the trousered legs and flowing skirts.

She hadn't been back to the pier since then, having left for Beverley the following spring, but she looked around now and recalled the thick carpet laid out on the planking for her majesty to walk on, the sun shining, and the estuary crowded with steamers, barges and yachts. She ran her hand over her abdomen. I never told Christy about that day, she thought. I must remember to tell his son.

The next morning she took a train to Beverley. No-one offered to see her off or asked her to write. 'Shall I let you know about 'babby?' she ventured to her mother as she picked up her bag ready to depart.

'If you like,' her mother replied indifferently. 'Let me know about Aggie anyway. If she dies, I mean. Not that I'd go to 'funeral. But I'd like to know.'

Can't think why, Jenny thought as she walked away towards the railway station. She's not been interested in her life, why would she want to know about her death? And then she considered her own sisters and brothers and thought that they were not interested in her, any more than she was in them. I'm fond of young Joe, she pondered, thinking of her youngest brother. But as for the others, there were so many of us. We hardly knew each other.

Saturday Market was packed with stalls and carriers' carts and thronging with both town and country folk when Jenny walked from Beverley railway station into the town. Villagers from miles around the district came in by cart, trap or waggon, to sell or buy. She made one or two purchases, bought a block of writing paper, pen and ink and pencils, needle and thread, and a new pair of stockings, for her only pair were well darned, and as she was counting out her money realized that there had been no mention of whether or not she would be paid for being with Aunt Aggie, or if she was expected to work for her bed and board.

And what will happen when I give birth? she wondered. Who will help me then? Is Aunt Aggie so sick that she won't be there? Well, Jenny, she thought stoically. It's into the unknown again. But there's one thing certain and that is that I won't find another like Christy. She took a deep breath as the events of the last few weeks overcame her. I'll only have his memory; and when his child is born, well – she glanced around Saturday Market – we'll see. They said I had to leave Beverley but they didn't say I couldn't come back; and my child's heritage is here.

Across the street she saw Billy come out of his father's shop, and catching sight of her he came over. 'Jenny,' he said. 'You've come back!' There was a ray of expectant hope in his face, which she quickly quashed.

'I have,' she said. 'But I'm only passing through. I'm on my way somewhere. I've to get a lift with a carrier and get down in Etton. I don't know how far it is.'

'It's not far. Four or five miles, mebbe.' He bit anxiously on his lip. 'Why are you going there? There's nowt much doing in Etton, not at 'moment anyway. They might be having a railway line. Have you got a job of work?' He spoke quickly and urgently.

She nodded. 'Somebody's picking me up.'

''Carriers might be full. They're busy on a Saturday. I'll come across with you, if you like. I know some of 'em.'

They walked to where a group of drivers were waiting and smoking their pipes by the inn door. Billy went up to one of them. 'Can you drop my friend off in Etton? She needs to get there urgently.'

'Friend o' yourn, Billy? Aye, I reckon so. I'm setting off in a half-hour, so you've time to kiss 'little lady goodbye!' The carrier grinned as Billy blushed, but Jenny, straight-faced, paid him the fare to make sure he didn't go without her. They turned back into the market until it was time for departure.

'Why aren't you at work, Billy?' she asked. 'I thought Saturday was your busiest day.'

'I am at work,' he said. 'I've just nipped out for a hot pie from the baker's for my dinner. Da's got an extra lad to help him out, cos when our new shop's ready in Toll Gavel, I'll be in there. Well,' he added, 'except that my ma's going to give me a hand. She knows about butchery.'

'I'm really pleased for you, Billy,' Jenny said. 'When I next see you you'll probably own a string of shops!'

He blushed and shuffled. 'I hope I see you again before that, Jenny.'

'You might not, Billy,' she said gently. 'The magistrates said I had to leave. For my own good, I expect.'

Billy looked down at his feet. 'Aye, until folks forget, mebbe.'

'Yes,' she said. 'That's it. I'm going now, Billy, and you'd better get back to your customers. Don't keep them waiting.' She smiled at him, though she felt like crying. It was hard for them both, meeting again so soon when they had just said goodbye. But worse for Billy; he looked so miserable and she knew he wanted to say something to her, but didn't have the right words. Which is just as well, she thought as she walked away, for I don't want to hear them.

Jenny kept her eyes straight in front as the carrier's cart drew out of Beverley. There was just one other passenger, who chatted to the carrier, leaving Jenny able to gather her thoughts. They drew out of Saturday Market, along North Bar Within and past St Mary's church, under the arched North Bar, and on towards New Walk and the hamlet of Molescroft. She closed her eyes as they passed the Ingrams' house but on opening them saw the chestnut trees where she and Christy had first pledged their love. She put her hand to her mouth to still her trembling lips as she remembered all that had passed. They said that I should leave Beverley, but I vow that one day I will come back.

It was further than she imagined, and if she hadn't felt so miserable she would have enjoyed the ride through the green gently rolling countryside. The air was clear and there was a smell of autumn, of wood smoke and crisp falling leaves. Hawthorn hedges were already dressed in bright red berries and in the distance, the corn-fields had been harvested and opened to grazing stock. They passed the road marked for the village of Cherry Burton where the other passenger got down and wished her good day, then continued on for another few miles until they came to a road signed to Etton.

Jenny jumped down with her bag as they came into the village and looked around. 'Is this it?' she asked, for it was a very quiet sleepy kind of place with an inn and a collection of houses and cottages.

'Is somebody collecting you?' the carrier asked. 'Cos this is the usual stop.'

When Jenny replied yes, he remarked that he hoped she wouldn't have a long wait and drove on. She glanced up and down the road, but there was no waggon, cart or trap in view so she settled down on the grass verge and prepared to wait. It was a warm sunny afternoon, and after sitting for some time she put her head on her bag and closed her eyes. She must have fallen asleep for she awoke with a start as a voice called, 'Jenny?'

For a second she thought she was dreaming, for the voice was like Christy's. She gave a gasp and clutched her throat as she sat up.

'Jenny?' A very tall, thin man stood above her. His dark hair was long and shaggy with grey streaks at his temples. He wore corduroy breeches and a clean but stained flannel shirt. He stared at her from intense blue eyes. 'I didn't mean to startle you. Are you Jenny?' he repeated.

'Yes.' She scrambled to her feet. 'Sorry. I must have dozed off. I didn't hear you come.'

He nodded. 'Come along then. Get in.' He indicated an old high scarlet waggon, the like of which she hadn't seen before, with the back wheels larger than the front ones, and pulled by two horses. 'Where've you been? This is the third time I've been to look for you!'

'Sorry,' she apologized as she threw her bag in and sat beside him. 'I only found out I was coming on Thursday. My ma made 'arrangements.'

'Without telling you?' He turned to look at her. 'Does she usually do that? I'd have thought you were old enough to make your own plans!'

'I am,' she said. 'I've been working in Beverley, but I – I left my employ and went back to Hull. Then Ma told me she'd arranged for me to come to Aunt Aggie's.'

'Agnes,' he said sharply. 'That's your aunt's name. Not Aggie!'

He pronounced the statement in such an authoritative imperious manner that she was startled and realized that this was no common or labouring man. His voice and bearing was as Christy's had been. He was an educated man, not of her class at all, and she wondered how he came to be collecting her, and why he was dressed in working men's clothes.

'Begging your pardon, sir,' she said in a small voice. 'It's what my mother called her. I've never met my aunt. Does she work for you?'

He gave a wry grunt. 'No. She doesn't. We work together.' Then his mouth tightened into a thin line. 'Or we did,' he muttered and she saw him swallow and his Adam's apple moved in his throat. 'She's sick.' He glanced at her again. 'That's why you've come, isn't it? To look after her!'

'I can do, sir,' she said. 'Though I've no experience of nursing.'

He made a dismissive sound and stared straight between the horse's ears. 'I can't think why she wrote to her sister. Not after so long.' He gave a deep breath and groused, 'But I suppose blood is thicker than water. We won't keep you on, though,' he said abruptly. 'Not if you don't shape up. You must realize that. Even if you are family.'

'Yes, sir,' Jenny said quietly. 'Aunt Agnes might not want me to stay when she meets me. I might not be suitable.' Especially when she finds out I'm expecting a child, she thought. 'So – might I ask who you are, sir? Begging your pardon for my ignorance.'

He nodded solemnly. 'Certainly you can ask. My name is Stephen St John Laslett. Your aunt Agnes is my wife.'

CHAPTER NINE

They travelled for several miles along a narrow road and Jenny asked timidly, 'How far is it to your house, Mr Laslett?'

'Not much further.' His tone was clipped and abrupt. 'We're quite isolated. We live on the Etton Wolds.' He shook the reins to encourage the horses up a track. 'So if you're looking for the delights of town you're going to be disappointed. It's quiet. We don't get visitors and that's how we like it.'

As he spoke, the track widened and rose, with blackthorn and hawthorn hedges and the fading flowers of dog rose on either side. Above the hedges she saw meadows with sheep grazing and heard the cooing of pigeons and the trill of song-birds. 'Look!' she exclaimed, as a large white-winged bird flew alongside them behind the hedge.

He gave a ghost of a smile. 'Barn owl. Going out to supper.'

She glanced sideways at him. He must have been handsome when he was younger, she mused. Still is, I suppose, except he seems so tense and withdrawn, as if he can't smile or laugh. Perhaps he considers it beneath him to be driving a servant girl. It's odd, though. Why is he driving me? Do they not have any other servants? Ma said Aunt Aggie – Agnes – had run away with a swell. I didn't realize she meant a gentleman.

They topped the rise and as they drove through a white farm gate, the thatched roof of a cottage came into view. At least it seemed like a cottage until they drew nearer and the track to it dipped down. She saw that the house was sitting in a hollow and that there were two storeys to it and a barn to the side, making it a substantial building, though not as large as Mr Ingram's which was her only comparison. It was pleasing to the eye, with sweet-smelling honeysuckle round the door and lavender bushes lining the path from the gate.

A woman was standing in the doorway. She was middle-aged but pretty and plump and Jenny couldn't imagine that this could be her aunt, for she was nothing like her own mother. But it was, for she came out to greet her. 'Jenny!' she said. 'Welcome to Lavender Cott. How very nice to meet you. I've often wondered about my sister's sons and daughters. I can see that you favour your father. You have none of your mother in you!'

Jenny bobbed her knee. 'And you are nothing like my mother, Aunt Agnes,' she said shyly, thinking that if anyone looked ill, then it was her mother, who was pale and scraggy, whilst this aunt was not at all.

'No, we were never alike,' Agnes smiled, 'not in looks or temperament. But do come in, dear, and take off your things and we'll have a cup of tea. You must be tired after your journey?'

'She was asleep on the verge when I found her.'

Stephen St John Laslett came into the house and flopped into a chair by the fire. 'I almost didn't see her and came on home.'

'Just a bit tired,' Jenny confessed. 'I left Hull early this morning.'

'And how is your mother?' Agnes was about to make the tea when her husband sprang up from his chair and took the kettle from her and poured the water into the pot.

Jenny was so astounded to see him perform this task, something she had never seen her father do, that she was almost lost for words. 'She's well, Aunt,' she said. 'But I saw her only briefly before I left. I've been working away in Beverley for the last five years.'

'So why did you go back to Hull?' Stephen St John Laslett placed the tray of tea and cups and saucers close to his wife so that she might pour. 'Did you not like Beverley?'

Jenny felt her face flush and was grateful to her aunt who, seeing her discomfort, said quickly, 'I'm sure Jenny will tell all later when she's settled in.'

Jenny drank her tea, conscious of St John Laslett's eyes on her. What a very long name, she thought. I've never come across such a name before. Will I have to say it each time I speak to him? Or maybe he won't let me stay when he discovers that I have been in prison.

'I liked Beverley very well, sir,' she said. 'But my circumstances changed.'

'Mm,' he said, then, quickly finishing his tea, once more sprang to his feet. 'Must go.' He kissed his wife on the forehead. 'I'll be in for

91

supper,' he told her, and crossed the small room with long loping strides like a cat.

'So tell me about your mother,' Agnes said. 'She was the only one of my four sisters who replied to my letters.'

'She's probably the only one who can read or write,' Jenny said, 'even though not very well, and I think that one of *my* sisters probably read your letter to her. But, yes, she seems well enough. Though she doesn't look as well as you, Aunt. The country air must be beneficial to you?'

Her aunt sighed. 'Ah. If that were only so. That's why I asked for your mother's help. There's no-one else I could have asked. I have no children of my own.' She gazed into the flames of the fire. 'It's the one regret of my life that we were not blessed with children.'

Jenny thought of her own family home, crowded with brothers and sisters, and wondered if her aunt really knew what she was missing, but she saw the sadness in her eyes and knew that she should not discuss the merits of family life. She thought that whilst her aunt's husband was out, she should confess her pregnancy, and then if necessary be prepared to leave.

She began her story hesitatingly at first, telling of her employment in Beverley, and then of Christy's unfortunate accidental death and her imprisonment, and as her explanation gathered speed she saw her aunt's eyes cloud with sympathy and anxiety, and before she could stop herself she was sobbing, crying as she hadn't cried before. She had wept on the day of Christy's death and again at the indignity of being locked

92

up, but she hadn't poured out her heartache as she did now. Neither her mother nor her sister had asked her about Christy, or about her own feelings, and she had kept them hidden away. Now they were released and fell in an unstoppable torrent of sorrow, rage, and fear of what might happen to her and her child.

'My mother didn't know about 'child when she wrote to you.' She wiped her reddened eyes on the handkerchief which Agnes had silently handed to her. 'So she can't be blamed, though it was 'first thing she asked me. But I thought I'd take 'chance of coming. I'd nowhere else to go, and I couldn't stop at home. I'm sorry.' She blew her nose. 'I didn't mean to upset you. You've troubles of your own, I'm sure, but if you or your husband don't want me to stay, then I'll leave first thing in 'morning, if you'll give me a bed for tonight.'

Her aunt leant towards her and grasped her hand. 'I'll speak to Stephen later and we'll talk about what we should do. But first you must come upstairs to your room, unpack and have a rest before supper.' She smiled at Jenny in a sad way. 'And then I will tell you *our* story and you will realize that we probably do understand.'

That night Jenny sat at the table in the small neat room that had been prepared for her, and by the light from a candle she took up her pencil and added, in her best hand, to the continuation of her life that she had started whilst in Beverley prison.

'I knew from what my mother told me that her sister had run away from her husband and set up with a young man, but no more than that; yet there is so much more to tell. Aunt Agnes confided that she had been married at seventeen to an older man, an innkeeper. Her father had arranged the marriage one night when he and the innkeeper were in their cups at the inn. He'd thought it would be a convenient arrangement, particularly as the innkeeper was a crony of his.

"But John Bolton was a brutal man," Agnes told me. "I was little more than an unpaid help, and he was cruel. He used to beat me when he was in drink or if I'd displeased him." She sighed very deeply and said that she'd thought that that was going to be her life for ever. Her only consolation was that she didn't bear him any children. And then ten years later she met Stephen and they fell in love.

'He was twenty,' Jenny wrote, 'and from a good family, and here the story is similar to mine, except that they eventually came to spend their life together, whereas my life with Christy has ended in tragedy as theirs, it seems, will also.

'Stephen St John Laslett's family are wealthy, and I have discovered from my aunt that his name is spelt not Sinjun as I'd ignorantly supposed when he told me it, but as in Saint. But to continue: his family were horrified that their only son was taking up with an older married woman, especially one from a poor background, and I suppose they would consider her poor, being from a serving class. Stephen, though, was determined to be with her, rather like Christy with me, though poor sad Christy didn't really know how to go about things. But Stephen borrowed money from a friend to enable them to live, and went out of his family's life.

'That is as far as I have got with their story,' she wrote. 'Agnes's husband died, and so she and Mr Laslett were eventually able to marry and are now man and wife, though seemingly his father isn't interested to know that.'

Jenny put the page with the others. And now she's ill, she thought. The beatings her first husband gave her have damaged her in some way, and that's why she's never had children, though she's had miscarriages, poor soul. Now her husband can only look forward to sorrow and she to pain.

She picked up the pencil again and added a postscript. 'She wants me to stay.'

Birdsong, the rustling in the thatch and the bleating of sheep woke her the next morning, and for a moment she couldn't remember where she was. Then she heard the barking of a dog and a man's voice calling to it. She rose from the bed and went to the window. Her room was at the back of the house and had a view across the meadows towards low hills, a stream and a small woodland. The windows downstairs looked over a garden surrounded by a briar-rose hedge, but the view was restricted on account of the house's sitting low. It's so tucked away, she thought, that no-one would know it was here. Perhaps that is why they chose to live here, away from prying eyes.

She quickly washed and dressed and went downstairs into the kitchen. She found a white apron hanging behind the door and put it on, then taking the kettle from the shelf beside the fire she shook it slightly, found that it was almost full of water, and put it on the fire bar. The coals had already been riddled and more fuel put on the flames, and soon the kettle was boiling.

'Morning!' Stephen St John Laslett came in through the kitchen door and Jenny turned from the table where she was preparing a breakfast tray for her aunt.

'Morning, sir.' Jenny thought he looked sternly at her and she said hurriedly, 'I was preparing a tray for Aunt Agnes. Is that all right?'

'Yes, perfectly. It's why I came in. I generally take her breakfast up. There's tea and preserves in the cupboard. Milk in the larder. Bread in the crock. Agnes doesn't eat much in a morning.' In a sudden movement, he put his hand to his forehead and pressed his fingers over his brows and took a deep breath. Jenny bustled into the larder, knowing that he had become emotional.

'Perhaps you'd like to carry it up, sir?' she said when she had set the tray.

'Yes, I would,' he said. 'And Jenny, don't keep calling me *sir*. Mr Laslett will do.'

'Yes, Mr Laslett. I will. And what would you like for breakfast, sir? I mean Mr Laslett!'

A sudden smile lifted his gaunt features and he picked up the tray. 'Nothing just yet. I'll be in later. Then I'll have two rashers of bacon, two fried eggs and three slices of bread. You'll find everything in the larder.'

After he had taken the tray upstairs and then come down and gone out again, Jenny went up and knocked on her aunt's door. Agnes was sitting at a dressing table with her back to the door and looking into a mirror. 'Come in, Jenny.

96

Come and see me as I really am.'

Jenny smiled and went across the sunny room towards her. 'As you really are–' she began, but her smile faded as her aunt turned towards her. Agnes's rosy cheeks and bright eyes had gone, as had her pretty curls. Her face was sallow and dark shadows sat beneath her eyes, whilst her hair hung listlessly about her neck.

'Are you not well today, Aunt?' Jenny whispered.

'I am not well on any day, Jenny,' Agnes replied softly. 'It takes a great deal of effort to make myself as presentable as I was yesterday. Stephen is the only one who has ever seen me looking like this. Not that we see many people. We live very quietly, just the two of us.' She smiled and nodded. 'And now we are three. Perhaps you will be able to help me be presentable for a little while longer?

'Look.' She opened a wooden box. 'This is my beauty box. Stephen sees me as I really am every morning, then when he comes in later he sees the woman I once was, except of course,' she added, 'a little older.'

She took out a palette of colours. Peach dusting powder for her face, carmine for her lips, and powdered rouge to uplift her cheeks. 'Watch what I do, Jenny,' she said, 'so that when I am too tired to do it myself, you can do it for me.' Holding her powder brush with a pale languid hand, she first hid her deep shadows with white chalky powder, then proceeded to colour her face, blushing her cheeks, touching her lips with a hint of red and darkening her eyebrows with soot which she kept in a small box and applied by delicately spitting

97

on a miniature brush, then dipping the brush into the soot.

'Now for my hair.' She opened a drawer and took out some false fair curls. 'Perhaps you would fasten these for me?'

Jenny took the hairbrush and gently untangled her aunt's hair, smoothing it out and trying not to notice the loose strands which came away with the brush. She carefully twisted it into a chignon and pinned the curls around her face.

'Goodness,' Agnes exclaimed, turning her head this way and that as she looked in the mirror. 'How well it looks. Thank you, Jenny.' She gave a brilliant smile, which quite transformed her face into the one Jenny had seen on her arrival the day before. 'Stephen is going to think he has found another wife.' There was a catch in her voice as she spoke of her husband. 'My poor darling,' she whispered. 'He tries so very hard.'

Jenny suggested that her aunt rested in her room until Mr Laslett returned for breakfast and she had finished some chores. 'I could bring Mr Laslett's breakfast up here, Aunt,' she said. 'If we put the table in the window you could sit with him whilst he eats.' She didn't know if she was being very forward in suggesting such a thing, but she thought how pleasant it would be to look out over the countryside whilst eating. Agnes thought it an excellent idea and said she would have coffee at the same time.

'I'm so glad you came, Jenny,' she said. 'You are going to be an asset, I can tell.'

'Did Mr Laslett mind about my baby, Aunt Agnes?' Jenny asked.

'He said if I didn't mind, then neither did he,' Agnes said. 'And I told him about Christopher Ingram. He knew of the family at one time. He was sad for you.'

He didn't seem sad, Jenny pondered later, when Stephen Laslett questioned her about Christy. He must have been merely considering his wife's feelings, not wanting to upset her.

'Why were you so sure that young Ingram would marry you?' he said brusquely after he had carried his breakfast tray downstairs. 'He might have been just playing games.'

Jenny choked back her tears. 'He did play games,' she said. 'But he believed they were real. No-one understood him like I did. I wasn't bothered about getting married. But I wanted to be with him, to look after him.' She turned her face away. 'I loved him, and he loved me.'

'Yes,' he said after a moment. 'Of course,' and then went on, 'Agnes looks very well this morning. She'll come downstairs shortly. Perhaps you'd help her down?'

CHAPTER TEN

'I thought Beverley was country,' Jenny admitted to her aunt one morning as she dressed her hair. 'I didn't know that 'country was like this.'

'And do you like it?' Agnes wheezed. Sometimes her breathing was laboured. 'Or are you bored? We see few people.'

99

'No, I think it's lovely,' Jenny assured her. 'I love all 'smells of meadow grass and sound of bird-song and the way that 'animals seem so content.' There were a few sheep, a dairy cow and a pig, and a dozen or so hens and ducks.

Her aunt smiled. 'It looks so idyllic, doesn't it? I thought 'same when I first came here. I didn't know what hard work lay in front of us. Lavender Cott was nothing more than a hovel when we first saw it.' She stretched and grimaced, but put on a smile, which didn't fool Jenny at all. She knew that before the morning was over, Agnes would want a dose of the medication that Stephen had obtained from the doctor.

'There's so much to do, Jenny,' her aunt went on, 'and I don't mean just in the house. The cow has to be milked, 'pig to be fed, 'vegetable garden to see to, apples to pick and store for winter. We don't have much money; we have to grow the food we need.'

'Yes,' Jenny said. 'I know.'

Stephen Laslett had shown her over the land he had bought from a local farmer. The farmer was reluctant to sell the ten acres but he was in need of cash, which Stephen Laslett was willing to pay. On the land set into a hollow was a dilapidated shepherd's hut, built of chalk and flint, and there was a stream running through the sloping pastureland. Rabbits which had escaped from a neighbouring warren swarmed over the land.

He and Agnes had made the hut habitable, had the roof thatched, rerouted the stream so that it ran close by the building and dug and built a brick well. They bought two lean and thin-ribbed

100

shire horses, which was all they could afford, and fed and cosseted them until they were fit and able to pull a single-furrow plough. Then they ploughed an acre of grassland and sowed corn. Stephen trapped and sold the rabbits at market and so they were provided with food and money. Over the years they grew vegetables, planted fruit trees, kept hens and ducks, bought sheep and pigs, cut down timber, extended the house and waited in vain for children to fill it.

Could we have done that, Jenny wondered, Christy and me? And she knew that they couldn't. Christy wouldn't have had the stamina for such hard work, she decided. He couldn't have dug ditches or laid hedges as Stephen had. He would not have noticed the sly fox which stole the hens, or the shy deer which grazed the hillside, nor seen the distinction between the owls that hooted at night and the kestrels which hovered by day. He was made for a gentleman's town life, she realized. He would have allowed me to do everything for him.

'I'm strong,' she told her aunt as she put in the final hairpin. 'I can do all of those things that you did. I just need to be shown how.'

'When is your child due, Jenny?' Agnes asked. 'Do you know?'

'I think sometime in 'spring,' Jenny said. 'March or April. I'm not quite sure.'

'We must take care of each other over the winter then,' Agnes murmured. 'I hope I shall still be here.'

'Oh, Aunt.' Jenny was distressed. 'Please don't think such things.'

'I must,' Agnes said softly. 'I must plan for Stephen.'

Jenny understood that, for hadn't she planned with Christy? Though those schemes had gone disastrously wrong. But what would she do if her aunt died? Would Stephen Laslett allow her to stay on? Would he stay here, left only with Agnes's memory? Or would he go back home to his family?

'Are Mr Laslett's parents still alive, Aunt Agnes?' she asked. 'Does he ever see them?'

'His mother died some years ago.' Agnes got up from her chair, then leant on the bed and took deep breaths. 'His father is still alive. He would welcome Stephen back if it were not for me. He's never forgiven me for marrying his son, though if we had had children,' she said pensively, 'I think he might have done. There's no-one else to take the family name, you see; there are no other sons, only daughters.'

She gave a wistful glance at Jenny. 'But Stephen doesn't see him. He says he won't ever go back, not after the way I've been ostracized. Even now I am not accepted, though we are legally man and wife, married in church before witnesses.'

'It's a pity that Mr Laslett's father doesn't know you, Aunt,' Jenny said softly. 'He would recognize your worth, if he did.'

'He calls us peasant farmers.' Agnes gave a dry laugh. 'And of course that is what we are. Stephen's father has hundreds of acres of land, whereas we have only ten. We hire itinerant labourers, Irish migrants or tramps to help us with haymaking and harvest. Everything else we do ourselves. Or we did.' Her voice softened. 'Now, Stephen does it all.'

Although she couldn't do outside work Agnes still cooked and baked and showed Jenny how to bottle fruit, make jams and chutneys, pluck a chicken and preserve eggs in brine. Jenny had never baked anything in her life. At her home in Hull pies and pastries had been bought from the baker. Now she took great delight in producing a golden crusty rabbit pie out of the oven, or making a pot of steaming vegetable soup.

'We'll make a countrywoman of you yet, Jenny,' her aunt said as they ate a dish of game stew one evening. 'Won't we, Stephen?'

Stephen glanced at Jenny and then at his wife's plate. She had eaten little. He nodded. 'Just as we did of you.' He got up from the table, excusing himself, and went from the room.

He doesn't want to think of me taking Agnes's place, Jenny thought, watching as her aunt's eyes grew wistful again. I shall have to move on. He won't want me here.

'I was a town girl, just like you, Jenny,' Agnes said with a catch in her voice. 'But I learnt by my mistakes and Stephen was always a farmer at heart. Since he was a child he had watched the men on his father's land, though once he had thought of being a soldier.'

As autumn turned into winter, Jenny grew heavier and more cumbersome. She thrived on the fresh food, eggs and milk; her complexion was rosy and blooming whilst in contrast her aunt, day by day, grew paler and thinner.

'Aunt Agnes told me', Jenny wrote in her notes,

'that Stephen said he loved her as she was, and that there was no need for her to paint her face, but I believe that she wants to. She doesn't want to look into the mirror and see someone there that she doesn't recognize. So I carefully apply the powder to cover the shadows beneath her eyes and give a little blush to her cheeks, and they both pretend that that is how she really is.

'I grow fatter by the day. My skin is good and my hair is glossy and if Christy was here to see me, he would say I was beautiful. When my son is born, I will call him Christopher in memory of his father and to remind me of happier times before disaster overtook us.'

Winter came on fast and hard. The sheep were brought down into the barn. Water from the stream was carried in to them every morning and a pail filled for the house, for the iron pump to the well was frozen. The disconsolate pig grunted in its pen and the ducks huddled in a corner of the barn, occasionally paddling across the snow to the stream, where they dipped their heads and cleaned their breast feathers before they waddled back to the warmth of the straw-filled barn. The hens stopped laying, so some of the older ones had their necks wrung and were put into the cooking pot.

'It's going to be a long winter,' Stephen said one morning as he brought in a pile of wood and kindling for the fire. 'For goodness' sake don't give birth until the spring, Jenny. The roads are impassable. The doctor wouldn't be able to get through.'

Jenny was plucking a chicken and had feathers all over her aproned lap, but she stopped what she was doing and stared at him. She had felt so well. She hadn't given thought to having a doctor visit her. 'The doctor?' she said. 'Would I have to pay?'

Stephen glanced back at her. 'Do you have any money?'

She shook her head. She hadn't been given any wages. It hadn't been mentioned, and she didn't know quite how she stood. Her situation wasn't the same as a hired servant's. It hadn't seemed right to ask her aunt about such a thing and she was still rather in awe of Stephen Laslett, even though he wasn't quite as distant as he had been, and had recently told her to call him Stephen, which she did only rarely.

'I have a friend who's a doctor,' he said. 'He's been giving Agnes medication for her illness. We were at school together,' he muttered. 'He's the only one who has kept in touch. I'll ask him nearer your time.'

Christmas came and Jenny cooked her first Christmas dinner. Stephen carried Agnes downstairs and she sat in an easy chair with her feet on a footstool and a blanket wrapped around her. 'What a fraud I am,' she said weakly. 'Letting you two do all the work.'

'You must tell me what to do next, Aunt,' Jenny said. 'I've been boiling this plum pudding for hours, since first thing this morning. It's surely done by now?' She took the rattling lid off the pan where the pudding was steaming, wrapped in a cotton cloth.

'A little longer,' her aunt smiled, 'and then if Stephen can find a drop of rum, I'll tell you how to make a sauce.'

Stephen rummaged in a cupboard and brought out a half-bottle of rum. 'I've been saving this for a special occasion.' His voice was tight. 'And I can't think of any other occasion that will be more special.' He poured some into a jug for Jenny to use in the sauce, then took four eggs from the larder, cracked them into a bowl, whisked them with honey and melted butter and stirred in a glassful of rum. He poured half a glassful of the mixture and kneeling down by Agnes's side handed it to her. 'There you are, my darling. This will pick you up.' His voice broke and he put his head on her knee.

She stroked his face and took a sip of the mixture. 'I feel better already,' she said softly, and Jenny hustled out of the room, too choked by emotion to stay.

In January they were marooned in the house and yard, the snows too deep to venture further than the stream, which fortunately didn't freeze. Jenny looked at the white landscape, at the peaks and troughs and the trees bowed down by the weight of snow, and marvelled at the beauty of it. She saved crumbs and scraps of meat to feed the birds, and a cock pheasant daily braved the dog to feed by her feet. For gathering the few eggs and milking the cow, which Stephen had taught her to do, she wore an old coat of his and a pair of her aunt's stout boots, for she had come ill equipped for country weather.

By the beginning of March Agnes was confined to bed, too weak to venture downstairs, and Stephen rode to the nearby village of Etton to fetch the doctor. When Dr Hill came, he nodded amiably at Jenny as he passed her to follow Stephen upstairs. 'You look well, young lady,' he said. He was a tall, broad-set man who topped his friend Laslett by several inches. 'Will you be needing my assistance or will you manage on your own?'

'I don't know, sir.' Jenny blushed. 'It's my first time.'

'I'll get a woman to come to you,' he said. 'Don't worry.'

When he came down alone a quarter of an hour later his demeanour had changed. He motioned to Jenny to come and sit beside him. 'Birth and death,' he said. 'Both perfectly natural occurrences. But one brings joy and one brings sorrow. Are you prepared for that?'

'I've already had sorrow in my life, sir,' she answered. 'I shall be glad to have some joy.'

'Stephen will take it hard when Agnes leaves him,' he said in a low voice. 'As leave him she will. Can you help him?'

'I don't know, sir,' she said. 'He might not want me to stay. I'm not his responsibility.'

'No, I realize that.' He rubbed his chin thoughtfully. 'But perhaps you can help each other.' He got up to leave. 'I'll come again next week. The weather is improving, spring will soon be here.' He looked squarely at her. 'A spring birth, I think? A renewal of life!'

Jenny went into labour, though she didn't know that was what it was, on 31 March 1860. She felt some discomfort during the morning and put it down to overeating the night before. 'I'm such a pig,' she said to Agnes as she propped her up in

107

bed and plumped up her pillows. 'But that rabbit pie, if I say so myself, was scrumptious. I wish you'd tried it, Aunt. Stephen ate hardly any, so that's why I ate so much.'

Jenny was doing her best to be cheerful, though it was hard when she saw Agnes getting weaker and frailer, and spending every day in bed.

'You're eating for two,' her aunt said hoarsely. 'I'll try some tomorrow. But persuade Stephen to eat. He needs his strength.' She put her hand over Jenny's. 'You'll stay with him, won't you, Jenny?'

'If he wants me to, Aunt Agnes.' There were no secrets between them. They were both aware of the inevitable. It was only when Stephen was with them that they all pretended that life was continuing as normal.

'I'll tell him that you must,' Agnes said. 'You must have a place for your child.' She gazed wistfully at Jenny. 'It's what we have always wanted. A child around the house.'

As Jenny continued with her tasks during the day, she thought of how when Agnes was still able to come downstairs she had followed her with her eyes, watching her every move. Not checking on her work, but as if she was reassuring herself that all would be well after she was gone. By little hints on what to do during the year, it seemed as if she was planning for Jenny to take her place.

By teatime, Jenny was decidedly uncomfortable. She pulled herself upstairs to take Agnes a cup of tea and paused to breathe deeply. 'I'm a bit out of sorts, Agnes,' she said. 'That pie is giving me some gyp. I'll have to go and have a lie down.'

'All right, dear.' Her aunt was half asleep.

Stephen had given her a dose of opium an hour before and it was taking effect. 'Don't you worry about me.'

Jenny roused herself at suppertime and, groaning and panting a little, went down to prepare Stephen's meal. She gave him the leftover pie and heated up potatoes, and took it upstairs to him where he was sitting at Agnes's bedside.

An hour later when darkness had closed in, and she had cleared away and built up the fire, she shouted up to him. 'Mr Laslett – Stephen!'

'What is it?'

She called back, 'I don't feel well.'

He came to the top of the stairs and looked down to where she was holding on to the stair rail. 'You haven't– Is the baby coming?'

She turned incredulous eyes up to him. 'I don't know. I thought it was 'rabbit pie that had upset me!'

He gave a short laugh and came down. 'Rabbit pie! Don't you know when you're due? What did Hill say when he was last here?'

'He said a spring birth.' She felt embarrassed talking to him about it.

'Go and sit down,' he said briskly. 'I think you're in labour.'

'I can't,' she said. 'Sit down, I mean. It's too uncomfortable.'

He drew in a sharp breath. 'I'll go and fetch the midwife that Hill told us about. Will you be all right until then?'

'I think so,' she said. 'I'll go up and stay with Agnes until you come back.'

'Please, if you will!' His eyes were dark and

brooding. 'I don't think it will be much longer, Jenny,' he said quietly. 'She's in a great deal of pain.' He gave a shudder. 'I hate to see her suffer.'

'So do I,' she said. 'But she needs you there. Go quickly,' she added. 'I'll be all right.'

Jenny paced the floor of her aunt's room, not wanting to disturb her but not wanting to be alone either. 'Jenny,' Agnes whispered. 'Give me your hand.'

Jenny did as she was bid and a sudden spasm gripped her, causing her to clutch Agnes tightly. 'Sorry! Oh, I'm so sorry!' she cried out.

'It's all right. Squeeze tight if you want to,' Agnes said breathlessly. 'I won't mind.'

Jenny knelt by the bed and clutched her aunt's hand. 'I didn't want to make a fuss,' she said. 'But I hadn't thought ahead to the birth. I somehow didn't expect–' She took a deep breath as another spasm creased her.

Agnes stroked Jenny's head. 'I wish I could help you, Jenny, but I'm so weak.' She added in a whisper, 'Yet I'm so glad that you're here and that I'm with you. I shan't mind dying now – I feel involved in creation.' Tears trickled down her thin cheeks. 'I feel as if this baby is part of me and your pain is mine.'

They heard the slam of the door and Stephen's hurrying feet up the stairs. 'She's not there,' he exclaimed as he came into the room. 'She's gone to stay with her daughter in Driffield.' He looked from Jenny kneeling by the bed to his wife lying in it. 'Look,' he said, biting his lip. 'There's no time to fetch the doctor. I've never delivered a child. But I've delivered lambs and calves since I was a boy, so if you'll let me, I will help you at the end.'

Jenny stared at him in horror, then considered and nodded. The doctor was a man; he would have helped her had he been here. Perhaps, she thought, as Stephen is a farmer, he'll know what to do, whereas I don't. When her mother was giving birth to her younger brothers, Jenny had been turned out of the house.

'You'll have to get through it now as best you can,' Stephen said, 'but when you think you're ready, call me and I'll come.'

'How will I know?' she asked.

'You'll know,' Agnes croaked from the bed. 'Be sure of that.'

Jenny went to lie down on her own bed, but she couldn't settle and paced the floor, holding on to the bedrail when the pain was intense. Then as the sky started to lighten and the birds began their morning chorus, she knew that the time had come. 'It's a new month,' she gasped. 'A new day, and my son – Christy's son – is about to be born.'

'Stephen,' she called. 'Come now. Hurry.'

CHAPTER ELEVEN

Stephen had been reassuring and patient as Jenny had cried and cursed him as he'd urged her to push. 'For God's sake I am pushing!' she'd screamed at him, and then immediately apologized. 'Sorry. Sorry. Sorry.'

'It's coming! It's coming,' he'd urged her, then

111

gently laid his hand on her naked belly to calm her before easing the baby from her. He held up the slippery newborn infant and gently patted its back until a mewling cry issued from tiny lungs.

There was a transfixed look of wonder on his face as he gazed at the infant, then turning to Jenny he said, 'You have a beautiful daughter, Jenny.' She heard the catch in his voice and saw the glisten in his eyes as he placed the baby in her arms. 'A lovely little girl.'

But it should have been a boy, was Jenny's first thought. That had been my plan. To produce a son as Christy's heir. I would have taken him to the Ingrams when he was grown up and said, here he is, the rightful successor to the Ingram name. She looked down at the child and then gave a start as she realized that Stephen was speaking to her.

'"Put her to your breast, Jenny," Jenny wrote in her book that night. 'That's what he was saying, and I saw the look of tenderness as he gazed at my child. He didn't turn away as I unbuttoned my nightgown, and I didn't feel at all embarrassed as I lifted out my breast and placed her on my nipple, for hasn't he seen more of me than any other man? More even than Christy, for our inexperienced fumbling was always under cover of darkness, beneath chestnut trees, petticoats and shirt tails.

'He sat beside me on the bed as the infant suckled my breasts and then asked if he might show her to Agnes. I said of course he could, for she must have been most anxious and disturbed by the noise I had been making. So whilst I sat on my chamber pot for the afterbirth to come away, as Stephen said I should, he wrapped the babe in a sheet and took her into Agnes's room opposite. I saw them through the partly open door and watched as he placed her in Agnes's arms. She kissed the top of the baby's forehead and then Stephen leant forward to kiss Agnes on the cheek. She whispered something to him and I saw him sit back as if she had said something startling, and he shook his head. She spoke again and touched his cheek, and he put his hand to his head and I could tell by the way his shoulders shook that he was weeping.'

Dr Hill called two days later and found Jenny going about her usual chores and the baby sleeping in a padded drawer in the corner of the kitchen. 'You've been delivered safely, I see,' he commented. 'Did Mrs Burley come in time?'

'No,' Jenny admitted. 'Mr Laslett delivered her.'

'Did he, by Jove!' The doctor gave a hearty laugh. 'Well, he was always practical. And are you well?' he asked, putting on his medical manner. 'No difficulties?'

'No, sir, none at all.' Jenny glanced towards the stair door. 'Not with me, but my aunt is very ill. Mr Laslett spends all his time with her.'

'And are you prepared for the inevitable?' The doctor raised his eyebrows, but lowered his voice. 'You have your child to comfort you, of course. Mr Laslett will take it very hard, having no-one.'

'I've promised my aunt that I'll stay if he wants me to,' Jenny told him.

'And if he doesn't want, where will you go?' Dr Hill looked at her quizzically.

Jenny shook her head. 'Nowhere,' she said. 'I'll have to apply to 'parish.' She was prepared for that. When she had seen Agnes and Stephen talking on the day of the birth, she was sure that Agnes was imploring Stephen to let them stay, and that Stephen was refusing, not because he didn't like her, but because he couldn't bear to have another woman in Agnes's place.

The doctor took in a deep breath as he pondered. 'I see!' was all he said before turning to go upstairs.

Stephen's face was ashen when the two men came downstairs. Jenny put the kettle on the fire and placed the teapot ready to make a brew of tea.

'Something a little stronger, I think, Jenny,' Dr Hill said. 'If you have it.'

Jenny glanced at Stephen. She never went into the cupboard where he kept one or two bottles of spirits, which he gave sparingly to Agnes with hot water and honey. But he nodded and motioned her to go to it. There was half a bottle of whisky and an almost empty rum bottle. She brought out the whisky and fetched two glasses, setting them down on the table in front of the men.

'Shall I go up to Aunt Agnes?' she asked Stephen. 'Or is she sleeping?'

'She's sleeping.' The doctor answered for him. 'Let her rest for a while, then go up.'

Jenny swung the kettle off the fire, and picking up the baby went outside. She walked up to the gate and leant against it. The day was bright and sunny, and here and there splashes of early white blossom were emerging in the hawthorn hedgerows. There was a smell of new grass, the bleat of young lambs in the meadow and the distinctive call of yellowhammers. She hugged the child to her. 'This could be a new beginning,' she whispered. 'If only we can stay.'

She heard the door creak open and the doctor came up the path towards her. 'What name have you given her?' he asked as he approached.

'Christina April. But she hasn't been baptized yet.' Jenny gazed down at the baby. Though she had at first been disappointed at her not being a boy, already she loved her and was making other plans. 'Mr Laslett wanted me to call her Angel. He said that's what she is!'

'I'm sure that she is. Jenny,' he spoke gravely, 'your aunt hasn't much longer. I've given Stephen medication to give to Agnes to ease her pain and help her depart this life. He might not be able to do it. I'm asking if you will, if he can't?'

A sudden image of the prison cell swam into Jenny's head. 'Will I get into trouble?' she whispered. 'Will it be a crime?'

'No,' he said gently. 'It will be a kindness.'

That night after supper Stephen called Jenny into the bedroom. 'Agnes wants to speak to you,' he said hoarsely, and as Jenny approached the bed he positioned himself outside the door.

'Come close by me, Jenny,' her aunt whispered and motioned her to come nearer. 'I can't speak for long.' Although she was pale with dark rings below her eyes, she seemed peaceful. 'I'm not afraid,' she said. 'And I'm quite happy, especially since you had the baby. She's a renewal of life, so we mustn't be afraid of death.'

Jenny felt a lump gathering in her throat and found it hard to speak, but Agnes seemed to gather strength to say, 'I want you to stay here and Stephen has agreed. I've asked him to promise me something and although he hasn't yet agreed, he says he will try.' She closed her eyes for a moment. 'He'll tell you what it is when 'time is right.' She put her hand into Jenny's. 'I'm going to rest now. Go and see to your baby. I can hear her calling you.'

There was no sound coming from the baby, but Jenny leant towards her aunt and kissed her cheek. 'Dr Hill asked me to give you your medicine,' she said, picking up the bottle from the side table. 'Just a small dose to help you sleep.' She spooned the liquid into her mouth. 'Sleep well, dearest Agnes,' she choked. 'Thank you for what you've done for me.'

She passed Stephen as she went out of the room but neither of them spoke, and he again took up his vigil by the bed.

Jenny took him a cup of tea an hour later and he was slouched half asleep in the chair. He jumped when she touched his shoulder and looked towards Agnes, who was sleeping. 'Thank you,' he murmured, but when Jenny suggested he lie down on the bed to rest, he refused. 'I might fall asleep,' he said, 'and not hear Agnes if she should wake.'

Jenny went to her own bed, first asking Stephen to call her if she was needed. She tucked the baby into the crook of her arm and dozed off and was awoken by her nuzzling against her, her tiny mouth searching for her breast. The dawn was just breaking and a rustling and twittering was coming from the ivy around the house walls as the birds roused themselves. 'Breakfast time,' she murmured, gazing at Christina. 'That's what they're saying. Another day has begun.'

She fed her and then, getting out of bed, placed the infant in the middle of the bed with a pillow on either side of her. Then Jenny put a shawl round her shoulders, and padded in bare feet to the other bedroom. Stephen was still sitting in his chair but leaning over with his head on the bed, fast asleep. She tiptoed in and saw Agnes lying still, her eyes closed. She's gone. Jenny took a deep breath. She went to sleep and didn't wake up.

Jenny tiptoed out of the room again and went downstairs, riddled the fire and put on more wood, then placed the kettle over it. Best if he makes the discovery himself, she considered. He won't want me there. Not yet, anyway. She waited five more minutes and then set about some tasks, making a noise so that Stephen would hear. She opened the kitchen door and spoke to the dog whose kennel was outside, and rattled the water pail, and then as the kettle steamed she made a pot of tea.

She was sitting by the fire, a cup of tea in her hand, when Stephen came down. Jenny looked up enquiringly, but didn't speak. Stephen's face was drawn but calm. He swallowed hard and said, 'She's gone, Jenny. Agnes has left me.'

He went to the door and, opening it, looked out. 'Such a lovely morning,' he murmured, 'and she's not here to see it.'

Jenny came behind him and tentatively put her

hand on his arm. 'Perhaps she's got a better view of it than we have,' she murmured. 'Perhaps her spirit is out there looking over the land and her home.'

He gave a crooked, trembling smile. 'I'd like to think she is,' he said. 'I'll try to hold on to that.'

Jenny washed and dressed, putting on a dark skirt and blouse out of respect for Agnes, and looked in at her. Stephen had straightened the bedspread, smoothed the pillows and arranged Agnes's fine hair across them. She looks younger now that the pain has gone, Jenny thought, then, turning to the drawer where Agnes kept her face powders and false curls, she took out the curls and pinned them carefully around Agnes's face.

'What are you doing?' Stephen stood in the doorway.

'I'm – Aunt Agnes liked to look nice,' Jenny stammered. 'I thought – if anyone should call – to pay their respects, I mean.'

'No-one will call,' Stephen said bluntly. 'Except Hill, when I fetch him. But – yes, she did. You can leave them on.' He turned to go downstairs. 'I came to tell you I don't want any breakfast. I'll be in the barn if you want me.'

'But ... shouldn't we be doing something?' Jenny halted him as he took a step down. 'I mean – arrange something?' She had never been involved with funerals, but she knew that preparations had to be made.

'It will be taken care of. Once Hill has been to certify death, we can get on with the burial. Agnes didn't want a priest.' He gazed at her from the lower step. 'I'm about to make a casket, and then she'll be buried in the top meadow.'

'Oh!' Jenny gave a small gasp. 'I didn't realize that was allowed.'

He grunted. 'Whether it is or not, that's what is going to happen. It's what Agnes wanted.'

'That's all right then,' she murmured and tears began to fall for the first time that morning.

'Yes.' He nodded. 'It is.'

She could hear the sawing and hammering all morning, and at midday she took him a bottle of cold tea and a bacon sandwich. 'You should eat something,' she said. 'It'll keep your strength up.'

'You sound like Agnes.' He sat down on an upturned pail and took the food from her. 'Or is that what all women say?'

'I don't know,' she answered. 'I can't remember my mother ever having to remind me to eat.'

'What's your mother like?' he asked. 'Is she like Agnes?'

'No. Nothing like her. I think Agnes was quite different from all her sisters. Was she beautiful when she was young?' she asked.

'Oh, yes.' His voice took on an enthusiastic lilt. 'When I first saw her – it was in her husband's inn, you know.'

Jenny nodded. Agnes had told her that.

'I'd gone in with some friends. We'd travelled into Hull for a jolly and were on our way to one of the theatres.' He gazed into space as he looked back in time. 'We'd already had a few glasses of Hull ale, but decided to have one more before going to the show. The inn was in the Market Place and Agnes was serving at the tables. I saw that she'd been crying and that there was a bruise on her cheek. I spoke to her, but she didn't answer and looked away in the direction of the innkeeper. I realized that he was the reason she was crying. She was obviously frightened of him. He was a big brute of a fellow.'

He bit into his bread and bacon and pondered. 'I stayed behind. The other fellows went on to the theatre, but I stayed. I had a young man's notion of rescuing her. I didn't know then that he was her husband.'

'And you fell in love with her?' Jenny asked.

He nodded. 'Yes. Immediately.' He glanced up at her and smiled. 'Some people don't believe in love at first sight. But I know, Jenny. It can happen.'

'Oh, yes!' Jenny said. 'Of course it can!'

They seemed more at ease with each other after their conversation and throughout the rest of the afternoon, as he continued with his hammering and planing, she occasionally heard him whistling. It's done him good to talk, she mused, but then gave a wry smile as she thought he would comment that that was what a woman would say.

Later in the day, he came in, washed and changed and said he was going to ride over to tell Dr Hill about Agnes. 'He'll come tomorrow,' he said. 'And that's when we'll have the burial. You don't have to come if you don't want to.'

'I do want to,' she said. 'Agnes was my kin. It's only right that I should be there.'

The sun had gone down when he returned, and after having some supper he changed into his oldest clothes and went out again. She watched him as, with a spade over his shoulder, he went out of the garden and along the track. Then she lost sight of him, so she went upstairs into the room where Agnes was lying, and looked out of the window. 'There he is, Aunt Agnes,' she said softly. 'He's preparing a place where he'll always be able to see you.'

Stephen had reached a high point in the meadow where the ground levelled out into a flat area. It was here that he put his spade to the earth, taking off the top sods of grass and placing them to one side. Then he started to dig. Jenny turned away. *What love he has for her.* She held back her tears as she felt a profound sorrow that her love for Christy had been snatched away. Then she heard the baby Christina crying. She took a deep, deep breath. *But I have my child. That is love enough.*

CHAPTER TWELVE

There were just three of them at the burial, four including the baby Christina who slept in Jenny's arms. Dr Hill said a few comforting words, then the two men lowered the plain wooden casket into the grave. Jenny and the doctor threw in a handful of soil and Stephen picked up his spade and began to fill up the deep space.

'A cup of tea, I think, don't you, Jenny?' the doctor said and they turned away down the hill, leaving Stephen alone in his task.

Jenny had prepared a plate of bread and butter and cold chicken and brought out a fruit cake, which she had made the day before. 'Delicious,' the doctor proclaimed. 'You've got a good hand for baking!'

'Never baked before I came here, sir,' she said. 'Agnes showed me how.'

'Then she's left you a fine legacy.' Dr Hill took another slice. 'If you feed Stephen as well as this he won't want you to leave.'

'He's not said yet whether he wants me to stay, Dr Hill,' Jenny said anxiously. 'And I've not liked to ask him. Would it be proper, do you think, if I do stay?'

The doctor raised his eyebrows. 'Depends whose opinion you care about. Your parents might not be pleased, but then, you are already an unmarried mother. What do they say about that?'

'I've not written to tell them that I've got a daughter, though my mother knew I was expecting.' Jenny shook her head. 'She wasn't bothered about knowing about the birth, but she asked me to write and tell her about Agnes.'

'Strange, isn't it, that some people like to know about the close of a chapter, but not about the beginning of one? I'd say that if she is so uninterested, don't bother to say anything.' He held out his cup for more tea. 'There is no-one else who needs to know. Stephen and Agnes lived quiet lives with few visitors, just the itinerant workers and they don't count.'

'Who don't count?' Stephen came into the room in his stockinged feet, having left his muddy boots at the door.

'The itinerant workers when they come to help with haymaking,' Dr Hill said, looking at him over his cup.

'They do count. I couldn't manage without them.' Stephen flopped into a chair and Jenny got up to make another brewing of tea.

'No. What I was saying,' explained the doctor, 'was that it doesn't matter to them or to anyone else that Jenny is living here as your housekeeper, now that Agnes is no longer here,' he added.

'What do you mean? Of course it doesn't matter. Why should it?' Stephen's voice rose tensely. 'It's nothing to do with anyone else what I do. It never has been and it never will be.' He took a cup of tea from Jenny. 'I live as I please and Jenny should do the same.' He looked across at her. 'So if you want to stay, that's fine by me. I'd expect you to do your share of the work, of course. You've seen what there is to do.' He shrugged and added brusquely, 'But if you're uncomfortable with the situation and would rather leave, that's up to you.'

'I'd like to stay, please,' Jenny said in a small voice. 'I've nowhere else to go.'

Stephen nodded. 'I can't pay you. You realize that? You can keep the money from the eggs if you sell any; they'll sometimes buy them down in Etton if you want to take them.'

The baby started to whimper from her drawer in the corner and Stephen, being nearer, got up and went to her. He bent down and to Jenny's surprise he picked up the baby and put her close to his cheek. 'Little angel,' he said softly and rocked her gently in the crook of his arm. 'Do you know what I'm going to do next?' He continued speaking to the child. 'I'm going to make a fine crib for you to sleep in instead of this old drawer, and your mama can sew you some fine linen sheets and proper baby gowns.'

Dr Hill smiled reassuringly at Jenny, and stood up to go. 'I'll leave you to it then, old fellow.' He offered his hand to Stephen, who hitched the baby into his other arm, took hold of his hand and shook it firmly.

'Thank you, George,' he said quietly. 'For all you have done for us, especially for Agnes. It has been appreciated, as you know.' He blinked rapidly. 'Your help and friendship over the years, when all others failed, has meant everything to me.'

George Hill patted him on the shoulder. 'Reciprocated, dear fellow,' he said gruffly. 'And it won't end here. We shall meet again soon.'

He turned to Jenny. 'Goodbye, Jenny. Good luck in your new position as housekeeper and cook! What was your work before, by the way?'

Jenny paused for a moment, lost in thought as she pondered on her elevated role. 'Kitchen maid,' she murmured vaguely. 'I was Jenny kitchen-maid.'

Stephen started work on the crib, but first he opened a chest of drawers in his bedroom, revealing crisp white linen, cotton and flannel which smelled of lavender. 'Use it,' he said briskly to Jenny. 'Agnes bought it years ago from the packman when – when she thought we would have children.'

Well, another thing that Miss Smithers taught me, as well as to read and write, was how to turn a good hem, Jenny thought as she sat of an evening stitching small flannel gowns and hemming cot sheets. The child, between her birth and Agnes's death, had been wrapped in a cotton sheet and shawl with a triangle of old towel for a napkin.

Christina was a small baby with straight dark hair. Like mine, Jenny mused, but will she look like an Ingram when she's grown or will she look like a Graham? She has a touch of my da in her, I think.

A week after giving birth, Jenny was feeding the hens and collecting eggs, and a week after that was helping Stephen to milk the cow twice a day, though he insisted that she should rest for an hour after their midday meal. 'You'll lose your milk if you get overtired,' he said. 'I can manage for the time being, but I'll need you to help with the lambing and the farrowing.' He gave a rare smile. 'But you'll know all about that now!'

There had been some lambs born during the harsh days of January and February but the second lambing season had now started and the pig was due to farrow. 'You'll have to show me,' she said, and then suddenly blushed. 'I mean – it's not 'same as having a baby yourself.'

'Almost,' he said. 'But not quite. You won't have to do anything, just check on the sow every couple of hours and make sure she doesn't lie on them.'

The ewes had been brought down into the barn. Some had started to lamb, and because the weather was cold the lambs had to be put to their mothers' milk as soon as they were on their feet. Jenny had dashed, in between feeding Christina, checking the sow, feeding the hens and preparing a meal, to take Stephen a hot drink, a slice of pie and a chunk of fruit cake. I'm a town girl, she thought, as for the third time that morning she had trekked across to the small meadow and the pigpen to check on the sow. I never in my life imagined I would be tramping in mud and pig dung.

She heard Stephen shouting to her from the barn, waving his arm for her to come. 'I've lost one of the ewes,' he called. 'And the others won't take to her lamb.' He picked up the lamb and put it into her arms. 'Take it home and feed it with the bottle or we'll lose that as well. Keep it warm.'

Jenny scurried back and as she approached the house door could hear Christina crying. 'You're going to have to wait, my darling,' she called to her. 'I know you're not as cold and hungry as this little creature.' She looked down at the baby, cosy in her new cot, and gently touched her cheek. Christina moved her head towards her, gave a hiccup and stopped crying. 'Too much rich food,' Jenny murmured, and turned her attention to feeding the lamb.

Half an hour later she went again to the pigpen and found that the sow had a litter of six piglets. Four were snuffling at her teats, but two were lying quite still. 'Oh no! Are they dead?' Jenny gingerly touched one. It was still very slightly warm, as was the other. She picked them both up and wrapping them in her apron scurried back to the house. She placed them in front of the fire, whilst she poured warm water from the kettle into a bowl and then put the piglets into it. Ten minutes later they were again in front of the fire and starting to snuffle and squeal and the lamb was curiously nosing them.

When Stephen arrived back at the house late for

his midday meal, he found Jenny sitting in a chair with Christina at her breast, the lamb trapped between her knees whilst she fed it with a feeding bottle, and two piglets squealing at her feet.

His look was one of pure amazement, and then he started to laugh. 'What on earth–'

She grinned triumphantly and nodded her head towards the piglets. 'Poached pig,' she said. 'They were nearly dead, so I put them in hot water to see if they would revive. And they did! I fed them with milk from the bottle too. I hope I did right?'

He took the lamb and the bottle from her and sitting down opposite her took over the feeding. 'You've done wonderfully well, Jenny,' he said quietly. 'I'm proud of you.'

This unusual praise took her by surprise and she felt tears spring to her eyes. 'I only did what I thought was sensible,' she murmured.

He gazed at her for a moment. 'Yes,' he said. 'Keep them warm and well fed. Just as you do with a baby.'

'Mr Laslett and I are getting along very well,' Jenny wrote. 'Though there is so much to do that we have barely time to talk. I'm very tired by the evening, so much so that when we've finished supper and I've shut up the hens and given Christina her feed, I'm almost too weary to climb the stairs to bed. I fell asleep in the chair one night as I was feeding her and when I woke, found Mr Laslett watching me. I realized that I was sitting in Agnes's chair and felt such remorse, for he must have been thinking of her, and how she used to sit across from him, and how much they wanted children of their own. He took Christina from me when she had finished, and patted her back to bring up her wind, and I thought what a good father he would have made. Few men would have known to do that, since child rearing is generally left to the women, but perhaps it's because he's a farmer and cares for his animals. I moved the chair to a different place the next morning.'

By June the air was filled with the smells of summer. The honeysuckle and roses were in bloom and the perfume so heavy and sweet that Jenny felt she could eat it. The hedgerows were filled with twittering, nesting birds and in the little orchard the hens and cockerel clucked and crowed and the pig scratched beneath the apple trees. Foxgloves hid their bright colours in shady places and buttercups glowed like golden stars at dusk.

Jenny was rolling pastry for a rabbit pie. The door was wide open as the day was warm and the fire built up with wood for the oven to get hot for the baking. Christina was in her cot outside the door where Jenny, when she looked up, could see her toes and plump little legs kicking. She put the rabbit pieces into a pie dish and placed the pastry over it, crimping the edges with a fork as she had seen the Ingrams' cook do, then looked up as she heard an unfamiliar sound.

The rattle of wheels and clop of horses' hooves made her wipe her hands on a cloth and go to the door. A chaise was pulling up at the gate. The driver jumped down and opened the carriage door to help a young woman out. They're lost, Jenny thought. They've missed their way somehow. She waited as the woman, dressed in a

128

white muslin gown and pink bonnet, opened the gate and proceeded down the path towards her.

She stopped abruptly in front of Jenny and looked her up and down. 'This *is* Mr St John Laslett's house, is it not?' Her tone was high and haughty. 'I believe my directions are correct?'

'Yes, miss. This is Mr Laslett's house.' Jenny gazed back at her. 'He's not here just now. He's haymaking.'

'Oh!' The young woman looked down her nose. 'And you are?'

Jenny bridled at her arrogant manner. I don't have to tell her, she thought. Stephen said it doesn't matter about other people. I can live as I please, as he does. 'Who are *you*, miss?' she asked. 'Is Mr Laslett expecting you?' She remembered that when she worked for Mr Ingram, he would never see anyone without an appointment.

The visitor looked astonished, then with a sudden gasp put her hand to her mouth. 'You're not – are you – Agnes?'

'No!' Stephen came from round the back of the house. He had a hayfork in his hand and a battered felt hat on his head. 'She's not! What are you doing here, Bella?'

'That isn't a very warm greeting for your sister, Stephen,' she said.

'What do you expect? I give what I receive, and I've received nothing from you. Any of you.' Stephen stared grimly at his sister and Jenny looked for a likeness between them and found none. This young woman was slight and fair with a pettishness on her pretty face.

'It's not easy with Father,' she began. 'Are you

129

going to ask me in?'

'I don't know! Are we going to ask her in, Jenny? This is Arabella, by the way,' he remarked casually. 'The youngest of my four sisters.'

'Please come in, Miss Laslett,' Jenny said, moving the cot to one side to make room for the visitor's hooped gown.

'St John Laslett,' she corrected her and stared down at Christina. 'Whose child is this?'

'Mine,' Jenny said fiercely and stood aside to let her enter. She saw Bella's questioning glance at her brother, but Stephen's face was impassive and he remained silent as he led her into the house.

'Oh, this is so sweet, Stephen,' Arabella enthused as she looked around the room. 'How very cosy!'

Jenny suddenly realized that the pie hadn't been put in the oven and dashed to retrieve it. 'Sorry, Mr Laslett,' she said. 'I didn't think you'd be down yet.'

'I wouldn't have been.' He wiped his sweating brow with the back of his hand. 'I saw the carriage.'

Arabella glanced curiously from one to another. 'Erm – I was expecting to see Agnes.'

'Were you? Well you're too late!' Stephen's voice was harsh and intimidating. 'You're all too late if you want to make amends. Agnes is dead!'

His sister drew in a breath. 'I'm – I'm so sorry.' She sat down uninvited and her skirt billowed around her. 'I – I didn't know.'

'How could you know? We might both have been dead for all any of you knew – or cared!'

Her mouth trembled at her brother's anger. 'But

that's why I came,' she whimpered. 'Papa doesn't know I'm here! We're not supposed to even mention your name. He's so difficult, Stephen,' she implored. 'I came to ask you – well, if you would ever reconsider coming home?'

'With or without Agnes?' Stephen asked cynically.

She looked down, unable to meet his eyes. 'You know you couldn't have come with her.'

'And you expected me to come without her?' he said bitterly. 'Of course I wouldn't have come!'

'But now?' Arabella glanced at Jenny who was clearing up the table from the baking and trying not to listen to the conversation. 'Is there any reason why you can't come now?'

Christina gave a sudden yell and they all looked towards the door. Stephen glanced down at his sister, then turned and went outside. He came back carrying Christina who grabbed at his hat. He took her hand and blew raspberries into it. 'Yes, there is a reason why I can't come,' he said tersely. 'A very good reason.'

Jenny stopped what she was doing and stood looking at him, then she shifted her gaze to his sister who was flushed with embarrassment.

'I see.' Arabella rose to her feet. 'I beg your pardon.' She put her pert nose in the air. 'Then I won't bother you again.'

Stephen grimaced. 'For heaven's sake, Bella. Sit down! Make her a cup of tea, will you, Jenny?' He patted the baby on her back and took her outside again to her cot. When he returned, he stood staring down at his sister. 'Agnes is buried on the hillside,' he said softly. 'She's facing the home we made together. Do you think I could leave her here alone and go back to that loveless house of my father's?'

Arabella fished for a handkerchief and delicately blew her nose. 'I'm sorry,' she said. 'I know how much you must have loved her.'

'You don't know.' His voice was low and bitter. 'You can't possibly know, because you haven't experienced love.'

Jenny poured boiling water onto the tea leaves and took cups and saucers from the cupboard. But I know, she thought. Stephen and I understand what real love is. That's why we are getting along so well together.

'Well, that's just it, isn't it?' Arabella said petulantly. 'I have no chance of knowing, because Papa will expect me to stay and look after him, and by the time he is dead, I shall be too old. I'm too old now,' she wailed. 'I'm twenty-four and an old maid!'

'Excuse me, miss.' Jenny handed her a cup of tea. 'If you don't mind me interrupting, how would it help if Mr Laslett went home?'

Arabella recoiled as if someone had put something nasty in front of her, but Stephen asked mockingly, 'Yes, how would it? Tell us!'

'Well, because.' She sniffled. 'You would be the head of the household and gentlemen could call on me. Papa won't allow it. He says I'm all right as I am, at home with him!'

'You think that Father would allow me to be head of the household whilst he is alive and still with his wits? How ridiculous. Of course he wouldn't,' Stephen admonished her. 'He would never be party to that! I'm sorry, Bella. Father told me when I left to live with Agnes that he didn't want to see me again, and the only time he did was when I came to Mother's funeral, and then he barely spoke.'

He stared at her, hostility on his face. 'I was never allowed to see Mother whilst she was alive, and my letters to her were returned unopened!'

'I know,' she said dejectedly. 'Mama was very unhappy about it, but she could do nothing. She always said, though, that if you'd had a son, it might make a difference.' Her eyes flickered between Stephen, Jenny and the door where they could hear Christina gurgling and letting out little shrieks. 'Is it a girl or a boy?' she asked.

'What?' Stephen exclaimed, whilst Jenny drew in a breath.

'She's a girl,' she declared. 'And she's mine, not Mr Laslett's,' and as she spoke she remembered that she hadn't yet registered Christina's birth.

CHAPTER THIRTEEN

'I haven't registered Christina's birth,' Jenny told Stephen, as they sat down for their midday meal. Arabella had declined the invitation to eat with them and had left. 'I'd forgotten that was what had to be done. Do I have to go into Beverley?'

'Oh!' Stephen gave a gasp of exasperation. 'Hill reminded me to notify Agnes's death! He gave me a certificate. What did I do with it?' He

133

glanced vaguely up at the mantelshelf and over at the dresser.

'I took a piece of paper from one of your shirt pockets before I washed it.' Jenny got up from the table and fished in a jug on the dresser. 'Weeks ago. I meant to tell you. Is this it?'

'Yes, that's it.' Stephen stared down at the crumpled certificate. Then he put his hand to his head and pressed his temples. 'I suppose I didn't want to think about it. I've put it to the back of my mind.' He looked across at her. 'But I can't put it off for ever. We'll take a trip into Beverley, Jenny, now that we've finished lambing. We can register both at the same time.'

Jenny hesitated. 'I'm not supposed to go back to Beverley,' she said.

'Who says?' he asked brusquely.

'The magistrates said I should leave and go elsewhere until people had had 'chance to forget what happened to Christy.'

He grunted. 'Well, I'm sorry to say, but I'm afraid people will have forgotten already. Apart from his family, of course; they won't ever forget.' He drummed on the table with his fingertips for a moment, and then began to eat again. 'Anyway, you were acquitted, weren't you? No-one has the right to say you shouldn't go back. You were not banned, merely advised to stay away.'

She trusted him to be right and though she had misgivings, later in the week they took the waggon and drove into Beverley to register a birth and a death. They sat apart in the small office of the registrar, Jenny holding Christina and Stephen staring up at the ceiling. Jenny went into the inner office first.

'Date of birth?' The registrar glanced at Jenny. 'Of the child.'

'April the first 1860.'

'Name of child?'

'Christina April Ingram,' Jenny said boldly.

'First names only please,' he said, without looking up. 'Male or female?'

'Christina April. Female.' She suddenly felt intimidated by this sombre little man.

'Name and surname of mother?'

'Jenny Graham,' she said, quietly but firmly.

'Married or unmarried?'

She took a breath. 'Unmarried.'

'Occupation?'

'Housekeeper – domestic.'

'Informant?' When she hesitated, he added, 'Who gives the information?'

'I do. The child's mother.'

He asked where the child was born; dated and signed the certificate, blotted it and handed it to her. 'Good day, Miss Graham.' He looked over his spectacles at her. 'I wish you and your daughter both well in your lives.'

'Oh! Thank you,' she said at this unexpected courtesy. 'That's very kind!'

He nodded and, opening the door, showed her out. Then he called, 'Next, please.'

When Stephen came out, he seemed very low-spirited. He didn't speak as they went out of the register office but ushered Jenny towards Saturday Market.

'Are you all right, Mr Laslett?' she asked. 'Was it very bad for you?'

'Yes,' he said dully. 'It was.' He pressed his lips together and she let the moment pass, until he'd recovered enough to say, 'I'm going across to see Akrill at the gun shop. I need some powder and shot. Go and look at the shops and I'll meet you in half an hour. Do you need any money?'

'Yes please,' she said. 'I'll get some thread and darning wool. You've got holes in your socks.'

He took some coins out of his pocket and handed them to her, then gently pinched her, then the baby, on their cheeks. 'We sound like an old married couple, Jenny,' he said softly. 'You should be making yourself a pretty dress, not darning socks for an old fellow like me!'

'You're not an old fellow.' She smiled. 'And I'm grateful to you, Mr L– Stephen. I can't begin to tell you how much.'

She made her purchases at the haberdasher's and was pleased that no-one seemed to recognize her. She gave a brief look into the butcher's shop but only Billy's father was there, and then, as she still had plenty of time before meeting Stephen, her feet took her down towards Toll Gavel. Just to look, she told herself, at the draper's and the boot maker's shops.

William Brown's Son, the sign above the new butcher shop proclaimed, and as Jenny looked in she saw Billy serving a customer, and a woman whom she presumed to be his mother was stringing sausages.

She heard Billy wish his customer a good day and as he turned to the window to replace a tray of meat he looked up. He stared at her for a second, then wiping his hands on his apron he came outside, first saying something to the woman in the shop.

'Jenny!' He gazed at her as if lost for words. 'Jenny, wh–' He glanced at the child in her arms and then back at her. 'Whose is 'babby?'

'Mine,' she said, knowing he was really asking was it Christy's. 'We've come to register her birth.' She looked up at him and smiled. She'd almost forgotten how blue his eyes were. It was a year since she had last seen him. He seemed to have grown taller, broader and thicker-set than before, and although he was clean-shaven he had long sideburns, which suited him, she thought. He's groomed and spruced up; I wonder if he's courting a young lady?

'Who's we?' he asked bluntly. 'Are you still in 'same job of work?'

'I went to work at my aunt's house, Billy, out in 'country. You remember when I caught 'carrier?'

'Aye, I do. Up Etton way, wasn't it?' He shuffled his feet as if he was embarrassed, just as he used to do. 'I've often wondered about you, Jenny. Wondered if you'd been back.'

She shook her head. 'I don't get much free time.'

'They kept you on then, even after you had 'babby?' He glanced down again at the sleeping infant.

'My aunt died a few weeks back, Billy. I looked after her when she was ill. That's why I went there in 'first place. Now her husband needs somebody to help him around 'farm. I look after the house and feed 'hens and milk 'cow. Mr Laslett doesn't mind the baby.' Loves her to bits, she thought, gazing tenderly at Christina as she

137

stirred. He spoils her to death.

'I see,' Billy mumbled and sighed. 'Well, I'm glad it's worked out for you, Jenny. What have you called her?' He peeked at the baby as she opened her eyes.

'Christina,' she said. 'Christina April. She was born on 'first of April.'

'Ah!' He averted his eyes from her. 'Aye, of course.'

'What about you, Billy? Is 'shop doing well? I see your ma's still helping out!'

'Aye.' He sighed again. 'She likes to keep an eye on me. Thinks I can't manage on me own! She says when I wed and have a wife to help me, then she'll leave.'

'And have you got somebody in mind, Billy?' she asked. 'Have you met anybody?'

His eyes gazed into hers. 'No,' he said abruptly. 'At least – I've been meeting this lass, Annie Fisher, but there's nowt to it.'

'Be careful, Billy,' Jenny said softly. 'She might think there is. You could get caught.'

'Like you did?' he muttered.

She shook her head. 'I didn't get caught. I loved Christy then and he loved me.' A sudden emotion made her shudder and she looked away, and as she did, she saw Stephen Laslett coming down the street towards them.

'Aye, except–' Billy began, but broke off as Jenny waved to Stephen.

'I'll have to go,' Jenny said. 'That's Mr Laslett, my employer. He probably wants to get off home.'

Billy gazed towards the tall lanky figure coming

their way. 'He's not an old fellow, then?' he muttered. 'Not old at all!'

'Erm – I suppose not,' she said, and pondered that although Stephen Laslett was wearing his rough cord breeches and old tweed jacket, with his felt hat on his long hair, his bearing proclaimed him the gentleman that he was.

'I mean – not as old as my da?'

'No. He was younger than my aunt. Mr Laslett,' she said as he approached. 'This is my friend, Billy Brown. I knew him when I worked in Beverley.'

'How de do, Brown.' Stephen put one hand out to Billy; with the other he held a parcel from the gun shop.

'I'm a bit bloody, sir,' Billy said, refusing his handshake. 'If you'll excuse me.'

'Is this your shop?' Stephen said. 'Are you Brown the butcher?'

Billy drew himself up. 'Aye, that's me.'

'Billy Brown, butcher boy!' Jenny murmured, a sadness washing over her.

Billy looked at her, and then muttered. 'I'd better get back in.' He glanced into the shop. 'I've things to do. It's been good seeing you again, Jenny.'

'You too, Billy,' she said softly, knowing that he still cared for her.

'Jenny.' Stephen took some money out of his pocket. 'Shall we treat ourselves? What about some beefsteak? Make a change from rabbit pie?'

'It would,' she said. He gave her some more coins and took Christina from her. She followed Billy into the shop where he sliced up two thick pieces of beef. He wrapped them up and handed

139

them to her. 'With my compliments,' he said, his voice expressionless. 'It's best beef, it'll cook well.'

'No, Billy. I must pay you!' She was conscious of his mother turning round to look at her. 'Mr Laslett will be cross. He doesn't like favours.'

He shook his head. 'Next time,' he said.

'It's not what you think, Billy,' she whispered. 'Really it isn't!'

'Oh aye? Nowt to do wi' me, anyway.' His voice was controlled but with an undertone of pique. 'Bye, Jenny. Be seeing you.'

She went outside to where Stephen was pacing up and down with Christina in his arms. 'Shall we get back?' she said, wanting to leave. She felt tearful and emotional but didn't know why, except that she knew that Billy was upset, and she didn't want him to be. 'It's almost time for Christina's feed. Have we got everything?'

He was about to answer when a middle-aged woman dressed in black walked by. Stephen lifted his hat and murmured good day. She inclined her head, then her eyes turned to Jenny. It was Mrs Ingram. Christy's mother.

Though it was only seconds that their eyes met, to Jenny it seemed an interminable time. Mrs Ingram stared with obvious hostility, then lifted her chin and walked on, scurried almost, past Billy's shop. A small sob escaped Jenny's throat and she wanted to chase after her and confront her, saying, look, this is your grandchild, your dead son's daughter. She could bring you comfort as she has to me. But she wouldn't want to hear it, Jenny thought miserably. Wouldn't believe me anyway.

Billy's mother came out of the shop and stared after Mrs Ingram's retreating back. Billy followed her. Mrs Brown sniffed and muttered something and Jenny heard him say, 'Leave it, Ma. There's nowt to be done.'

Jenny put her hand to her mouth and swallowed away tears. Billy watched her. His manner changed to one of solicitude when he saw her distress. 'Don't expect owt from them, Jenny,' he said quietly. 'They're in a bad way.'

They collected the horses and waggon from the hostelry where they had left them, and as soon as they left Beverley Jenny put Christina to her breast with her shawl covering her. Stephen stared straight ahead without speaking. The day had been a strange one.

'We shan't need to go again,' Stephen said abruptly as he handed her down at the gate. 'Not for a while, anyway.' He looked up at the hillside to where the stone, set beside Agnes's grave, gleamed white against the meadow grass. 'We've everything here that we need.'

'Yes.' Jenny heaved a sigh. 'It's good to be back.'

Billy stood gazing out of the shop window after Jenny had left, looking at nothing but exceedingly preoccupied.

'Who was that?' His mother turned curiously towards him, pausing momentarily at the job in hand of stringing sausages.

'Somebody,' Billy muttered. 'A friend.'

'It was Jenny Graham, wasn't it?' He didn't turn round to answer so she addressed the back of his head. 'Did she do it?'

He turned abruptly to face her. 'She was acquitted! You know very well.'

She was about to reply but her words were held in check by the appearance of a young woman, with her bonnet askew, dashing in at the shop doorway. Billy could always tell his mother's humour by the tone of her voice, but mostly by her facial expressions, which she was never able to hide. Now her nose wrinkled distastefully and her pinched lips turned down, a feat she had perfected to make her own; he would have known even without turning his head who was the cause of her disapproval.

'Billy! Guess who I've just seen!'

'How do, Annie,' Billy answered morosely.

'Guess who I've seen!' Annie looked triumphantly at Billy and then more cautiously at Mrs Brown. 'I've just seen that lass, Jenny Graham, that was up for 'murder of Christopher Ingram.'

'She was acquitted,' Billy said sourly.

'Oh, aye!' Annie gave a wry disbelieving smirk. 'She was carrying a babby. Bet it was his!'

Mrs Brown moved to the counter. 'Can I get you summat, Annie?'

'No, thanks. I was just passing 'time of day.' She looked from one to the other and her mouth drooped. 'I'll be off. Shall you be at 'Green Dragon tonight, Billy?'

'Mebbe,' he said. 'Depends.'

She sniffed and turned for the door. 'Suit yourself.'

'Like I was saying,' Billy's mother continued as Annie Fisher scurried past the window. 'Did she do it?'

Billy gazed at her unblinkingly. 'I just said. She was acquitted.'

CHAPTER FOURTEEN

Jenny drew the lamp nearer to her and began to write. 'When I look back I realize how little time I have had for writing about my life. The days, weeks and months have passed so quickly since we visited Beverley, and neither Mr Laslett nor myself have expressed any wish to go back. I had been very happy there, but it was also the place where I had known much pain, fear and sorrow, and it is that thought which throws such a dark shadow over me that I cannot bring myself to return.

'Mr Laslett told me on the evening after our visit that whilst he was waiting in Akrill's gun shop, he had met someone he knew, a mere casual acquaintance. This man chatted and asked if he had heard about the proposed railway line from Beverley to Market Weighton; then in almost the same breath asked if he had heard the news of Mr John Ingram, who was well known in the town. When Mr Laslett professed that he knew of the railway proposal but not of Mr Ingram, the gentleman proceeded to tell him that Mr Ingram was on the verge of bankruptcy and that he owed money all over Beverley. He owed the butcher, the baker and candlestick maker, according to this man, and various friends and benefactors who had lent him money. It needs but one creditor to call in his debt, the man said, and he is bust. Those were his very words.

'It seems, this fellow gossiped, that Ingram had been expecting an inheritance after his son's death, but it had gone instead to some other relative.

'Mr Laslett said wasn't it odd that we had seen Mrs Ingram that very same day, and he wondered if she knew how bad things were. I could make no answer to that, for I had felt very dismal after seeing her and feeling her hatred towards me.

'We have few visitors here, apart from the occasional itinerant workers and tramps who come to help on the land, and none have expressed any surprise at seeing me here instead of Agnes. Apart, that is, from a young gypsy woman who had come with her husband. She came to the door one hot afternoon and asked if she might have some milk for her children. She had two with her, a boy and a girl of about four or five.

'We had plenty of milk, the cow was yielding more than I could cope with and I seemed to be for ever in the dairy at the back of the house, churning butter and making cheese, and I'm not very good at either I've decided, for there is definitely an art to getting it right. I gave the children a cupful there and then and filled a jug for her to take back to their camp, asking her to return the empty jug when she had finished with it.

'"Where's the other *manushi?*" she asked. "The other wife?"

'I told her that Agnes had died; she nodded and

144

said she had expected it. She had read Agnes's palm and seen it coming. She also told me that Agnes was watching over us, and I knew that to be true, knowing that she is lying peacefully up on the grassy hillside.

'A parson came to visit. He had somehow heard of Agnes's death and came to offer his belated commiserations. Mr Laslett wasn't in, but this man of God expressed great displeasure when he found that I, a young woman with a child, was living with a man who wasn't my husband. No matter that I explained that I was Mr Laslett's housekeeper, he demanded to know where the child's father was. When I said that he was dead, he stormed off immediately to find Mr Laslett and remind him of his moral duties. When Mr Laslett came in for his supper, he said that he had sent the parson off with a flea in his ear, and threatened him with his shotgun if he should come near again.

'The packman has been with his dusters, pins, needles and thread and local gossip; two harvests and one winter have been and gone,' she wrote, 'and now another winter is upon us. The logs are stacked for the fire and the cow is in the barn with the hens. The milk yield is not so great and there are just enough eggs for the three of us. This summer I had to go down to the villages to sell some for we had such a glut, and Mr Laslett went to Driffield market to sell the rabbits, so we have a little money put by.

'Mr Laslett came in one day in a very irritable mood. A surveyor had called on him to discuss the railway line to Market Weighton, which if it goes ahead would run across his land. Mr Laslett said he had told the man to go away for he wouldn't allow it, even if there should be compensation as he had said.

'Christina is walking and chattering and I have all on to watch for her. She tries to follow Stephen when he goes out and puts up her little arms for him to pick her up. It worries me rather that she dotes on him so, and he on her. Perhaps the parson was right. It is an unusual situation.'

Jenny had bathed Christina and tucked her up in bed. She slept with her now as she had outgrown her cot. Stephen kept promising that he would make her a little bed of her own, but he never had the time; there was always something else more pressing. She put some eggs on to boil and sliced ham for their supper, then brought a cake out of the cake tin. She turned down the lamp to save the oil, put another log on the fire and swung the kettle over it. Then she sat down and waited for Stephen to come in from checking the animals and making sure all was locked up securely. There had been a fox about; a week ago one had come into the barn and killed some of the hens before Stephen could shoot him.

She'd closed her eyes for a moment and must have dropped off to sleep, for she woke with a start when she heard Stephen moving the steaming kettle.

'You're tired!' he said. 'You're overdoing it.'

'No, I'm all right,' she said, stretching. 'It's just 'end of 'day, isn't it? You must be tired too.'

'I'm not chasing after a child all day.' He looked

down at her. 'Nor feeding her. You should finish weaning her, Jenny. She's too big to be at the breast.'

There had never been any embarrassment over her feeding the child in front of him, though she always tried to be discreet. But Christina often pulled at her breasts when she wanted comfort or was tired, and Jenny found it hard not to give in to her. But she blushed now as he admonished her.

'Give her a bottle, if she needs it,' he said bluntly. 'You're wearing yourself out.'

And so she did. When Christina demanded her, she gave her a bottle, or else distracted her in some way; then Stephen brought in a puppy and within a week she had forgotten about her mother and the bottle and turned her attention to the wriggling pup that escaped her entreating arms.

'I want to talk to you, Jenny,' Stephen said one night. He'd been edgy for a few days and Jenny had wisely let him alone, knowing that sometimes he became morose. She had seen him walking up the hillside towards Agnes's grave, and in the evenings when they sat opposite each other, she with her sewing and he perhaps mending a lock or adding up accounts, he had gazed into the fire, but occasionally she had caught him surreptitiously watching her.

'Is something wrong, Mr Laslett?' The name slipped out. 'Stephen, I mean,' she said lamely. 'Something's bothering you. Have I done something I shouldn't?'

'No,' he assured her. 'You haven't. It's me. I wondered – well, I think perhaps I haven't been

147

fair to you. Here you are, a young woman, cooped up in an isolated cottage with a grumpy old fellow.'

'You're not grumpy,' she said. 'Neither are you old.' She thought of what Billy Brown had said, that he wasn't as old as his da. 'I'm nearly twenty-one, not a young girl any longer. How old are you, Stephen?'

'Thirty-four, thirty-five next birthday.' He ran his fingers through his shaggy hair. 'A few grey hairs to prove it.' He sighed and looked away from her. 'I never told you this, Jenny, but Agnes asked me something before she died.'

'Oh!' She felt it must be serious, but why had he waited so long? 'She asked you to let me stay because of Christina, didn't she?' she said fearfully. 'I won't hold you to it if you want me to leave.' But where will I go? Her spirits plummeted. I won't give up my child. Not ever. Not after the anguish I have suffered.

'Nonsense! There's no question of that.' He seemed tense and his voice was sharp. 'None at all. If you're happy with the situation here, then so am I.'

'Oh, I am,' she said earnestly. 'I don't want to go anywhere else. I don't know where I would go,' she said. 'There's no-one else who would want me.'

'Then that's all right,' he said, and seemed relieved, though she felt there was something else he wanted to discuss. But what was it that Agnes had asked him? Jenny remembered that her aunt had told her that she had asked her husband to promise something, and that he hadn't yet agreed. Whatever it was, however, would have to wait, for Stephen got up abruptly and announced he was going to bed.

Jenny thought that Stephen was trying to avoid her over the next few days. He rose earlier than usual and helped himself to his own breakfast, though he came in for his midday meal, which they ate together, usually in silence. The weather became colder as November turned to December, and when Christina had her afternoon sleep Jenny went out to help him with feeding the horses and bedding them down with clean straw; then they fed the pig, and checked the sheep which had been brought down into the shelter of the bottom meadow.

They ate their supper and she bathed Christina and prepared to take her to bed.

'Come and give me a kiss, angel,' Stephen said, putting his arms out to the child, and she leant towards him in his chair to receive his kiss. His arms brushed against Jenny as he hugged Christina and she pulled back awkwardly from his closeness.

'Say night-night to ... I don't know what name she should call you,' she said to cover her confusion. 'I suppose she'll find something of her own eventually!'

'Yes, I suppose so.' He rubbed his hand across his chin. 'She could just call me Stephen as you do when you remember!'

She hitched Christina up into her arms; she was getting almost too heavy to carry. 'I try not to forget that I work for you, that's why,' she said. 'I don't want to become too familiar. You're my employer, after all.'

'Even though I don't pay you?' he said gruffly.

'You do pay me,' she insisted. 'I have bed and board, and I have 'egg money when there is some. I'm far better off than if I was in service. And I have Christina with me,' she added.

He nodded. 'That means a lot to you, doesn't it? Having the child?' He stood up and took Christina from her. 'I'll carry her up,' he said. 'And then I want to discuss something with you.'

Jenny climbed the narrow stairs carrying a flickering candle. Stephen followed and Christina patted his cheek at this unaccustomed pleasure. He handed her back to Jenny to put into the narrow bed in her room, and went into his own bedroom, the one he had shared with Agnes. He went across to the window and stood looking out.

'Jenny!' he called, as she came out of her room across the landing. 'Will you come here a minute?'

'What is it?' She hesitated at the door. She only went into his room to sweep and dust or change the bed linen, or occasionally if she needed linen from the big drawer where it smelled of the lavender which Agnes had always laid amongst the sheets, and Jenny now did also.

He half turned from the window towards her. His face was in shadow, though outside a full moon shone. 'I just want to show you something.'

Slowly she went towards him. What was it that he wanted her to see? She felt strange being alone with him in his darkened room, which is ridiculous, she thought, for aren't we always alone and have been ever since Agnes died.

'Look,' he said, pointing up the hillside. There was a sharp frost tingeing the grass with silver and as she followed the direction in which he was pointing, she saw the white stone brilliantly illuminated in the moonlight.

'Agnes,' she breathed. 'She's watching over us, just like the gypsy woman said.'

'What?' He looked down at her and she saw the glint of moonlight reflected in his eyes. 'Who?'

'During haymaking,' she explained. 'One of 'gypsy women came to the house. She asked about Agnes and when I said she had died, she said she had seen it in her palm. She also said that Agnes was watching over us.' She gave a small smile. 'I didn't tell her that she was buried up there on 'hillside.'

He gave a dismissive grunt. 'She would have known. The gypsies used to make their camp up there. Now they don't. I expect it's because they've seen the grave.'

'Perhaps,' she said, though she was inclined to believe in the gypsy's words.

'Do you believe that she's watching?' he asked quietly.

'I don't know,' she said. 'I'm not sure what I believe – except–' She paused.

'What?'

'Well, sometimes it's as if she's showing me what to do, like when I brought 'piglets in that time, or when I don't know if 'oven is right for baking. It's as if she's telling me.'

He turned back to the window. 'I do know what you mean,' he murmured. 'I sometimes get that feeling too. Though I don't believe in all that,' he

151

added brusquely.

'Oh! So if you don't believe it, why...?'

'It's my conscience that's telling me,' he said firmly. 'Agnes asked me to do something and although I didn't promise that I would, I know it's what she wanted. I've let her down and that's why I feel that she's watching. It's as if her spirit won't rest until I've done what she asked. Which is the most ridiculous notion,' he said testily. 'And quite out of the question!'

'Was it something very difficult?' Jenny asked. 'Couldn't you find your way to doing it? It might make you feel more settled. Oh!' she said as a thought occurred to her. 'Did she want you to make it up with your father?'

He gave a sudden start and glanced at her. 'In a way, yes. That might come into it.' He put his hand on her shoulder. 'The trouble is, Jenny, I still love her so much that what she asked of me seems quite improper.'

She hardly dared to ask what it was, if it was something so terrible. 'Sometimes...' She hesitated and gave a shiver. 'It's as if we have to do something against our nature in order to make something right,' she said. 'And Agnes would surely never ask you to do something wrong. She was a good person.'

'She was, wasn't she?' he answered softly. 'But perhaps it isn't so much wrong – as not being right.'

She saw the Adam's apple move in his throat as he swallowed, and she thought how strange that he seemed so vulnerable, whereas usually he was strong and positive. 'So, what was it?' she

152

whispered. 'Do you want to tell me? Would you feel better for having confided in someone?'

'It concerns you, Jenny, so if I tell you, I must ask you to promise not to be angry or afraid. Though I would understand if you were both, and I will apologize now before I even say it.' He took a breath to compose himself and she saw from his anxious expression that whatever he was going to say wasn't going to be easy for him, or even for either of them.

'When Agnes saw Christina that first time, she was overjoyed,' he said quietly. 'She felt she had had a renewal of life.'

Jenny nodded. Her aunt had said the same thing to her. 'Yes. She gave her great delight,' she murmured.

'Well, she asked me – if I would ask you–' he paused, 'and I will understand if you put on your bonnet and walk out when you hear what I have to say.'

'I won't do that,' she said. 'Not tonight anyway. It's starting to snow.'

He turned to glance out of the window. A flurry of snowflakes were falling and dissolving on the glass.

'She said, would I ask you to bear me a child.'

Jenny stared at him, the silence of the night throbbing in her ears. Whatever was he thinking of? He had just said that he still loved Agnes.

He took hold of her hand and gazed down at it, unable to meet her eyes. 'So, will you, Jenny?'

CHAPTER FIFTEEN

'I can't believe what you're saying,' Jenny breathed. 'How could you ask such a thing? It wouldn't be right! We don't love each other.'

'I said, didn't I, that it wasn't so much wrong as not right? But Jenny.' A flicker of a smile touched his lips. 'People do – erm – make babies, though perhaps unintentionally, and do not necessarily love each other. They are – erm – attracted to each other, or perhaps swayed by passion!'

'But – we're not!' She pulled her hand away from him and clutched her throat. 'I mean – I work for you, and Agnes was my aunt and you are – were – her husband. And – and why would she want us to?' she stammered out in a flurry. 'What reason would there be?' She looked wildly around the bedroom. 'I want to go downstairs!' she said. 'It doesn't seem right talking in such a way in here.' She glanced out of the window and saw the stone stark white on the hillside.

'I'm sorry, Jenny,' he apologized. 'I'm really so very sorry! But I had to ask you here in this room where Agnes had been. Will you discuss it downstairs?'

She agreed, though reluctantly. I'll have to leave, she thought. How can I stay now? How could he suggest it? He said he loved Agnes. It's a strange kind of love! And yet he is doing it for her. She was the one who asked it of him.

Stephen went to the cupboard where he kept his spirits and brought out half a bottle of brandy. He poured himself a glass and a small one for Jenny. 'I know you don't usually drink, Jenny, but this might calm you. I'm sorry. I didn't mean to upset you, but I had to say it. I've been mulling this over for weeks. My conscience – as I said before,' he said ruefully. 'But now that it's said, we can forget about it. Agnes wouldn't want you to do anything you were unhappy about. And it does seem most bizarre.'

Jenny took a tentative sip of the brandy and shuddered at its raw potency. 'I don't understand,' she murmured, avoiding his eyes. 'I know that Agnes wanted children of her own, but to ask you to – to go with another woman!'

'It shows the strength of her love, doesn't it?' His voice was wistful as he sat across from her. 'But she wouldn't have considered it with any other woman. She had grown increasingly fond of you, Jenny.'

'Like a daughter?' She raised her eyes to him. 'That makes it worse!'

'No. More like a sister,' he asserted. 'Like a sister who might have supported her in the past. You would have done that, wouldn't you?'

'I don't know,' she declared. 'I'm not so close to my own sisters; but yes.' She considered. 'Probably. I was very fond of Agnes. I felt I knew her better than my own family – even more than my mother. But I still don't understand why she would ask such a thing of *me*. Unless... It's because I'm young and fertile, isn't it? She thought I could give you what she couldn't!'

He nodded. 'Agnes knew that I wanted a son. It was what we both wanted, even though it wasn't a source of conflict between us. She was also aware of how bitter I became when my father wouldn't accept her as my wife, even after her brute of a husband died and we married legally. We had lived together – in sin, as my father called it – when she had been a married woman.'

He gulped his brandy straight down and stared into the fire. 'She always thought that if she'd had a son, my father would have forgiven us and accepted the child. I never told her that he wouldn't. He wrote to tell me that, after I informed him of our marriage.'

'He sounds like a very hard man,' Jenny said. 'And not deserving of grandchildren!'

Stephen gave a little smile and shook his head. 'He wasn't hard when I was young. He didn't entertain his children, of course, his generation didn't, and we had to obey his rules. But he took an interest, especially in me as his only boy: he taught me to shoot and hunt, to track and fish.' He sighed. 'So many things that I would have liked to teach my sons. Father spoiled the girls too when they were young, but he was quite out of his depth as they grew older, as you must have observed with Bella.'

'But you surely don't think he'd accept a child from someone who's your housekeeper and had once been a kitchen maid?'

He leant back in the chair and folded his arms. He gazed at her for a moment, and then said, 'It does sound improbable, but if we were married and hadn't had a romantic liaison, yes I think he might. He needs an heir.'

She put her hand to her mouth. 'Married!' She breathed the word. 'You'd want us to marry?'

'You contemplated marrying Christopher Ingram, didn't you?' His tone and question was direct. 'But yes, of course! Otherwise any children we might have would be bastards and he wouldn't accept them. Sorry,' he added quickly. 'I wasn't thinking. It was not intended as a slur on Christina. She's an adorable child. I think the world of her, as you know, and, if we had married, which I now realize is out of the question, then I would have adopted her.'

She was even more flabbergasted than before. The thought of having Stephen Laslett's child had shocked and unnerved her. The idea of becoming his wife astounded her. But it was true; she and Christy had planned to marry. Whether they would have been allowed to would never be known.

'Your sister has seen Christina,' she reasoned. 'She'll surely tell your father that I have an illegitimate child?' She couldn't bring herself to call her daughter a bastard as he had done. Yet a responsive stirring was beginning to take effect. He said he would adopt Christina!

'Arabella doesn't know that she's illegitimate, and besides, you saw how she was. She's desperate to have me home again.'

'And would you go?' she asked. 'Would you leave here and go to your father's house?'

'No! Of course I wouldn't!' His eyes held hers. 'My father would expect me to inherit and live there when he's dead. But how could I leave this place, knowing that Agnes is here? But Arabella would live in hope that eventually we would go back.' He gave a wry grin. 'Whereas I would only want the estate for my son.'

We? she thought. It would mean that I'd be part of the Laslett family! But would his sisters resent me because of who I am, a mere nobody? Yes, they would. But if I had a son, they'd have to accept me, and, she thought, as a tingle of excitement ran through her, if Arabella should marry, perhaps then I would be mistress!

'I need to think about it,' she said. 'It's come as a big shock.'

'Will you think about it?' He looked amazed. 'Heavens! I thought you'd be packing your box and leaving in the morning!'

'Well,' she said wryly. 'You must be considered a good catch, Stephen, which makes me wonder why you don't ask someone of your own class to marry you and give you sons? There must surely be plenty of young ladies around who would be willing?' She recalled the score of eligible young women who were paraded before Christy.

'I'm sure there are. Arabella would know of them.' He smiled, but she saw the sadness written in his expression. 'They wouldn't understand me, Jenny. I'm a rough and ready kind of man. A peasant, my father called me. I wouldn't behave as a young lady would expect. But you know how much Agnes has meant to me! I was little more than a boy when we first met, not much more than twenty, and our love sustained us through many difficulties. I couldn't marry a giddy young thing who would expect undying love and devotion. You understand me.'

He got up from his chair and stood in front of her. He lifted her chin with his fingers. 'We understand each other. You have shared such love with Christy, which is what Agnes recognized. We are romantics, you and I, Jenny. We both believe that that kind of love comes only once and therefore would not expect more from each other than what we could honestly give.'

She felt an overwhelming sadness for what might once have been, and, her mouth trembling as she spoke, said, 'So – so you wouldn't expect me to love you, but only to respect you as my husband?'

'Exactly. It would be a marriage of convenience for us both. I can't promise you riches at this stage, but you would have the advantage of being a married woman, and I would have the sons I've always wanted.'

'I thought Christy's child would be a son,' she reminded him, and took out a handkerchief to blow her nose. 'I wanted him to claim the Ingram name. But I had a daughter. What if I don't produce a son?'

'You will.' He smiled. 'Sooner or later.'

'Do you trust me?' she asked. 'Once we are married I might not want to come to your bed.'

'I do trust you, Jenny, but perhaps I should remind you, before either of us makes any kind of commitment,' his gaze was penetrating, 'that as my wife you would be bound to allow me my marital rights. It might be distasteful to you – to us both.' He shrugged. 'But until we have a son...'

'Yes,' she said quietly. 'I understand.'

She barely slept that night. She turned over and

159

over in her mind the complications that such a marriage would bring. I won't ever love him, she deliberated, even though he is more considerate than I had previously given him credit for. I won't ever love anyone again. Loving is not easy and I could not endure it again. It brings such sorrow. If I'd wanted to marry anyone, I reckon Billy Brown would have asked me if he thought he had a chance. But he knew that he hadn't. But this is a chance for me. Should I take it? Grasp the opportunity to better myself? If I don't, will he look for someone else to marry and give him sons? In spite of what he says, there's bound to be a willing woman who would accept him as he is, for I understand perfectly well that in his society they do not marry for love but for status.

She got out of bed, being careful not to disturb Christina, and, wrapping her shawl around her, went to the window. Snow was falling quite heavily, covering the ground and grassland with a dense whiteness. Without Stephen Laslett, Christina and I have nothing, she meditated. Nothing at all: no home, no money. I should have to go to 'parish for help if I left here. I could end up in 'workhouse.

She heard a movement on the landing. Stephen, she guessed, wasn't sleeping either. I'll make us a cup of tea, she decided, seeing as we're both awake.

When she went downstairs, Stephen had already swung the kettle over the banked-up fire. He was wearing only his nightshirt, which because he was so tall only just covered his knees. His calves, she noticed, were hard and muscular.

He was bleary-eyed and his hair was tousled.

'Couldn't you sleep either, Jenny?' His voice cracked huskily with fatigue. 'You don't have to make a decision. We can forget I ever said anything. It's offensive to you, I realize now, and perhaps–' He hesitated. 'Well, I've been wondering – Agnes was very ill. She might not have been thinking lucidly, if you know what I mean.'

'I do know what you mean,' she said softly. 'And Agnes was perfectly right in her mind. She told me that she had asked you to promise something. She was quite clear about it.'

He poured the boiling water into the teapot and then gave it a stir. He smiled. 'Agnes showed me how to do this,' he said fondly. 'I'd never done it before. I'd always had a cook and a parlour maid to do such things. Agnes said that every man should know how to make his wife a cup of tea!'

'She was quite right,' Jenny responded and took the cup he was offering. She took a sip. It was hot and strong. Agnes had obviously not told him the cost of tea. 'So as your future wife, I can tell you that you make a very good cup.'

He turned to look at her. 'What? You mean that you will?' He shook his head. 'Really? I never thought that you would!' He ran his fingers through his hair, making it stand up on end so that he looked quite boyish. He took a breath. 'I must tell you, Jenny, that I'll never do anything to deliberately hurt you, and that when we have a son and my father accepts him, if you want to leave me I won't stop you. You have my promise on that.' He put his hand on his heart as he vowed it.

'It seems very odd, doesn't it?' Jenny remarked.

'That we can sit here in the middle of the night drinking tea and discussing our marriage!' She pressed her lips together as she felt a raw emotion sway her. 'It's not as romantic as I might have imagined when I was just a young girl. Dreams don't always materialize, do they?'

He put down his cup and came across to her. He took her own cup from her and put it on the table, then he held her hand and gently squeezed it. 'Sometimes they do, Jenny,' he said softly. 'And other times they don't turn out the way we want them to. But you are still young. Keep your dreams for a little longer.' When she shook her head, he added, 'I know that being with Christy was your dream, but he's gone, as has Agnes who was mine. Find another dream to cling to. I have mine now that you've agreed.' He smiled. 'I shall have a son.'

He bent to kiss her on the cheek. 'This is my marriage vow,' he said.

She gazed at him. That wasn't unpleasant, she thought. He will perhaps be considerate in the marriage bed. She wasn't experienced in such things; she had only known Christy and he hadn't been experienced either. She blushed and stood on bare tiptoe to return his kiss. 'And this is my promise,' she whispered.

CHAPTER SIXTEEN

'I wasn't sure what to do next. After all I haven't been in this situation before.' Jenny started on a fresh sheet of paper. It seemed appropriate as she was about to begin a new stage in her life. 'But Mr Laslett took charge, and it seems only proper that I call him by his surname until we're married. I noticed when I worked at the Ingrams' house that Mrs Ingram always called her husband by his surname, or at least whilst the servants were about. But as I say, Mr Laslett took charge of the arrangements and said that there was no reason for us to wait, but that we could be married immediately. He first of all wrote to his friend Dr Hill, to ask him if he would stand as witness to our marriage. Then he wrote to his sister Arabella to inform her of the situation, and ask if she would be willing to come and stay, and also be a witness. He told me that he had mentioned to her that Dr Hill would be at the ceremony, and was sure that she would be swayed by that intelligence.

'As we were in the parish of Etton the banns had to be read in the church there. We went to hear them being read for the first two Sundays but didn't get there again on account of the cow being sick. I had to stay with her whilst Stephen, I mean Mr Laslett, went to fetch the veterinarian. She was a good milker and we didn't want to lose her.

'Miss Arabella came as requested and braved

the muddy roads, for after the snow we have had a good deal of rain, and she is staying with us until after the ceremony, which is to be in two days' time. I think she will be better for knowing, though she is inclined to be conceited and pretentious, and likes her full surname to be used. Mr Laslett teases her about this and tells her that she is too proud. He has given her his bed and I've put clean, sweet-smelling sheets on it. He has been sleeping downstairs on the floor, which can't be very restful. As the time for the ceremony comes nearer, I am becoming very nervous and apprehensive over what is in front of me. I have written at last to my mother and father to tell them of Agnes's death, my daughter's birth and my impending marriage, though I avoided telling them either the name of my future husband or where or when it would take place. They will be relieved, I think, to hear that I am married. I have made myself a new gown with some material I found at the back of a cupboard. It's a pretty blue and came up looking lovely after I'd washed it to get rid of the fustiness.'

'Jenny!' Arabella called to her from the doorway on the afternoon before the wedding. Jenny was feeding a new young pig with old potatoes and scraps of food left from their midday meal. 'Should you not be preparing yourself?'

'What do you mean? Prepare myself?' Jenny straightened up and climbed out of the pen. 'I'm ready.'

'Just look at you!' Arabella pulled a face. 'Covered in mud and an old sack over your head. You can't get married looking like that! Whatever will Stephen think?'

'I won't look like this, I shall be clean and tidy.' Besides, she thought, Stephen knows what I look like. He's seen me knee-deep in dung and scrubbed clean on washdays, just as I've seen him. But Arabella doesn't know that he's also seen me giving birth, and would be shocked to the core if she should find out. Neither does she know that we are marrying for one purpose only and that is to produce a son.

Nevertheless, that evening, after bathing in a tub by the fire whilst Stephen was out and Arabella had gone discreetly upstairs, Jenny washed her hair and cut her toenails, and then pampered herself with scented powder which Arabella had given her. She emptied the tub of water outside and then dried her long hair in front of the fire.

'Will you let me brush it for you?' Arabella asked when she came down. 'It's what my sisters and I used to do when we were all at home. I do miss them,' she said plaintively. 'It's lonely being the only one at home with just my father and the servants.'

'I'm sure it is,' Jenny murmured, cringing as Arabella pulled at her damp hair. 'I have three sisters but none of them ever offered to brush my hair.'

'Oh! And brothers? Do you have brothers?' Arabella paused in the brushing, but didn't wait for an answer. 'I would so like to have had more brothers. It would have been such a comfort to know that I could go to any of them, if for instance I don't marry, though I do always hope to. It would have been impossible, of course,' she

165

confided, 'to have come to Stephen when he was married to Agnes!'

'Not sufficient room,' Jenny agreed. 'And not what you were used to.'

'Oh, Father wouldn't have allowed it,' she asserted. 'He had such plans for him, you see, and then *that woman*, as he called her, came along and spoiled them all.'

'And what will he think now?' Jenny asked uneasily. 'I'm not Stephen's equal, as I'm sure you realize.'

'Oh, I told him that,' Arabella said airily, 'and Father said that Stephen obviously has a taste for the lower orders.' She smiled sweetly and inoffensively at Jenny. 'But I explained that although you were a plain girl, you were not at all vulgar, and, in your favour, being a widow with a child,' she lowered her eyes modestly, 'and therefore fertile, you might give him the grandson he wanted. He appeared to be mollified by that,' she added, 'and didn't fly into a fury as sometimes he can.'

This isn't a role I ever envisaged, Jenny thought, staring into the fire as Arabella brushed and chatted, giving her opinions on this and that. A plain girl, able to produce babies for other people. She felt a tightening lump of anger in her chest. Is this what I have agreed to? To hand over my son to an arrogant landowner who thinks he can make rules to suit himself? I must speak to Stephen again before I take the final step.

'Your hair is lovely,' Arabella was saying. 'So thick and shiny. Will you let me put it into rags for you, ready for tomorrow?'

'Rags?' Jenny asked. 'What do you mean?'

'To give it some curl.' Arabella patted Jenny's head. 'It would suit you, I think.'

'No, thank you,' Jenny said. 'As you say, I'm a plain girl. My hair suits me perfectly well as it is.'

'Oh, very well.' Arabella pouted. 'Perhaps you're right. I shall go up, then. I have yet to decide what to wear for the ceremony. It will be a long day tomorrow I expect, with the service and everything – you have prepared food, I suppose? – and then I shall go home in the evening. I've asked Collins to collect me.'

Jenny had prepared extra food, even though they would only have two extra guests. They had killed a pig a few weeks earlier, so she had cooked a ham, which she had boiled for two hours then studded with cloves and baked for another two; and she had made a dish of brawn, potted chicken livers and cooked a rabbit and bacon pie to eat cold. When Stephen saw all the food he had asked if she was expecting the whole of the county.

After Arabella had gone upstairs she went to the larder, and was putting a cake which she had left cooling there into a tin, when Stephen came in. 'Still busy, Jenny?' he asked, taking off his heavy jacket. 'Preparing for the big day?'

He seemed a little edgy, she thought, as his eyes flicked over her, and she wondered if he was having second thoughts or maybe even thinking of his marriage to Agnes.

'I want to say something,' Jenny said nervously. 'I've been talking to Arabella – at least, Arabella has been talking to me.'

'Oh, yes.' He gave a ghost of a smile. 'Arabella is good at talking. What has she been saying?' He

167

frowned. 'Not upsetting you?'

'No. Not really.' Jenny wasn't sure how to say what it was that was troubling her. 'It's just – she said that she had told her father – your father – about me, that although I wasn't the same status as you, I might be able to deliver him a grandson.' She swallowed. 'I – I don't want anyone to think that if I should give birth to sons I would ever give them up – hand them over – for I wouldn't! They would still be mine, until they were older at least.'

He gave a sigh, shaking his head, and came towards her. 'Jenny! Of course not! That wasn't my idea at all. How could I look after a child? A child needs its mother.'

'But your father – what if he–'

'No! It will be your child. Yours and mine. Though the law says a child belongs to its father.' He looked down on her. 'You can still change your mind, you know,' he said bluntly. 'You don't have to go through with this if you're not happy about it. I would understand.' His eyes gazed into hers and she thought how honest they were, though very searching. He bent towards her and wrinkled his nose. 'You smell nice,' he said. 'And your hair – what have you done to it?' He fingered it as it lay on her shoulders, unleashed from its customary plait. 'It looks like polished mahogany.'

'Only washed it.' She blushed. 'And Arabella gave me some scented powder. She wanted to curl my hair, but I wouldn't let her.'

'Quite right,' he said gruffly. 'It needs no addition.' He let his gaze linger a moment longer before asking, 'So! What is it to be? Do we marry tomorrow or not?'

168

Jenny took a deep breath, and then nodded. 'Yes. I think so.'

She said good night and went upstairs to her room. Christina was sleeping soundly and Jenny turned to the window to look out as she always did before climbing into bed. It was raining, a steady drizzle from a low cloud which obscured the view, but she heard the clank of a pail and saw Stephen outside in the yard drawing water from the pump and guessed that he too was about to prepare himself for his wedding day.

It was still raining when Jenny rose at five o'clock. The hens and pig had to be fed and the cow milked, and they all had to have breakfast before they set off to the church for eleven o'clock. Stephen was already outside and he gave her a cursory nod and greeting before handing her a bucket of pigswill.

'This might be your life from now on, Jenny,' he said. 'I can't promise you more. Are you sure it's what you want? You might have a better chance with that young butcher in Beverley. He seemed taken with you.'

She looked at him. He was older than her, handsome in a gaunt kind of way, and inclined to be impatient. Aristocratic and proud, she thought, as Arabella is. A different upbringing has made them what they are. But then, Agnes lived with him and married him. What was it that she had seen, to love him in the way she did? And he, giving up a position in society in order to marry her, what had he seen?

'We've agreed that there won't be love between us,' she said softly. 'But if we trust each other and

169

can live together in friendship, then I think this marriage will survive; so I'll take 'chance with you.' She swallowed and looked away as a blush suffused her cheeks. 'I just want to ask that you'll be patient with me. I've only known Christy. I'm not experienced in such matters as ... 'marriage bed and I'm ... quite nervous of tonight, if I'm truthful.'

He gave her a sad smile. 'And if *I'm* truthful, Jenny, so am I! I lived with Agnes all those years. I can't imagine how it will be to take another woman to my bed.' He reached across and patted her shoulder. 'We don't need to do anything in a hurry. Let us be honest and understanding and just take things as they come.'

Arabella threw up her hands when Jenny and Stephen came into the house together. 'It's unlucky to meet,' she shrieked. 'You should have stayed apart until you met in church!'

'Oh, dear!' Jenny threw a sly glance at Stephen. 'If only you'd told me before, Miss Arabella. I'd have stayed in bed and you could have fed 'hens and 'pig instead of me. But as it is, Mr Laslett and me have been chatting away.' She assumed a disconsolate face. 'So misfortune'll be upon us.'

'What superstitious nonsense, Arabella!' Stephen mocked. 'Where is your common sense? How could we possibly keep apart in such a small house? Jenny is my housekeeper until later this morning, and then she will be my wife, and in the meantime there are jobs to be done. We can't abandon the animals and our livelihood for the sake of such silly conventions. And besides,' he added, 'who would cook your breakfast?'

Jenny dressed Christina in a velvet dress, which she had made from a faded curtain, and then slipped into her own gown. It fitted her well and she was pleased with her sewing. The style showed off her trim waist and firm breasts and accentuated her plump hips. Arabella knocked on her door.

'Jenny! Would you be terribly offended if I offered to lend you a bonnet? I brought several with me – unless you already have one of your own?'

'I only have my plain bonnet,' Jenny said and looked admiringly at the ones that Arabella was holding. 'I was going to put some ribbon on it to dress it up, but I ran out of time.'

'Then borrow one of mine, please do.' Arabella seemed anxious to be agreeable. 'Here is a grey with blue flowers which would match the colour of your gown, or this one is pretty, look. White with pink ribbons. Or this one–'

Jenny took the last one from Arabella's hand. 'This one,' she said. 'If I may?' The bonnet was a deep blue ruched velvet, which she set back from her face so that her shiny brown hair, parted in the middle, showed beneath it. White lace at the side of the bonnet framed her face and wide dark blue and white velvet ribbons fastened beneath her chin.

'How lovely you look,' Arabella enthused, clasping her hands beneath her chin in delight. 'Why, Jenny. You're not a plain girl at all!'

'Time we were off,' Stephen called up the stairs. Arabella went down first in her hooped gown of cream silk, which brushed the walls as she descended. Jenny followed, carrying Christina who immediately put out her arms for Stephen to carry her.

Stephen blinked, and then opened his eyes wide as he took the child from her. 'You look very – fine, Jenny,' he murmured. 'Very fine indeed.'

They were to meet Dr Hill at the church, so the three of them, with Christina on Jenny's lap, rode in the waggon, which Stephen had swept clean of straw. Arabella complained constantly that if she had known that this was the only mode of transport, she would have asked Collins to come with the carriage.

'There's many a poor farmer would be proud to have a waggon such as this,' Stephen argued. 'It's perfectly adequate and suitable for our status, is that not so, Jenny?'

Jenny nodded that it was. As the morning wore on she was feeling more and more nervous and tongue-tied whenever Stephen spoke to her. When they reached the church, Dr Hill was pacing up and down at the gate. She and Stephen glanced at each other as they climbed out of the waggon, and both knew that this was their last chance of turning back.

'Are you sure about this, Jenny?' he murmured. 'It's not too late.' He gently touched her cheek with a fingertip. 'You could be wasting your youth on an old man like me.'

She smiled shyly, her cheeks dimpling. 'We both know you are not so old, Mr Laslett,' she said softly. She placed her arm on his and with the other hand took hold of Christina. 'Shall we go and make our vows?'

CHAPTER SEVENTEEN

Dr Hill took charge of Christina whilst Jenny and Stephen made their vows. Arabella standing by his side seemed very petite.

After the ceremony Jenny and Stephen drove back to the house in the waggon, whilst Dr Hill offered to drive Arabella and Christina in his trap. Arabella eagerly accepted, though was clearly uncomfortable with Christina on her knee.

'Well, Jenny. For better or for worse, we've committed ourselves,' Stephen commented. 'But I give my word of honour that if you are ever unhappy with your situation, I'll set you free.'

'But – we've promised, haven't we?' she said. 'I know that's what we agreed, but we've vowed in church before God and the priest! It's binding, isn't it? I hadn't thought how binding it would be. You knew because you've been married before. We can't take it lightly!'

He took a deep breath, then shook the reins and urged on the horse. 'Agnes was married to a man who beat her and treated her as a servant. Do you think she should have stayed with him because she had promised God?' His voice was low and hard and she knew that he was still hurting over Agnes's death. 'Do you think that God would have wanted her to?'

'I don't know,' she whispered. 'I don't know.'

Stephen, Arabella and George Hill chatted over

the wedding breakfast whilst Jenny served the food, first putting Christina to bed for a sleep. They talked of people they knew from their childhood, but Jenny didn't know any of them and concentrated on seeing that everyone had all they wanted in the way of food and drink.

Finally, Dr Hill filled everyone's glass with wine, which he had provided, and rose to give a toast to the newly married couple. 'To Stephen, my dear friend who has honoured me with his fellowship for so many years, I wish good health and companionship with the worthy, sincere and amiable young woman you have chosen to be your wife in marriage. To Jenny, whom I have known only a short time, yet with her undoubted good sense, tenderness and housewifely skills has impressed me greatly, I wish contentment and joy in your union with Stephen, and may the two of you go forward together into a bright future.'

He raised his glass and Arabella, with flushed cheeks, gazing at the doctor, did the same. 'To Stephen and Jenny.'

Arabella's carriage came shortly afterwards and she reluctantly took her leave. 'I can't invite you to visit, of course,' she said to Jenny as she fastened on her cloak, for it was raining again. 'Not until Father says so.'

Stephen heard her and put his hand lightly on Jenny's shoulder in a show of harmony. 'We don't need his condescension, Bella, and besides we're too busy for socializing. We have a living to make. But *you* may come to visit us.' He bent his head towards Jenny. 'May she not, Mrs St John Laslett?'

Jenny took in an imperceptible breath and then

hid a smile at the astonishment on Arabella's face, as she comprehended his words.

'Wh-why, that's very kind of you, Stephen, and you too … Mrs St John Laslett.' She swallowed and licked her lips. 'So kind.'

'Call me Jenny, Arabella,' Jenny said. 'We don't have to be so formal now that we are sisters!'

'Oh!' Arabella breathed. 'No, indeed not. Goodbye.' She extended her hand to Jenny and gave a slight bob of her head. 'Thank you for inviting me.'

Dr Hill, behind them, nudged Stephen as Arabella hurried up the path towards the chaise. 'You are very unkind, Laslett,' he murmured. 'Go and wave your sister off properly. At least she came to the wedding. None of the others did.'

'That's because I didn't invite them,' Stephen growled, but nevertheless he chased after Arabella and, after kissing her on the cheek, assisted her into the carriage and waved her goodbye.

'You'll need to be patient with him,' Dr Hill advised Jenny as they stood in the doorway. 'I don't think he's recovered from Agnes's death.'

'He hasn't,' Jenny interrupted.

'Yet he is marrying again! You are a remarkable young woman to take on a man who still loves his dead wife!' He gazed curiously at her. 'You're not marrying him for his wealth, that's for certain.'

'I'm not,' she agreed. 'I've not had a penny to call my own since I first came here. I loved–' she took a breath, 'still love Christina's father, who also died. Stephen and I – we–' How can I say that we are marrying because it is what Agnes wanted? she thought.

'Ah!' The doctor intervened. 'So you have something in common and you both need companionship?' He smiled. 'But you are young, Mrs Laslett, you need gaiety in your life. You must persuade your husband not to hide himself away like a recluse.'

How strange her new name seemed. 'Please call me Jenny,' she said, as she had said to Arabella. 'I'm 'same person as I was before.'

'But you will not remain the same,' he said. 'And you must expect and receive consideration as Stephen's wife. You are no longer Jenny the kitchen maid! You are a respectable married woman and your husband is a gentleman. The fact that he is poor doesn't make him any less of one.'

'Agnes didn't receive respect.' Jenny lowered her voice as Stephen came back down the path.

'No, she didn't,' the doctor agreed quietly. 'But circumstances were different for her. She came here as a woman already married to someone else, and she was never forgiven for that.'

'What are you two whispering about?' Stephen asked. 'Talking about me behind my back?'

'Yes,' said Dr Hill. 'That's it exactly. Now, I must be off. There will no doubt be someone hammering on my door.'

'Thank you for coming, Dr Hill,' Jenny said, and put out her hand for him to take.

He gave a little smile of approval as he bent to kiss it. 'The pleasure was all mine, Jenny. I trust we'll meet again soon.'

Stephen held out his hand and gravely shook Dr Hill's. 'Many thanks, George. I rely on your friendship, as you well know. Our paths will cross again ere long.'

George Hill nodded. 'Good luck,' he murmured. Turning, he walked away up the path and towards his horse and trap tethered near the gate. He lifted his hand in farewell, leaving Jenny and Stephen gazing after him. They both stood for a moment, aware that they were alone as man and wife and no longer employer and housekeeper.

'Best get on,' Stephen muttered. 'I'll get changed and start the milking.'

'Yes,' Jenny replied, and to her relief heard Christina's shout as she awakened from her sleep. 'I'll see to Christina and then clear up.'

The rest of the afternoon and evening saw them carrying out their various tasks, but towards the close of evening the sky, which had been dark and overcast all day, suddenly became brighter with long thin shafts of red and gold. Jenny looked out of the kitchen window as she washed the last of the dishes from the wedding feast and saw Stephen striding up the path with his long-legged lope towards the meadow and Agnes's grave.

She'll always be with us, she mused. If I was a young wife in love with my husband, I could be very jealous. But as I loved Agnes too, I understand his feelings: I have so many mixed emotions about Christy. But I have his daughter by my side and she is a constant reminder of that time.

Stephen came in half an hour later and poured himself a glass of wine, then suddenly started. 'Sorry, Jenny,' he apologized. 'I'm forgetting my manners. Would you like a glass?'

'No thank you,' she said. 'I had a glass of wine

177

when we ate. It's as much as I want.'

They sat in silence on opposite sides of the fire, Jenny gazing into the flames and Stephen contemplating his drink. Then he gruffly cleared his throat. 'Forgive me, Jenny, but this is not going to be easy. Not for either of us, but especially not for me. Agnes and I lived here for so many years without company that I think we became almost reclusive. Until you came to join us, I hadn't had any conversation with another woman. Is it any wonder then that I am forgetful of my manners? I ask you to excuse me if at times I seem churlish, for it will be nothing to do with you, but everything to do with me.'

'Yes,' she said quietly. 'I see.'

'Tell me how you feel,' he said. 'Tell me how you felt about young Ingram when he died, and if you still miss him?'

A pulse throbbed in her throat and the blood hammered in her ears, just as it had on that day. 'On the day he died, all I felt was disbelief and shock,' she whispered. 'But–' She swallowed, trying to retain her composure. 'But I have Christina. She makes up for the loss.'

'You must have wanted to die with him?' he said sympathetically. 'All your dreams shattered.'

'Oh no!' Jenny shook her head. 'I didn't want to die! I wanted to live. Christy wanted us to die together.' She stared at Stephen, not seeing him. It was the first time she had confessed it. 'He wanted us to commit suicide,' she whispered.

'What?' Stephen leant towards her. 'But why didn't you say? Why didn't you tell the police that? You wouldn't have been charged!'

Hot tears gathered in her eyes as, trembling, she remembered. 'I didn't think they would believe me. And suicide would have been a terrible thing for his family to bear, so I didn't tell them.'

'How could he have expected you to agree to suicide?' Stephen was aghast. 'It is abhorrent. Against all our teachings!' He looked at her searchingly. 'Did it seem as if his mind was going?'

Jenny hesitated, then took a deep lingering breath. 'Christy had strange ideas sometimes. He wasn't sensible or straightforward, and latterly, when he thought his parents were against him, he locked himself in his room and didn't eat or drink; and that was when he came up with the idea of us always being together – in death. But he didn't tell me until that day,' she added.

'You poor girl,' he murmured and reached for her hand. 'I'm so sorry. You must have been terrified when he suggested it to you. Was there a struggle? Is that how the gun went off?'

Jenny looked away from him, her eyes gazing steadfastly into the fire. 'I don't want to think about it.' Her voice was composed. 'If I do, I can still feel the cold metal in my hand.'

'Of course.' He patted her sympathetically. 'You must put it behind you. It was a dreadful thing to have happened, and amazing that you were uninjured.'

They again sat in silence until Stephen admitted, 'I gave Agnes an extra dose of medication, you know. To ease her pain. Hill said that I should.'

'I know,' she said, still with her eyes on the flames. 'He said 'same to me.'

'I went up there tonight. To her grave.'

Jenny nodded. 'Yes.'

'It was as if she was gone. Usually I feel that there's a response from her. Does that seem strange?' He ran his hand over his chin. 'But tonight there was none. I think she was telling me to leave her in peace.'

He got up and stretched. 'I'll just go and check around everything before I lock up.'

'Yes.' Jenny gave herself a mental shake. 'I think I'll go up to bed.' She hesitated. 'Where shall I sleep?'

He stood by the door, one hand on the sneck, and glanced towards her. 'Wherever you feel comfortable, Jenny. I told you there was no hurry about anything. Sleep in your own bed if you wish.'

Jenny undressed by the low light of the lamp, which she had left on in case Christina awoke. It seems odd, she thought. Here I am a married woman preparing to spend my wedding night alone. She pulled her nightshift over her head and brushed her hair. Then she padded to the chest of drawers where there was a mirror on a mahogany stand. She looked into it and, beyond her white-clad figure and streaming dark hair, saw the reflection of a single bed with her child softly sleeping, and the glowing lamp on a side table.

She turned and, going to the lamp, put out the flame. Bending, she gently kissed Christina before going to the door, leaving it slightly ajar as she crossed the landing to Stephen's bedroom.

CHAPTER EIGHTEEN

Jenny was almost asleep when she heard footsteps on the stairs and then the creak of the door as it opened. She hadn't lit the lamp and the room was illuminated only by the night sky, which, though moonless, was quite light in spite of the earlier rain.

Stephen sat on the side of the bed and removed his trousers and unbuttoned his shirt, and as Jenny moved slightly in the bed he turned. 'Jenny!' He barely breathed her name.

'Yes,' she whispered. 'It didn't seem right sleeping in 'other bed. I've promised to be your wife and bear your children. I can't do that from across 'landing.'

She thought that he laughed for she heard a slight breathy sound, though she couldn't be sure, as his face was in shadow, but she watched as he took off his shirt and his under drawers, and then pulled back the sheet to lie naked beside her. They neither of them spoke, and Jenny almost held her breath as she considered that she had never before lain beside a man, let alone seen one completely naked.

He reached out and clasped her hand, then quickly withdrew it and sat up with his head in his hands. 'I'm sorry, Jenny. So sorry. Your being beside me brings back so many memories of Agnes, especially of when we were both young.'

She sat up beside him. 'It'll take time, I expect,' she consoled him. 'I feel strange too and nervous. It's 'first time I've been in bed with a man.'

'Is it?' He turned towards her. 'But what about Christy? Surely–'

'No. We were never in bed together. How could we? I was a servant. We used to meet on Beverley Westwood or beneath 'trees in New Walk. We – it was always quick; we were afraid of being caught. Christy wanted it and I didn't mind.'

He smiled down at her. 'So you're still an innocent in spite of having a child?'

'Innocent? I didn't think I was.'

'Innocent in the ways of love,' he murmured. 'It can be so beautiful.'

'Then yes, I am,' she admitted. 'I didn't rate it all that highly, even though I loved Christy.' She swallowed nervously. 'Perhaps we'll just go to sleep, shall we? We've had a long day.'

She lay down and moved as far from him as possible, facing the window. She knew that Agnes had slept on this side of the bed, but she hadn't wanted to take Stephen's side, nearest the door. She sighed. I hope I've done the right thing in marrying him.

He lay down beside her on his back, and soon she felt sleep stealing over her and images of the day jumbled together in her drowsiness. Her breathing became deeper as she sank softly into the feather bed and she was only just aware of Stephen's deep sigh as he turned his back.

It was some time later, when she came to turn over, that she found that her hair was trapped beneath Stephen's shoulder. He must have moved at some point and lain upon it as it was stretched across the pillow. She pulled her head but she was held fast, with his body close to hers. She reached one arm behind her to push him away, but in his sleep he came closer.

'Stephen,' she whispered. 'You've caught my hair. I can't move.'

He murmured something and put his arm across her and kissed her shoulder. 'Mmm?' he mumbled.

'I can't move. You've trapped my hair.'

'Sorry!' he croaked, and lifted his head. 'I'm dreaming. Jenny?' He leant on one elbow and looked down at her. It was lighter now; a pale grey dawn was breaking and the birds were beginning to chirrup and trill in the roof. 'How lovely you are!'

'No.' She smiled sleepily as she turned over. 'Not me. I was always known as a plain girl.'

He touched her face with his finger. 'Whoever said that was wrong.' He lay down to face her. She opened her eyes to see his, glazed and tender, softly gazing at her. 'You're very beautiful: warm and flushed in sleep.' He ran his fingers from her cheek down her throat and she felt a sudden craving sensation in the pit of her stomach as they continued down, and he cupped her breasts in his hands.

He leant towards her and kissed her lips, closing his eyes as he did so, and she wondered if he was thinking of Agnes. His hands slipped beneath her nightshift to stroke her thighs, belly and naked breasts. 'So soft,' he breathed. 'Like silk. So young and lovely.'

183

She drew in a breath, but didn't speak, couldn't speak, for as she felt his hands and mouth traverse her body, she could only moan. A pulse throbbed in her throat, her breasts felt tender and aching, whilst from between her thighs came an impulsive yearning. This wasn't something she had experienced with Christy. The quick couplings to give Christy urgent release had left her largely unmoved. This was a pleasure previously quite unknown as she felt Stephen's body enticing and exploring hers, and she, tantalized and intoxicated by his seduction, let her own hands stray across him. Over his shoulders and down his chest, then running her fingers down his back until, gasping in an overwhelming surge of desire, she clutched the roundness of his buttocks and felt his strong thighs straddle her.

She stretched back her neck on the pillow and gave out a low, quivering moan as unhurriedly he slipped inside her: demanding and persistent, yet tempting and entreating by the penetrating throb of his body until she was urged to respond. She ran her tongue around her lips and he, seeing the gesture, covered her lips with his own. She started to pant and he, with a low hankering groan, eased his mouth away as she cried out.

'No, don't stop,' she begged. 'Please don't stop. Oh, is this right? We said we didn't love each other. We don't, do we?' She grasped him and with her clamorous body urged him on.

'No,' he breathed hoarsely, as he reached a crest and then came down. He suckled her nipples with a voracious appetite, bit her neck and devoured her open mouth and climbed the peak once more.

184

'No, we don't. We love other people. But we're flesh and blood,' he groaned, 'man and wife, and you are so desirable. Ah!' He gave a rampant cry. 'Jenny!' He clutched her so tightly that she might have bruised, but she was melting and past all perception.

They fell asleep with their arms round each other, both murmuring words of contentment. They woke again to find the sun shining through the window and knew that they were late for milking, and feeding the hens and letting out the horses, but Stephen gathered her into his arms and made love to her, swiftly and urgently, then they scrambled into their clothes and rushed downstairs, touching and kissing as she put the kettle on the fire and he struggled into his outdoor boots.

She made tea and took a cup out to the dairy where he was sitting on a three-legged stool milking a disgruntled cow. 'Christina's still asleep,' Jenny said. 'I'll feed the pig.' He looked at her and then away, concentrating on what he was doing.

'Did I – I hope I didn't hurt you?' he muttered.

'No.' She shook her head shyly. 'No, you didn't.'

'It's been a long time. Agnes was – well, she was ill for a long time, even before you came.'

Still he didn't look at her and she bent her head to hide the flush on her cheeks. 'Yes,' she murmured. 'I understand what you mean.'

'Do you?' He stood up and picking up the almost full pail emptied it into the wooden churn. 'I don't think so.'

'Yes,' she repeated after a moment. 'I understand that men have a need, and – and it must have been very difficult for you – for both of you, because I know how much Agnes loved you.'

He glanced at her but didn't answer and slapping the cow gently on her rump he led her out of the barn.

She let the pig into the orchard, collected the chicken and duck eggs and went back inside to cook breakfast. The elation of the night and the morning had left her, and she felt curiously deflated. I must try to remember that he's a man with a man's needs, and that the reason we married was so I could give him a child and he would give Christina and me a name. He doesn't love me and I don't love him, and perhaps ... perhaps I shouldn't have enjoyed what we did. Maybe it was even wrong that I should want him to do the same things again. But I do, she confessed to herself, confused and guilty. I do.

She sighed and went to the cupboard, took out a bowl, cracked four eggs into it and whisked them with a fork. She heard the kitchen door open and then close and, looking up, saw Stephen leaning against it.

'Breakfast's not ready yet,' she said, and for some unknown reason felt tears prickle her eyes. 'Another ten minutes.'

He came towards her and taking the bowl from her set it on the table and put his arms round her. 'I didn't come in for breakfast!' he said softly, kissing her on the mouth. She lifted her face towards him, responding to his touch, and saw in his eyes a look that she knew to be desire: a longing which bewitched her, was received and returned. There was no time to run upstairs. He took her into his urgent grasp and they pulled and tugged at awkward clothing and sank to the floor, crashing into table legs and chairs. They heard the chortling cry of Christina from the bedroom, but the sound was lost in the thudding of heartbeats, the pounding of pulses and the deep moans of eager passion.

Later, when they had finished breakfast, Stephen lifted Christina high in the air. 'Your mama,' he said, giving her a little shake until she squealed in delight, 'will be giving you dozens of brothers and sisters if we carry on the way we are doing.'

Jenny sat back in her chair and breathed out. 'And we shall have to work twice as hard to keep them.'

He came towards her, Christina in his arms, and gently stroked Jenny's cheek. 'I will,' he vowed. 'I'll let nothing stop me. I've wanted a family ever since I lost mine. I'll work for you and my children, Jenny. Have no fear of that.'

'Even though you don't love me?' The words were out before she could stop them. 'Even though we love – have loved – others?'

He gazed down at her. 'Even so.' He bent and kissed her. 'You won't ever forget him, will you?'

She swallowed. 'Christy? No. Never.'

He nodded. 'He must have been very special to you. First love always is.' He smiled wistfully. 'Did he think you were beautiful?'

'He said that I was.' She gave a small laugh. 'But I didn't believe him.'

He put Christina down. 'But he was right.' He

went to the door. 'Must be off.' He sounded reluctant. 'I'll be down at midday.'

'You're wearing me out, Jenny,' he said a week later. 'You forget I'm an old man compared to you, a sprig of a girl. I'm going to sleep in Christina's bed tonight and she can sleep with you!'

'You don't seem like an old man,' she laughed. 'An old man wouldn't have your energy, or vitality. But yes, go in the other bed. I could do with a good night's sleep!'

But they both awoke and met on the landing and in silence they returned to his bed where he held her close and, without the searing explosion of eagerness, tenderly and gently made love to her.

They awoke one morning a few weeks later when the sun was newly up with a brightness that had been missing over the long cold wet winter. 'It's almost spring,' Stephen said as he stood by the window. 'At last. There's another lambing due. Crops to be sown. It's going to be a good year, I can feel it in my bones.'

Jenny, sitting up in bed, noticed that he didn't glance up at the top meadow with the same intensity as he once did, when he had looked towards the white stone that faced them. She had looked, though, and had seen the greening over as moss started to cover it, and long stalks of grass growing around it, and knew that he hadn't been up to cut it lately.

She put her hand to her mouth and the other to her ribs, as she felt bile rise inside her. 'Stephen,' she muttered. 'Will you put 'kettle on 'fire? I feel sick.'

'Sickening for something?' He turned towards

her. 'The pork wasn't off?'

'No!' She grimaced. 'I don't think so. I'd salted it well.' She gasped and threw back the covers and, tumbling from the mattress, fished under the bed for the chamber pot. 'I think I'm pregnant. We're going to have a baby.'

CHAPTER NINETEEN

'Stephen is the most caring husband,' Jenny wrote from the comfort of her bed. 'I wasn't allowed to go downstairs that first morning after I'd retched and retched, and was brought hot water for drinking, as I couldn't face tea. Then he made thin gruel and poached a new-laid egg and brought it upstairs so that I could have breakfast in bed. I couldn't help but think of Agnes, and how he must have cared for her when she was ill before I came to help them, and I confess to feeling a touch of envy for the love that they once shared.

'I will never know of course, but I don't think that Christy and I would have had the same contentment that Stephen and Agnes had, for the more I think about it, the more I come to realize that our life together would not have worked out well.

'Stephen rode over on one of the crossbreed shires to give George Hill the news, taking Christina up in front and leaving me in bed. As soon as they were gone I got up and continued with my usual tasks and had the dinner ready on the table when they returned. Dr Hill, of course, refused to come immediately, as Stephen had asked him to. He said I was young and healthy and childbirth was perfectly natural, and that there was no danger of my giving birth within the hour! It is very surprising to me that Stephen is so concerned, when he knows quite well that I gave birth to Christina with only his help. It is different now, I suppose, when I am carrying his child.'

Stephen took the waggon and made the journey to Driffield market to sell some rabbits. He came back with a young heifer for fattening and trailing a small pony for Christina.

'She's too young to ride,' Jenny said fearfully when he returned with the pony trotting behind the waggon. 'She'll fall off and break her bones.'

'She won't.' He grinned. 'I shall teach her how to sit and ride properly. She's just the age to start: she'll have no fear.'

He sat Christina on the pony's back and, to her delight, led her slowly round the bottom meadow. Stephen glanced up towards Agnes's stone. 'I heard more news about the railway line when I was at market,' he said. 'We shall be having another visit from an official of the North Eastern Railway Company before long, I don't doubt.'

'What will it mean?' Jenny asked, walking alongside them. 'Will it affect us? Will you be forced to give up land?'

He shook his head. 'Not without a fight, I won't. I've been talking to some of the other farmers. It's gone before Parliament already but if we band together we have a chance of turning the proposal, but some of them won't hold on, and others are looking for compensation.' He grunted. 'This Beverley to Market Weighton line has been talked about for years. When Agnes and I first came to live here George Hudson was about to buy the Londesborough estate, so that he could build new lines from Market Weighton to York, and stop any other company from linking up with them from Beverley. Lord Hotham refused to let them put a track across his land, but now he's agreed to it, providing they build a station at Kiplingcotes.'

'But don't you think it's exciting?' Jenny said. 'People could go all the way to York from Beverley by train if a line was built!'

Stephen stopped the pony and looked at her. 'Yes, of course. I believe in advancement, but I don't want it here.' He turned and pointed up the meadow. 'That's where it would come, right across our land which we can't afford to lose. Besides, there'd be soot and sparks flying, perhaps setting fire to the crops. The noise would startle the animals. There'd be hissing steam and thick smoke – you should know, you've travelled by train!'

'Yes,' she said reluctantly. 'I agree it's dirty, but I still think it's a good way to travel.' But, she thought, there's another reason why Stephen doesn't want the line there. It would cut right across Agnes's grave.

'Well, I shall try to stop it,' he said stubbornly. 'They've already started the Market Weighton section, but they'll not come on my land!'

'So if you tell them about Agnes you think they'll take another route?' Jenny kept her eyes firmly up at the stone, now not as white as it once was.

'Tell them about Agnes? What do you mean?'

191

Stephen stared at her.

'Well.' She shifted uncomfortably. 'They surely wouldn't – can't – move her for the sake of a railway line?'

'Good God!' he breathed and followed her gaze up the hillside. 'So that's why–'

'What?' she said, feeling unaccountably weepy and wanting to go inside the house to lie on her bed, Stephen's bed, which had also been Agnes's.

'That's why Agnes wanted to be buried there! She insisted that it shouldn't be anywhere else.' He lifted Christina down from the pony's back and went to lean against the fence, rubbing his hand against his chin. 'She said it had to be there. I want to be part of the landscape for ever, she said. She even chose the stone,' he added softly, 'said it would always show where she had once been.'

'I'm so sorry,' Jenny began brokenly, feeling guilty and confused. 'She thought, then, that the line would eventually come up here?'

He nodded, his eyes still gazing upwards. 'Yes. As I say, it's been on the cards for years, but there have been objections by landowners, and the terrain will be difficult.' He took a deep breath. 'But Agnes was practical. She was convinced that one day it would come, and that it would take a miracle to stop it.'

Jenny turned away. 'I need to go and lie down,' she said, taking Christina by the hand. 'We'll go and have a rest, shall we, Christina?'

'You're not feeling unwell?' Stephen asked uneasily.

'No,' she said heartily. 'But I need to put my feet up.' And, she thought, I need to get rid of this grudge inside of me. How can I be resentful of poor dead Agnes, when I have so much? But I am, and I don't know why.

In Jenny's seventh month the midwife came to visit. She'd hitched a lift on a carrier's cart, sitting atop a pile of sacks, and then trudged up the long track and path to their door. Jenny made her a cup of tea, for Mrs Burley, who was heavy in build, was hot from the walk.

'I'm in a fair old lather.' She wiped the sweat from her forehead. 'But I thought I'd better come and see how you're getting along. I didn't realize it was such a trek.' She sipped gratefully at the tea. 'Dr Hill asked me if I'd been to see you. Said that Mr Laslett had particularly asked me to call. I'm right sorry I wasn't here last time.' She nodded at Christina who was playing on the floor at their feet. 'But you managed wi'out me?'

'We did,' Jenny said. 'She was an easy birth.'

'Aye? Good. She'll be gone two, is she? You do well to space 'em out. I allus says to my young mothers, try and space 'em out if you can. They're healthier for it.' She leant towards Jenny with her cup to accept more tea. 'But of course, their husbands are young and eager – and thick as two short planks, most of 'em. They don't seem to realize how babbies are made.'

She looked round the kitchen. 'Nice and cosy,' she murmured, 'and if I might tek a look upstairs? Just so's I know where everything is.' She glanced at Jenny. 'Is Mr Laslett from a branch of 'St John Laslett family, up Driffield way, might I enquire, ma'am?'

'Y-yes, he is,' Jenny answered.

193

'Ah! I did wonder.' Mrs Burley pursed her mouth. 'I thought – well, I'd heard – you know how rumour gets about? But I thought that the Mr Laslett who lived up here was married to an older woman, and his family had disowned him! Course it was a long time ago, so it might have been somebody else!' she said, raising her eyebrows enquiringly.

Jenny took a breath. There was no need for her to lie, but Stephen would be furious if he discovered he was being discussed. 'I am Mr Laslett's second wife,' she stated in a matter-of-fact manner. 'His first wife died some time ago.'

'Ah! Well, I never heard about that. Beggin' your pardon. It's a pity I hadn't heard, cos I could have come to attend to her. With laying out, I mean.' She smiled and nodded affably. 'But at least he'd no children for you to mother or argue with? It can be difficult when you're a second wife. I know. I've seen it. I know what trouble they can bring. Specially when 'new wife is only young and can't allus cope. But there, you'll be satisfying him with two bairns and a few more besides I shouldn't wonder.'

She took a look upstairs and decided that the single bed would be best for the confinement. 'Then your husband can have a good night's sleep in his own bed if you tek ower long,' she said. 'Though if your first was quick your second will be quicker, so be sure to send for me as soon as you get 'pains. I've no more due that month so I can come straight away.'

Stephen came in as Jenny was showing Mrs Burley to the door. 'Your wife's doing right fair,

194

Mr Laslett,' she told him. 'We'll not need to worry our heads about her. But fetch me when she's ready and I'd appreciate a ride here and back to Etton, for it's a fair pull up 'road to here.'

Stephen said that transport would be arranged, and as he was wishing her good day she turned back. 'Will 'railway line affect you, Mr Laslett? They're breaking 'first sod 'day after tomorrow at Cherry Burton. I'd go and see 'em 'cept I've a bairn due about then.'

'No,' Stephen said emphatically. 'It won't affect me. They won't be coming on my land.'

She must have sensed some tension coming from him. 'Dirty noisy things,' she said in agreement. 'I allus said them trains wouldn't catch on, but I've been proved wrong and folks seem to think they're here for good. There's a few carriers out o' work cos of 'em. Well,' she said at last. 'I've chattered a bucketful and I'd better be off or I'll miss my ride back.'

Stephen closed the door behind her. 'Is she going to be all right? I bet she wanted to know all about you? About us both?'

'She'd heard already about you and Agnes,' Jenny said. 'But she assumed that Christina was yours and I didn't put her right about that.'

He gazed at her. 'What?'

'Well, she said we were right to space 'children. She didn't know that Agnes had died or that you had married again.'

'Not that,' he said bluntly. 'About Christina. Don't I treat her as my own? For heaven's sake, Jenny. I was there at her birth.' There was a flash of anger in his eyes. 'She'll think of me as her father. Will you tell her that I am not?'

'I don't know.' She looked down at her feet. 'I just don't know.'

'You still think of him, don't you?' It was almost an accusation.

'Sometimes,' she admitted. 'I can hardly forget him, can I, after what happened? And,' she added, 'when I have his child.' Then she lifted her head and gazed directly at him. 'But probably not as often as you think of Agnes. Her memory is constant, isn't it?' She swallowed hard to hide her tears. 'But we agreed, didn't we, that we understood how the other felt towards those we have lost?'

He blinked rapidly, then sat down at the table and put his hand to his forehead. 'Yes. Yes, of course we did. I'm sorry, Jenny. I'm forgetting how overpowering young love can be. How unforgettable.' He reached out to clasp her hand. 'Sorry! It's just that I do care for Christina as if she was my own, and when our child is born I will do as I promised and adopt Christina – if that is what you would like,' he added swiftly. 'Better for her to have an adoptive father than none?'

'Yes,' she replied huskily. 'You're a good father.'

'A better father than a husband?' he asked, his gaze holding hers.

'I have no complaints on that score.' She blushed, for his lovemaking was more passionate than she could ever have dreamed of, and she admitted that if she hadn't known that it was only desire, and had thought that there was real love there also, well then, she tried to shake the thought away, well then, it would be perfect.

That night he was tender, treating her as if she was made of glass, but touching her so seductively, so fondly, while whispering of tempting allurements and need, that she felt she would swoon with craving and wishful appetite. He pulled away from her. 'I don't want to hurt you or the baby,' he said softly. 'So send me away if you want. Lock the door on me. Don't let me share your bed.'

She breathed heavily. 'It's your bed,' she said. 'I should be the one to move out.'

He leant over her and traced his fingers over her cheekbones. '*Your* bed, yours and mine.'

A small breath of wistful longing escaped her lips. 'Only by chance,' she whispered. 'If it were not for Agnes's request, I wouldn't be here. I'm but a thief stealing another woman's bed.'

'What? What are you saying?' His voice was testy and in the lamplight she saw outrage. 'What about Agnes?'

'I – I don't mean anything against Agnes! She was thinking of you and perhaps even of me, but I'm racked with guilt sometimes. I think of how happy you both were and that – well, perhaps you wish that she was here instead of me.'

'I have – never – wished–' He got out of bed and paced the room, shaking his fist. 'Jenny! Does it seem–' He came and knelt at her side of the bed. 'Am I so inadequate? I know that I'm not young as Christy was, but don't I show you how I care?'

She sat up in bed and started to weep. 'It's just that ... I'm jealous!' she confessed and felt relief at last at her own acknowledgement. 'I'm jealous of 'love that you shared with Agnes. I want it! I want your baby but I want your love too, more than anything I've ever wanted before!'

'Stop! Stop!' Stephen put his fingers to her lips. 'Are you telling me, Jenny, that you love me as I love you? As I've loved you since the day of our marriage and dared not tell you?'

She nodded and wiped her eyes on the sheet. 'We entered into a marriage of convenience.'

'So we did.' He pulled himself onto the bed and put his arms round her. 'But you have insinuated yourself into my very being, and I cannot think of life without you, even though I told you at the beginning that I would let you go if you wanted to. Now, if you left me, I would follow you to the ends of the earth to bring you back.'

He kissed away her tears and licked her wet cheeks. 'I thought that you'd love Christy for ever, that no-one else could take his place.'

'I didn't know that it was possible to love again,' she said softly. 'I thought that when he died there'd be no other love in my life, apart from my child.'

He kissed her lips. 'When I lost Agnes, I thought too that there would never be anyone else. We were so wrong.' He stroked her face. 'But we have found each other and life has taken on a brightness again, which I thought had gone for ever.'

CHAPTER TWENTY

Life seemed somehow sweeter after they had made their confessions of love for each other. Jenny was lighter in spirit and Stephen not as impatient as he sometimes was, for he admitted he was by nature inclined to be fractious when events didn't go the way he wanted them to.

'It's my father's fault,' he said irritably. He had been to Cherry Burton and watched the navvies turn the first sod for the railway line. On returning home he then had to go and search for the sheep, which had escaped through a hole in a hedge. 'He was such a cantankerous man sometimes and I have inherited his humours. I shall be a crabby old fellow, Jenny, if I live so long, so be warned now.'

'You told me not long ago that you were already an old man,' she teased. 'Have you rediscovered youth?'

'Well, yes, of course I have.' He grinned. 'Now that I am married to a slip of a girl. But,' he gave a false groan, 'that girl is wearing me out very fast!'

Jenny heaved a deep breath. 'I feel fair worn out myself. I'm really tired and have been for 'last few days. I'll be glad when this is over.'

'Then you must rest,' Stephen insisted and urged her to sit down. 'Perhaps I'll ride over for George to come and take a look at you.'

'Better going for Mrs Burley. She'd know better

than 'doctor,' Jenny said, not wanting to admit that she felt not only tired but also unwell, something she hadn't felt with Christina.

'Shall I go for her?' Stephen looked troubled. 'How much longer before it's due?'

'Four or five weeks, I think,' Jenny said. 'Too early yet.' And she hoped that the child wouldn't arrive before its time. I wouldn't like Dr Hill or Arabella to think that Stephen and I had been sharing a bed before our marriage.

'All the same, I'll go first thing in the morning,' Stephen decided. 'We'll feel easier if she comes, and then she can decide if Hill should visit.'

The next morning it was apparent that he should fetch the midwife without delay. Jenny had woken during the night with pains in her back and had been sick. Stephen hitched a horse to the waggon and set off even before milking and as Jenny paced the floor she could hear the cow complaining.

She went downstairs and felt the weight of the kettle. There wasn't much water in it, for she had forgotten to fill it the night before, but she swung it over the fire anyway, not trusting herself to go outside to the pump. Christina called to her and Jenny stood at the bottom of the steep and narrow stairs as she came down.

'Careful. Don't fall,' she said, as Christina took one step at a time. 'I shall tell your da how clever you are.'

'Tell Papa,' Christina pronounced. 'Not Da! Tell Papa Christy is very clever girl.'

Jenny held out her hand as she reached the bottom step. 'Christina,' she said. 'Not Christy!' She led her towards a chair and sat down, lifting her onto her knee. Hugging her, she began to weep.

Christina patted Jenny's face and then began to cry herself. 'Christina make you cry,' she wailed. 'Naughty girl.'

'No, sweetheart. You're not a naughty girl. You're a very good girl and now you're going to help me by setting 'table for Papa's breakfast for when he comes home.'

Christina eagerly trotted to and from the larder, the door of which was open, for she wouldn't have been able to reach the sneck, and brought out one by one a loaf of bread, which she only dropped once, the milk jug, which she held in both hands and only spilt a drop, and the butter dish which proved to be empty when she took off the lid.

'Fetch some from the dairy,' the little girl piped, but Jenny emphatically declined the offer, afraid to let her out of sight until Stephen returned.

'Get two dishes from the cupboard,' Jenny told her. 'One for you and one for Da.'

'One for Papa, not for Da,' Christina chanted and Jenny gave a small ironic smile as she realized that her children, hers and Stephen's, would have a different upbringing from the one she had known. Though they might not know riches, Christina and the child she was carrying would speak differently, act differently and have higher expectations than Jenny had had as a child.

'And one for Mama.' Christina reached into the cupboard for another dish. 'One, two, free, six.'

'Did Papa teach you to count?' Jenny asked in astonishment, and then took a deep rasping breath as a pain shot through her.

'Christina count sheep,' Christina said proudly.

'And chickens.'

Stephen brought Mrs Burley back within the hour, but by now Jenny was creased with pain.

'You'll have to fetch Dr Hill, sir.' After she had examined Jenny, the midwife went outside to find Stephen. 'Your wife's starting in labour early and she's not looking very good.'

Once more Stephen rode off with Christina in front of him, but not before he had kissed Jenny and whispered that he loved her. 'I'm so afraid for you,' he murmured. 'So afraid of losing you.'

'You won't,' she said, 'but I'm worried for 'babby. It's very still.'

When George Hill arrived ahead of Stephen, riding at a faster pace on his sturdy cob than his friend could achieve on the shire, Jenny was about to give birth. Dr Hill took off his jacket, rolled up his impeccable shirtsleeves and delivered a girl child. The midwife glanced at him and gave a slight shake of her head.

'I'm sorry, Jenny,' the doctor murmured sympathetically. 'The child is stillborn. A girl. So very sorry.'

'A girl?' Jenny turned her head to look at the babe who was being wrapped in a sheet by Mrs Burley. 'Let me hold her for a moment.'

Mrs Burley handed her the child, whose tiny face was in repose, and she tucked her against her breast and kissed her brow. 'Wasn't meant to be, Mrs Laslett,' Mrs Burley said kindly. 'She's onny a little mite; wouldn't have survived even if she'd drawn breath.'

Wasn't meant to be, Jenny thought as tears rolled down her cheeks. Is this a punishment for marrying for a purpose and not for love? Next time, our child will be born because of our love and not for any other reason. She glanced towards the window. It was dark and wet; the clouds hung low and grey. She heard Stephen open the kitchen door and the murmur of voices as George Hill acquainted him with the news, and knew how grief-stricken he would be. He had wanted this child, more than she had, and she had failed him. Failed him twice, for he had also wanted a son.

Mrs Burley took the child from her as Stephen came into the room. His hair was wet and his coat damp. He glanced at the child and drew his finger across her still cheek. 'God bless her,' he murmured, and then looked towards Jenny.

'I'm so sorry,' she wept as he sat beside her on the bed. 'I know how you wanted this child. You and Agnes,' she said in a low voice as Mrs Burley went out of the room. 'But we'll bury her with Agnes, then they can be together for always.'

'Jenny, Jenny! Stop. Please. Don't say that.' His voice was anguished and he clasped her hand tightly. 'This was *our* child, yours and mine. Don't torment yourself in this way. I told you that I loved you from the day we married. This was *our* child,' he repeated.

'But we wouldn't have married if Agnes hadn't suggested it,' she continued, and now her head was beginning to spin. 'I would have gone on my way with Christina – and – and – you–'

'And what would I have done?' he asked in distress. 'What would have happened to me if you hadn't stayed? We can't think of what might have been, Jenny! We can only think of what is now.'

Dr Hill came into the room and Stephen turned to him. 'Jenny is overwrought,' he said worriedly. 'Can you give her something to calm her?'

The doctor nodded. 'Don't distress yourself,' he told her. 'There'll be other babies. Lots of them, I shouldn't wonder. You're young and healthy, even if you are married to this old man.' Then soberly he said, 'Babies don't always survive, but sometimes it's nature's way. Better to lose them at birth than later when you've grown to love them. She was a tiny baby; she would always have been weak.

'Take Jenny back to her own bed,' he told Stephen. 'I'll give her a mild sedative, then let her rest for a few days before she gets up. But what would you like to do about the burial?' he murmured.

Jenny heard him. 'We're going to bury her next to Agnes. We must, Stephen.' Jenny's eyes were bright and feverish. 'But we'll have a parson here – if one will come – to say a prayer.'

That proved to be more difficult than they had imagined, for whilst Jenny lay in bed, sedated by medication and with the curtains drawn, Stephen rode around the villages with Christina, trying to find a parson willing to come and bless a stillborn child who was going to be buried in unconsecrated ground. Eventually he was directed to a young parson who said he would come to talk to them and visit the burial site.

'Because there's already a grave here, it could be considered to be sanctioned by usage,' he said earnestly, rubbing his smooth chin and gazing down at Agnes's stone. 'And I see no reason why

I should not bless this place. It is as good as any other. Shall we do it now?'

Stephen went back to the house to tell Jenny and at once she insisted on getting up. He wrapped a shawl around her and lifting her in his arms, he carried her downstairs, through the house and up to the meadow, with Christina following behind.

'I cannot write what I felt.' Jenny took up her pen again a few days later. 'When the tiny coffin, which Stephen had made on the day she was born and died, was lowered into Agnes's grave, I felt only numbness. No emotion or tears, but strangely, a kind of release or freedom. I dare not say this to Stephen, or indeed to anyone, for they'd surely think that I wouldn't have loved the child had she lived, when of course I most certainly would. The release came, I think, because I had fulfilled my duty towards dear Agnes, who had so badly wanted a child by her husband. And now she has one. Stephen's child, carried by me, now lies with her. We have named her Agnes.

'The freedom is because Jenny kitchen-maid who was once accused of murder and cast out of Beverley, and who masqueraded under the name of the second Mrs Laslett, has now disappeared. That part of my life has closed as if in closing a chapter in a book. The next part of my life as Mrs St John Laslett, with my husband, Stephen, my daughter Christina and the child I hope soon to carry, is about to begin.'

CHAPTER TWENTY-ONE

'Mama, Mama! There's a man! Look!'

Christina was playing outside the kitchen door and had looked up to see a man opening the gate to their path. Behind him was another man. She ran inside and clung to her mother's skirt.

Jenny went to the door and screwed up her eyes. It was hot, a bright May day, and the freshly washed sheets, which she had draped over the hedge to dry, were throwing off a dazzling brilliance. Though she didn't know the man who was making his way to her door, she at once knew, by the manner of his dress, why he was there. He wore a dark frock coat and a top hat, and in his hand he carried a measuring staff.

'Good day to you, madam.' He airily touched his hat. 'Is your husband at home?'

'He's out somewhere,' she answered. 'What is it you want? If it's about the railway line–'

'It is indeed about the railway line.' He gestured towards the man waiting by the gate, who was holding, Jenny now saw, a length of chain, a flag and another piece of equipment, which she didn't recognize. 'My man and I wish to take some measurements of the land.'

'Of *our* land,' Jenny corrected him. 'Of my husband's land!'

'Indeed, indeed,' he answered with an ingratiating smile. Taking a notebook out of his pocket, he consulted it. 'Of Mr Laslett's land.'

'St John Laslett,' she said reprovingly, and had the satisfaction of seeing him take an open breath of awe.

'Ah!' He made an amendment in his book and asked in a fawning tone, 'Where may I have the pleasure of finding Mr St John Laslett?'

She hid a smile and said sternly, 'I'm afraid it won't be a pleasure, if you do find him, Mr...? For he won't wish to speak to you.'

'Stockton, madam,' he pronounced, 'Isaac Stockton, surveyor for the North Eastern Railway Company. It is a matter of urgency that we survey this land. Mr Las– Mr St John Laslett has not been co-operative so far.'

'Well, he's coming right now,' she said, pointing up the meadow to where she could see Stephen striding towards them with a crook in his hand and his dog at his heel. 'So you can speak to him in person.'

'Off my land!' Stephen shouted before he had even reached the hedge which enclosed the garden. 'I know why you're here and the answer is no!' He came out of the field through the bottom gate. 'I sent the last fellow off and told him he couldn't survey it.'

'Sir,' Stockton said. 'We must survey the terrain. The railway is coming whether you like it or not. The Hull to Hornsea line is now open and we cannot let single individuals prevent progress in this area. Beverley needs this line. It does not necessarily mean that we will build on your land. The parliamentary committee decide whether or no!'

'Off!' Stephen said. 'Or I set my dog on you.'

The man glared at him and turned away. 'We can survey it without your permission,' he said before marching back up the path. 'We can do it first thing in a morning or last thing at night. You can't be everywhere at the same time!'

'Why not let them come?' Jenny asked as they went back into the house. 'Let them take their measurements and tell them about the grave. Perhaps then they would make a detour.'

'I know where they would want it to be,' he said testily. 'They'll cut the land in two. It's hard enough trying to make a living. How can we farm the land with a railway line running through the middle of it? The sheep wouldn't know it was a railway line; there'd be dead mutton all over the place!'

'All the same,' Jenny reasoned. 'You should tell them about 'grave and maybe they'd rethink.'

'Perhaps,' he agreed reluctantly. 'Perhaps I will. I'd like to think the issue will be resolved soon.' He gave her a smile, his fractious mood evaporating. 'We have other things to think of. How are you feeling today?'

'Better!' she said with feeling. ''Sickness has gone, thank goodness.'

They had waited until Jenny had recovered from the birth of the stillborn child, but she had conceived quickly and was now in her fourth month of pregnancy. Her sickness had dissipated and she felt healthy and vital and was back helping Stephen with the chores. Christina wanted to help too and was allowed to feed the hens.

'It will be good for Christina to have a brother

or sister to play with,' Stephen mused. 'I'd never felt isolated before, but now I realize that we are, and that she should have company.'

Jenny agreed. Christina was shy of any strangers who called, such as the packman, or tramps looking for work.

'Perhaps,' Stephen deliberated. 'Perhaps when the child is born I'll write to Arabella and ask her to call.'

'I can do that,' Jenny said. 'The invitation would be better coming from me; but we don't need to wait. She won't come in the winter anyway. She could come and stay, couldn't she? She could have Christina's room and Christina could sleep with us.'

'In our bed? I suppose so.' Stephen seemed dubious. 'I never ever saw my parents in bed,' he said. 'I only ever saw them fully dressed.'

Jenny gave a pealing laugh. 'How very strange! We often slept four or more to a bed, with Ma and Da at 'top and us bairns at 'bottom.'

'Us bairns!' He grinned. 'You don't often say things like that!'

'I try not to,' she said bashfully. 'Christy used to tease me sometimes, whenever I forgot.'

'I won't,' he said. 'But if ever – well, if ever you became mistress of my father's house, perhaps it might be important to try to remember.'

'But Arabella is mistress, isn't she?' Jenny frowned. 'She wouldn't want me there, and,' she added quietly, 'you once said that you couldn't live in your father's house and leave Agnes here!'

'I know I did.' He bit hard on his lip. 'I know that's what I said, and I've been thinking about that a lot, especially since we buried the child there too – but as for being mistress,' he changed the subject rapidly, 'Arabella would be subordinate to you.'

'Subordinate?' Jenny asked hesitantly. 'What does that mean?'

'It means that she would be below you.'

'But that doesn't seem fair!' Jenny said. 'She's lived there all her life. How can another woman come along and take over?'

He shrugged. 'That's the way it is, I'm afraid, so unless she marries...' Again he shrugged, and then smiled teasingly at her tense expression. 'You would be in control, Jenny. You would be mistress of the house.'

Jenny thought about it over the next few weeks and when she received a reply from Arabella in response to her letter, saying she would like to come to visit, she felt a sense of guilt, even though the situation hadn't arisen and might never arise. Am I bound always to live in a house where another woman has belonged? she thought. Though I like this little house, it did once belong to Agnes.

'Someone come!' Christina shot into the house in scared excitement one morning and clung to Jenny. 'Quick! Quick!'

'It's all right, Christina,' Jenny assured her. 'It will be someone come to help Papa.' Stephen had been to Etton a few days before to ask if there was a labourer available to help cut the hay in the meadow.

'No, not help Papa,' the little girl piped. 'Another Mama.'

Jenny went to the door. The gypsy woman who

had called once before was there with her little girl at her skirts and a baby strapped to her chest. 'Hello,' Jenny greeted her. 'I remember you. Won't you come in?'

'I'll not come in, lady, but can I beg some milk for the *chavi?*' She pointed down to the dark-haired child. 'And for myself.'

'Yes. Yes, we have plenty.' Jenny was quite relieved to talk to someone other than Christina. Stephen had been out since early morning, only coming in for a quick breakfast at eight o'clock and then going out again. He had started on the haymaking alone, as he hadn't had any offers of help. Everyone was busy at this time. 'Come with me,' she said. 'It's cooler in the dairy.'

The gypsy agreed to come into the dairy where she sat at the wooden table, on the chair nearest the door. Jenny gave her and the child a beaker of milk each, and then stroked the little gypsy girl's dark curls, darker than Christina's straight glossy hair. The two children looked at each other.

'What's your name?' Christina asked shyly.

'Kisaiya Lee,' the little girl said, lowering her dark lashes.

'Can she play with me?' Christina asked her mother.

The gypsy hesitated for only a moment, and then nodded and the two children clasped hands and ran outside. 'We have *gorgio* family,' she told Jenny. 'My mam has a cousin who is half Romany, half *gorgie*. Sometimes we see them at Hull Fair.'

'What is *gorgio?*' Jenny said, puzzled. 'Someone who isn't a gypsy?'

'Yes,' the woman said. 'Someone who lives in a

211

house, not a bender as we do.'

Jenny poured her another beaker of milk. 'Will your husband help us with the haymaking?'

'Yes, and our son. He's big enough now.' The woman, though her feet were bare, was covered entirely by her long skirt and shirt with a shawl over her head. She unfastened her blouse and began to feed the baby. 'Your *manush* said we could stay on your land for the summer.'

Jenny smiled. 'Good. We don't see much company and my husband will be glad of the help. What's your name?'

'Floure Lee. I was a Boswell, but I married a Lee. We are from the very best Romany families.'

'Oh,' Jenny said thoughtfully. 'That's nice. I'm not anybody, though my husband is – was.'

Floure Lee glanced at her and then changed her baby to the other breast. 'As your *chavvies* will be.'

'What do you mean?' Jenny said.

'I mean your children. They'll belong to the best families, though that doesn't mean they will be better people. Have you a son?' she asked, a frown deepening above her nose. 'You have two children?'

'No.' Jenny felt a shiver down her back. 'We lost a child, a girl.'

'Ah! The stone on the hill.' She shook her head. 'We don't camp there. There's a spirit watching, though it is not unfriendly.'

'Agnes!' Jenny breathed. 'Yes, she's there with our child.'

Floure gazed silently at her. 'You've had some unhappiness, lady? There's something troubling you about your past life!'

Jenny took a breath. How much did the Romanies know? Were they really able to look into the future and see what was coming?

'Sometimes we can read fortunes,' the gypsy said, and Jenny looked at her in astonishment. 'And sometimes we can sense another person's feelings. My grandmother Shuri could do that, and I have inherited the gift of duckering from her.' She fastened up the buttons on her blouse and, putting the now sleeping baby on her shoulder, gently patted her back. 'You'll have changes in your life and not always what you expect. Some disappointments and sorrow, and you'll go back to where once you were happy.'

'Go back?' Jenny said. 'To where?'

Floure shook her head. 'I can't tell. I only knows that you will.' She leant forward and took hold of Jenny's hand and turned it over to look at her palm. She drew in a sudden breath and her eyes widened. Jenny pulled her hand away, clenching her fingers so that the gypsy couldn't see.

'I'm not sure that I want to know what's in front of me,' she said.

The gypsy rose to her feet, wrapping the baby under her shawl. 'It is not what is coming,' she whispered, and her eyes flashed nervously. 'It's what has already been.'

Jenny felt uneasy after she had gone and watched her as she tramped up towards one of the fields where the gypsies had camped. What had she seen? Could she really see anything? Her thoughts slipped back to Christy. She surely couldn't know about that? Could she read? Had she heard

213

rumours? But she can't have, she assured herself. No-one up here knows about me or where I come from. But the encounter unsettled her and Stephen commented on it that night as they ate their supper.

'Are you unwell?' he asked. 'You're very quiet.'

'I never thought that I was ever anything else,' she said.

'It's true, you are inclined to be reserved,' he agreed. 'But I meant quieter than usual. Is something troubling you?'

'The gypsy woman asked the same thing,' Jenny said, but then remembered that the gypsy had pinpointed the past, rather than the present, which was what was concerning Stephen.

'You shouldn't encourage her,' he said sharply. 'She'll be round every day, begging for something or other!'

'I don't think so. She only ever wants milk for 'children. She's never asked for anything else.'

Stephen grunted. 'Well, count the chickens before you close them up for the night,' he said.

'Would you begrudge them?' she asked. 'They've got nothing much.'

'They have as much as we have, apart from the land,' he said grumpily. 'They have a roof, of sorts, over their heads and a chance to work, which they do only when it suits them. If they asked for a chicken they could have one, as long as they worked for it. I can't afford to give anything away.'

He sounded so sour that she looked at him in alarm. 'Are we so very poor?' she said, and when he nodded, she asked, 'What can we do?'

'Go cap in hand to my father,' he said bitterly.

'He's sitting on a fortune that could be mine if I grovel on my knees before him.'

'But you won't?'

'No. Not yet,' he asserted. 'I'd rather he came to me. And one day he will!'

CHAPTER TWENTY-TWO

It was the end of summer and there was a scent of autumn in the air, of dying foliage and wood smoke. Arabella sat by the fire in Lavender Cott sipping tea. 'It is a pity that one cannot choose when to have a child,' she said thoughtfully. Since she had arrived for her visit, she and Jenny had strolled in the meadows, she had watched the cow being milked, had thrown corn for the hens, and enthusiastically joined in with Christina's games. 'It would be more pleasant – I imagine,' she added, blushing slightly, 'for of course I wouldn't know, to have a child in the summer instead of the winter when it is so cold and the roads are bad.'

Jenny raised her eyebrows. It surprised her that Arabella, a well brought up unmarried young woman, should choose to discuss such matters, but she did, quite often asking questions on subjects which shouldn't have concerned her.

'I was sorry to hear that you have lost a child,' Arabella continued. Glancing around the room, she remarked, 'I do hope you will excuse my saying so, but, although it is very sweet here, it is a little primitive. Perhaps the child would have

215

survived if the conditions had been better?'

'There's nothing wrong with 'conditions,' Jenny replied rather sharply. 'I had 'services of Dr Hill and a midwife. The child never drew breath, there's nothing can be done about that. It wasn't meant to be, that's all.'

Arabella nodded. 'Well, perhaps the next child will be a son,' she said sagely. 'Then it will have been worth the wait. Did you give the other child a name? Is that permissible?'

'Yes, of course. We named her Agnes, after Stephen's first wife.'

'Oh!' Arabella's eyes widened. 'Really? Did you mind that?'

'Not at all,' Jenny answered quietly. 'She always wanted a child.' She swallowed hard. 'And so we gave her one.'

'And buried her with her!' Arabella exclaimed. 'I think that was very sweet and kind of you, Jenny. I declare, I don't think I could have been so benevolent to another wife. And the child that you are carrying – if it is a son, what will you name him? After Stephen? Which is also our father's name,' she added, 'though Papa is known as John, his middle name. Yes,' she said thoughtfully. 'I think he would be pleased to have his first grandson named for him.'

'We haven't yet considered names,' Jenny said. 'I don't want to bring ill luck by naming him before he arrives.' Why did I say *him?* she wondered. The gypsy asked if we had a son. Was it her influence?

'When you have given birth,' Arabella said chattily, 'I shall broach the subject of your visiting us with my father. He does sometimes ask if I have heard from Stephen, and if he has a son yet. He will, I think, look favourably on you, Jenny, in spite of your background.'

'Because I am a bearer of children?' Jenny replied, but if there was a trace of sarcasm in her voice Arabella did not appear to notice.

'Why yes,' she smiled. 'He does quite like his grandchildren. My sisters have three children each, all girls, and Papa dotes on them. Laura and Maud are both expecting again, and if one of them has a boy, then the estate will go to him if you don't produce a son.' She leant towards Jenny. 'I do hope that you do,' she confided. 'I can't stand my sisters' husbands, they are so very arrogant. If any one of them has a son, they would want to run Father's estate until their child is old enough to do it.' Her face puckered. 'And I don't know what would happen to me then!'

'Surely your father would leave you well provided for?' Jenny said. 'Especially if you were unmarried.'

'He's very old-fashioned.' Arabella's eyes became moist. 'He would leave me an annuity, I expect, but I wouldn't have a house. He would expect my sisters and their husbands to have me live with them. And they won't want to.' Her bottom lip trembled. 'I know that they won't.' She took out a lacy handkerchief and dabbed at her eyes. 'That's why I am desperate to get married, Jenny,' she confided. 'It's such a pity that you haven't a good background, for it would have helped me enormously if you had had friends of the right kind. My sisters do not help at all, they are so wrapped up in their own lives.'

Jenny gave a sudden laugh. 'You poor thing, Arabella! There must be thousands of people wishing they were in your shoes, wearing your clothes and enjoying your comfort, instead of struggling to find work, pay their rent and buy food for their families. If they only knew how difficult it is for you, they would be so very sorry for you!'

Arabella gave a huge sigh. 'They would. They really would. Nobody understands my situation.' She gave a brave smile and took hold of Jenny's hand. 'But perhaps you do, Jenny. I think we could be friends, you and I, in spite of our differences, and if ever you should come to live at my father's house I will treat you very kindly.'

Jenny had opened her mouth to outline the situation as Stephen had explained it to her – that she and not Arabella would be mistress of the house – when Stephen came in asking if there was a pot of tea, and so the chance was lost.

'Arabella's all right,' Stephen conceded two days later as they waved her goodbye. 'She's not terribly bright, but she could be a friend to you, Jenny.'

'That's what she said.' Jenny turned away from the gate as the chaise disappeared from view. 'About being friends. She thought we could be; she said she would treat me kindly!'

'How very patronizing!' Stephen exploded, and then he laughed. 'But she doesn't mean to be. She was taught by our mother to be benevolent to the poor or those who have less than she has, and she obviously thinks of you in that way.' He stroked Jenny's cheek, and then bent to kiss her. 'She doesn't realize that *you* have so much more than her.'

'Yes. I have you.' She looked up at him lovingly. 'I am so lucky.'

He smiled and tucked her arm into his as they walked back down the path. 'I didn't mean that, you little goose! I meant that you have the ability to think for yourself. You're not constrained by convention or society, with rules which you cannot step over.'

'But I have stepped over,' Jenny murmured. 'First with Christy and then with you. If I'd married Christy, his family wouldn't have accepted me, and he wouldn't have fitted in with mine. Arabella said she's going to speak to your father about my visiting him after our child is born.' She shook her head. 'We're deluding ourselves if we think that I would be accepted by him, or your other sisters, or anybody else in your family or society. It just won't happen. I'll be ostracized.'

'But you married me knowing this,' he said quietly. 'You haven't just thought of it?'

'No,' she answered, 'but I never thought that I would be expected to live anywhere else but here. I only thought at 'time that Christina and I would be safe with you. I didn't think that I might have to meet 'rest of your family.'

'You don't have to,' he maintained. 'Not if you don't want to. You can stay here for ever, as long as we're not run down by the trains,' he added, tight-lipped. 'But one day I shall want my son – or sons – to inherit the estate which should've been mine!'

'Which *would* have been yours,' Jenny reminded him, 'if you too hadn't crossed that line.'

'Yes,' he agreed. 'You are quite right. But I was influenced by love, not money or power.' He smiled and opened the door for her. 'Twice in my life.'

As autumn drew on and leaves began to fall, Jenny grew heavier; her legs ached and walking made her breathless. She confined herself to the house and could no longer dig up a bucket of potatoes or bend down to collect the eggs.

'It's going to be a massive boy,' Stephen said one night as he lay down next to her and gently stroked her belly. 'He'll come out six feet tall and weighing twelve stone.' He sat up and looked at her. 'Are there any giants in your family? You're not going to produce one like William Bradley?'

'Who's he?' she asked sleepily, wishing she could turn over, but she couldn't, it was too uncomfortable.

'The Market Weighton giant. The tallest man in England. He was nearly eight feet tall and weighed over twenty-five stone. He was a curiosity at the fairs, poor fellow.'

Jenny sighed. 'Not a relation of mine,' she said. 'But one of my father's sisters bore twins. Maybe there are two babies.'

'My God!' he breathed. 'Perhaps there are. I hope they're not both boys or they'll fight over the inheritance.' He lay down again, and as Jenny was drifting off to sleep she heard him say, 'I think I'll ride over to Hill and get him to come back and take a look at you.'

Twins, a boy and a girl, were born to her in the first week of October. The boy came first and his first cry was a lusty bellowing bawl. The girl, three minutes later, gave a serene hiccup. 'A proper lady,' George Hill said as he placed her in Jenny's arms, whilst Stephen looked down in emotional bewilderment at his red-faced, squalling son. 'She knows how to behave.'

'You should write to Arabella,' Jenny said to Stephen a few days later. 'She'll want to know. And perhaps ask her if she will stand as godparent?'

'I will when we've decided on the names. Are we agreed on John Stephen?'

'It's impressive, though a mouthful.' Jenny smiled. 'John Stephen St John Laslett! And for this little darling...' She stroked the soft cheek of her daughter whose rosebud mouth was searching for her breast.

'Serena!' Stephen said. 'She couldn't be anything else, but would you mind if we also called her Mary? After my mother? Unless you'd like her named for your mother? She could have three names.'

'Poor little mite, would I saddle her with Augusta?' Jenny laughed. 'My grandmother must have had ideas above her station! My mother was always called Gussy.'

Stephen shuddered. 'Aggie and Gussy! No, I think not. We'll keep to Serena Mary.'

A letter of congratulations came back from Arabella who said she would be delighted to stand as godmother to the babies, and a few weeks later a brief letter from Stephen's father came addressed to Mrs St John Laslett inviting her to come and stay with the children in the New Year, if the weather was suitable for travelling. He added that if she would let him know the date of her intended visit he would send a carriage and a maid for her assistance.

Stephen, stony-faced, read the letter when she handed it to him. 'I won't go, of course,' Jenny said. 'Not without you.'

'He won't invite me,' he said, his eyes dull and his lips turned down. 'That is patently obvious.'

'Then I shall write to him,' Jenny said, 'and explain that I cannot possibly travel without my husband.'

'Do,' Stephen muttered, 'but it won't make a scrap of difference.'

There was no reply to the letter sent to Stephen's father, but Arabella wrote to tell them that her sisters Laura and Maud had both been safely delivered of daughters. She also said how very cross her father was that Jenny had refused his invitation. 'I shall mention it again in a week or two,' she wrote, 'but he is a very stubborn man and I doubt he will change his mind about Stephen.'

'Then nor shall I change my mind,' Jenny said, as she read out the letter to Stephen. 'We don't need him and I shan't go without you.'

Stephen looked worried. 'Well, although I don't like to admit it, we do actually need him, Jenny. I don't want my children to be paupers. How will I ever pay for their education? How will we buy them clothes and shoes? There isn't enough here to feed all of us. And I'm sick of eating potatoes, pork and eggs!'

'You should think yourself lucky,' Jenny chided. 'There are people who'd think it riches to have a slice of pork, let alone eggs and bacon for breakfast! And you have your own house,' she added.

'Yes, I know,' he said, his voice sharp and

irritable. 'I don't need reminding about the poor! But you forget, Jenny, I once had more, therefore there is more for me to miss!'

She stayed silent for a moment, then she muttered, 'It was your choice. You didn't have to marry again. You knew Agnes was dying. You could have waited and then gone back home.'

'No. I wouldn't have given my father the pleasure of seeing me return in those circumstances. Besides, I wanted a family, I told you that right from the start.' He got up from his chair and came and stood beside hers. He stroked the top of her head. 'I'm being an old grouch, I know. But I want what is best for you and the children. I want what is rightfully theirs. I don't want you or them to suffer.'

She pulled him towards her and kissed his forehead. 'This isn't suffering,' she said softly. 'I've seen suffering. When I was at home we always had just enough, though you might have considered us poor. We have riches, Stephen! We have food on 'table every day. We might not have a carriage, but we've got a waggon and horses. You told Arabella on our wedding day,' she reminded him, 'that many a farmer would have been glad of a conveyance like ours. And we have a roof over our heads.'

He nodded, but she knew he wasn't convinced. 'It's because of the children,' he said. 'I knew you and I and Christina would manage, but now we have two more hungry mouths to feed.'

As if in confirmation of his words, an angry bellow came from the cot, and then a mewling one, as the twins woke for a feed. It's because of Johnny, Jenny thought as she picked up her

223

squalling son and put him to her breast. Stephen doesn't want his father's estate for himself, he would be content to stay here for ever, but he does want it for his son.

It was May before Arabella wrote again and said she had gained permission from her father to invite Jenny and the children. 'Please do come, Jenny. If Father sees the children, he may relent. He is suffering with gout at the moment and so I cannot leave him to visit you, even if you were so kind as to invite me. I am *desperate* for company; my sisters are all away, our neighbours are all busy with their own affairs and there are no social events whatsoever.'

'What should I do?' Jenny asked Stephen.

Stephen drew in a deep breath and exhaled. 'Go! Go and see the old devil and show him his grandson. But don't take any nonsense from him,' he warned, raising his voice and shaking a finger. 'Let him know you're only there under sufferance.'

She smiled. 'I shall make it plain that you insisted I come. That I didn't want to come alone. That I was being a dutiful wife in bringing our children to visit their grandfather.'

Stephen laughed. 'You'll do, Jenny, you'll do. Just let him know that you're not frightened of him.'

'I'm not,' she stated. 'I have you; I don't need him. But perhaps he needs us.'

He put his arms round her and nuzzled into her neck. 'You are such a sensible practical woman. You are probably right.' He held her at arms' length and kissed her on her nose. 'Whatever will I do without you? Don't stay away too long. I shall be lonely while you're away.'

CHAPTER TWENTY-THREE

When the carriage arrived to collect her, Arabella came as well as a maid. 'I persuaded Papa he could manage without me for half a day,' she said. 'I did so want to get out of the house and I couldn't wait to see the babies. I suppose they have been baptized without me?' she added petulantly.

'Yes,' Jenny said. 'Dr Hill stood as godfather and Mrs Burley, the midwife, stood as proxy for you. She was pleased to do so.' She didn't add that Mrs Burley was moved to tears when asked, and said that she felt honoured, as the babies were as dear to her as her own godchildren, of whom she had many.

After Arabella had taken some refreshment, they were ready to be off. The maid took the bags, the coachman carried the cots, and Stephen held Christina's hand, whilst Jenny brought the babies. 'Who will look after poor Papa?' Stephen mourned to the little girl. 'I shall be all alone.'

Christina's eyes filled with tears and she clung to Stephen. 'Poor Papa,' she wailed. 'I stay with you. Mama, I stay with Papa!'

'Stephen, don't torment her so!' Jenny admonished. 'She'll cry all 'way there now.'

Arabella looked on in astonishment. 'How very strange! I can't ever recall crying for Father when he went away,' she said. 'You have a singular relationship with your children, Stephen. I cannot but think that it is unique.'

Stephen lifted Christina up and kissed her wet cheek, whispering something in her ear, which made her give a tearful hiccuping laugh.

'And,' Arabella continued in a low voice, 'it isn't as if the child is your own, which makes it even more unusual.'

The smile on Stephen's face vanished and Jenny glanced anxiously at him. 'She's as much mine, even though I did not father her, as these two.' He looked down at the sleeping twins. 'She can expect and will have the same throughout her life as Johnny and Serena.'

Except, Jenny thought, that Johnny will be extra special as he is your eldest son; though probably not the only one, she considered, and wondered if she had been caught again. She had seen only one flux since the twins' birth seven months before.

Stephen passed Christina into the carriage and then hugged Jenny, putting his arms round her and the babies. 'Don't let Father bully you,' he whispered, 'and you must ask to come home if you are unhappy.'

'He won't bully me. I'm the mother of his grandson,' she whispered back. 'And I shall only be there a week, so you mustn't worry.'

'I'll miss you, Jenny, even though I shall be busy day and night.' The haymaking was about to start and the gypsies were again camped in the meadow.

'Don't forget to eat,' she said, 'and give milk to 'Romany children.' She had baked and prepared enough food for an army for a fortnight, even though she knew he was just as likely to fall asleep after a day's work as sit down to eat.

They were ready for off. The horses were stamping and snorting and the coachie was sitting with his whip raised. 'Come along, do,' Arabella implored. 'I promised Papa we would come straight back,' and Jenny reluctantly handed the babies to the maid whilst Stephen assisted her into the carriage.

'Wave to Papa,' she said to Christina. 'Blow him a kiss.'

The little girl did so, her head bobbing up and down as she tried to see through the window. As the carriage rattled down the track Jenny waved until she could no longer see Stephen and then she sat back against the leather upholstery, which she noticed was very cracked and worn. Arabella would think it very strange if I told her this was the first time in my life that I have travelled in a carriage, she thought, and then out loud she asked, 'Do you travel much by train, Arabella?'

'Good gracious no!' she answered. 'Do you?'

'Not now, but I did. Many times.' Jenny smiled at her, withholding the fact that her rail travelling had only been between Hull and Beverley.

'Oh! How exciting! Father won't go on the trains and will not allow me to either, even though the Driffield railway is so close and would be *very* convenient. He says it isn't safe, though I feel sure the trains are just as safe as this old boneshaker. He objected years ago when the line between Driffield and Malton was being built; he was so sure that they would want to come on his land that he stood guard with his shotgun; but as it happened they didn't want to.' She gave a little chuckle. 'I think he was quite disappointed; he so wanted to take a pot shot at somebody!'

There must be something about landowners, Jenny mused. Stephen is the same as his father in that respect. They don't want to give up any part of their land, even if it benefits the community as a whole. She began to feel nervous and apprehensive about meeting this fierce old man. He knows already that I am of the *lower orders*, because Arabella has told him so. I hope his house isn't too grand or I shall be quite out of place and will want to hide in the kitchens.

Laslett Hall where the Laslett family lived was near the country town of Great Driffield, which was new to her. I only know Hull and Beverley, she thought, and the villages where I've been to sell eggs. We lead such a solitary life. Rarely do we have contact with neighbours, and there are no friends or visitors to call except for Dr Hill and Arabella, or Mrs Burley when I'm childbearing.

For the first time since coming to live at Lavender Cott, she felt a sense of isolation. I've been in self-imposed exile, she thought; yet it's what I wanted. I needed to lick my wounds and escape from prying eyes and wagging tongues, which would have followed me had I defied the magistrates and stayed in Beverley. Stephen and Agnes wished to hide away from gossip too; they didn't want their love to be contaminated by whispers, scandal and rumour.

'Do you see many people, Arabella?' she asked. 'Do you entertain?' At least I know the right questions to ask, she thought. My time in the kitchens at the Ingram house wasn't wasted. I know what time luncheon, afternoon tea and supper are served, and what to expect from the servants.

'Not now that my sisters are married.' Arabella sounded gloomy. 'We often had house parties when Mama was alive so that they could meet suitable young men. All the farmers and the gentry round about did that, trying to match up their sons and daughters.'

Her mouth turned down and she lowered her voice, though the maid sitting across from her, holding a sleeping Serena, must have heard, unless she was deaf, Jenny thought.

'Father isn't keen any more,' Arabella continued in a whisper, 'now that Mama isn't here to organize everything. I'm stuck!' she moaned. 'And there are not so many young men left, not who are suitable anyway.'

'I suppose you have to marry someone suitable?' Jenny said. 'Someone with money and position?'

'But of course!' Arabella stared at her in amazement. 'Who else is there?'

The countryside grew hillier and greener as they travelled and the crops in the fields varied from barley for brewing to hemp and flax for rope and textiles.

'Is Great Driffield a large town?' Jenny asked. 'Like Beverley?'

'Yes, but we're not going to Driffield!' Arabella said. 'We don't live there. Did Stephen not tell you anything?'

Jenny shook her head. Nothing, she thought, nothing at all. He had never wanted to talk about his former life.

'Driffield is a very busy town,' Arabella informed her. 'It has a brewery, a tannery, a market, and shops with everything anyone could want. I could almost wish that we lived there instead of where we do. I shall take you one day if Father can spare the carriage.'

They came off the road that led to Great Driffield, and took small roads which were signposted to Kirkburn, and Eastburn, which Arabella said was medieval, and travelled past isolated farmsteads and smallholdings. 'We're coming towards our land now.' Arabella languidly pointed a finger. 'Isaac Johnson farms over there.' She indicated a distant farmhouse at the end of a long track. 'He has three hundred acres, two sons and a rabbit warren. Over there' – she pointed vaguely north – 'is an old manor house, which is practically a ruin. Over the brow to your left is the Masons' farm; they have six hundred acres, two daughters, a son and a nephew. They are both eligible,' she said with a sigh. 'The gentlemen, I mean, but terribly dull.

'This is the beginning of our land,' she went on, as they turned a bend in the road and pulled up a hill. 'It is quite extensive and we have three farms which Father rents out.'

But just as isolated as Lavender Cott, Jenny thought as she gazed at the vista, so no-one will know about me here either. There's no wonder that Stephen is perfectly happy where we are. It's quite what he is used to.

After another quarter of an hour of bumping along potholed lanes, they turned up a long track. Jenny could see what appeared to be a large farmhouse at the end of it. Not a grand house, then, she pondered. Perhaps Stephen's father is a working farmer after all and not a gentleman as I'd supposed.

'Does your father have many employees?' she asked Arabella tentatively. 'On the land, I mean?'

'He hires labour every Martinmas,' she said. 'Some of them live in, and then the gangs come in the summer for harvest.' She tutted impatiently as a carriage wheel hit a deep hole and they were all thrown about. 'Then we have the horse lads. Some of them live above the stables and the others live at the back of the house with the hind and his wife, and she cooks for them and does their washing, I believe. House servants like Dolly' – she indicated the maid with them – 'all live in. Mama always liked them to. She said she didn't want then going home to the villages where they might get into trouble.'

Jenny glanced at Dolly, whose face was impassive as if she didn't know she was being spoken of, and thought of Cook at the Ingrams' house who said she liked to employ country girls so that they weren't always running home.

As they approached Laslett Hall, Jenny saw that it was much bigger than she had first thought. A rambling brick house, built originally to be square, it now had additional wings to the east and west with high gables and tall chimneystacks. The carriage pulled up at the front entrance, a heavy oak door opened and a tall but bent elderly man, with a curly grey beard and side whiskers, in a rough tweed jacket and cord breeches and wearing muddy boots, hobbled down the steps to greet them.

'Thought you were never coming home,' he barked at Arabella. 'I told you my gout was playing up! Come along then. You, girl,' he said to the maid, 'Look sharp. Get that luggage inside; you've wasted enough time for one day. Now then, Bella, who's this then?'

Jenny felt her cheeks flush at his manner. What a rude man he was, certainly not a gentleman, like his son. She gave a dip of her knee.

'Papa, this is Stephen's wife, Jenny,' Arabella said. 'And these are their children, John Stephen and Serena Mary.'

'Hmph,' he grunted and cast his eyes towards the children. Jenny was holding the twins and Christina was hiding behind her skirt.

'How do you do, sir?' Jenny wished that she had a hand free so that she could offer it as she remembered Mrs Ingram's friends used to, but her arms were full of squirming babies who at any moment would be demanding food. She moved towards John Laslett. 'This is your grandson, Johnny,' she said, moving her right arm so that he could see the boy, 'and this is your granddaughter, Serena.'

'Hmph,' he said again. 'And who's this hiding behind your skirts, eh?' He nodded towards Christina. 'Is this a child I don't know about? He hasn't wasted much time in this marriage, I'll say that for my son.'

'Christina is Stephen's adopted daughter, sir.' Jenny could feel tension rising within her. 'She means as much to him as his own children.'

'Does she indeed.' The old man gazed down at Christina who was now sucking her thumb as if her life depended on it. 'Well, no wonder. She's a pretty little thing. Break a few hearts in time, I don't doubt.'

Jenny heaved a breath; perhaps his bark was worse than his bite. And to her astonishment, he put out his hand to Christina to help her up the steps and told them to follow him.

Arabella pulled a face and raised her eyebrows as Christina and her father went in front of them. She took hold of Jenny's elbow to assist her and they entered the hall together.

Jenny's eyes opened wide at the size of the inner hall. It's as big as a ballroom, she thought, looking up at the panelled walls and down the flagged floor towards the fire burning in the huge fireplace at the end. In front of the fire on a ragged carpet lay two large dogs, who lifted their heads as they entered, then put then down on their big paws and surveyed them from mournful eyes.

'Come on, lads, out of the way!' John Laslett shouted at the animals. 'Go on. Outside! Let somebody else see the damned fire.'

The two dogs turned their reproachful eyes on him, then slunk out through another door. Jenny shivered. Though the sun was warm and bright outside, the house was cold and she hoped that the other rooms were not as big or as draughty as this one.

'There,' he said to Christina. 'You stand there by the fire and get warm. What did they say your name was?'

'Christina,' she piped, 'and I'm not cold. I've got my winter drawers on, cos Papa said it would be as cold as charity here.'

There was a glimmer of a wry grin on the old man's face. 'Did he, by Jove? Well, perhaps he's right. Better make sure the bricks are put in the beds, Bella. Don't want these children catching a chill.' With that he was off, muttering about things to do, and Arabella said with some relief in her voice that they wouldn't see him again until supper.

Jenny asked if she could go upstairs immediately as the babies needed feeding. Johnny was starting to squall and she always had to make sure his demand was met before Serena's, otherwise he turned into a red-faced screaming monster.

Her bedroom was large and filled with heavy old-fashioned furniture. The tester bed was lavishly draped with brocaded hangings in need of repair and a faded rose silk bedspread was thrown over it. A fire burned in the grate and an upholstered armchair was placed beside it. A pleasant view of meadows with flocks of sheep grazing could be seen from the window.

'Thank you,' she said to Arabella, who had come up with her. 'It's a lovely room. Very comfortable.'

'It's our best room,' Arabella said. 'Mama always used this one for our special guests. It's the warmest bedroom in the house; the fire always draws well in here. I've asked Papa if I can have it instead of mine, but he says not, that we must keep it for when we have company. Not that we do very often.'

'Do your sisters visit?' Jenny asked as she sat down and started to suckle the babies. 'They must fight over it? Or perhaps they still have their old rooms?'

Arabella lowered her eyes away from Jenny. 'Oh, they don't stay! They live quite near and so always go home. They always say they have to get back on some excuse or other, but really it's because it's so cold, especially in winter.'

Dolly knocked on the door and entered, carrying the luggage. 'Beg pardon, ma'am.' She seemed uneasy. Though she spoke to Jenny directly, her eyes glanced briefly at the feeding babies. 'But Mr Laslett has just come back in again, and says he'd like to speak to you before supper.'

'Give Mr Laslett my compliments,' Jenny said calmly, 'and tell him that I'm busy with 'children at present, and will be down as soon as it's convenient.'

Dolly took in a breath, and Arabella quickly said, 'I'll tell him, Dolly. You unpack for – Mrs Stephen, whilst she is seeing to the twins.' She gave a nervous smile at Jenny and hurried out of the room.

So, he's used to being obeyed immediately, Jenny thought, as she gently patted Johnny's back. He gave a satisfying burp. She looked up at the maid who was watching her intently. 'Perhaps you'd bring Christina a glass of milk and a piece of cake, Dolly,' she said. 'Or would you like to take her down to the kitchen and introduce her to Cook?'

Christina is such a little angel, they'll love her if I know anything about kitchen staff, she thought. And then Dolly can tell them that I feed the babies myself and don't have a wet nurse, and we'll see what they make of that!

'Yes, ma'am. I'll take her down. They've been

looking forward to you coming.' Dolly gave her a sudden warm smile. 'And I'll bring you a glass of milk, shall I? Or mebbe you'd prefer a glass of ale? They say 'tis 'finest thing when you're feeding bairns.'

Jenny, who hardly ever drank, simply because Stephen only ever drank a tot of whisky when he could afford it, which wasn't often, and they never had any other alcohol in the house, remembered with a sudden clarity her mother sending out for a jug of ale after the births of Jenny's young brothers. 'Thank you,' she said. 'That would be very nice. I am quite tired. Perhaps it will perk me up.'

Dolly appeared ten minutes later carrying a tray with a glass of ale, a plate with a slice of bread and butter, and two small bowls on it.

'Hope you don't mind, ma'am, but I've left Miss Christina downstairs having a bit o' supper, and Cook says she hopes you likes her ale. And she's sent up a bowl o' pobs for 'little bairns, for when I told her what an appetite young master John has–'

'Johnny,' Jenny interrupted. 'We call him Johnny.'

'Master Johnny, and how big he was, she said he might benefit from a bit extra, and save you as well, ma'am.'

'That's very kind,' Jenny said. 'Most thoughtful.' It was true that she was feeling tired and exhausted by Johnny's constant hungry demands, and she had started to supplement his feeds with bread and milk and mashed up potato. 'Perhaps tomorrow when we are settled in I could bring the twins downstairs and introduce them?'

'Oh, they'd like that, ma'am. They want to know if the boy looks like Master Stephen. I never met him, but Cook's been here a long time and knew him, and Peg who's worked here off and on as kitchen maid remembers him as well.'

Jenny nodded and bit into the bread. And what would they think if they knew I had been a kitchen maid too? she wondered. Or has Dolly guessed already that I'm the same status as them? She smoothed down her plain dark gown, the only one she had brought with her, for her only other was very faded and shabby. Or will they think that I am one of those bohemian women who lead an unconventional life, feeding their own babies and caring nothing for fashion or rules?

'Oh, and ma'am.' Dolly flushed guiltily. 'I nearly forgot. Mr Laslett is still waiting to speak to you. He's down in 'great hall, and isn't looking ower pleased.'

'How long to supper, Dolly?'

'Fifteen minutes.'

Jenny straightened her back and took a deep breath. Well. Whatever he had to say, he should be able to say in that time. He didn't seem to be the kind of man to beat about the bush. 'Good.' She took a long draught of ale, as if she wasn't in any hurry. 'This is exceedingly good, tell Cook.' She smiled at Dolly, remembering the time when Mrs Ingram didn't know her name. 'And would you like to give the children their pobs, Dolly?'

'Yes, please,' Dolly said enthusiastically.

'Then I'll go down. We don't want to keep Mr Laslett from his supper.'

CHAPTER TWENTY-FOUR

John Laslett was waiting for her in the hall. He had changed his jacket for a dark tailcoat and a white shirt with a high collar, but still wore his cord breeches and boots. He was standing with his back to the fire, holding up his coat tails to warm his nether regions. The dogs had come back in and were lying on the carpet by his feet.

'I want to talk to you,' he barked. 'I'm not used to being kept waiting.'

'I beg your pardon,' Jenny said civilly. 'I came as quickly as I could, but I'm afraid 'children had to come first, otherwise you wouldn't have liked the noise they would have made.'

He frowned. 'In my day children were not allowed to dictate to their elders!'

'I'm sure that's right, sir,' Jenny said patiently. 'But perhaps you could afford wet nurses and servants to look after them so that they didn't disturb you?'

'Hmph,' he said. 'So you don't have any help? My son can't afford them, is that it?'

'We manage.' She wasn't prepared to give him the satisfaction of gloating.

'The other woman died, then? Didn't take him long to grieve if he was married soon after!'

'He did grieve. I was there. He was devastated when Agnes died. He loved her.'

He grunted again. 'And why did you marry

him? Housekeeper, weren't you? Did you think he was a good catch? That he might get the estate back now that *she'd* gone?' He fired the questions at her. 'It's not guaranteed, you know. Not fixed in stone. I can give it to anyone I want!'

Jenny sat down, even though he hadn't asked her to, and folded her hands in front of her. She was breathing hard. 'Why did you ask me here, sir?'

'What! What do you mean?'

'I understood I was invited here so that you could meet your grandchildren. I refused once because you didn't invite my husband. I was persuaded to come this time. There was no ulterior motive on my part.'

He glared at her. 'You speak well enough for a former servant. How come?'

'I've had some schooling,' she said, 'and living with Stephen has improved my knowledge.'

'Mm – well, the servant class has to fend for itself, I suppose. There are some pretty sharp folk about. So what did you do before you were housekeeper to Stephen and that woman?'

'That woman, sir, as you call her, was my aunt!' Jenny felt her anger rising and knew she couldn't stay in the house with him. She would ask to be taken home first thing in the morning. 'I was asked to go and look after her; she was dying and your son badly needed some help.' She put her chin in the air. 'They went to Agnes's family for that help, not yours! And as for what I did before, I was a kitchen maid and then upstairs maid.'

There, she thought. It's out! He'll probably ask me to leave now and Stephen and Johnny will have lost their inheritance completely.

He sat down opposite her, stretching out his booted legs and pursing his lips as he gazed at her. She saw that his eyes were as blue as Stephen's were. He nodded his head very slowly as if considering. 'Well,' he said at length. 'I admire your candour. Can't abide folks who make up stories about themselves just to impress. Now, about these children. You say my son has adopted the little girl? But the twins are his? He fathered them?'

'Yes,' Jenny replied stonily.

'Were you a widow?'

She hesitated. If she were to tell the truth, say that she hadn't been married to Christy, it would be the same in his eyes as it had been when Agnes lived with Stephen. Yet he had said he admired candour. Perhaps if I tone down the truth without actually lying, he might accept it.

'Christina's father died before we could marry,' she said quietly. 'So I wasn't a widow, though almost 'same as.'

'Ah! Got caught, did you?' He nodded again and kept his eyes upon her. 'It happens in the best of circles. But he intended to marry you, did he?' he asked sharply.

She met his gaze. 'We had our plans made.'

'Righty ho!' He rose to his feet just as a clangorous din erupted as someone pounded the supper gong. 'Damn and blast it,' he bellowed towards the bottom of the hall. 'How many times do I have to tell you? I'm not deaf! You'll waken those children!'

Christina stood by the brass gong, the striker in

240

her hand and her mouth open, with a scared-looking maid behind her. 'Sorry, sir,' the maid gasped. 'It was meant as a treat. I didn't think she could strike so hard!'

The old man stared at Christina, then suddenly grinned and wagged a finger at her. 'Just this once then. Go on, strike once more and then off to bed with you.'

Christina smiled prettily and heaved up the striker with its padded end and crashed it once more onto the gong.

'Come and say good night, Christina,' Jenny called to her and glanced up the stairs to where Dolly was coming down.

Christina put her face up for her mother to kiss and then turned to Mr Laslett and pursed her mouth towards him. He seemed nonplussed for a moment, then he bent down and kissed the child on the cheek.

'Hrmph.' He cleared his throat and then, turning to Dolly, snapped, 'You can put her to bed whilst her mother has her supper! Somebody else can do whatever you usually do. Where's Bella? Tell her to organize it.'

'Yes, sir,' Dolly said, and put out her hand to Christina, who glanced at her mother. At her nod, she took hold of Dolly's hand.

'Night-night, Mama. Will Papa be lonely without us?'

'Just a little.' Jenny smiled at her daughter. 'But he'll know we're thinking of him.'

That night as she sat in bed with the drapes partly drawn around her to keep out the draughts, Jenny began to write in her notebook, something she hadn't done for weeks as there never seemed to be any time.

'It seems', she wrote, 'that Mr St John Laslett is a man of irritable disposition. Stephen told me that he inherited his temper from his father and now I know what he meant. Mr Laslett senior could make a saint blaspheme. He has, however, taken a liking to Christina and ordered the maid, Dolly, to stay with her until she was asleep, in case she was nervous in these strange surroundings. At supper, Arabella asked her father if we might take the carriage tomorrow and ride into Driffield so that I can admire its industry. He refused us the carriage, but said we could take the trap and then needn't hurry back. I had to explain to Arabella privately later that I could not stay out long because of the babies, and she didn't at first understand, but Dolly did and said if I feed them in the morning, she will give them some pobs which will last them until I get back again. It seems very odd to me that such things had to be explained to Arabella, but I suppose she has led a sheltered life.

'I now appreciate Arabella's desire to marry, for she must get very lonely in this rambling old house with just her father for company. It has been a fine establishment and I suppose when Mrs Laslett was alive and all her family living here, it would not have appeared as gloomy as it does now. As it is, there is great room for improvement if Mr Laslett was prepared to spend money on it, but from what I've seen of him, he wouldn't notice if the roof was falling in as long as his supper was on time.

242

'After we had eaten supper, Mr Laslett got up from the table, went to the door leading to the hall and yelled out "Boots!" at the top of his voice. A young boy came running and he reminded me of Jem who used to be the general lad at the Ingrams' house when I was a kitchen maid. He positioned himself in front of Mr Laslett who had taken a seat by the fire and was holding fast to the chair arms. "Ready, boy?" he said and lifted a leg. Whereupon the lad took hold of his boot and pulled and pulled until it came away from his foot. Then they did the same with the other leg. Mr Laslett left the room shortly afterwards in his stockinged feet and we didn't see him again that evening. That then solved the mystery of why he came down to supper in his muddy breeches and boots, for he couldn't get out of them by himself and I don't suppose he would notice that he was putting mud all over the stairs.'

'I hate driving,' Arabella said irritably as they climbed into the trap the next morning. 'The mare always has a mind of her own.'

'Shall I try?' Jenny said. 'Though I haven't driven before. We only have our old waggon, which of course you have ridden in,' she added, remembering Arabella's horror at being taken to their wedding in the waggon. 'Stephen won't allow me to take 'reins in case I crash it or let 'horses run off. He says he can't afford any more horses or another waggon.'

Arabella refused her offer. 'Poor Stephen,' she said. 'It must be hard for him, not having any money at all. However do you manage?'

Jenny shrugged. 'We just do. We have to.' She

243

took a deep breath as they bowled along and revelled in the freedom of being out without the children, for Christina had said that she wanted to stay with Dolly too. Jenny guessed that she had probably been promised a treat downstairs in the kitchens.

The weather had been warm and in many of the fields the hay had already been cut, and farm labourers with their sleeves rolled up showing dark sun-browned arms were turning the tumbled heaps with wooden rakes to dry in the sun. This was a mixed farm, and cattle grazed in the lower meadows and sheep dotted the hillside. Stephen's father had told her he had invested his money in steam threshers, ploughs and cultivators. 'Still need the hosses though,' he said. 'Can't ever manage without them or the lads to work 'em.'

As they came into Driffield, Jenny noticed that several people, some men and some women, greeted Arabella. The men lifted their hats or touched their foreheads and the women raised a hand, and she surmised that the family were well known. They pulled into an inn yard and Arabella explained that her father regularly visited here to attend meetings or occasionally have supper with other farmers.

'I need to buy some thread and new ribbons,' Arabella said and shepherded Jenny along the main street. 'And then– Oh, Maud!' she called, not loudly but lightly and genteelly, to a young woman across the street and waved her hand, signalling to her to wait.

'Maud,' she said, when they crossed over to meet her. 'This is Stephen's wife, Jenny. She's come on a visit with the children. Jenny, this is my sister, Mrs Herbert Graves.'

Mrs Graves glanced at Jenny, her eye sweeping over her, then she inclined her head. 'How do you do?' she said in a brittle voice. 'I understand that you have been safely delivered of a son?'

She must be very disappointed that Stephen has fathered a son, Jenny considered. 'And of a daughter,' she replied. 'We have been doubly blessed. I understand that you also have a new daughter?'

'I now have four daughters,' Mrs Graves said caustically. 'And it is not a blessing when you consider that they will all have to be married off!'

'I'll be thankful if my children reach marriageable age,' Jenny murmured. 'I shall consider myself very fortunate.'

'Mm, I suppose so, but it must be difficult for you, living hand to mouth?' Mrs Graves looked down her sharp nose. 'And no prospects of improvement? Father is in very good health and not likely to change his mind over Stephen's indiscretions!'

'We must be going, Maud,' Arabella interrupted. 'Jenny has to get back to the children. Perhaps you'll call? You could see the twins,' she added, her eyes brightening. 'They are dear little things.'

'Really! I have never known you enthuse over my babies!' her sister said. 'Are these so special?'

'Well, there are two, you see,' Arabella flustered. 'And besides, yours were never brought down to look at; they were always in the nursery.'

'But of course! Herbert would never tolerate the discord that children bring. And anyway, the nurse knows best what to do. It's only labourers' wives or the very poor who look after their children. But I might call if I'm up to it. You can tell Papa you have seen me.'

She gave a slight inclination of her head to Jenny, kissed Arabella on her cheek and rushed away.

'Oh,' Arabella breathed. 'Jenny, I am so sorry. Maud was very rude. She's cross about Johnny being the first grandson, I expect. But she shouldn't have said what she did about only the poor looking after their children.'

'But she's right.' Jenny stared along the street after Maud. 'That is what we do, and I'm very glad of it.' And she is living in hope that her father will continue to cut Stephen out of his inheritance, she thought. 'There was never any chance of my family squabbling over possessions,' she told Arabella, 'for we had none.' She smiled. 'And as for Stephen's indiscretions, if he'd stayed at home and never met Agnes, then I wouldn't be married to him now.'

Arabella tucked her arm into Jenny's. 'And I'm glad that you are, Jenny, and I'm sorry if in the past I have offended you in any way, by presuming that you were inferior, for I now know full well that you are not, and I'm very pleased to welcome you as a sister, even if my own sisters don't, for I fear that Laura will feel the same towards you as Maud.'

Jenny was touched. Arabella had formerly assumed a patronizing superior manner and here she was now being very warm and friendly. 'Thank you, Arabella,' she said. 'I appreciate having your friendship.' And an ally, she considered, who

246

might help Stephen to claim his rightful place.

Arabella's two other sisters came to visit, or to inspect her, Jenny decided, and asked to see the children. Laura, Mrs James Banks, had had another daughter, but Pearl, Mrs Edwin Smith, who was the eldest of Mr Laslett's family, stated quite firmly that she hoped she had finished with all of that nonsense as she had three daughters already and considered that was enough for anyone.

'Oh, but I have four,' said Laura, 'and James will want to continue until we have a son!'

'Hmph,' Pearl grunted. 'Tell him to have them then! There'd only ever be one child if men had to give birth. And anyway, daughters run in our family so your chances of having a son are fairly small.

'And what about you, young woman?' She turned a beady eye on Jenny. 'You've had one son. Are you likely to have more or will you produce girls like the rest of us?'

'I don't know.' Jenny quaked under her gaze and put her hand protectively across her body. 'I have six brothers and three sisters so I suppose I could have either.'

Pearl gave a grim laugh. 'So there you are, Laura; you can tell your husband to desist and go back to his own bed, for there's little chance of any son of yours taking over Father's estate. Stephen's wife has a head start already and likely to have more.'

'Pearl! Really!' Arabella's cheeks flushed. 'You shouldn't speak so.'

'Oh, sorry, Bella, I forget how innocent you are!' Pearl didn't seem at all sorry for Arabella's discomfort and settled back comfortably in her chair. 'Ring for the children, then,' she ordered. 'Let's take a look at this fine son of Stephen's.'

Dolly brought the children down, a baby in each arm, and Christina came to stand by her mother, putting her thumb in her mouth and gazing with her dark eyes at the company. Pearl took Johnny from Dolly and sat him on her knee and he immediately started screaming and struggling and kicking his feet. 'Take him back,' she demanded of Dolly. 'He's a Laslett all right with that temper! Let's take a look at the other one.'

Dolly gave her Serena, who chortled and reached to pull at the beads round her neck. 'This one will be easy to handle,' she said to Jenny, 'which is just as well, for that young fellow will cause you some trouble. He's got it written all over him. And who's this?' She raised a finger for Christina to come to her. 'Now this one isn't a Laslett, that's for certain.'

'No,' Jenny said quietly. 'She isn't.'

Pearl scrutinized Jenny, though didn't question her further, then gently pinched Christina's cheek and propelled her back to her mother. 'So there you are, Laura, you might as well give up, and Maud too. You can tell her I said so.' She gave a wicked satisfied chuckle. 'Her nose will be put right out of joint.'

Laura put her own small nose in the air and reprimanded her sister. 'You are being quite ridiculous, Pearl, and I shall do no such thing! And in any case, we all know how Papa is. He won't tell us anything about what he intends to do until he is ready. And,' she added petulantly, 'if he doesn't forgive Stephen' – she glanced quickly at Jenny – 'for consorting with ... with his first wife, then he'll want someone to take over when he is unable to manage, and James is the obvious choice, being a farmer himself.'

'Don't count on it, my dear,' Pearl replied, and nodded at Jenny. 'Stephen will be back, mark my words.'

CHAPTER TWENTY-FIVE

'If it is convenient I'd like to go home 'day after tomorrow,' Jenny said to Arabella when she had been with them almost a week.

'Oh, so soon? Please stay a little longer!' Arabella was quite downcast.

'Stephen will be missing me,' Jenny explained. 'And there is so much I can do to help him. Feed 'hens and milk 'cow, and make sure he's eating properly.' Besides, she thought, I miss him. 'And I miss not having the children around me,' she said, 'even though it's been very restful for me with Dolly looking after them.'

'But we go up to see them in the nursery several times a day, and they come down every evening before they are put to bed! Even Papa has asked to see them.' Arabella smiled indulgently.

Dolly had commandeered a spare room and put the twins and Christina and herself in there. She had also found three child-sized chairs, a small table, and a musical box and a ball to entertain them.

'It's not 'same as having them around all the time,' Jenny said. 'I could almost forget I had any children when they're upstairs where I can't see them.'

Arabella sighed. 'That's the difference between you and my sisters, I suppose. I think they would be quite happy not to have any more children, unless they could be sure it would be a son. And that of course is quite impossible!'

'And then the human race would die out,' Jenny laughed. 'We have to have at least one of each kind. But,' she said, going back to her original conversation, 'I must go home.'

'But you'll come again, won't you?' Arabella pleaded. 'I've so enjoyed having you here.'

'I will,' Jenny agreed. 'And I'd invite you to stay with us, but we haven't any room, nor even a bed.'

'If I brought a truckle, I could sleep with the children,' Arabella murmured and Jenny looked at her in astonishment at the suggestion and thought how much she had changed.

Dolly was upset about their leaving. 'I wish I could come with you, Mrs Laslett,' she said to Jenny. 'I've really enjoyed looking after them bairns.'

'You've been very good with them,' Jenny told her. 'Especially with Johnny. But I'm afraid we don't have room for anyone else. We live very simply.' Nor could we pay you, she thought. I worked for nothing but my bed and board when I went to look after Agnes. But I was desperate.

'Why don't you try to get a position as a

nursery maid, Dolly?' she suggested. 'If you like being with children. I suppose I could give you a reference.' And a little thrill went through her at the idea of it. 'Or you could ask Mrs Banks or Mrs Graves.'

'They've got somebody already. But I wouldn't work for them anyway. I'd never do owt right for them.' Dolly considered. 'No, I'll stay here. I don't mind Mr Laslett. I've got used to his humours, and I'm near enough to home to walk to see my mother on my days off. I've worked away before and didn't like it.' She pondered for a second, her eyes shifting away from Jenny. 'And mebbe you and Mr Stephen'll come back to live here one day and then I can look after 'next little 'un.'

Jenny took a breath. Was it so obvious? If it was, then she must go home, for Stephen didn't yet know.

'What? Are you sure!' he exclaimed when she told him soon after arriving home, and he ran his hand over her belly. 'I can't believe it could happen so soon!'

'You're the farmer, Stephen. You're supposed to know about these things!' She put her arms round him and hugged him. It was good to be back again even though she saw how the jobs had piled up. There was dust everywhere and stale bread and dirty dishes lying on the table. She saw that the hens had been in the house for there were feathers and mess on the floor. She also noticed how tired Stephen seemed and saw the lines of tension round his mouth.

Stephen saw her looking around her normally

251

clean kitchen and said abruptly, 'Sorry. I've been worn out at the end of each day and didn't do anything more than have a slice of bread before I fell into bed.'

'Did you take your boots off first?' she said in a mock-disgruntled voice. 'Or are you really so like your father and kept them on?'

'Does he? Not in bed!' he exclaimed, frowning. 'He was always eccentric but I can't believe he's so outlandish!'

She laughed. 'No. He yelled for 'young lad every night after supper to help him pull them off. When I asked Arabella why her father didn't ring the bell for him to come, she said it was because he liked to shout and see the lad come running. He said it kept him on tenterhooks and stopped him from sloping off.'

'He's got worse, obviously,' Stephen said tensely, 'and having Arabella to tend to his every whim has spoiled him even more.'

'Poor Arabella. Even if she found someone who wanted to marry her, I doubt that your father would agree to it. Now,' she said briskly, 'if you'll listen out for 'babies and keep an eye on Christina, I'll prepare you some supper.'

He groaned. 'I'm not sure I wouldn't rather be out in the fields!'

'Not when you see what I've brought you.' She smiled. 'Your father's cook has sent a basket of food: a beef and ale pie, some slices of venison, a fruit cake and something which she said you had always loved, a Yorkshire curd cheesecake.'

'Not a *crud chiskeeak*,' he murmured, his ill humour dissipating as he peeked into the basket.

252

'There's an art to making these and Cook has it.' He looked wistful for a moment, then took a knife and cut a large slice, holding his other hand under it so that he didn't lose any of the delicious crumbs or fruit. 'Now, if you could learn to make these, Jenny,' he said with his mouth full, 'you'd be the perfect woman.'

A cry came from upstairs. 'Sorry,' she said. 'I hate to disappoint you, but there are other things I'm better at.'

He caught hold of her. 'I know that.' He kissed her lips. 'And I've missed all of them. Go and see to the young varmint and then I've something to tell you.'

'What? Tell me now.' There was something bothering him.

'No. It will keep,' he said. 'Feed the children first.'

'I'll bring them down. They'll be forgetting who you are otherwise.' She brought the twins down and fed them on bread and milk as Stephen told her what had happened whilst she was away.

'The railway surveyors came back. I'd had a really hard day cutting the hay. The Romanies had come, as you know. I told them they could camp if they would help to cut the hayfield. They were a great help. It was so hot; I'd never have done it so quickly on my own. As it was we got it cut and stacked in a couple of days.

'Anyhow, the woman – Floure? – knocked on the door one night whilst I was having my supper, to tell me that men were measuring up the land. I raced up to the top meadow and found that the gypsies and the railway men were in the middle of a confrontation. The surveyors were telling the gypsies that they had no rights, so they could move off out of their way. I came along just in time to tell them that the gypsies were on my land with my permission, and that *they* were not.'

'So then what happened?' Jenny looked anxiously at Stephen. 'Is the line coming after all?'

'Oh, yes, it's coming all right and it will be up here before very long, but what was odd was that as we were arguing, I noticed that the gypsy woman had gone back to her bender–'

'Her bender? Ah! Yes, her tent.' Jenny remembered.

'Her tent – and another woman came out, older than her so I guessed it might have been her mother. The surveyor had his back to them, so he didn't see them walking towards us. Then this older gypsy, I think her name was Kisaiya or something, took hold of his arm and asked him to go with her. He was very taken aback for she must have seemed to come out of nowhere, but he didn't have much option,' Stephen gave a wry grin, 'because he was immediately surrounded by all the men. But this Kisaiya assured him he wasn't in any danger and led him towards the grave. I watched them from where I was standing and–' He gave a little shudder. 'It was getting dark and a mist was starting to come down and shrouding everything, and I could see the gypsy with her hands held up as if she was explaining something. The other railway fellow, who was standing with me, was beginning to get jittery and said it was time they were off.

'Then they came back and I don't know what

she had said to the surveyor, but he was quite ashen and shaking. He told me that it was now too dark to do anything more and they both scuttled away.'

He took the last slice of cheesecake; he'd eaten it all as he'd talked. 'And then?' Jenny asked. 'What happened? Did they come back?'

He shook his head and wiped his mouth of buttery crumbs. 'I got a letter three days later.' He reached to the mantelshelf above the fire and took down a piece of paper. '"Dear Sir," it says. "With regard etc. etc ... following the completion of a survey of your land on behalf of the North Eastern Railway Company, we are of the opinion that the terrain on the original plan is unsuitable for a line."' He raised a hand as Jenny gave a relieved sigh. 'There's more,' he muttered. '"And will therefore proceed with construction half a mile to the north as outlined on the enclosed plan. You will of course be compensated for any loss of land and revenue and we will ensure that the grave will not be disturbed and will be fenced."'

'So we lost?' Jenny stared at him, wide-eyed. 'What does it mean? They're cutting your land in half?'

'Not quite half,' he said glumly, 'but the grave will be on the other side of the railway line which means that we can't tend it without crossing the line.' He put his hands to his head and rubbed his forehead. 'I'm so tired, Jenny, I can't fight any more. The money they have offered as compensation is reasonable and it means I can pay George back some of the money I owe him.'

'George?' Her eyes were filling with tears.

255

'George Hill?'

He nodded. 'I borrowed from him when Agnes and I first came here. He always said there was no hurry but he's waited for years and never once asked for it back.'

'But my baby – and Agnes,' she wept. 'They'll be all alone and we won't be able to see them from the bedroom window as we can now. We'll only see the railway line and the trains!'

He nodded wearily. 'I know. They'll dig out and build up the embankment, so they'll be hidden. But at least the line isn't going right through where they are, as they originally intended. I'd move them,' he muttered, 'but it would seem like sacrilege. It's where Agnes wanted to be.'

'It's not right.' She wiped her eyes and continued feeding Johnny, who was reaching out for the bowl of pobs. 'Is it too late? Is there anyone we can complain to so that they'll change their minds?'

Stephen shook his head. 'I don't think so. The line's already out of Beverley. They'll be up here in a matter of weeks; the area will be swarming with navvies.' He glanced at her and the twins on her knee. Christina, wrapped in her own little world of imagination, was playing on the floor. 'There's something else. You might as well have all the bad news at once.'

'What? There can be nothing worse!'

'There can,' he said wearily. 'We must worry now about the living, not the dead. There's no more milk. That's the last.' He nodded towards the milk jug. 'Daisy's dried up. Somebody's coming to fetch her tomorrow. I can't afford to feed her if she's not milking.' He shook his head. 'And there's not enough money to buy another cow in calf.'

She stared at him. 'We must have milk for the children! Can't you sell the hay?'

'I wouldn't get enough for it. Besides, the hay's needed for the sheep and the horses.'

'Should we keep the sheep?'

'We'll get mutton,' he said glumly. 'And I'll kill the pig in the autumn. At least we'll eat.'

'Can we afford a goat? The children could have goat's milk.'

Stephen nodded. 'Yes. I've done a deal with a farmer. He'll let us have a goat and kid and a pig in litter, and he'll take half our corn when it's ready.'

'Oh!' she breathed. 'And what'll we do next year?'

'God knows,' he said. 'I don't.'

'You managed before because there were just two of you, you and Agnes,' Jenny said slowly. 'Now there are three extra to feed and clothe, four before long.'

'I wanted children,' he said sharply. 'And now we've got them. We'll manage, one way or another!'

They couldn't afford to pay the midwife and Stephen delivered Thomas just after the twins celebrated their first birthday. It was an easy birth as he was a small child and Jenny was up and about the next day. He was a placid baby, born with a little frown above his nose and similar in temperament to Serena who loved him from the first, as did Christina. Johnny lifted a

257

plump fist to smack him the first time he saw him, and no amount of coaxing from Jenny could ever convince him that Thomas wasn't there just for him to fight with.

'At least we'll be popular with Father now,' Stephen said as he sat down to write to Arabella and tell her the news.

'And unpopular with Maud and Laura,' Jenny said. 'They can't possibly catch up now!'

'Not at the rate ours are arriving,' Stephen groaned. 'Four children! I'm going to have to sleep out in the barn!'

Jenny shared his concern. They didn't want any more children. Not yet, anyway. They had a vegetable patch for growing potatoes, beans, onions and cabbages and kept back some of the barley crop for making bread and soup. The soup was nourishing enough if she flavoured it with onions and mutton fat, but the barley bread was bitter and dry. But they had no money for clothes or boots and Christina wore only woollen stockings, as she had outgrown her last pair of boots.

Arabella had given Jenny some cotton sheets when she had stayed with her and these she cut up to make sheets for the babies, and dyed another to make Christina a dress and pinafore. For herself she still wore the skirt she had first arrived in, altering it and letting it out at the seams whenever she was pregnant.

'If I wasn't so proud I'd go cap in hand to Father.' Stephen bit on his thumb as he deliberated on their situation.

'But you won't!' she said. She had asked Stephen to ask his father, if he had any influence with the railway chiefs, to persuade them to reroute the track so that the grave remained on their side of the line. But he wouldn't and forbade her to either.

'He didn't approve of Agnes when she was alive,' he said angrily. 'He's hardly likely to have a change of heart now she's dead!'

'But baby Agnes?' she said tearfully. 'What about her?'

'He has no sentiment.' He regretted his outburst and reached out to comfort her. 'She was a female child and didn't draw breath. He won't think of her as a person.'

She knew that he was right, and, she considered, it was probably too late. The railway line was getting closer. If the wind was in the right direction it carried the sound of the clang of metal and the muffled shouts of the navvies.

He stood up and walked to the window, looking out. 'I'm going to apply for labouring work.' The ground was hard with winter frost and the sky hung dark and heavy with the threat of snow. He'd brought in logs and kindling for the fire and a bucket of potatoes from the store in the barn. The beans and cabbages were finished.

'What?' Jenny turned to him. She was feeding Thomas and drinking water to increase her milk. 'What kind of labouring work? On one of the farms? Do they need anyone at this time of year?'

'No,' he said, keeping his back to her. 'Not on a farm. On the railway.'

CHAPTER TWENTY-SIX

'But – but you can't! You're not a labouring man. You're a gentleman.' She stared aghast at him. 'Stephen!'

He turned to her. 'I don't think you appreciate how bad things are, Jenny.' His voice was strained. 'A gentleman!' He gave a harsh exclamation. 'Look at my hands.' He held them up for her to see. 'I'm a yeoman farmer! A labouring man and not ashamed of it! I've been labouring for years, ever since I was a young man.'

'But for yourself,' she insisted. 'Not for anyone else.'

'Does it make a difference?' He came towards her and put his face close to hers and she felt alarmed by the anger she saw there. 'Yes. In fact it does, and I'll tell you what the difference is! I can make up to five shillings a day as a navvy. It means we can buy food and shoes for the children.' He shook his head in despair. 'We're not making any money, and the children have to be fed and clothed!' He pressed his lips together. 'It's no use pretending that I'm the gentleman farmer I might have been. I've sold one of the shires, and Christina's pony,' he said abruptly. 'I must have been mad to think we could afford to keep it.'

Things are bad, she thought. He would never have done that otherwise. He knew how Christina loved that little horse and how proficient she

260

was becoming at riding it.

'Shall we think it over?' she asked quietly. 'Try to think of some other solution?'

'I don't think so,' he said wearily. 'I've been thinking it over for weeks. The railway company need men now; they're aiming to have the line up and running by May next year. I shall go tomorrow and tell them I can start immediately.'

Whilst he was away the following morning, Jenny busied herself washing clothes, making barley soup and bread and trying to calm a fractious Johnny. 'Play with him, Christina,' she implored the little girl. 'Try to make him laugh.'

'He's teefing,' Christina said solemnly. 'Getting some new toofs.'

Jenny smiled. Christina was such a delight. She was always happy, never irritable or cross. 'I'm sure you're right,' she agreed. She looked down at Johnny as he sat grizzling on the rug in front of the fire. His right cheek was red and his chin was wet. 'He needs some oil of cloves to rub on his gums.'

Christina looked puzzled. 'I need some new cloves too. Papa said.' She nodded her head. 'He's gone to get some.'

'We'll get some soon,' Jenny sighed. 'Not yet,' then looked up as she heard the rattle of the gate.

'Papa! He's come back!' Christina abandoned Johnny and rushed to the door. Johnny started to scream at her departure. Serena, who had been playing quite happily until then by banging two wooden spoons together, started to cry. The noise woke Thomas who had been sleeping in his cradle and he started to wail too.

'No. No, it's not Papa,' Jenny said. It was too

261

early for Stephen to come back. He'd taken the horse and waggon to drive into Beverley to ask about railway work. She tried to shut her ears to the crying children and lifted the sneck of the door. It was Stephen's sister, Pearl.

'Well! Are you going to ask me in?' Pearl was dressed in a grey travelling gown and feathered hat with neat black-buttoned boots and black gloves and stood determinedly in front of her.

'S-sorry. I was just surprised to see you.' Jenny opened the door wider and invited her sister-in-law in. 'I'm afraid there's rather a noise,' she apologized, raising her voice above Johnny's wails.

'Hmm. He does rather a lot of that, doesn't he?' Pearl looked sternly down on the youngster who immediately stopped crying.

'He's cutting teeth,' Jenny said lamely and was suddenly aware of how poorly clad the children must appear. Christina was barefoot.

'It's cold in here!' Pearl said abruptly. 'Can you not make a better fire?'

'The wood isn't burning very well.' Jenny went to stir the fire with the poker. 'It's too green.'

'And I suppose you can't get coal brought up here? It's too far for delivery?' Pearl glanced round the room. 'Do you have fires upstairs?'

'Yes. But I only light them in the evening when it's very cold,' Jenny answered in a low voice, suddenly feeling tired and inadequate. 'The wood has to last us all winter.'

'Where is my brother? Out in the fields? I must say I was surprised at how cut off from civilization you are.'

'We're not,' Jenny said defensively. 'No more

262

than at Laslett Hall. We're not so very far from 'villages. It's just that we're tucked away. Did Arabella tell you where we were?'

'Oh, we've always known. It's just that we didn't come. Father would never allow it. Well,' she admitted, 'I suppose I could have come, but I was a young wife and mother when Stephen first went off and I was always busy with my own family, and then the years slipped by. Should have made the effort really,' she said bleakly. 'Stephen was always on my conscience, but it went against the grain, you know, him going off with a married woman the way he did. Arabella was the one who missed him the most. She was only young when he left, too young to understand how shocked everyone was and what a disgrace it was for the family.'

'Yes, I suppose so,' Jenny murmured, thinking of what her own mother had said, about no-one mentioning Agnes's name after she had left her husband.

Pearl gazed at her. 'Where did you say Stephen was?'

'He – he's gone into Beverley. He had a few things to see to.'

'Papa's gone to get some cloves,' Christina suddenly piped up. 'For me.'

'Cloves – the twins are teething.' Jenny gave an uneasy laugh. 'Christina thought he said clothes. Would you like a cup of tea? Though I haven't any lemon,' she added, remembering that some ladies took lemon with their tea. Tears suddenly filled her eyes. 'I'm sorry; I'm not very hospitable. You've caught me at an awkward time. I haven't baked. I'm – I'm expecting Stephen to bring back some provisions,' she lied.

'Are things very bad, Jenny?' Pearl asked gently. 'Have you food for the children?'

Jenny took a breath. 'No, not at all. Thank you, yes,' she said. 'They've had gruel this morning and bread, and tonight I'll stew a rabbit. And we have a goat now instead of the cow. We manage very well.'

'That's all right then.' Pearl continued to gaze at her. 'Because I've come on a mission. Father said would I ask you if you'd like to come with the children and spend the winter at Laslett Hall.'

'Is Stephen invited?' Jenny saw the hesitation on Pearl's face as she asked the question.

'Would he agree to come? Or is he as stubborn as his father?'

'I don't know,' Jenny said honestly. 'Not if he was expected to grovel.'

'Would you come without him? You came without him before, but it would be for longer this time. The farmers are saying it will be a hard winter. You could be away for several weeks.'

Jenny suddenly felt weary. It would be nice to eat well and have someone prepare the meals and do the washing and help look after the children. And if Stephen did obtain work on the railway it would mean she would be here alone all day and probably into the evening. 'I'll have to speak to Stephen first. He might not want me to come. He likes to see the children.'

Pearl nodded. 'I'll come back in a day or two. Perhaps Stephen would see me? I hope that he will.'

'Why didn't Arabella come with you?' Jenny asked.

'I decided to come alone,' Pearl said. 'I wanted to try to make amends for all the bad feeling that went before. As I said, Arabella was only young when Stephen went away and she didn't know of the things that were said, of the language that was used in anger against Agnes. I realize now that she and Stephen did care for each other; enough,' she added, giving a wistful smile, 'to leave behind all those who cared for them. I can speak only of Stephen, but Agnes too must have been sad to leave behind her own family.'

Jenny didn't answer. She was quite sure that Agnes had always looked forward and never back. There was no-one who had cared for her as much as Stephen had.

After Pearl had gone, Jenny sat in the chair by the fire and took Christina on her knee. Johnny had curled himself up on the rug and gone to sleep and Serena had lain down next to him. Thomas was asleep in his cradle. The little girl cuddled up to her. 'Shall we go and see Dolly?' she asked. 'And Grandpappy?'

'Would you like that?' Jenny replied. 'Would you like to go for a visit?'

Christina looked up at her and with a start Jenny saw how like Christy she was becoming. The coaxing expression in her eyes was just as Christy's used to be when there was something he specially wanted. 'Yes,' she lisped. 'And Papa come too?'

No, he wouldn't go. Stephen was adamant. 'I

265

haven't been asked, and I've just got work,' he stated. 'I can start tomorrow. Four shillings a day and extra if I work on Sundays. If I work over the winter when there's little to do here, we can accumulate a tidy sum before the spring. But you could go,' he said. 'The children would benefit. There was always a good table at home.'

'Meaning there isn't here?' Jenny was stung to reply.

'You know I don't mean that,' Stephen answered quickly. 'I know how well you manage, but right now there's nothing to manage with!'

'But what about 'pig, and 'hens? And the goat? You'll need to feed them.'

'I'll see to them in the mornings and shut them up when I get home at night.'

'It'll be dark. 'Fox will get the hens.' She strove for reasons why she shouldn't go.

He shrugged. 'I'll chance that. Unless you don't want to go?' He looked anxiously at her. 'Don't you want to, Jenny? If you don't, say so. But the days will be long.' He reached out to hold her. 'And I'll worry about you being alone here.'

'It'll be a long winter,' she said softly. 'I'll miss you.'

'And I'll miss you too, and the children,' he said. 'But there'll come a time when Father will want me to go back. And I will, but not with a black mark on me. Not begging for forgiveness. I'll go back on my terms.'

When Pearl returned, with Arabella, three days later, Jenny and the children were ready. There was little to pack. Johnny, Serena and Thomas

266

were wearing the cotton petticoats and baby gowns that Jenny had made from the cotton sheeting for Christina. Neither Christina nor the twins were wearing shoes and Jenny saw Pearl cast a glance at their grubby feet.

'Is Stephen not here?' Arabella asked. 'We were hoping to see him. Pearl especially wanted to see him.'

'I'm sorry.' Jenny gathered Thomas up from his crib. 'He's had to go back into Beverley – on business.' She felt bad about the lie, but Stephen had particularly asked that she didn't tell his sisters about his working on the railway line. He had come home from his first day at work aching and weary. He had been employed all of the day in digging out a trench in preparation for the line, and throwing the resultant earth into a waggon.

'Some of these navvies can shift twice as much as me,' he'd said. 'I thought I was strong but they have muscles like iron and can dig a yard deep whilst I've got my back turned.'

She thought when he fell into bed beside her that she could smell alcohol on his breath, but then considered that she must be mistaken. Where he was working there would be nowhere he could have bought any, even if he had had any money.

He had said goodbye to her this morning and said he guessed that his sisters might come that day. 'I hope that they do,' he said. 'I don't get any wages until the end of the week.' There were no rabbits caught in the trap he had set the night before and therefore nothing to cook for dinner. Jenny had made barley broth and fed it to the children and then baked bread which was hard and bitter; there were a few hens' eggs which she saved for Stephen's supper. The ducks had stopped laying but each day she had searched along by the stream to see if they had laid away from the barn.

'We'll have to kill another hen,' she'd said reluctantly before he left. 'Otherwise there's nothing to eat but the last of the potatoes.'

He'd nodded. 'Do that,' he said, 'if they don't come. But if they come don't tell them how hard it is. I don't want them gloating!'

'They won't gloat, Stephen!' She'd spoken more sharply than she intended. 'Pearl was concerned when she came before. Her intentions were good, I'm sure of it.'

He'd just grunted and gone out of the door, but he returned a minute later and gave her a kiss on her cheek. 'Sorry,' he muttered. 'I'll make it up to you one day.'

She'd heated some water and washed the children and brushed Christina's thick hair and tidied the kitchen as she waited and hoped that Stephen's sisters would come.

'What kind of business has he gone on?' Pearl said perceptively. 'Or is it an excuse not to see me?'

'No,' Jenny said quickly. 'Of course not. We didn't know which day you'd be coming. We – we thought it might be tomorrow, that's why he went today.'

'Papa's building a railway line for the trains,' Christina piped up, 'and when he comes near here I'm going to wave to him.'

The two sisters looked silently at Jenny, whose

lips trembled. 'I'm sorry,' she whispered. 'He didn't want you to know.'

'Stubborn!' Pearl said, her mouth set tightly. 'Stubborn, stubborn man! Just like his father!'

CHAPTER TWENTY-SEVEN

'We've new servants starting tomorrow,' Arabella moaned as they travelled towards Laslett Hall. 'I do hate this time of year. I never know what I should tell them to do. Cook is staying on, fortunately, and Dolly; but we've two new maids coming and a general lad.'

'Did the other one leave?' Jenny asked, thinking of the boy who pulled off Mr Laslett's boots.

'Yes. They never stay longer than the year,' Pearl sniffed. 'Not the young ones anyway. Father is very hard on them.'

'It's not easy being a servant,' Jenny murmured. 'Being at everyone's beck and call.'

The two women glanced at her and Jenny blushed. 'Though it must be worse working in a mill or a factory – for a woman I mean,' she added feebly.

'Very true,' Pearl broke in. 'And if a servant can get into a good house at least they're fed and supplied with clothes to wear.'

Which comes out of their wages, Jenny thought. It doesn't come free. She glanced down at her own old skirt, which though clean and washed was stained with years of usage, and she

269

surreptitiously compared it with the travelling attire that Pearl and Arabella were wearing, which was warm and practical and of good cloth. Has Stephen's father told them that I was a kitchen maid? she wondered. They know I was Stephen's housekeeper, which is quite a good status, in my eyes at any rate.

'You must learn to be more practical, Bella,' Pearl commented to her sister. 'You must tell them how you like things to be; otherwise they'll only do the minimum. Perhaps Jenny could help you. Could you, Jenny? You know how to run a house and how to cook. I'm amazed that you can do so much and look after the children as well.' She smiled reassuringly at Jenny, and then raised an eyebrow. 'Arabella is such a dizzy thing sometimes.'

'I'd be glad to help,' Jenny said. 'If Arabella doesn't mind.'

'I wouldn't mind at all,' Arabella said enthusiastically. 'I would welcome your help. I'm quite sure the servants take advantage of me because I don't notice when something wants dusting or the sheets need changing.'

Jenny was astonished. 'Good servants should have a routine,' she said. 'Though usually a housekeeper would organize them.'

'Papa won't have a housekeeper.' Arabella pouted. 'Though we had one in Mama's day. He says I should be able to tell them what to do. Will you tell them for me, Jenny? Please!'

'But – I'm a house guest. I thought you meant just to advise you on what to tell them. I didn't realize you meant me to give them orders!' Jenny knew that the servants wouldn't take kindly to a virtual stranger's giving them instructions.

'But the new maids won't know who you are. Cook has taken them on.' Arabella's eyes sparkled. 'Suppose I pretend to be unwell and you can say that I've asked you to advise them! How would that be?'

Pearl gave a deep sigh and shook her head. 'You see!' she said. 'Arabella is quite impossible!' She eyed Jenny keenly. 'Might be worth a try, though.' She gave a little smile. 'It would be good practice for you, Jenny. In case Stephen ever decides to come back home.'

I'm on trial here, Jenny realized. Although Arabella probably does need some help with the servants, Pearl is testing me, trying me out to see how I shape up to becoming part of the family. And I wonder if Mr Laslett is part of this plan? 'All right,' she agreed. 'If you're sure.'

When they arrived at Laslett Hall, Pearl departed immediately for her own home, and Arabella started to swoon with apparent fatigue, and with her hand to her forehead swayed across the hall. Dolly had opened the door to greet them and followed Arabella, Jenny and the children into the sitting room. 'I'm pleased to see that you're still here, Dolly,' Jenny said, 'and not gone on elsewhere.'

'Yes, ma'am.' Dolly dipped her knee. 'I've stayed on but we've two new maids coming in 'morning.'

'So I understand. Miss Arabella is unwell, as you see,' Jenny said, looking at Arabella who was reclining on the sofa fanning herself, even though the room wasn't very warm. 'Would you bring her a little brandy and hot water, please?'

'Yes, ma'am. Have you caught a chill, Miss Arabella?'

'I think so,' Arabella said faintly. 'Take your instructions from Mrs Laslett, Dolly. Do whatever she says, for I think I'm going to be laid up for a little while.'

'Very well, miss. Is there anything else, Mrs Laslett?' Dolly glanced from Arabella to Jenny.

'A tray of tea and bread and butter, please, and milk and biscuits for 'children.'

Dolly smiled down at Christina and put out her hand to her. 'Are you coming down to 'kitchen wi' me?' she asked the child, and Christina jumped to her feet.

'Not yet,' Jenny said firmly. 'She must eat first and take a little rest, and then she can come.' And I must tidy her up before anyone else sees her in her old clothes, she thought, or there'll be some gossip.

'Pearl has had a trunk taken up to your room.' Arabella spoke languidly from the sofa after Dolly had gone out. 'It's full of clothes that belonged to her daughters. She asked if you would mind sorting through them, and said if there was anything that would fit Christina to take them, and if not hand them on to the servants. Dolly has a sister with children. She'd be glad of them, I expect.'

How thoughtful of Pearl. Jenny heaved an inner sigh. She'd obviously noticed how shabby we all looked when she called last time. Hand-me-downs! Stephen would be furious if he knew, yet it seems quite normal to me. It's what we always did when I was a child. Seems a waste otherwise.

After she had fed Thomas and the twins had drunk their milk, she put them to bed for a nap and then asked Christina to help her sort out the trunk. 'Let's see what's in here,' she said, making it into a game. 'Let's see what Aunt Pearl has sent us.'

She opened the lid and removed the top layer of brown paper and brought out a child's dress of spotted muslin.

'Oh!' Christina clutched it. 'Mine.'

'It's too cold for wearing now,' Jenny said. 'It's a summer dress, and look, Christina, here's a little coat to match. We'll keep that until summer, and it will fit you then. It's too big for you to wear now.'

She lifted another layer of paper. There was a navy wool dress with red stitching round the hem, and a crisp white pinafore to go over the top. A green one in a similar style, and a grey wool coat, several pairs of white and black stockings, shoes and buttoned boots, which looked brand new in spite of the scratches on the soles, which Jenny suspected had been done deliberately, to hide their newness.

Christina fumbled with her buttons, undressing so that she could try on the new clothes, and Jenny, digging deeper into the trunk, found wool and flannel skirts, cotton blouses, a grey dress, and numerous petticoats, all of which would fit her or could be cut down to make clothes for Christina. These must have been Pearl's own, she thought, perhaps before she had her children, for they certainly wouldn't fit her now. Pearl was well rounded and comfortably plump, unlike Arabella who was thin, like Stephen.

Jenny rocked back on her heels. Am I being greedy keeping all of these? she thought. Is my need greater than that of Dolly's sister? She shook out one of the skirts. It was made from plain grey flannel and was wide at the waist. I'd have to take it in anyway, she thought. I could leave that; there are enough here for me. I don't need so many garments. I've never had more than one change of clothes in my life. Why would I want more?

Christina was struggling to fit into the green dress. 'It's too small, sweetheart,' Jenny said. 'We'll give it to another little girl.'

'I want it,' Christina pleaded. 'It's for me!'

'No. The other one is for you, and the pretty one.' She held up the muslin. 'Or shall we give this to another little girl instead?'

'No. This is mine.' Christina snatched it back and struggled out of the green dress. 'The little girl can have this one. What's her name?' she said. 'Can I play with her?'

'I don't know her name,' Jenny smiled, 'and I don't know if you can play with her for I don't know where she lives. But perhaps you could play with some of your cousins. I'll ask Aunt Arabella about that.'

'What are cousins?' Christina asked.

Jenny hesitated. Of course, strictly, they were not Christina's cousins at all. Would it matter? she wondered. That Christina wasn't a Laslett? That she didn't have a father whom she could name?

'We don't see them,' Arabella said, when she

274

asked about the cousins later that afternoon. 'Laura and Maud hardly ever come over with the children, though they could; they both have a carriage. Father frightens the children.'

Jenny laughed. 'He doesn't frighten Christina!'

'No, he doesn't, does he? Odd that!' Arabella rose from the sofa. 'I think I'll take a lie down on my bed, Jenny. It might do me good to have a sleep as I'm a little unwell.'

'But–' Jenny gazed at her in astonishment. 'You're not really unwell, Arabella. We're only pretending!'

Disappointment showed on Arabella's face. 'Are we? Oh, but I do feel a trifle out of sorts, and besides, if Father comes in, he'll expect me to have primed Cook and Dolly to arrange the tasks for the new servants. And I haven't.' She pressed her lips together. 'Will you do that for me, Jenny? Please!'

'What will your father say?' Jenny asked. 'I'm supposed to be here on a visit. He might be angry.'

'He won't be at all bothered as long as he isn't inconvenienced.' Arabella slid towards the door, opened it, smiled and was gone.

Well, this is a fine thing, Jenny thought. Am I now supposed to twiddle my thumbs until supper? She gazed out of the window and towards the rolling grassland. I could take Christina for a walk whilst the babies are asleep, but it's getting dark and looking like rain, or snow. She sighed. Stephen, I wonder what you're doing? Will you have finished work and come home to find an empty house? I hope you remember to eat. She sighed again, and then turning to the fireplace she

275

pressed the bell on the wall beside it.

Dolly answered the bell and brought Christina with her. Jenny had dressed her in the navy dress and white pinafore, and brushed her hair, and she thought how sweet she looked.

'Mama!' She rushed towards Jenny. 'Dolly said that one day I'll be able to play with her children.'

Jenny gazed enquiringly at Dolly who smiled and said, 'My sister's bairns, ma'am. Sometimes she comes over this way and drops in to see me. She doesn't stay long,' she added quickly. 'It's onny to say hello.'

And pick up a slice of meat or a loaf of bread, I'll be bound, Jenny thought, but said nothing, only nodded, for she knew how things went on downstairs, where friends of the servants would knock on the kitchen door in expectation of a little treat.

'Dolly!' she said. 'Miss Arabella has gone to her room. She's feeling unwell and has asked me if I will organize the duties for 'new servants who are starting tomorrow. Can you tell me first of all what you do?'

Dolly stared, then, licking her lips, said, 'Well, Mrs Laslett, right now I'm maid of all work, cos there's onny Cook and me what's left. All of 'others have gone, and nobody ever before has ever thought to ask me what I do.' She warmed to her theme. 'If it wasn't so convenient for me, being near home, I wouldn't stop either.'

'Yes, I understand. There's far too much to do for one person. What about Cook? Does she have any help at present?'

'Just a scullery lass. She's from round here. I got her meself. She started just a day or two ago. Cook said she wasn't going to wash any pots and pans, and I didn't have time to do them, what with doing 'fires and making 'beds, waiting on table and a bit o' dusting. I'll be glad to have these new young women!'

'And who chose them?' Jenny asked.

'We did, ma'am. Cook and me. She picked one for 'kitchen and I picked one to help me upstairs. Oh, and Mr Laslett picked 'lad for general.'

'Well, send them up to me when they arrive and I'll tell them their duties. Have they had positions before? Did they come with references?'

Dolly looked down at her feet. 'Onny in a manner of speaking. They're relatives of mine, you see, Mrs Laslett. But I checked with Miss Arabella; she said it would be all right,' she hastened to add. 'But they'll not take advantage. I'll make sure of that.'

'That's right, they won't,' Jenny said firmly. 'What I'll do, Dolly, is make you senior house-maid, seeing as there is no housekeeper at present.' She hoped that it sounded as if there might be one in the future, which would keep Dolly on her toes. 'The other upstairs maid will answer to you and you'll answer to me, until Miss Arabella is feeling better,' she added.

'Thank you, ma'am.' Dolly beamed at her, then said worriedly, 'I hope as Miss Arabella isn't seriously ill?'

'No, she's not,' Jenny assured her. 'Just a little under 'weather at the moment. She'll soon be up and about. I'll tell 'upstairs maid her duties, which of course you know already,' she continued. 'She'll be up at five thirty, draw 'curtains or 'shutters in all the rooms, clean the fireplaces and prepare 'fires for lighting. Then she'll clean the rooms, shaking 'rugs outside to be rid of any soot or coal.' Jenny drew heavily on her own experience at the Ingrams' house. 'It will be your responsibility to make sure that 'work is finished and a fire lit in 'breakfast room before Mr Laslett comes down for his breakfast. The other fires can be lit after he has gone out.'

'Yes, ma'am,' Dolly said in a small voice. 'And what about 'kitchen maid? Will you see her as well?'

Jenny knew very well who ruled in the kitchens, and it wasn't the mistress of the house. It was imperative, if the household was to run well, that the cook was kept sweet. 'I'll come downstairs and see Cook myself,' she said. 'Tell her I'll be down in twenty minutes and we'll discuss what she would like 'new kitchen maid to do.'

'Twenty minutes, ma'am?' Dolly said.

'Yes,' Jenny answered. 'Any later than that and Cook will be busy preparing supper. Tell her I won't keep her long.' She also knew that it would give the cook sufficient time to finish what she was doing, wash her hands and straighten her cap, but without giving her time to become disgruntled at someone from upstairs interfering.

It would have been more usual for Cook to be summoned upstairs, but Jenny wanted to see the kitchens for herself and find out how well they were run. Cook was obviously good at her profession for she produced nourishing food and excellent pastries and pies, as Stephen had testified on receiving the curd cheesecake, but Jenny wondered how she managed with so little help.

When she went down exactly twenty minutes later, Cook was standing by her well-scrubbed table with a large mixing bowl, a crock of flour and a dish of butter in front of her as if she was ready to start baking.

'I won't keep you, Cook,' Jenny began. She cast her eyes round the spacious kitchen and saw the worn flagstones, the grimy kitchen range which was in need of black-leading and the cracked kitchen window. 'I realize you have supper to prepare, but I wanted to ask what you needed from the new maid.'

'I need her to transform herself into three people, ma'am, for one maid isn't enough.' Cook's tone was sharp. 'Can't expect one young maid to clean this lot,' she waved her arm around the kitchen, 'and help me cook as well. But 'master won't hear of it.'

'But you have a scullery maid,' Jenny said. 'So you'll have two.'

'She's onny good for scrubbing floors and pans, no experience at all. I need another maid to help with 'vegetables and watch over 'stove.'

There are usually only two people to cater for, Jenny thought. Mr Laslett and Arabella. Why should she want more people to help than there are people to serve?

Then the cook's remark broke into her thoughts. 'We've farm hands to cook for as well, ma'am. It's not just 'master and Miss Arabella. Mr Laslett's been to Hirings and tekken on more farm lads. And he's took on a new hind, but he's a single man without a wife to help wi' cooking. I wish they could live out, but he's put 'em at back of 'house and in 'stables so that means I've to feed 'em.'

'I see! I didn't realize,' Jenny said. 'Well, then, of course you must have more help.' She gave a little frown. 'I'll try to speak to Mr Laslett about it,' she said. 'Although of course I am only acting on Miss Arabella's behalf whilst she is – er – unwell.'

Cook sniffed. 'Aye, well begging her pardon, but I've mentioned it afore and nowt came of it.' She looked at Jenny with a kind of pleading. 'You could tell him that I'll leave if I don't get some help.' She sighed. 'But he wouldn't believe it for he knows I won't.'

Jenny nodded. 'I'll see what I can do,' she promised, and as she walked to the door, remarked, ''Kitchen could do with a lick of paint, couldn't it?'

Cook gave a disgruntled laugh. 'If you could manage that, and more staff, I'd think you'd been sent from heaven – ma'am,' she added.

CHAPTER TWENTY-EIGHT

'More servants!' John Laslett bellowed. 'I've just taken on two new maids! Why should we want more?'

'Cook needs extra kitchen staff, Mr Laslett,' Jenny explained. 'She's cooking for 'farmhands as well as 'house.'

'If she can't manage, then she'd better leave and I'll find somebody who can,' he said irritably.

'That's what she said,' Jenny agreed. 'Will you be able to find someone before she leaves? I think she might be willing to give you a month's notice.'

'God damn it,' he roared. 'It's not my job to find a cook! Where's Bella? She should be doing this!'

'She's unwell,' Jenny said. 'She's taking supper in her room.' Although she had been doubtful of this ruse when Arabella suggested it, she realized now that it had been a good idea. Arabella's father would have shouted her down and insisted that there would be no more servants.

'What's the matter with her? Damned women are always ailing!'

'That's it, sir. It's a woman's complaint.'

That shut him up altogether. That subject was not for discussion.

'Of course, to run the house properly, you really need a laundry maid as well as an extra kitchen maid. And then 'laundry maid could help in the kitchen.'

He glared at her. 'What do you mean – run the house properly? It runs properly now!'

'Begging your pardon, sir, but I'm afraid it doesn't.' Jenny turned her face away from him.

'Out with it, woman. What do you mean?'

'Well.' She hesitated. Was it up to her to point out the cracks in the ceiling, the peeling paint-work and the cobwebs on the highest reaches of the cornices? 'It's not very clean, sir. I don't sup-pose there's been any decorating since Mrs

Laslett died? Not in 'kitchens, anyway. If you could see your way to taking on temporary staff to clean through, then it would make life easier for 'regular staff to manage.'

He frowned. Then pursed his lips. 'Place looks perfectly all right to me! And I'm not about to make life easier for servants. They get on with what they have to do and if they don't like it they can leave!'

'Yes.' Jenny took her place at the table as Dolly brought in the supper dishes. 'I expect that is what they do.'

He glanced sourly at her but said nothing. Jenny dished up a large slice of game pie onto a plate and handed it to him. Then she pushed a tureen of steaming potatoes towards him for him to help himself, followed by a dish of buttered carrots. Dolly opened the door carrying a gravy boat. 'Sorry, sir, I forgot to bring 'gravy.'

They ate in silence and Jenny felt a tight knot in her chest, which was preventing her from enjoying her supper. 'Of course,' she said quietly, 'if Cook leaves, I expect Dolly will go too. You'll perhaps need to get a housekeeper then, as well as a cook.'

His mouth was open and about to take a bit of game pie. He put down his fork and glared at her. 'Can I finish my supper? If you don't mind!' His voice was heavy with sarcasm. 'I might discuss it later.'

'Sorry.' Jenny wondered if he might send her packing tomorrow if he thought she was being a nuisance. 'The children are settling in,' she said brightly. 'Johnny is walking well now, though he

282

was a week or two behind Serena. I caught him trying to climb 'stairs to the attics.'

Her father-in-law grunted, then said, 'You'll have to watch him. Mind he doesn't get into mischief. If he's anything like Stephen–' He broke off suddenly, then passed his plate towards her. 'I'll have another slice of pie.'

Dolly cleared away when they had finished and brought in an apple sponge pudding and a jug of custard. Jenny felt that she hadn't eaten so well in weeks.

'Beg pardon, Mrs Laslett,' Dolly said, and John Laslett started and stared at her and then at Jenny. 'I can hear one of 'babbies crying,' she said. 'Shall I go up?'

'No, I'll go,' Jenny said. 'You have enough to do.' She put down her napkin and, excusing herself, ran up the stairs to the children's room. 'It's freezing in here,' she muttered and put another piece of coal on the low fire. She picked Johnny up, for he it was who was crying. His legs were cold under his nightgown, for he had kicked off his blanket and had climbed out of bed. He babbled at her on being picked up and patted her cheek with his fist.

She smiled, and on a sudden impulse wrapped him in his blanket and took him downstairs. 'I hope you don't mind, Mr Laslett,' she said as she went back into the dining room. 'But he's cold and won't go to sleep again until he's warm.' She sat down again at the table with Johnny on her knee and continued to eat her pudding. Johnny, with his mouth open, reached out for her spoon, and she fed him a small amount of custard. He pointed at

283

John Laslett, who was watching them closely, then at his mother and then at the pudding.

Jenny smiled. It was nice when Johnny was happy. Quite often he was a demanding child. 'Grandfather has his own pudding, Johnny,' she murmured. 'He doesn't want ours.'

Johnny slid out of his blanket and off her knee and toddled towards his grandfather. He stood looking at him as curious children do, pointed at his boots, which he was wearing as usual, and then patted his grandfather's knees with both hands. John Laslett pushed back his chair and bent towards him. 'Now then, young fellow-me-lad, what do you want? Time you were asleep in bed.'

Johnny put both arms up to him and to Jenny's amazement her father-in-law picked the child up and placed him on his knee; and there he still was when Dolly came in to clear away. Dolly opened and closed her mouth, and when Jenny asked would she take Johnny back up to bed, she gulped and cleared her throat. 'Yes, Mrs Laslett,' she said.

'Our children never came downstairs after supper,' John Laslett remarked, as he left the table, but she didn't take it as disapproval. 'Not when they were small, anyway.'

'Stephen likes to see his children,' she said. 'And as we live in a small house without a separate dining room, we have to eat together.'

'Hmph,' he grunted, looking at her from beneath shaggy eyebrows. 'Manage all right, do you? For money, I mean?'

'We manage,' she said, remembering that they had had a similar conversation on her last visit.

He paused for a moment and then said, 'We'll go into the sitting room.' She led the way across the hall, where the dogs were lying by the fire, into the sitting room and closed the curtains. Then she threw another log on the fire. She sat down and folded her hands on her lap and waited for him to stop prowling about the room and say something.

'I could never work out how he paid for that house and land. He had nothing when he left. Not even his allowance.' He sat across from her and stared into the flames. 'He wasn't even twenty-one when he went off. He was just a lad.'

'He was a man,' she said quietly. 'He knew what he wanted.'

'So where did he get the money from?' he demanded, his brusque manner returning. 'Borrowed it?'

'I don't know,' she said, even though she now knew it had come from George Hill. 'I didn't know him then.'

'It can't have been hers,' he muttered. 'She'd have come with nothing.'

'A love match then?' she suggested softly. 'It must have been very hard for them both. She giving up a home and a husband.' Though she was well rid of him from what I have heard, Jenny thought, which Mr Laslett doesn't know.

He gave a deep sigh and nodded. 'And him giving up his inheritance.' He glanced around the room. 'All of this. House. Land. Farms. Everything. All for a woman!'

'Stephen would have come back,' she said. 'If you'd accepted Agnes.'

'Never,' he snorted. 'It was a scandal! My wife lost face. Didn't go out for almost a year!'

'He wanted to see his mother,' Jenny said softly. 'He was denied that.'

His eyes narrowed as he looked at her. There was something hidden there, some regret or sorrow, but he simply barked at her: 'Well, that was his punishment, wasn't it? He gave us all up for that woman. His mother. Sisters. Me!' He was silent for a moment, and then said, 'And how do you feel about that? Do you feel like second best, being a second wife?'

'I love Stephen,' she said. 'And he loves me.' But his words hurt and she wondered if it was true. Was she second best? It was true they hadn't gone into marriage with love, but then not everyone did, she pondered. Not the people of the St John Laslett society, anyway. People of my background do, if they have the chance. But then she realized that that was wrong too, for Agnes had been forced into a loveless marriage by her father.

'We have to take a chance, now and again,' she said, her eyes lowered. 'And I took one with Stephen in spite of our differences. He had loved and lost, as I had. We were able to comfort each other.'

'Hmph.' He gave a low grunt. 'Yes,' he said, almost apologetically.

They sat in silence for a while, and Jenny, unaccustomed to being idle, began to fidget and consider going up to her room. She had brought scissors and sewing materials from home and thought she could make a start on altering the clothes that Pearl had given her, and possibly cutting up one of the skirts to make Christina a day dress.

'So what about this servant business, then?' Mr Laslett abruptly interrupted her flow of thought. 'What do *you* think we should do about it? I'll concede to one more maid, if it's necessary, but no more than that!'

'Well, it's not really for me to say,' she began, but he interrupted.

'You've already said. You told me the house wasn't being run properly.'

She blushed. Perhaps she had gone too far. It really should be Arabella's decision. She was mistress of the house. 'I'm only a guest, Mr Laslett. Perhaps I shouldn't have commented.' And who am I to say anything, she thought. I've only been a servant myself. But then, I can see it from both sides.

He stared full at her. 'You're not just a guest! I invited you here as family. To bring the children. My grandsons who might–' He lifted a warning finger. 'Only might, mind – inherit one day. That's if they don't do anything stupid like their father did. So what's needed? Arabella's not going to say, even if she noticed! Why, when her mother was alive, everything ran like clockwork. The servants knew their place – and they stayed, weren't asking for their wages or giving in their notice every quarter!'

'That's because they knew who was in charge,' Jenny said. 'And I expect she knew who they all were and what they did. It's very important, that,' she said, remembering again that Mrs Ingram hadn't known her name. 'Everybody needs to feel

287

that their work is important.'

'Huh,' he humphed. 'Well, of course it's important! Even a general lad has to do a good job otherwise he's of no earthly use. But you've got to tell 'em what to do! They've no sense of their own. Rules are rules. No use in spoiling 'em or standards slip!'

She gave a small sigh. That was true, anyway. He wasn't going to change his attitude, but if he was willing to compromise she could lay down some rules for Arabella to follow when she had gone.

'I quite agree.' She smiled. 'So you're willing to take on another kitchen maid, and have 'kitchen painted?'

'Did I say I would have the kitchen painted? Good God, woman. You'll have me bankrupt!'

'It would only take one man, sir, and 'general lad could help to clean up.'

'He's a bit lame,' he said gruffly. 'The lad I've got. I took him on at Driffield Hirings. But he reckons he's strong. And I suppose I could set one of the farm lads on whilst we're a bit slack. Aye,' he conceded. 'All right then.'

Jenny hid her astonishment. Maybe Mr Laslett wasn't as hard as he appeared to be. He just needed to be persuaded.

'Another kitchen maid? And 'kitchen painted? By heck! That's nobbut fine, ma'am.' The cook fairly beamed at Jenny. 'I wonder if he'd find his way to painting yon back room?' She nodded towards a door set back and to the side of the range. 'Where 'farm men eat,' she added.

'Don't they eat in here?' Jenny hadn't noticed

the door when she had come to the kitchens last time. 'What's through there?'

Cook waddled across to the door and turned the large iron key. It opened into a large room with a fireplace, a table and several wooden chairs. At the end of the room was a wooden ladder leading into what appeared to be a loft. A cold draught was blowing down and it was quite cheerless.

'Is this where the men live?' Jenny asked. She had never seen such a place before. 'It's very cold,' she said. 'Don't they have a fire?'

'Aye, if we've time, 'fire's lit afore they come in at 'end of the day. Otherwise they light it themselves, although they don't allus bother but go straight up to bed.'

Jenny went to the bottom of the ladder and looked up, then lifted her skirt and climbed four or five steps so that she could peer into the void. She saw a row of straw mattresses and several wooden trunks: the farm boxes which would contain the men's possessions. She carefully stepped down. 'Get the scullery maid to light a fire at least an hour before they come in,' she said to the cook. 'And tell the lad to clean it out in a morning and lay it ready. They need a bit of comfort if they've been out in the fields all day, and they might not want to go to bed. They might prefer to talk or play cards after their supper.'

Cook eyed her cautiously. ''Master'll say we're setting a rod for our own backs,' she said. 'They're not used to such comforts.'

'How often does Mr Laslett come down here?' Jenny asked.

'Why, nivver, ma'am. Not so far as I know.'

'Well, there you are then,' Jenny said triumphantly. 'Unless he asks, he's not going to know,
and if he does ask then refer him to me.' She took
a breath. I might as well be hanged for a sheep as
a lamb, she thought. 'And when the kitchen has
been painted,' she told the cook, 'ask the painter
to put a wash over these walls as well.'

'I'm right glad you're here, ma'am,' Cook said.
'You'll be stopping for a bit, will you?'

'I'm not sure,' Jenny replied. 'For a few weeks
anyway.' She found it strange, yet exhilarating, to
be giving out orders to the servants and being
able to ensure that the house ran well. But I must
be careful not to get above myself, she pondered.
No-one here knows that I was just a kitchen
maid, only Mr Laslett and he's not likely to say
anything. And he doesn't know my history. But if
it should get out and anyone should have heard
of me– She felt a cold shudder down her spine.
Then I would be barred from here, and my
children too, just as Agnes was.

CHAPTER TWENTY-NINE

A week later another maid was hired as well as
the two new ones taken on by Cook and Dolly;
the painter had started on the kitchen and the
young lad, Ben, was assisting him. The weather
had turned to sleet and so one of the farm
labourers was given the job of scraping down the

walls in the room used by the men. He'd lit a fire to air the place, he'd told Cook, who passed on the word to Dolly, who then passed it on to Jenny, and said he could be heard whistling.

'He'll think it a treat, ma'am,' she said. 'He's warm and dry and is getting extra cups of tea!'

'I'm feeling much better, Jenny,' Arabella said one morning, having come down to breakfast. 'I'm so glad that you are here. I don't know what I would have done if you hadn't been around to see to everything.'

'But, Arabella! You weren't ill,' Jenny reminded her again. 'Don't make yourself ill by thinking that you are. My ma used to say–' She stopped. Better not mention her mother, Arabella might start to enquire.

'What?' Arabella yawned lazily. 'What did your mama say?'

'Oh,' Jenny hesitated. 'Just that thinking about a malady might bring it on.'

'Mothers are so wise, are they not?' Arabella remarked. 'Mine was very sensible. I declare if I was a mother I don't think I would be half as practical as she was.'

'She would have taught you to be, if she had lived long enough,' Jenny replied cautiously, thinking that her own mother was not at all wise, but she was shrewd.

'So was your mother displeased with you when you went as housekeeper to Stephen?' Arabella continued. 'She probably had something else in mind for you, such as governess or teacher?'

Jenny blushed. 'I don't think she had anything in mind at all,' she said. 'It was my decision.'

'Ah!' Arabella nodded her head significantly. 'She would have preferred you to stay at home until you married? Or did you have a position before you went to Stephen's?'

'Oh! Please excuse me, Arabella. I can hear one of 'children crying.'

'Can you?' Arabella leant her head to one side. 'I can't hear anything, but I suppose your ears are attuned to their every little sigh!'

'Yes, that's so.' Jenny hurried out of the breakfast room and upstairs, where she met Dolly on the landing. She was holding Christina by the hand. 'All 'babbies are fast asleep again, Mrs Laslett,' she said. 'And I was going to tek Miss Christina into 'kitchen to see Cook.'

'I'd like her to stay with me, thank you, Dolly.' She put her hand out to Christina, who pouted. 'Aunt Bella is waiting to see you, dear.' She took a deep breath. If Christina were with her, perhaps Arabella wouldn't ask such awkward questions.

'I'm so afraid of being found out,' she wrote in her diary that night. 'As Arabella questioned me I was conscious of being here under false pretences. My pleasure at being able to delegate and arrange responsibility has evaporated, and I'm aware that I'm just the same as the people downstairs. I'm masquerading as someone better who is called ma'am by the servants, when they should be calling me Jenny. If only Stephen could be here to protect me from the questioning. He knows who I am and some of what went before. Though not all. I have never told all of what happened that last morning with Christy. It is, and always will be, too painful to relate entirely.'

'I'd like to go home for a day or two,' Jenny told Arabella three weeks later. 'Would your father mind, do you think? I'd take Thomas and Christina with me, of course, but Dolly would perhaps look after the twins?'

'But how will I manage?' Arabella looked aghast. 'And why would you want to travel when it's so cold?'

'But the weather is good,' Jenny exclaimed. 'It is cold, yes, but bright and sunny and no sign of snow.'

'Oh, but it will come, be assured of that, Jenny. I would hate to think that you couldn't get back.'

'I will get back.' She smiled. 'But I really do want to see Stephen. I worry as to how he's managing alone. I must do some baking for him and see if he's all right.'

'Cook will give you something to take,' Arabella said. 'Then you needn't stay too long.'

'Don't you worry about your brother, Arabella?' Jenny asked.

'No,' Arabella said candidly. 'He's been away from home so long that I rarely think of him at all now. I was worried at one time, of course, which is why I came to see him, but he has his cosy little house and his needs are negligible from what I can see.'

'You came to ask him to come back,' Jenny said, frowning. 'You didn't want to be left alone here with your father!'

'That's right.' Arabella smiled brightly. 'And now I'm not. And' – she leant forward towards Jenny – 'I'm going to try to persuade Father to start entertaining again; some of his farming

293

friends, you know. I shall tell him that we should introduce you to our neighbours.' She gave a little giggle and a shrug of her shoulders. 'And it will mean that we shall be invited back and then who knows whom we might meet.'

The young men you might meet, I think you mean, Jenny thought, and she worried again that she might be asked personal questions about her background. 'I can't meet anyone unless Stephen is with me, Arabella,' she said. 'People might think that we are estranged, and we are not.'

She travelled home the following Saturday morning with Thomas and Christina and it was arranged that she would be collected the next afternoon. Mr Laslett was reluctant to let her stay longer and made the excuse that he couldn't spare the driver or the carriage on any other day. The day was cold and sharp and the roads rutted, and they bumped and jarred uncomfortably along. Christina started to cry and complain that they would turn over, and that she wanted to go back.

'It's better than walking, Christina,' Jenny told her. 'Think how long it would take us to walk to see Papa, and how your feet would ache.'

Christina stuck her feet out and looked at them. 'I shall show Papa my new boots,' she said. 'And my coat.' She was wearing the coat which Pearl had sent to them.

'Papa will hardly know you.' Jenny smiled. 'You've grown since we've been away.'

Christina nodded, her discomfort forgotten. 'Perhaps Papa has grown too,' she said.

But he wasn't there when they arrived. Christina ran down the path, shouting, 'Papa. Papa, we're here. We've come back. Where are you?'

The door was closed but not locked and as Jenny lifted the sneck to open it, a bedraggled hen flew out. She glanced down the side of the house and saw that the hen house door was open, but only a few hens were scratching around in the neglected vegetable garden. The pigpen was empty but as she looked down towards the orchard she saw her snuffling and rooting around the base of the apple trees. She also saw up on the hillside a wide embankment with horse-pulled waggons filled with rock and chalk running along it, and gangs of men working alongside. The tracks are laid, she thought. The railway has come.

'Look. Look,' Christina shouted from inside the kitchen. 'Here's an egg.' The hen, trapped indoors, had laid an egg on a chair.

'You can have it for your supper,' Jenny told her and looked despairingly around the desolate kitchen. The table was littered with dirty plates, the floor was muddy and the hearth was unswept, with ashes still in the grate. Jenny put her hand towards it. It was quite cold. 'All right,' she said. 'I'll put Thomas for a sleep, then Christina, will you go outside and collect some kindling, please? I'll light a fire so that when Papa comes home it will be a nice treat for him to see a warm blaze and 'kettle singing.'

'And a pie for his supper,' Christina piped, for she had seen Cook pack up a basket of food.

'Yes,' Jenny said. 'That too.'

It took her the rest of the day to clear up. She made a fire, then went upstairs and opened a window, and saw that the gypsies were camped in one of the fields. She took her broom and swept the floors and stairs, brushed the kitchen floor and washed the dishes. She was sitting down with a cup of tea when she heard the bark of dogs, the door opened and Stephen walked in. He looked at the tidied room, at the fire burning in the grate and Jenny in her usual chair, Thomas in his crib and Christina sitting on the rug in front of the fire, and put his hand to his forehead.

'Oh,' he breathed. 'I thought I was imagining things when I saw the smoke from the chimney.' He put his arms out to Christina, who jumped into them, and leant towards Jenny and kissed her. 'What are you doing here? I thought you'd be gone until the spring.'

'I was worried about you,' she said. 'I wondered what you were eating, though I can see you haven't eaten much. You've lost weight, Stephen,' she admonished. His face looked thinner and his eyes were shadowed.

'No time to eat,' he mumbled, glancing at the sleeping Thomas. 'The job has to be done. You'll have seen the track up above?' He gave a toss of his head in the direction of the embankment.

'Yes,' she said quietly. 'And the–'

'Grave?' He finished for her. 'It hasn't been disturbed. A fence has been put round it, and a gate, so that we can go and tend it. But we have to cross the track to get to it.' He looked and sounded very weary.

'And the compensation for the land?' she asked. 'Have you had that?'

'No. Soon,' he said. 'But I don't want to talk now. I'm so tired. I just want to go to my bed.'

'Eat first,' she said. 'There's food ready.'

He pulled a chair up to the table. 'I nearly didn't come home tonight. I'm working further down the track and almost stayed in the hut with the other navvies.'

'What would you have done for food?' She put a bowl of mutton stew in front of him.

'Nothing,' he muttered. 'Somebody would have had a bottle of whisky and a hunk of bread. We'd have played cards.'

She gazed at him. She had thought she could smell alcohol on his breath when he had bent to kiss her, but had dismissed the thought as her imagining. 'Would you have won?' she murmured. 'Or lost?'

He paused in the act of putting the spoon to his mouth. Then he said scathingly, 'I work hard, Jenny. I have to have some relaxation!'

'Yes, I know that. But you took this work on so that we would have money to spend on food and clothes for 'children.'

She didn't mean to sound petulant, but he got up from the chair and angrily paced about. 'You've been comfortable enough, haven't you?' he snapped. 'You've had good food and new clothes too by the look of you.'

'These were your sister Pearl's clothes, Stephen. Hand-me-downs, not new. I don't mind,' she added quickly. 'It's what I've always been used to. Don't let's quarrel,' she implored. 'Please. I came home because I wanted to see you. I missed you.'

He sat down again and passed his hand across his forehead. 'Sorry. Sorry.' He looked down at Christina, who was watching him with tearful

297

eyes. He gave her a wistful smile. 'You look very pretty,' he said softly. 'You've got a new dress.'

'And new boots,' she said. 'Aunt Pearl gave them to me.'

He nodded. 'It's very kind of Aunt Pearl to give to her poor relations,' he said sardonically, and Jenny sighed impatiently. 'No, I mean it,' he said. 'I never thought of her as being a philanthropist, but obviously I was mistaken.'

'She's doing it for *your* children, Stephen,' Jenny admonished. 'I think they'd like you to go home.'

'I am home,' he said sourly. 'And I'd only consider it if my father asked me. And he won't.'

Jenny tucked Christina up in her old bed, lit a lamp in her and Stephen's room and turned down the bed covers. When she went downstairs again to fetch Thomas, Stephen was asleep in the chair. She put her hand on his shoulder and he awoke with a start. 'Go to bed,' she murmured. 'I'll be up in a moment.'

He shook himself awake, then said, 'I want to talk to you, Jenny.'

'Not tonight,' she said. 'In 'morning.'

'No. It has to be now whilst it's in my mind. I've been thinking. I need to tell you what should be done.'

'About what?'

'This business of the compensation for the land. I'm going to put the money into your name. I'll have to pay George Hill out of it, of course, and I shall put Lavender Cott into Christina's name. That way she'll always be independent of my father.'

'Stephen!' She was alarmed. 'Why are you

doing this? You're not an old man!'

'One of the navvies was killed a week ago,' he told her bluntly. 'A tip-waggon crashed over. A load of metal track and wood fell onto him. His wife was sent his wages and nothing more. If anything should happen to me, you'll be secure. My father would look after the twins and Thomas. But Christina isn't mine; he might not want to take responsibility for her.'

'He's very taken with her,' she told him.

'Yes, I dare say,' he muttered. 'But the other children are his flesh and blood and he'd look after them until they came of age.' He gave a sneering grimace. 'Unless they go off with someone unsuitable, as I did. And he'll look after you if you keep on the right side of him. But if you ever cross him, be warned, he'd take the children from you.'

'He couldn't do that,' she said, alarmed. 'They're mine!'

'He could,' he said emphatically. 'And he would!' He got up and went across to the cupboard, brought out a half bottle of whisky and poured himself a large glassful. He drank it down in one gulp. 'I'm going to bed.'

Jenny sat on by the fire after Stephen had gone upstairs. She felt nervous and fearful. This wasn't the Stephen she knew. Could it just have been the death of the navvy that had brought on this decision to secure their future? She gave a deep sigh. But it was good to think that Christina would be safe. With her own property she would always have a roof over her head.

She riddled the fire, built it up with damp wood

and rolled back the hearthrug in case of sparks, then let her hair down, putting her hairpins on the dresser. She noticed that Stephen had emptied his pockets and put the contents there, including an opened envelope. Idly she picked it up. It was his wages envelope for that week with the amount written on the front. Fifteen shillings. A huge amount of money! More than enough for them to live comfortably. But there was nothing in it save a few coins.

Slowly she climbed the stairs, carrying Thomas on one hip and with a guttering candle in her other hand. What had happened to his wages? Had he lost them playing cards or spent them on whisky? She slipped into bed beside him. He was already asleep but the movement must have disturbed him. 'Agnes!' he cried out. 'Hush!'

CHAPTER THIRTY

He still thinks of her. In his unconscious state, she's still with him. Jenny lay motionless beside Stephen, with Thomas in the crook of her arm. Do I dream of Christy? Only sometimes if I'm suddenly awakened and I feel the fear that I felt then. Stephen turned over and put his arm across her and kissed her shoulder. Is he kissing me, or her? she thought, but then he murmured, 'Jenny? You've come back.'

Christina climbing in between them awakened them the next morning. 'Time to get up,' she said brightly. 'Time to feed the hens and let the piggy out.'

'The piggy's out,' Stephen groaned. 'And there aren't many hens. Your mama's friends the gypsies have seen to that.'

'What?' Jenny sat up. 'I thought 'fox had got them.'

'Fox or gypsies, I don't know. I only know that I forgot to lock them up one night and the following morning most of them had gone.'

''Cept for the one in the kitchen,' Christina gurgled. 'She hidied away and laid an egg for my supper.'

Stephen caught one of the hens and wrung its neck. He plucked it, and Jenny cooked it whilst Christina cried over its loss. 'Who shall have it for dinner?' Jenny asked her. 'Papa or the fox?'

She roasted it, boned it for the breast and the legs and then made a large pot of chicken soup with the carcass. 'This should last you for a few days,' she told Stephen. 'Don't forget to eat it.'

He seemed rather vague. 'Don't worry,' he answered. 'There's a lodging house near to where I'm working. I can buy food there. I can sleep there too if I want to.'

'But it'll cost you.' She was thinking about the empty wage packet. 'You've a comfortable bed here.'

'It's the company,' he said. 'If I come home, I'm alone.'

'We'll come back,' she declared. 'I'll go back and collect 'twins and come home.'

'No. Stay there until winter is over. There's snow on the way. The line is due to be completed

301

by May, but I'll send for you to come back before then. I don't want you and the children here alone in winter whilst I'm away.'

'Send for me? How? Will you come in person?'

'And darken Father's doorstep?' he said sardonically. 'No. I'll send one of the gypsies.'

She left him that Sunday afternoon and saw him as a lone figure watching her from the doorway. Christina ran back several times to give him a hug and a kiss, before climbing into the carriage which was waiting by the gate. I've heard of families living separate lives, she mused. But I never thought that it would happen to me. I only ever wanted to be with someone who would love me and want me with them always.

The snow came a few days later and lay thick and crisp on the ground. The leafless trees and hedgerows stood out in stark contrast to the pristine whiteness. The pond at Laslett Hall froze and Dolly dressed Christina in hat and scarf and woollen gloves and took her skating. Now that she had an under maid to help her with the household chores Dolly took charge of the children, dressing them every morning and washing their clothes.

Dolly had reason to be grateful to Jenny who had one day wandered up to the attic and discovered that although there was a fireplace in the maids' room, the fire was hardly ever lit. 'There's plenty of wood and coal,' Jenny said. 'Tell Janet to lay it each morning, and you can light it in the afternoon so that the room is warm by bedtime.'

'Thank you, Mrs Laslett,' Dolly said. 'Nobody's ever considered how cold it gets up there in 'attic.'

Ah, Jenny thought. But I remember.

December was halfway over without a word from Stephen. The weather was bitterly cold but Jenny was seriously considering going home. She was upstairs sewing late one afternoon and was called down. 'A gypsy woman, ma'am,' the maid told her. 'She's at 'back door. Said she had to speak to you privately. Won't give a message.'

At last, Stephen's sent for us, Jenny thought. But Mr Laslett won't want to send the carriage out when the roads are icy.

'Bring her into the hall,' she said to the maid. 'And ask Cook to give her some bread or pie.'

'She won't come in, ma'am. She asked if you'll go outside.'

'Oh. Very well.' Jenny hurried down the back stairs to the kitchen and out of the back door, leaving a flurry of disarray among the new maids who hadn't seen her down there before.

It was the gypsy, Floure, standing outside the house, and further down the drive was a man, holding the reins of a shaggy horse.

'You'd better come, lady,' the gypsy said in a low voice. 'Your *manush* is sick.'

Jenny felt fear clutch her. 'Sick? What? How? Has he been hurt?'

Floure nodded. 'An accident. His leg was trapped in some ironwork; somebody brought him home. We put a poultice on it, but he wouldn't send for you. It's only now that he said I could come to fetch you. He's sick with fever.'

But why didn't he send for me before? Jenny wondered. Did he not want to let his father know that he was working as a navvy? 'Has he seen a doctor?' she asked and felt a nausea come over her when the gypsy answered that he hadn't.

I'll have to tell Mr Laslett, she thought. He'll want to know why I need the carriage in a hurry.

She sent the lad out to look for him and told him to say it was urgent. 'I have to go home, Mr Laslett,' she told him when he came hurrying in. 'I've had a message to say that Stephen is sick. He's had some kind of accident.'

John Laslett grunted. 'You'll need the carriage? Is that what you're saying?'

'Yes, please. I'm sorry if it's inconvenient. Perhaps if we could go first thing in the morning?'

'We? You're not thinking of taking the children?'

'Yes,' she said firmly. 'It's time we went home. We've been here for a long stay and it will save taking 'carriage later.'

'Nonsense,' he said. 'No use taking the children if he's sick. He'll need to be quiet. What's wrong with him, anyway?' He looked at her from beneath his shaggy eyebrows and she thought she saw concern.

'I – I'm not sure. He's had an accident and has a fever. I must go back straight away.'

'Mmm.' He considered for a moment. Then he banged on the floor with his stick as if making a decision, and the dogs jumped up and looked at him expectantly. 'Not you,' he growled at them, and they resumed their places by the hall fire. 'Very well,' he said. 'We'll leave the children here and go within the hour.' He nodded at her look of astonishment. 'Can't let you go alone,' he said gruffly. 'The weather's bad out there and it'll be worse tomorrow.'

'But I must take 'children – Thomas–'

'He'll manage for a few hours. We'll come straight back.'

'I'm sorry, you don't understand. Stephen has sent for me. I have to stay with him. *Want* to stay.' Her voice rose as she tried to convince him of her intentions.

'We'll bring him back.' He stared her in the eyes. 'He'll be more comfortable here and we'll get a doctor if he needs one.'

She gave a startled exclamation. 'Mr Laslett! Don't you know your own son?' She shook her head in disbelief. 'He'd rather die than come back here.'

The colour drained from John Laslett's face at her words. 'He told me once that I'd have to beg him to come back.' His eyes shifted away from her. 'Well, I'll do that if necessary. But I think he'll come back for the sake of his sons.'

'You'll make that a proviso, will you?' she said boldly. 'You'll tell him to come home or else you'll cut his sons off from their inheritance? Your own grandsons!'

'It's nothing to do with you,' he shouted. 'You don't know half of what happened or the angry words that were said. You're just a chit of a girl!'

'It is to do with me! I'm Stephen's wife and mother of his children and I won't be shouted at! And what's more,' she said, 'I do know half! I know what Stephen told me. I haven't heard your half of the story or what reason you had for robbing your son of his family – his mother and sisters whom he dearly loved.'

'He was under the influence of that woman.' He glared at her but lowered his voice. 'That's why he left. He was only a boy and she took him away from us!'

'No,' she declared. 'She did not. He left of his own accord. He couldn't give her up. He loved her. Still does,' she added, her voice breaking, knowing in her heart that that was true. 'He'll never regret Agnes, but he does regret not being able to see 'rest of his family. And that's why I must take his children home,' she said finally. 'He'll want to see them.'

He sat down heavily in a chair and slumped forward, his head in his hands. 'I've made mistakes, I admit that,' he muttered. 'But he gave up so much. More than I ever could for a woman. But damn it.' He lifted his head to face her. 'I want him back. I miss him and I want him to have what is his.' He gave a great sigh. 'I'm fifty-eight. I don't know if I can last out twenty years before young Johnny can take over the reins here. We must persuade him to come home.'

'Not *we*,' she said. '*You* must do that if you really want him to.'

She decided to compromise. Since John Laslett had suggested travelling that evening, rather than wait until morning, she was quite keen to agree, knowing that she would have an anxious night otherwise. She would leave Christina and the twins – it was almost their bedtime in any case – and would take Thomas with her. She could have left him with Dolly, but felt she should make some kind of stand and not let her father-in-law think that he could have everything his own way.

They didn't speak much during the journey; Jenny huddled into a blanket and kept Thomas close to her body. Dolly had given her and Mr Laslett a hot brick each to keep their feet warm and though the journey wasn't so very far, there was sleety rain and it took them over an hour as the driver negotiated the horses round the slippery dips and bends of the road in the darkness, with only the swinging lantern to light their way. Jenny thought of the gypsies and wondered if they were travelling back that night or sheltering and waiting until morning. There had been no question of asking Mr Laslett to let them ride alongside, for he would have refused and so probably would they.

Stephen's dogs were outside the house and barked and wagged their tails when they heard the carriage. She reckoned that perhaps they were hungry and glad to see her. A small beam of light shone from the kitchen window. Jenny turned to Mr Laslett as she lifted the sneck, and as if he knew what she was about to say, he said quickly and gruffly, 'I'll stay here. You must ask him first if I can come in.'

The oil lamp was low and the fire in the grate almost out. Jenny wondered if the gypsies had lit it, for Stephen was lying on a makeshift bed on the floor. A blanket covered him but one leg was exposed. The cloth of his breeches had been cut and a bloody bandage was wound over his knee.

She put the sleeping Thomas down on a chair and approached Stephen cautiously, afraid of startling him. 'Stephen,' she whispered. 'Stephen! I've come home!'

She knelt down beside him. He was asleep or unconscious, she didn't know which. His forehead, when she touched it, was wet with sweat and she put her hand to his chest and felt the heat. She got to her feet and called to Mr Laslett outside the door. 'You'd better come in. He needs a doctor.'

John Laslett looked down at his son and Jenny saw a pulse throb at his temple and he swallowed hard. 'Whom can I fetch? Do you know a doctor nearby?'

'Only Dr Hill. Stephen's friend. He lives near Etton. I can give you his address, though I've never been there.'

'George Hill? Does he keep in touch?' He rubbed his hand over his chin. 'I didn't know. I'll fetch him. I know where he lives.'

When he had gone, Jenny built up the fire with some wood which had been left in the hearth, then went outside to fill a pan from the water butt. The air was sharp, crisping her nostrils and making her ears tingle. The sky was full of stars, but as she lowered her gaze she saw the dark shadow of the embankment and the railway waggons upon it.

She poured cold water into a bowl and bathed Stephen's brow, and then heated the rest over the fire to wash him down. He stirred and moved his head from side to side, murmuring something as she unfastened the buttons on his wet shirt. Then she saw the bruising and cuts on his chest. Black, blue and purple, from his collarbone almost to his waist. He had sustained a much worse injury than he had admitted to the gypsies.

'What's happened, Jenny?' George Hill knelt down

at Stephen's side. 'Where's he been to get injuries like this? It looks as if he's been run down by something – a waggon, or something heavy anyway.'

'I wasn't here,' Jenny admitted. 'I've been staying at Laslett Hall for the last few weeks. Someone came for me. We've only just arrived.'

Dr Hill's eyebrows rose but he made no comment.

'He's been working on that damned railway line, that's what he's been doing!' Mr Laslett broke in. 'I've always said those infernal trains were dangerous, but no-one ever listened!'

'Trains are no more dangerous than a runaway horse and waggon if you should get in the way of one, Mr Laslett,' Dr Hill said quietly, as he felt for Stephen's pulse. 'But why would Stephen be working on the railway? He's a farmer.'

'It was to earn some extra money over 'winter,' Jenny admitted. 'He had to give in to 'railway company and let the line come onto his land, so he said he might as well take advantage of it as sit and brood about it.'

Mr Laslett humphed. 'And I'll bet they haven't paid any compensation for the land yet, either? Nor will they pay his wages whilst he's injured.'

'And would you, sir, if any of your workers were off sick?' Dr Hill rose to his feet. 'Farm workers are notoriously ill done by, as I have often seen.'

'Please,' Jenny interrupted. 'What about Stephen? Is he going to be all right?'

George Hill took off his heavy coat and his jacket and rolled up his shirtsleeves. 'I'm bothered about his chest. He might have crushed

309

his ribs. But I'll take a look at his leg injury first. I'll need some warm water to clean it.'

'Why is he unconscious?' Jenny asked as she poured hot water into a bowl. 'Surely 'pain would keep him awake?'

'Nature's way,' the doctor said briefly, and set about cleaning the leg wound, which was deep and bloody.

John Laslett had been pacing the floor, one hand on his chin, and the other hand behind his back, clenching and unclenching. 'We'll take him home,' he said suddenly. 'We can take care of him there – hire a nurse.'

'He is at home,' Dr Hill answered, without looking at the older man. 'And he can't be moved at present. Anyway, Mrs Laslett is a good nurse. She can look after him.' He turned his head to her and smiled. 'Can't you, Jenny?'

She was grateful for his support and for remembering how she had looked after Agnes. She nodded. 'Yes. Of course I can. But what about 'children? I've only brought Thomas with me. They'll have to come home.'

'No,' Mr Laslett said quickly. 'They're all right where they are. They'll come to no harm. We'll look after them until – until Stephen can be moved.'

George Hill straightened up. He gazed directly at John Laslett. 'And then? What then do you propose for your son, sir?' There was heavy emphasis on the words 'your son', and Jenny realized that the doctor knew all that had gone before between Stephen and his father, and that John Laslett would not be able to take advantage of his son, whilst he was unable to make decisions for himself, or of her either.

Mr Laslett's cheeks flushed. 'Well, he can – if he wants to, that is – come back to Laslett Hall.'

CHAPTER THIRTY-ONE

'Don't let the old man bully you,' was George Hill's parting shot to her as he was leaving, saying he would come back within the next few days. Mr Laslett had already gone.

'That's what Stephen once said,' Jenny told him. 'And I won't. I don't.'

'You've changed, Jenny,' the doctor commented. 'You're a much more assured young woman than you were when I first met you.'

But I'm not, she thought as she returned to the house. I'm still the same inside; it's just a front that I put on to hide my real feelings, though I don't think I've ever let anyone take advantage of me. I've always marked out my own destiny.

She did her usual chores in between tending Stephen and Thomas. She drew water, baked bread, chopped wood and fed the few hens, though there were no eggs, and she wondered what had happened to the pig and the goat since she had last been home. The horse wasn't in the stable and neither was the waggon.

Stephen's father sent the carriage two days later with Arabella, a maid and Christina, who, Arabella said, had insisted on coming to see her papa. They also brought meat, vegetables and a game pie, which Cook had sent, and blankets and pillows.

'It's very thoughtful of your father, Arabella, but we have blankets and pillows.'

'He was most concerned that Stephen was sleeping on the floor,' Arabella said. 'If we could have found room for a truckle bed in the carriage he would have sent that too.'

'He's only on 'floor because we can't get him upstairs,' Jenny explained. 'As soon as he is able to he can go up to bed, though it's easier for me to have him down here where I can keep an eye on him and talk to him when he's awake.'

Stephen had woken, but was in considerable pain each time he took a deep breath. Dr Hill had left medication for him, and she wondered if it contained laudanum, for Stephen always dropped off to sleep after he had taken a dose. Just as Agnes did when she took it, she remembered.

'I'll be glad when you come back, Jenny,' Arabella moaned. 'I'm really not up to looking after everyone. My health is not what it might be.'

'There's nothing wrong with you,' Jenny pointed out. 'Nothing at all! And if Stephen doesn't want to come back to Laslett Hall then I won't either. I'll come on a visit but not to stay indefinitely.'

'But who will run the house if you're not there?' Arabella seemed astonished. 'And the children need you. Johnny cried for you the other night, it was quite pitiful. I could do nothing for him!'

'But the children will be back here!' Jenny stared at Arabella in dismay and hugged Thomas to her. 'We shan't leave them. They belong here with Stephen and me!'

'But, Jenny,' Arabella sat back in the chair and folded her hands on her lap, 'I overheard Papa telling Dolly that the children would be staying and that he would have one of the rooms made into a nursery. Dolly was pleased, because he said that she could have charge of them, whilst you were away, that is,' she added hastily as she saw Jenny's fierce expression.

'You can tell your father that I *did not* have children for his benefit,' she muttered between clenched lips. The young maid had gone outside with Christina who wanted to look for the hens, which were running amok in the orchard. 'And if Mr Laslett wants to see his grandchildren then he's going to have to apologize to Stephen before he comes back.'

A low weak chuckle came from the bed on the floor. 'Well said, Jenny, but it won't happen. Father's pride will not let him apologize. He'd rather cut the nose off his face.' Stephen gave a nod of acknowledgement of his sister's presence. 'Why are you here, Arabella?'

'I came because you're sick!' Arabella drew nearer to him. 'And Father said I had to come as he can't; his gout is playing up again.'

'Sick?' Stephen eased himself up and then winced. 'I'm not sick.'

'Stephen!' Arabella murmured. 'You're going to have to meet Father halfway, you do realize? If you're prepared to come home, then he will welcome you, in his own way of course. I think he's willing to say he might have made a mistake.'

'But he's not prepared to meet me here, in the

home I made because I was turned out of my own.' His voice was thick, his words slurred.

'He has been,' Jenny interrupted. 'Your father brought me when I first got the message from the gypsies. He wouldn't let me travel alone.'

'Message? What message?' He looked around the kitchen. 'What's going on? Why–' He winced again as he tried to get up. 'You'd better send for Hill, Jenny. I feel really bad.'

Jenny knelt on the floor beside him. 'Don't you remember what happened, Stephen? You've had an accident. The gypsies came to your father's house to ask me to come home.'

He closed his eyes in concentration. 'Something! Yes, somebody brought me back. Two men. In the waggon. But I don't know why. Or even where I was. Get Hill to call,' he repeated. He spoke quickly and breathlessly. 'How can we get a message to him? Arabella, could you go and fetch him?'

'He's coming again. He's been already,' Jenny reassured him. 'Your father went to fetch him.'

'Did he?' He seemed astonished. 'He's been here? Father has?'

'Yes. He wanted to take you back to Laslett Hall, but Dr Hill said you couldn't be moved.'

'Quite right,' he muttered. 'There's something tight round my chest. Have a look will you, Jenny? See what it is.'

'You're bruised,' she said, and repeated, 'You've had an accident.' She turned to Arabella. 'I think you'd better go, Arabella. Stephen obviously isn't well. Take Christina back with you and perhaps you'd come again in a day or two?'

Arabella hurriedly collected her gloves and

314

scarf. 'Yes. Yes. Or I'll ask Papa to call. Shall I, Stephen?' She observed her brother anxiously. 'Should Papa come?' She seemed like a little girl, unsure and about to cry.

Stephen didn't answer but closed his eyes as if he didn't want to make a decision. But he spoke as she reached the door. 'Do whatever Jenny says, Bella. She knows best.'

Christina bade a tearful goodbye to Stephen and covered the baby Thomas with kisses. Jenny promised that they would see her again soon. When they had left she propped Stephen up on the pillows which Arabella had left behind and spooned him some thin soup.

'I want to ask you something,' she said. 'Are you up to listening to me?'

He nodded. 'Yes,' he breathed. 'Only I wish that Hill would come.'

'He'll come,' she said. 'He promised that he would.' Though it is getting late, she thought. Perhaps he won't come until the morning.

'Do you recollect saying that you were going to leave this house to Christina, Stephen?'

'Yes.' He gave her a wry look. 'I'm not going to die yet, Jenny, even though I might feel like death right now.'

'Please don't joke,' she said. 'It's not funny. But as I was coming here with your father after I'd been told you'd had an accident, I wondered if you'd done anything about it. Drawn up any papers or whatever it is that you have to do?'

'I could have been killed, I suppose?' he murmured. 'Like that other poor fellow.'

'Yes,' she choked. 'You could have been. And I

315

would have been left with three babies and a small child!'

'Four babies,' he said softly. 'Christina's not much more than a baby, is she?' He pointed to the dresser. 'In there. In the drawer. I've written out a Last Will and Testament. It needs witnessing. I was waiting for George. Get it,' he said. 'Have a look at it.'

She insisted he took a little more soup and then looked for the paper. He had made it out as promised, leaving Lavender Cott and its contents in trust to his adopted daughter Christina and the rest of his estate, including his horse and waggon, to his wife, Jenny. He also stipulated that any monies owing should be paid out of the estate. But he hadn't signed it.

'Any monies owing?' Jenny asked. 'Do you owe anyone else apart from George Hill?' She looked at him. 'Not any of 'navvies? Not for playing cards or – or anything?'

'I'm not about to die, Jenny!' His voice was suddenly sharp.

'I hope not,' she said, contrite at even bringing up the subject. 'It's just – it's just that I don't ever want to go begging to your father.'

'No, nor do I. I'm sorry. No, there's nothing else owing, but that doesn't mean there won't be. I don't intend leaving this mortal coil just yet.' He took hold of her hand. 'There's not much, Jenny. I spent most of my wages,' he confessed. 'It's been such a long time since I had money in my pocket that I spent most of it unwisely. I went drinking and playing cards with the men. But I haven't spent the compensation,' he assured her.

'That still hasn't come, which is perhaps just as well or I might have spent that too.'

'Don't talk now,' she urged him. 'Take your medicine and try to have a sleep. I'm sure Dr Hill will come, if not tonight, then in the morning.'

Whilst he was dropping off into a doze, Jenny searched in the drawers and cupboards for a bottle of writing ink and a pen. When she found it, she dipped the pen in the ink and carefully carried it and the Will to Stephen. 'Stephen,' she said softly. 'Put your name on here.' She put the pen into his fingers. 'You forgot to sign it.'

With his eyes half closed, he put pen to paper and signed his name. She sighed. It was done. 'Please forgive me, Stephen,' she murmured. 'But I'm so afraid. Not for myself, but for our children.'

It was nine o'clock in the evening and Jenny had locked up. She had been upstairs and decided that it was too cold to sleep up there, and that she and Thomas would sleep in a chair by the fire, when there came a soft tap on the door. 'It's George Hill,' was the answer when Jenny came to ask who it was. 'I'm sorry I'm so late.' He took off his scarf and a flurry of snow floated off it. 'I've been kept by a young woman in a difficult labour, and the roads are very icy up here. How has he been?' he asked, looking towards Stephen.

'He's a little better, I think, and he's had some soup.' She felt nervous now that he was here, wishing that she had waited before getting Stephen to sign the Will.

'I won't waken him then.' The doctor put his fingers on the side of Stephen's neck. 'His pulse is steady.'

'He's not in any danger, is he?' Jenny asked. 'He didn't remember anything of what happened.'

He pursed his lips. 'Not so far as I can tell, but the injuries to his chest worry me; he may have broken ribs. The leg injury will heal providing it's kept clean and doesn't become septic.'

'He's not going to die?' she asked nervously, and then, taking a deep breath, she said, 'It's just that – he's made out a Will, and – and he wanted you to witness it.' She fetched it from the dresser and handed it to him.

A small frown appeared above his nose. 'But he's signed it already. He should have waited. I'm supposed to witness his signature, not what is in the Will!'

'Oh!' she breathed. Now am I to be found out?

'Did he think his death was imminent? Surely not!' The doctor sat down by the table and looked at the document. 'It's his signature anyway,' he said. 'It's an illegible scrawl, but he never did have a good hand. If you bring me a pen and ink, I'll sign it, even though it isn't strictly the way to do things. But it might put his mind at rest, and yours too.' He looked up at her as she brought the writing materials. 'You don't need to worry, Jenny. I would stand up to Stephen's father on your behalf if it ever became necessary.'

Her mouth trembled. How foolish I am, but I was – am – so afraid. 'Thank you,' she said. 'I'll remember that. And Stephen said that you are to be paid what he owes you out of his estate! But I'm sure he'll pay you back himself,' she added in a rush. 'When he's recovered.'

Dr Hill nodded. 'In time. All in good time. I've

never pressed him, Jenny. And I won't.' He hesitated. 'I shouldn't say this, for I have no real regard for Stephen's father after the way he behaved in the past, but if you could get them speaking to one another, it might be a good thing for Stephen to return to Laslett Hall to recuperate.'

'He won't want to go,' she said. 'He won't want to leave here.'

'It needn't be for long, just until the spring. Are there any animals left?'

She considered. There were only a few hens. The gypsies could have those in exchange for guarding the house. The pig and goat weren't there; Stephen must have sold them. There were just the two dogs and they could take them with them. 'Oh,' she said. 'The horse and waggon! Where are they? Surely he's never sold them!'

He hadn't sold them, nor did he know where they were when she asked him the next day. 'Stolen,' he exclaimed weakly. 'Whoever brought me back must have taken them! As soon as I can get out of the house, I must find out what happened.' He groaned and put his head in his hands. 'I'll never be able to afford another waggon!'

The gypsies confirmed that the waggon had been driven away after Stephen had been brought home. 'Two men,' Floure's husband, Paul, told Jenny. He was a man of few words. 'They came to ask us where you were, lady, then they drove off.'

'What did you tell them?' she asked.

'Nothing,' he said. 'We told them nothing.' He gazed at her from handsome dark eyes. 'Do you want us to find them?'

'Can you?'

He nodded and grinned. 'Yes. We can do that. A few days only and we'll bring them back.'

It was just two days later that Jenny looked out of the window and saw them. A child was on the horse's back between the shafts of the waggon, and a gypsy was leading it through the gate into the meadow. 'The *gav-engro* – constable – might come,' Paul Lee told her when he came to the door. 'Those thieves saw us.'

'If 'constable comes I'll tell them we sent you to get them back,' Jenny said. 'My husband will be so pleased. Thank you very much.' She hesitated and then said, 'We – we can't pay you for your trouble.'

Paul Lee shook his head. 'Your *rom* said we can stay here over winter. We won't be turned off?'

'You won't be turned off,' Jenny assured him, 'and if we go away for my husband to recuperate, I'd like to think you'd watch 'house? You can have 'hens in payment.'

He agreed and said she should leave the dogs. 'We'll feed them,' he said. 'They can guard the house.'

She was reluctant to leave them; she had seen the gypsies' dogs, which were thin and scrawny. 'One belongs to my little girl,' she said. 'You will look after them?'

'Don't worry, lady,' he said. 'You have the word of a Romany.'

The following day at noon, Jenny heard the click of the gate. She looked out and beyond the gate she saw the carriage. Running down the path was Christina and following her, leaning heavily on a stick, was Mr Laslett.

'Stephen!' She turned to where he was resting in a chair by the fire with a blanket round him. 'Your father has come.'

CHAPTER THIRTY-TWO

Jenny let in a rushing, laughing, excited child who flung her arms round her, and then dashed towards Stephen to hug him.

'Good day to you, Jenny.' Mr Laslett removed his ancient top hat and ducked his head as he entered the low doorway. 'I trust Stephen is feeling better?'

'Better than he was, but not fully recovered,' Jenny replied, taking his hat from him. 'His chest is still painful.'

John Laslett cleared his throat as he stood in front of his son, and then held out his hand. 'Good to see you are returning to health,' he muttered. 'We were worried about you.'

'Were you?' Stephen stared up at his father, and Jenny almost held her breath. Would he reject the hand of reconciliation? Then Stephen blinked and sighed and held out a pale hand. 'Forgive me if I don't get up,' he said in a low voice. 'My leg–'

'Yes. Yes, I know,' his father answered hurriedly. 'I saw it. It was a nasty wound.'

Jenny brought forward a chair for John Laslett and thought how fortuitous it was that Christina had come too, for with her chatter she broke the awkward pauses. 'Grandpappy said I can have a little pony, Papa.' Christina clapped her hands. 'Can we get Star back? He had to go away,' she explained to Stephen's father, 'because he ate too much.'

'We'll see.' Both men spoke in unison and Christina laughed merrily. 'Mama,' she gurgled. 'They both said we'll see!'

Jenny gave a nervous smile, and busied herself making a pot of tea and getting out cups and saucers. 'I'm sorry I've no milk,' she began.

'Don't touch it,' her father-in-law said gruffly. 'Drink it without.'

'Of course,' she said. 'I'd forgotten.'

Mr Laslett sipped his tea and there was a silence for a few minutes, then he cleared his throat again, and said, 'You'll have finished on the railway now, I suppose? After the accident?'

Stephen glanced at Jenny, then at his father. 'Who told you?' he asked abruptly.

John Laslett looked down at Christina sitting on the rug at their feet, and took another sip of tea. He rubbed the sides of his mouth with his knuckles. 'No grown-up,' he murmured. 'Just childish chatter!'

'Without prompting?' Stephen's voice grated.

'Entirely.' His father looked at him squarely. 'I've plenty of other things to occupy me without interrogating a child!'

'Yes. Sorry.' Stephen nodded.

'The line will be almost finished anyway, isn't it?' his father asked. 'Damned trains! I remember when they started talking about this line, must be nearly twenty years ago. Lord Hotham held it up, of course. Wouldn't let them on his land. But even he gave in, in the end. Just as you did, I suppose.' He gazed into space with a disgruntled look on his face. 'I heard that George Hudson is back in this country again, but trouble seems to follow him. Gossip is that he's still in debt, might even go to prison.'

'That's such a pity,' Jenny broke in. She had picked up Thomas and was gently rocking him. 'He's done so much for this country. People want 'railways. Ordinary people anyway!' she said defiantly. 'I don't mean landowners. Ordinary folk who can get about much easier.'

'You're probably right, Jenny,' Stephen admitted. 'It's just that I didn't want to give up any of my land, or my privacy. I don't like to think that people can look down from the trains and see my property. But yes,' he answered his father. 'This line is scheduled to be finished and in use by May. But they'll have to manage it without me.' He looked down at the leg wound, and the blood which was still seeping through the bandage. 'I didn't make much of a contribution and I wonder now if it was worth it.'

'Will you come home?' his father said suddenly. 'To Laslett Hall, I mean. See how we get on? I realize you won't want to leave here. Memories and all that.' He spoke in a brisk, abrupt manner. 'But now that you've children to consider.'

Stephen said nothing but stared down at Christina. Then he reached out and touched the top of her dark head, twisting a strand of her hair around his finger.

'You don't have to stay for good,' his father continued. 'But come at least until you are well

323

again. Close this place up until the spring. It will stand over winter. No harm will come to it.'

Jenny could see that it had taken a great deal of effort for John Laslett to ask, but Stephen's face was stony. Please, she thought, don't ask your father to apologize.

'I made mistakes,' the older man went on. 'I admit that. We should have talked things through, but we only ever wanted what was best for you.' His voice had a pleading quality to it.

'What was best for me?' Stephen said harshly. 'I knew what was best for me and we disagreed on that.' He pondered for a moment, then gave a hard swallow. 'But yes, we should have talked rather than argued.'

'Papa!' Christina's childish treble broke in. 'If I get a pony, can Serena ride on it too?'

He looked down at her. 'Serena's too small to ride,' he murmured, then patted her cheek. 'But we'll sit her on its back, just as we did when you were small. All right.' He relented, his eyes still on Christina. 'We'll come for the winter, but only on condition that George Hill can attend me whilst I'm there.'

A noticeable look of relief crossed his father's face. 'I've nothing against Hill,' he said. 'He's a fine doctor. Just a touch opinionated, that's all!'

Now that the horse and waggon had been recovered, Stephen insisted that they drive back in it to Laslett Hall. 'You and Christina can return in the carriage,' he told Jenny, 'and I'll drive the waggon.'

'You'll do no such thing,' she answered. 'You're in no fit state.'

John Laslett agreed with her. 'I'll drive the damned waggon if you insist on taking it,' he groused, 'and you and Jenny can travel in the carriage with the child.'

'No,' Jenny declared. 'Not with your gout! I'll drive it and Stephen can come with you.'

That wouldn't do either as Stephen didn't want Jenny to drive it alone; nor, she suspected, did he want to travel with his father. In the end, Jenny drove the waggon with Stephen propped up with pillows and blankets in the back of it, following the carriage which held Mr Laslett and Christina, who waved a hand from the window as they went at a slow and steady pace.

'We could have left 'waggon behind,' Jenny called over her shoulder to Stephen. 'And 'Romanies would have fed the horse.' She had given them instructions regarding the dogs: to feed them once a day and fasten them up in their kennel at night. The Romanies in turn had asked her to give them a letter stating that they could stay on the land, in case the law came and told them to move on.

'I dare say they would have, though I don't trust them entirely. But that's not why I wanted to bring them.' Stephen shivered with cold, despite the blankets.

The waggon was difficult to drive. The road was icy and the horse skidded going downhill. Jenny gripped the reins tightly. 'Let him take the lead,' Stephen shouted to her. 'Don't grip too hard, he'll find his feet. No,' he continued, 'if I have my own transport I can come back if Father and I fall out. I don't want to be stuck there waiting on his convenience!'

He's still embittered, Jenny thought, grimacing against the biting wind which blew in her face. But is he resentful against his father for refusing to accept Agnes, or against fate for taking Agnes away from him, when no-one else could? It's not easy being a second wife, she meditated. I feel as if I should make excuses for still being here, alive and well and mother of his children.

'Jenny!' Stephen called to her.

'Yes?' She half turned to see him.

'Thank you.'

'For what?' Her shawl slipped off her shoulders and she grabbed hold of it. He half stood, half knelt behind her and draped the shawl over her cape, one which Arabella had lent her, then taking one of his blankets he put it over her knees.

'Just for being you,' he said, kissing her on her cheek. 'I know I'm crotchety and it won't be easy at Father's. But I'm asking you to forgive me now for what I might do or say whilst I am there.'

She felt a sudden surge of emotion and took a deep breath. 'You must try to put 'past behind you,' she said, her voice wobbling.

'It's not so easy,' he said. 'I'm not strong like you. I'm driven always by passion. I can't think logically or rationally as you do.'

She was startled by his assessment of her. Is it true? she thought as they continued on their journey. I hadn't thought of it before; Stephen and his father share the same temperament, which is why they clash; whereas I, and I've never thought to give my behaviour a name before, I follow a chain of reasoning and deliberation. I have passion, though, hidden away, but – shrewd! That's what I am! Just like my mother. Jenny thought back over her life since first making the decision to go to Beverley, and the events thereafter. Yes, that's it! Shrewd! Though I'd never admit it. And that is why I have survived.

'I feel like the prodigal son!' Stephen muttered to Jenny as they drove up to the house. The servants had gathered on the front step to greet him. Cook, who had been there since before he left home, Dolly, who held Serena's hand and struggled to keep hold of Johnny; the other maids and the lad, Ben, who didn't know him at all. He nodded at them as the females dipped their knees and the lad took off his cap. He kissed Arabella, who stood behind them, and murmured to her, 'Whose idea was this?'

'Mine,' Arabella whispered. 'I thought it would be good for everyone to see you.'

'All right!' John Laslett boomed. 'Get back to work! You, lad, what's your name? Take the waggon into the barn, rub the hoss down and turn him out into the fold yard. Better give him a feed whilst you're about it. He's too lean by my reckoning.'

Ben touched his forehead and dashed off to do his bidding and the other servants dispersed, except for Dolly who stayed behind to hand over the children to Jenny and relieve her of Thomas. ''Twins have missed you, ma'am,' she said. 'Johnny's a right handful, but Serena's as good as gold. Mr Laslett said we could have one of 'top rooms as a nursery if you agree to it.'

'Thank you, Dolly. We'll discuss it later.' She

took the twins and Christina into the sitting room, where the little girl played with Johnny and Serena sat on her knee.

Stephen limped across to a chair and fell into it. He heaved out a breath. 'I don't understand it. The journey's exhausted me! I feel really unwell. I don't like the sensation. I'm not used to it.'

'You must rest now that we are here,' Jenny told him. 'I'll get Cook to make you a pick-me-up.'

'Yes.' He gave a wistful smile. 'Rum, honey, eggs. I made it for Agnes when she was ill.'

'I remember,' she said softly. 'But Agnes had a fatal malady. You haven't; you just need to rest.'

He nodded. 'And get George Hill to visit. I'll write. He won't know that we're here.'

'Doesn't your father like him?' Jenny asked. 'He said he was opinionated.'

'The pot calling the kettle black,' he grunted. 'George came to visit him when I went away with Agnes. He pleaded my case and when Father refused to listen, George told him a few home truths. Father didn't like that.' He put his head back against the chair and sighed. 'I think I will go upstairs. Write to George for me, will you, Jenny? Tell him I need to see him.'

When he had gone up to bed, Jenny sat pondering. Christina had brought a soft ball and was throwing it to the twins, but Johnny soon became bored with the game and stumbled across to the hearth where he attempted to pick up one of the fire irons. Jenny took it from him and put it back. It would be a good idea to have a nursery, she thought. Somewhere the children could play without endangering themselves or breaking anything. She glanced around the room. There were precious ornaments and glass bowls placed on child-height tables, which Arabella had previously told her had belonged to her mother; and which her father had kept in the same places since her mother had died.

None of this is mine, she thought. I would feel so guilty if the children were to break anything. Agnes had had nothing much, but what she and Stephen had was placed high where Christina wasn't able to reach it when she was a toddler with inquisitive hands. Jenny watched as the children played. Christina with her merry smile was supervising the twins, Serena watching her sister's every movement, but Johnny intent on playing his own games. They are all that I have, Jenny thought. I have nothing else of my own, not a dish or a wooden spoon, not a fustian sheet or a dishrag. But I have got my four precious children, worth more to me than any jewels or riches. She gazed fondly at Christina. No-one can ever take her away from me, she is mine alone. And because of her, this is my life. I must make of it what I can.

Arabella came into the room. 'I'm so glad that you've come back, Jenny. Shall we be able to persuade Stephen to stay, do you think?'

'Until he is well, yes. After that, I don't know. It will depend on how he and his father get along.'

'I'm going to have a little pony,' Christina piped up. 'So we have to stay.'

Jenny and Arabella glanced at each other. Little ears flapping, Jenny thought. 'And you're going to have a special room where you and the twins and Thomas, when he's big enough, can play,' she said to the child.

'And perhaps someone to teach you your letters,' Arabella said. 'Wouldn't that be nice?'

Christina clapped her hands, and Serena copying her did the same.

So? Jenny pondered. Is that how it is to be? It's for the best, I think. For the time being at any rate. 'That would be nice, Christina, wouldn't it?' she said. 'To read some books and write your letters?'

'I'll write a letter to Papa,' the little girl said. 'When he goes back home to Lavender Cott.'

CHAPTER THIRTY-THREE

Christmas came and went. Stephen and his father made an effort to be pleasant to each other, and although the three younger children were too young to understand or participate in the celebrations, Christina was petted and spoiled with presents and new clothes, for Pearl came with her husband Edwin and their three daughters for Christmas dinner, armed with parcels for everyone.

'It is what we like to do, my dear,' Pearl said to Jenny. 'So don't be embarrassed about not having presents for us. Our girls like to sew and make things and so we give them away at Christmas.' The presents were not large or expensive, but simple things such as embroidered handkerchiefs, lace caps and pleated cotton bonnets, all beautifully sewn. 'I do believe in young women being able to turn their hands to something useful, don't you agree?'

'Yes, indeed,' Jenny answered as she watched all the little girls play together, and thought that the daughters of the rich Mr and Mrs Edwin Smith would probably not need to be able to do much more than turn a fine hem, but that if by mischance they fell on hard times then they would make excellent seamstresses.

On Boxing Day Stephen's other sisters, Maud and Laura, with their husbands and daughters, visited them. The two women were rather distant towards Jenny, being the mother of sons she supposed, but they were warm towards Stephen. Christina became very excited at the prospect of having so many friends to play with. Arabella mistakenly referred to them as her cousins, but was immediately reminded by Maud that they were not, at which Christina cried, though not really understanding, and Mr Laslett gave her a bon-bon to comfort her and chastised his daughter for her insensitivity, which surprised Jenny.

The weather became very cold in January with a biting east wind, which kept them indoors. Stephen couldn't walk well though his wound was slowly healing. Dr Hill had been to visit him and listened to his chest which he said was still weak, and decreed that he should spend each morning in bed and not get up until midday.

Arabella abandoned any attempts at running the household, and Jenny found she was increasingly making household decisions. She saw Cook each Monday morning to plan the week's menu, and discuss the groceries and buying of food. She had to rely on Cook to tell her the best butcher for supplying a flitch of bacon, for they didn't keep their own pigs, a good grocer for butter as they didn't have a dairy maid; to say who sold the freshest fish and suggest the names of wild-fowlers who could supply game, for John Laslett no longer went out shooting. Grain from the estate was sent to a local miller who returned it in sacks as flour or oatmeal, and vegetables were grown in the kitchen garden.

'You're doing well, Jenny,' Stephen said one day. She had waylaid the maid and, taking the tray from her, had taken up his breakfast herself. 'Now all you need to do is marry Arabella off to some-body and you can run the house for Father entirely alone.'

'For your father?' She looked at him with a sinking heart. 'But – you'll be here.'

He took a sip of coffee. 'Perhaps. I don't know.' He put down the cup and said softly, 'I don't know if I can stay.'

'But you are getting on quite well with your father.' She pressed her fingers against her lips to stop them trembling. 'Once you are well, and up and about, you can take over from him, or at least help him so that he doesn't have to work so hard.'

Stephen shook his head. 'I've been away too long. I'm out of practice at running a big estate. I've been used to doing things my own way, on a small scale. Besides,' he said, 'my father would always be master here; he'd make the decisions, about the harvest, about selling and buying cattle or sheep. I'd simply be working for him until such time as he drops dead in his boots, for he'll never give up.' He took a huge breath and said, 'Only then would I be able to take over, and if I'm honest, I don't know if I want to.'

She sat on the bed beside him. 'So what shall we do?' she said in a small voice. 'Shall we go back to Lavender Cott? How will we manage?'

'I'll go back,' he said quietly. 'You'll stay here with the children. I can make a living for myself. I don't need much.'

'But what kind of a married life is that?' she asked. 'When a husband is in one place and a wife in another?'

'It does sometimes happen,' he said. 'It doesn't mean a separation; it means that it's best for all concerned. You and the children will be cared for, which is what I want more than anything. I don't want you to suffer, Jenny, and I want the best life for the children.'

'A life without their father?' But as she spoke she realized that he was reverting to his own experience of childhood. He hadn't been in close contact with his father, as she had been with hers by living within the confines of a small house with a large family. Their lives had been quite different.

'You can bring them over,' he said, 'or I will come to see you. We can still enjoy our marriage rites.' He spoke tenderly and lovingly and when he moved the tray from the bed and, holding her close, unfastened her gown and brought her into bed with him she was almost convinced. There were no children around to disturb them, no pressing tasks that must be seen to, and he was more loving, more passionate than he had been for a long time, when there had been so many worries and problems facing them. As she lay beneath him, she reflected that if she couldn't persuade him to stay with her aroused and willing body next to his, then she could think of nothing else to convince him.

'Just one thing I want you to promise me, Jenny,' he breathed into her neck.

'What?' she murmured.

He nibbled at her ear. 'If anything should happen to me–'

She pulled away and looked at him in alarm. 'Nothing will–' she began.

'No. No,' he soothed her. 'Nothing will. But if it ever should. If I should die.' He looked at her probingly. 'I would want to stay at Lavender Cott. I wouldn't want to be brought back here. I'd want to be buried in my own land.'

She licked her lips, which had suddenly gone dry. 'With Agnes?' she whispered.

'And our child,' he reminded her. 'Yours and mine.'

'And so he went back,' Jenny wrote at the beginning of March. 'Stephen did try to have discussions with his father about farming methods and the running of the estate, but Mr Laslett is very set in his ways and is convinced that the old methods are best, and needs therefore always to be cajoled into trying something new. Stephen, of course, is the last person who would attempt to persuade anyone. Like his father he thinks he knows best, and so they were at an impasse. Also, Stephen was becoming anxious about leaving his land any longer; he hadn't prepared it for sowing in the winter before we left, and thinks that now it will be too late. Also the gypsies will soon be on the move now that winter is over, and he doesn't want to lose the dogs. That is his excuse at any rate, but I worry that he is not as well as he might be. I fear that the accident might have left him with some internal damage.

'The children and I will visit him very soon. Mr Laslett is going to buy another dogcart which will be easier to handle than the present one, and Arabella said I will be quite welcome to drive it, as she is very nervous. I need to visit Stephen to tell him the news that next winter he is to be a father again. All the more reason, he will say, for us to stay here.'

'Dr Hill to see you, ma'am.' The maid dipped her knee. 'Shall I show him in?'

'Yes please.' Jenny glanced at Arabella who was reading a fashion catalogue.

'Shall I leave?' Arabella asked. 'Is he come about Stephen, do you think?'

'I don't know,' Jenny said worriedly. 'Please, Arabella, if you wouldn't mind.' He hasn't come about me, at any rate, she thought, for I haven't told anyone yet about the child.

Arabella held out her hand to Dr Hill as they crossed in the hall. 'It's always pleasant to see you, George.' She gave a charming smile and lowered her lashes. 'You should visit us more often.'

'That's kind of you, Arabella.' He nodded soberly. 'But I fear I have little time for social calls.'

She tapped him playfully on the arm. 'Nonsense. You must make time for old friends.' She made to turn away. 'I have just remembered I have an urgent letter to write, but I shall be down shortly. Perhaps you will stay for tea?'

'Regretfully I must leave immediately I have seen Mrs Laslett.' He gave her a brief smile. 'I have many sick people to see.'

'Stephen is not ill?' she asked in concern. 'Do say he is not!'

His face closed up. 'I must speak to Mrs Laslett,' he said. 'Please excuse me.'

'Dr Hill!' Jenny greeted him anxiously. 'You haven't brought me bad news?'

'Mrs Laslett – Jenny. All is not well with Stephen,' he said without preamble. 'He asked me not to concern you, but I felt it my duty to do so.'

Jenny sat down and indicated that he should be seated. He took a chair opposite and leant towards her. 'He really shouldn't have gone back until he was recovered, but he's a very stubborn man. Always was,' he said brusquely. 'He's been working the land by himself since the gypsies left. He said that he hadn't finished ploughing before he went to work on the railway, and so he's been out day and night to finish it. Now the leg wound has opened up again and his chest is also very painful. It was quite by chance that I called to see him, and he was almost collapsed. I believe he has damaged his heart.'

'I must go straight away,' she exclaimed. 'I should have insisted at the time that I went with him.'

George Hill shook his head. 'He was determined to go alone. I don't understand him. How could he leave you here?'

'He wants 'children to stay here,' Jenny confided. 'He's afraid that they, the boys, will lose their inheritance if they leave. He doesn't want them to go through the anguish that he did.'

'We must all make our own way in life,' Hill said sagely. 'Young Johnny might not want to be a farmer.'

'Perhaps not,' Jenny said quietly. 'But then there's Thomas and–' she looked across at him and said in a low voice, 'and whoever comes after.'

'Are you caught with child again?' he asked. 'If you are, then Stephen is right. You must stay here. This will be your fifth pregnancy, Jenny.' He counted on his fingers. 'Christina. The stillbirth in '62.'

'Baby Agnes,' she reminded him.

He nodded. 'The twins in '63, Thomas in '64, and now–'

'Late autumn I think, early November. I'm young and healthy,' she emphasized.

'Yes, I agree you are. But you must look after your health. Bringing up five children in a small cottage with little income would not be easy.'

'My mother had ten living children,' she said defiantly, but as she spoke she remembered the rush to the table at meal times, the sharing of beds, the handing down of clothes, and her parents being tired and irritable and her not understanding why.

'If you stay here, you could perhaps employ a wet nurse?' he suggested. 'Mr Laslett would surely be willing to pay for one?'

'No!' Her manner was determined. 'These are my children.' Her voice dropped. 'I have nothing of my own, Dr Hill. I have no possessions. I only have my children. And of those only Christina is my own entirely.'

'Yes, I do understand. Very well. Go to see Stephen. Does he know of the child yet?' When she shook her head, he said, 'You must gauge how he is as to whether you tell him yet. It might be just the thing to make him feel better,' he paused, 'but on the other hand, it might add to his burden.'

He offered to drive her there, but she refused, saying that she would drive in the dogcart which had been delivered only a few days before. 'If I go now, will I get there before dark?' she asked.

'It's too far for the dogcart. They're fair weather vehicles. It's cold and wet and you would be soaked before you were ten minutes down the road. You mustn't catch a chill,' he urged. 'Who would look after the children then? I will take you now or you must ask Mr Laslett for the carriage tomorrow.'

If I am to be mistress here, she thought, and it is looking increasingly likely that I am, then I should assert myself. 'I'll ask for 'carriage then,' she determined. 'And if necessary we'll bring Stephen back here to recuperate.'

John Laslett insisted on accompanying her again, and she reckoned that sometimes he didn't seem quite as black as he was painted, though she knew him already to be an impatient and irritable man. But his concern for his son seemed to be genuine. 'I know we've had misunderstandings,' he said, as they travelled. 'But it's hard for me to give up what I've been doing all my working life. If Stephen would work with me, by

338

my side, if we could try again, then I'll step back a pace, once I see that he is capable of running the estate. Sometimes', he sighed, 'I could wish to take things a little easier.'

Jenny considered what Stephen had said to her about being away too long, of being out of practice at running a large holding, and she brooded that perhaps he really didn't want to come back, but was happiest where he was, being his own master.

When they arrived at the cottage gate mid-morning, a chaise was already there. 'It's Dr Hill!' Jenny said. 'He must be concerned to come again so soon.' She was anxious and perturbed and her father-in-law took her arm to steady her and stop her rushing down the path.

'He's an old friend of Stephen's,' he said. 'Don't be alarmed. It's natural that he would call.'

But she knew it to be otherwise. George Hill had been to visit Stephen only the day before. He met them at the door. His face was grave and he looked tired. 'I've been here all night,' he told Jenny wearily. 'Some impulse made me call on the way back home after seeing you.' He glanced at John Laslett. 'Would you mind waiting down-stairs, sir?' he asked as they followed him into the kitchen. The room was cold and there was no fire.

Jenny shuddered. 'Is he worse?' she whispered.

George Hill nodded. 'Yes,' he said quietly. 'I'm afraid so. You must prepare yourself, Jenny, and you too, sir,' he said to Mr Laslett, whose face had turned pale.

The doctor helped her up the stairs, for her legs had suddenly gone weak. When they reached the landing, he whispered, 'There's nothing more I

339

can do for him, apart from giving him medication for the pain. His chest was crushed during the accident and, as I said before, I fear there was some internal damage.'

'But–' Jenny held on to the doctor's arm. 'He's so strong, surely–'

He shook his head and gently propelled her into the bedroom. 'Here's your lovely wife, Stephen,' he said heartily. 'Didn't I tell you she was on her way?'

Stephen didn't move, but half opened his eyes. 'Jenny! I'm on my way too. Has George told you?' His voice was low and breathless. 'What a mess I've made of everything. Shouldn't have done that ploughing. Who'll plant the corn now?'

'Sshh,' Jenny said. 'It won't matter if you miss a year.' She blinked away her tears. Stephen's face was ashen as if he was in pain and his chest was bruised and blackened. 'Your father's downstairs,' she said. 'I'll ask him if he knows someone who can help us out.'

'Don't forget this place is Christina's,' he said hoarsely. 'Did George sign my Will?'

Jenny turned towards George Hill who nodded. 'He did,' she said, taking a deep breath. 'Weeks ago. Don't you remember?'

He gave a shuddering breath. 'No.' He swallowed and closed his eyes again. 'Best get my father up here,' he whispered. 'I want to say something to him.'

Dr Hill hurried downstairs and Jenny took hold of Stephen's hand. 'I think you should try and put 'past behind you,' she choked. 'Your father said he's willing to try again when you're better.'

340

'I'll not get better.' His breathing was shallow and she had to bend her head to hear him.

'I've something to tell you,' she murmured, close to his ear. 'Something that will make you want to get better.'

But he had closed his eyes and his father came into the room and sat by the bed, took hold of his other hand and put his head down and wept. 'Am I too late after all?' he whispered. 'Too late to say I'm sorry?'

Stephen half opened his eyes and the corners of his mouth lifted. His lips moved but no words came out.

Jenny looked in alarm at Dr Hill. 'No!' she breathed. 'No! He – he can't–' Her words failed. 'When he's rested – if I'm here to look after him,' she implored. 'Stephen! We're to have another child.'

But he didn't hear.

CHAPTER THIRTY-FOUR

'I am now a widow and mother to the heirs of the Laslett Hall estate, and as such am deemed, by two sisters-in-law, to be in an enviable position.'

Jenny dipped her pen into the ink and bent her head over her notebook. 'Maud and Laura seem not to notice that I am full of sorrow, both for myself and my babies and my unborn child who will never know its father; and also for my poor Christina who feels Stephen's loss as much as I. I am now to be both mother and father to my children. Pearl and Arabella showed every commiseration and felt the sadness of losing a brother, although I'm a little suspicious of Arabella who is more than pleased that I am to be here permanently. I do not think it's because she has gained another sister, but because, once my period of mourning is over, I shall have full charge of the household and she will be able to go out visiting friends as she has always wanted to do, except that her father formerly objected, expecting her to stay at home.

'I am once again, therefore, in a situation of being *at home,* but without that home being my very own. We have shut up Lavender Cott and brought here everything of value such as the horse and waggon and the dogs. The furniture which once Agnes and then I polished, the cups hanging on the dresser, the plates and pans in the cupboard, and the memories, have all been left, until such time as we open the doors again.' She lifted her head and gazed out of the window at the greening corn. She sighed and dipped her pen into the ink again. 'And I also left Stephen in the grave he shares with his first wife and baby Agnes.

'I brought Stephen's Will safely back with me and have explained to Christina in the simplest terms that one day Lavender Cott will be hers. She became quite excited and said that she would like to go and play in it, and pretend that she was a mama, just like me. She does tend to become very animated when she is playing games, and I tend to worry that she is very like her father. I mean her real father.

'Dr Hill visits frequently; he has become a good friend and showed real concern for me when I was very ill following Stephen's death, and he feared for the child I am carrying. I have, though, made a full physical recovery and I am quite amused and can smile a little when Arabella chatters on, surmising what she thinks is the real reason for Dr Hill's visits. I gather that she thinks he is visiting her, under the pretext of attending me.'

'I shall go out for a drive,' Arabella announced one morning. 'Perhaps you'd like to come, Jenny? It's a beautiful day. Would it be seemly, do you think? If you wore a cloak no-one would notice.'

'I'm not ashamed to be carrying a child.' Jenny spoke sharply, feeling pettish. It was not the first time that Arabella had been coy about her going out into company, and Jenny judged that within Arabella's circle of friends and acquaintances, pregnant ladies would rarely be seen. 'Where will we go? I shouldn't want to be out too long. Dolly can't manage all of the children by herself.'

'Only into Driffield.' Arabella looked into a mirror and patted her hair, which was coiled beneath a lace cap. 'I need to buy some summer material and thought perhaps we might call on Pearl whilst we're there.'

'But Pearl is expecting visitors! We shouldn't call unexpectedly.'

'Oh, but we may. She's my sister, after all. I know that she won't mind. And anyway, I have met Mr and Mrs Horsforth before, so it wouldn't matter in the least. But if they are there,' she said, suddenly smiling and jolly, 'then we won't stay more than a moment or two. We'll simply greet them and leave.'

'Who else?' Jenny knew Arabella well by now. 'Any other company?'

'Oh – only their son, I believe,' she said airily. 'He is escorting them.'

'Escorting them? So he's a grown man? Not a child or young person?'

'N-no, he is about twenty-eight or so. A banker, but without attachments.' She beamed at Jenny. 'No attachments, Jenny! Do come with me. It would look so much better if you did.'

Reluctantly Jenny agreed and pondered that if Arabella married as she wished to, then she would be left in this great house with only her father-in-law, the children and servants for company. How my life has changed, she sighed, putting on her black hat and wispy veil and fastening up her cloak. From being a town girl and kitchen maid without aspirations, apart from earning a living, to running this country house. I never dreamed, she thought, but then dismissed the notion as she often did, for the past didn't always warrant thinking of, particularly as Christy's demise had come rushing back since Stephen's death, bringing the visions and nightmares which had made her so ill.

On impulse she called to Dolly to dress Christina in her coat and bonnet so that she could come too. She liked to have the child with her, even though Dolly found it easier to handle the other children when Christina was there, as she would entertain and watch out for Johnny who was becoming more mischievous and demanding by the day.

'Shall we need more help when 'next baby is here, Dolly?' she asked when the maid brought Christina down. 'A nursery maid perhaps?'

'Yes, ma'am.' Dolly looked flustered. 'It would help. Serena and Thomas are as good as gold, but Johnny needs my full attention.'

Jenny nodded and wondered how her own mother ever managed ten children. 'I'll speak to Mr Laslett,' she said, 'and ask if we could have a young girl for you to train up.'

Her father-in-law had been a great support whilst she was ill, ordering that she was to be indulged in anything she wanted. There had been nothing that she did want, for her life, she felt, had once more been shattered, but she understood that Stephen's father was full of remorse and was somehow trying to make amends through her.

If I was a scheming kind of woman, she had considered, during the early days of widowhood, then I could demand so much. But what I want now is a secure life for my children. That will be my aim. Has always been my aim. Again she looked back, but on seeing what had been, she shut it out.

Mr and Mrs Horsforth had already arrived on their visit to Pearl and her family. Arabella pretended a great deal of embarrassment at calling so inconveniently, but as her sister knew her intentions very well, they were invited in to take coffee with the visitors. Jenny was given a comfortable chair, and didn't take off her cloak, as, she explained, they were not staying long on account of shopping. Mr Paul Horsforth came in as introductions were being made, and he was,

Jenny decided, a very personable young man with a merry grin, which clouded when he was told of Jenny's recent bereavement.

'I remember meeting your husband,' he said, taking her hand and giving a courtly bow of his head. 'It was a long time ago and I was only young. I also remember thinking how romantic it was when I heard later that you had run away together.'

There was a sudden silence and Paul Horsforth glanced round at the company, realizing that he had committed some unwitting blunder.

Jenny came to his rescue. 'That was my husband's first wife, Mr Horsforth,' she said. 'Though you can be forgiven for 'misunderstanding. Agnes, Stephen's first wife, was never spoken of or accepted by his family. It was as if–' She hesitated. 'As if by not speaking about her they could ignore the fact that she had ever existed.' She smiled wistfully. 'And yet she and Stephen spent many happy years together until her death. That can never be denied.'

'How very brave you are, Mrs Laslett,' he murmured. 'I do admire your honesty and moral strength.'

Jenny saw Arabella's mouth draw in a tight line as Paul Horsforth chose to be seated next to Jenny, and as soon as they had finished their coffee she rose with excuses that they must be on their way to finish their shopping and that Jenny's children would be waiting for them.

'Not me,' Christina piped up. She had been sitting so quietly that she was almost unobserved. 'I'm not waiting. I'm a big girl and can come out

346

with Mama and Aunt Bella. Aunt Bella hasn't got any babies,' she said. 'But we've got three, and Mama's going to have another one soon and that will make four.'

Jenny blushed and Arabella put her hand to her throat in embarrassment. Pearl gave a cough and Mrs Horsforth looked away, but Paul Horsforth smiled and patted Christina on the cheek, and offered Jenny his best wishes for the future. 'I look forward to meeting you again, Mrs Laslett,' he said.

'Indeed, yes,' his mother boomed. 'I will be glad to hear that you are over your trouble.'

Jenny dipped her knee to the older woman. 'Thank you for your concern, Mrs Horsforth, but it's no trouble at all. It will be a joy.'

'How mortifying,' Arabella gasped as they drove away. 'So – so humiliating!'

'Why?' Jenny asked, hiding a wry smile. 'Do you mean because of Mr Horsforth's mistake over Agnes, or over 'forthcoming birth?'

'Well, both!' Arabella shuddered. 'And, I have to say, that is the difference between us, Jenny! Neither of those subjects should have been discussed! Especially in front of gentlemen, and,' she added, 'I really don't think you should have told Christina about – about–' She looked down at the little girl, squashed between them. 'You know!'

'I had to tell her,' Jenny explained quietly. 'It was 'only comfort I could offer her after Stephen died. Children feel grief,' she added. 'She misses him. She misses him a lot. She has to have something to look forward to.'

As Jenny's confinement drew near at the end of

the autumn, Arabella asked if she had chosen a name for the child.

'I haven't thought of a girl's name,' Jenny said. 'And as for a boy,' she gave a sigh, 'I would have liked it to be Stephen, but as Johnny is also Stephen, that won't do. Perhaps William,' she said. 'I once had a good friend called William, though he was always known as Billy. It seems a steady sort of name.'

'It does,' Arabella agreed. 'My father's brother was called William, so it is a family name and would be very suitable.'

And so it was that William St John Laslett came into the world. He was a big baby with large hands and feet and a good-natured temperament. Dr Hill delivered him with the help of a local midwife, who, though as efficient as Mrs Burley, lacked her warmth and solicitude after a long and difficult labour.

'Women like Mrs Burley make natural midwives,' George Hill said when Jenny commented on this. 'They actually like babies.' He sat at the foot of the bed, for he had insisted that after this confinement she should take a longer bed rest than she had ever done before. 'You don't need to get up,' he had said. 'You have servants to attend you.'

He looked at her now, a week later, as she lay propped up on pillows. 'You look well, Jenny. How are you feeling?'

'Empty,' she confided. 'And alone. Stephen's family are of course pleased that I have another son, but there's no-one to share with me in 'joy of a new child. But also,' she said, turning her head to look out of the window, for from this room the view was of undulating hills and meadows scattered with sheep. 'But also—' She swallowed. 'I know that this will be my last child.' She gave a deep sigh, and then faced him, giving a sad smile. 'And yet I am still quite young, not yet four and twenty.'

He gazed at her consolingly. 'There perhaps will be someone else who'll care for you, Jenny. It's too soon to say, but there could yet be another love in your life.' He patted her hand, the pressure lingering. 'You are too young to spend the rest of your life in widowhood.'

She shook her head. There was pain in her eyes. 'I'd be too afraid.' Her mouth trembled as she spoke.

'Afraid?' he asked softly. 'Of what?'

She licked her dry lips. 'Not for myself,' she whispered. 'But for any man who might become fond of me.'

This time he took firm hold of her hand and held it. 'What nonsense is this, Jenny? What are you saying?'

'There have been two men in my life,' she said. 'Christina's father and Stephen. Both are dead.'

'I know nothing of Christina's father, but Stephen's death had nothing to do with you,' Dr Hill insisted. 'He was run down by a waggon. It was those injuries that killed him in the end.'

'But if I hadn't been there when Agnes died, he would have come home to Laslett Hall. He wouldn't have had to work on 'railway line to keep me and the children.' Her voice had risen. 'So it was my fault, just as—' She stopped and

349

took a breath.

He gave a smile and softly teased. 'And if your father hadn't met your mother, then you wouldn't have been here, and you wouldn't have met Stephen, and I wouldn't have met you, either.' His eyes held hers as he added softly, 'And we would have been so much the poorer.'

There was something in his gaze, some hint of admiration or regard, which made her stir uneasily and withdraw her hand. Her emotions were still running wild. 'All the same,' she said weakly, and immediately he became the professional medical man.

'Don't think about the future,' he said. 'You're still feeling raw and bruised; think only about the present.'

'Yes,' she murmured. 'That's all I can think about. I can't think about 'past and I can't visualize the future.'

CHAPTER THIRTY-FIVE

'It has been my own decision to stay a widow,' Jenny wrote. 'Though I have had offers of marriage. It seems to me to be inconceivable that I, Jenny kitchen-maid, as was, should be looked upon as an eligible spouse. This is not because of any qualities of my own, of course, but because of my father-in-law who is rich, and by virtue of the fact that my sons will eventually be land-owners in their own right when they inherit. At least, I trust that they will inherit, but there is no knowing how things will turn out.

'Johnny, being the eldest boy, would naturally be the favoured grandson to take over the reins of the estate, except that he shows no inclination for farming, and since he was very small has marched around the house and grounds with a stick over his shoulder, and on his head a paper hat, which Christina fashioned for him, stating quite emphatically that he is going to be a soldier. He is now thirteen, tall and with the temperament of his father and grandfather, still of the same mind, and his grandfather is becoming impatient with him.

'Thomas, on the other hand, at twelve has a quieter nature, is stockily built, and has always watched the weather, the birds, the cattle and the corn. He tells us when rain is due or when the crops are ready for harvesting, and knows all the farm hands by name. He can handle horses, make hay and stook corn, whereas Johnny can't or won't do any of these things except under sufferance.

'My youngest boy, William, is an amiable placid child, which is surprising when I think of the circumstances of his birth, when I was so lonely and unhappy, but he has been such a comfort to me over the last eleven years, soothes my humours and makes me smile.

'My darling girls are beautiful. Serena is like her name, and so unlike her twin brother. She will one day make a good marriage and I'm sure want for nothing, yet how can we tell? Christina, my very own, is a good sweet child. Well, hardly a child at sixteen, yet she has childlike qualities, innocent and trusting and not at all worldly, which worries me when I think that she might become involved with someone who admires her beauty, but doesn't understand her naivety.'

Jenny put away her pen and placed her notebook with the many others which had chronicled her life. No-one knew that she wrote them. They were for her eyes alone and contained her hopes, fears, secrets and admissions. Sometimes weeks and even months went by and she didn't write at all, but whenever she was unsure of something or a worry assailed her mind, then she took out her notebook and wrote down her difficulties. She rarely looked back through them for she feared that there might be something which she would be tempted to change or erase, and that, she thought, would be dishonest, for I am writing of my life as I see it, without embellishment or fantasy. Yet as she pondered on this, she knew she was shutting her mind to some other unease of which she didn't write.

'Mama!' Christina knocked on her door. She was a pretty girl with dark glossy hair and rounded curves, bordering on womanhood. Whenever Jenny looked at her when she was merry and smiling, she could see in her the image of her father, Christy, and was struck forcibly by a mixed pang of distress, guilt and premonition.

'Could we go to Lavender Cott, Mama? We haven't been for ages, not since before the winter. Please?' Christina looked at Jenny with pleading eyes. 'The primroses will be out in the garden, and the narcissi. And the house will need airing. It's been closed up for months.'

Jenny smiled at her daughter. What did she know about a house's wanting airing, or of sweeping away cobwebs? But perhaps it was time she was taught. At other times, when the children were small and they had been to see the cottage, Jenny had tied up her hair and put on an old apron which had been left behind the door, and had swept and dusted whilst the children had played in the orchard. Perhaps now was the time for her to take Christina alone.

'All right,' she said. 'You and I will go tomorrow. Serena and William will want to come but they must stay behind for their lessons.' All the children had had the services of first a string of governesses and then a tutor. Jenny was not too happy about having a live-in governess; she was afraid of showing her own inadequacies in front of educated young women. Mr Laslett had insisted that was how it was to be, or else, he said, the boys should go away to school. She didn't want that either, as she knew Johnny would probably run away, or get into terrible mischief if she wasn't there to control him, and Thomas and William would have been very unhappy.

'If it's just the two of us, Mama, can we ride over? Oh, please,' Christina implored. 'The weather is going to be good all of the week, Tom says so, because the mist is low over the dewponds in a morning and there are a lot of midges about of an evening.'

'Well.' Jenny laughed. 'If Thomas says so, then it must be right. But I don't know about riding such a long way,' she said dubiously. 'I'd rather go in 'trap.'

'I'll take care of you,' Christina said. 'We'll ride nice and steady.'

Christina was a good horsewoman. Since her first rides on the pony Stephen had bought her and the subsequent mounts Mr Laslett had given her, she had ridden every day she could, groomed and tended the horses herself and latterly, with Mr Laslett, whom she always called Grandpappy, had chosen the horses herself. She was faster and more efficient than her brothers or Serena, and said that if she had been a boy, her desire would have been to ride in a horse race like the one at Kiplingcotes, which was the oldest horse race in the country.

Jenny, on the other hand, was a reluctant horsewoman and had only learnt to ride so as to accompany Christina. She rode an elderly plodding mare that seemed as reluctant as she was to go off the estate and into the surrounding countryside. 'All right,' she agreed. 'If it's a nice morning, but we must set off early, for it will take hours to get there at 'pace I ride.'

Mr Laslett, now that he was old, was more crotchety than ever, and constantly bewailed the fact that he couldn't do as much as he once had. Now, when Jenny went to tell him of the intended visit to Lavender Cott he was aghast. 'Two women alone! All that way? No, it's much too far! You must take someone with you. One of the stable lads, or ask Crowther. See if he can spare somebody. You see! I don't even know all of the men's names since he took charge. Interfering women,' he mumbled.

Jenny decided to humour him. It had been her suggestion that he employ a married hind who could live at the back of the house and take on the responsibility of the farmhands, whilst his wife would do the cooking for them. When the old cook had left because of infirmity, it had been difficult to find a replacement who was willing to cook for the men as well as the family.

'We don't need anyone to accompany us,' she said, knowing all of the men would be busy. 'We know the way.'

'You might take a tumble,' he insisted. 'You're not a good horsewoman. You could break your bones and what would we do then? Arabella's no good at organizing anything. I wish she'd get herself married off! I'd give her a good dowry,' he grumbled. 'But it's too late now.'

Jenny sighed and prepared to give way. In a way it was a relief and she didn't like to upset the old man. 'We'll take 'trap, then. Will that be all right?'

'I suppose so,' he muttered. 'But get back before dark. I shall worry otherwise. Tell Arabella to come in,' he said. 'I'll not be left kicking my heels on my own and feeling useless.'

'You know very well that you're not useless,' Jenny said. 'Crowther always comes in to discuss any issues with you.'

'He doesn't listen,' he grumbled. 'Why do you want to go anyway?' he asked. 'The place must be falling down. It should have been sold years ago.'

'It's not mine to sell,' Jenny said quietly. 'It's Christina's inheritance.'

John Laslett grunted. 'I wouldn't have left her out,' he muttered. 'You know I'm fond of the child.'

'Yes,' Jenny acknowledged. 'I realize that. But

Stephen didn't know that at 'time. He didn't want her to be left with nothing.'

He looked at her, narrowing his eyes. 'And I suppose he thought I might turn you off without a copper as well, did he?'

She shook her head. 'I don't think he thought that. He knew you would want his sons, and you couldn't have them without me.' It was a bold statement but she knew it to be true.

He nodded silently, then said, 'Have you ever told Christina that she isn't Stephen's daughter? I've never heard it mentioned.'

'I – I've never tried to keep it a secret.' Jenny trembled. 'But I've never discussed it with her. There have been times when I almost did.' Times when Stephen's sisters, Laura and Maud, had intimated that Christina wasn't a proper cousin to their children, but which had been glossed over or ignored.

'Tell her,' he said bluntly. 'She's old enough to know. Time that she did. Coming up to womanhood. Better that you tell her than she find out from someone else.' He patted his fingers on his mouth and gazed at her. 'You've never said who he was. Her father, I mean,' he said. 'At least, never in my hearing.'

'No,' Jenny murmured, thinking that it was to her father-in-law's credit that he had never asked any probing questions about her past, not since she had told him that she had once been a servant. She always assumed that he wasn't interested and was greatly relieved for that. 'No-one has ever asked,' she said. 'And I've never wanted to talk about it. It was a very painful time.'

'Mmm,' he muttered. 'Well, she'll want to know, mark my words that she will, so tell her. Get it over and done with. Was he a man to be proud of?' he asked abruptly. 'A good working man?'

He would assume that, Jenny thought, knowing that I'm from a working background. On seeing her hesitation, John Laslett added, 'Not that it matters now; it's water under the bridge after all this time. But tell the girl. Prepare her.'

'The gypsies are still here!' Christina exclaimed as they turned up the track to the cottage and saw the benders in the field and the drift of smoke from the campfires. 'I would have thought they might have moved on by now.'

'Perhaps they're waiting to see us.' Jenny smiled. 'Perhaps they knew we were coming.'

'How could they know, Mama?' Christina laughed. 'They haven't got second sight!'

'Haven't they?' Jenny murmured. 'I'm not sure about that.'

Christina jumped out of the trap to open the gate. 'Here we are,' she said gaily. 'Home at last!'

Jenny felt a stab of sadness. It had been so long since they had left. Johnny, Serena and Thomas had been too young to remember and William hadn't known the house at all. Christina had good memories of it. She had been born here, her early childhood years were here, and her memories were strengthened each year when they came to visit, to make sure the thatch was sound and that there were no leaks.

'Floure is coming,' Christina called to her mother as she fastened the pony and trap securely.

Jenny looked up and saw a figure walking across the meadow towards the house. Jenny waved and Floure waved back.

'We waited for you,' the Romany said when she came up to them. 'We must move off now. The spring fairs are starting; we have horses to buy and sell. Everything is all right here, lady. There's been no trouble this winter. The people hereabouts know that we can stay on your land.'

'Yes,' Jenny said. 'We're grateful that you watch over everything.' She glanced towards the embankment. 'Have 'trains bothered you?'

Floure shook her head. 'We moved further down with our backs to them,' she said. 'They're dirty and noisy and frighten the horses.'

There were several horses grazing in the meadow and Christina eyed them keenly. 'We should get another mount for William, Mama. He's outgrown Little Prince. Look,' she said excitedly, pointing into the meadow. 'There's Jay, do you see him? The brown cob. He used to be mine,' she said to Floure. 'He was so gentle and easy to ride.'

'Yes, miss,' Floure said. 'You sold him to Mrs Crossley up on the high Wolds some time back. She's my mam's cousin; half Romany she is. She's a good hoss breeder. Goes to Appleby fair.'

'Yes, that's right, we did,' Christina said. 'I went with Grandpappy and he bought me another in exchange. Oh, Mama! Can we buy him back for William?'

Jenny told her that she would think about it. Here is my dilemma, she thought. I have to ask my father-in-law whenever I want something extra. Although John Laslett was not ungenerous with the housekeeping allowance, and Jenny kept a meticulous book of expenditure, there was certainly never enough left over to buy expensive items. He always made the decisions about those.

The Romany had been looking at Christina as they were speaking. Now she glanced at Jenny. 'She's a grown woman now,' she said to her. 'One day she'll go back to where she belongs.'

Jenny clutched her throat. She didn't know why the gypsy made her feel uneasy, but she always did, and hadn't she said the same thing to her about going back? 'She belongs with me,' she muttered. 'She's my daughter!'

Floure nodded thoughtfully. Then she smiled and turned away. 'No need to be afraid,' she said, as she departed. 'It's for the best.'

'What was she talking about?' Christina asked as they went inside the house. 'What did she mean, go back to where I belong? I belong at Laslett Hall, don't I, the same as everyone else?'

Jenny picked up a cushion from a fireside chair and shook it. A cloud of dust flew around and she wafted it away from her face before replacing the cushion on the chair and sitting down. 'I don't know what she meant, but – but you and I don't really belong at Laslett Hall, not as the others do; Johnny, Serena, Thomas and William.'

Christina took a sudden breath. 'Why? What do you mean? Of course we do.' Her eyes flickered anxiously. 'Tell me what you mean.'

'I hadn't meant to – that is, I wanted to choose a time to tell you something,' Jenny said. 'I wanted to prepare myself, and you. I thought that here would have been an ideal place, but –

I'm not quite ready.'

'For what, Mama?' Christina pulled a chair nearer to her mother and sat down, leaning anxiously towards her. 'Is it something I did when I was a child?' She pressed her lips together. 'There's always been something, I don't know what. Something that somebody said, that made me unhappy.'

Jenny swallowed hard. Just how much should she tell about Christina's real father? Should she tell how he died and what had happened to her afterwards? She looked at her daughter's trusting face. Christina had worshipped Stephen and he in turn had treated her as his very own, in fact the one and only time they had almost quarrelled was over Christina, when he had demanded to know what she would tell her.

'Lavender Cott is yours, do you realize that?' she asked Christina. 'Stephen left it to you.'

'To all of us. Yes, I remember. I asked you if I could play in it.' Christina gave a wistful smile. 'I do miss Papa, even now.'

'Not to all of you,' Jenny said quietly. 'Only to you. Not even to me.' The compensation from the railway company had eventually been paid to her, but it hadn't been very much and she had insisted, despite the doctor's reluctance, on paying George Hill what Stephen had owed him for so long. 'He wanted to be sure that you had some security.'

Christina looked puzzled. 'Because we were dependent on Grandpappy otherwise? But so are the others – so are you! Why was I singled out?'

'Because.' Jenny took a deep breath. 'Because

all the others belong to the Laslett family.' She saw the expression on Christina's face fall as she spoke. 'And you do not.'

CHAPTER THIRTY-SIX

Christina flinched as if she had been struck and tears glistened in her eyes. 'Why?' she whispered. 'Why am I not the same?'

'Because Stephen was not your father,' Jenny said softly. 'Even though in his eyes and his regard you were his daughter.'

Christina's cheeks flushed. 'I don't understand. He was always there, ever since I can remember.' Her mouth trembled. 'How can he not – I mean, if he isn't – then who is?'

Jenny hesitated. Where to begin? 'I was living here at Lavender Cott,' she said, 'and was expecting a child – you! Stephen – your adoptive papa – brought you into the world. There was no time to fetch anyone and he – you mustn't ever tell Aunt Bella or the other aunts – he was 'only one there who could help me. I shall never forget 'look on his face when he held you. An angel, he said you were.'

Christina wiped away a tear that was trickling down her cheek. 'Yes, I remember he used to call me that,' she sniffled. 'I never knew why, especially when my hair was so dark. Angels are fair.'

'Are they?' Jenny raised her eyebrows. 'Who says so?'

Christina gave a slight shrug of her shoulder. 'But if he was there at my birth, where was my real father?' She started to cry. 'I can't bear it. Papa!' She put her face in her hands and wept. 'Papa!'

Jenny came and knelt beside her and put her arm round her. 'It doesn't matter,' she said, her own voice trembling. 'He loved you as his own, that's what matters.'

'The Romany! She knew,' Christina suddenly burst out. 'How did she know? She said I would go back where I belonged!' Her manner was distraught. 'What did she mean?'

'I don't know,' Jenny admitted. 'She was talking nonsense! Floure doesn't know anything about you. She first came here when you were only a little girl. She brought her own daughter and you played together.'

'Yes,' Christina took a sobbing breath. 'I know. And I've seen her since, when I went with Grandpappy to buy horses up on the Wolds.' She swallowed away her tears. 'So he's not my grandfather either? Do I have anyone, Mama? Or is it just you and me?'

'You have just 'same people who love you as you had five minutes ago before I told you.' Jenny tried to pacify her, patting her gently. 'Everything is just 'same as it was. Only your birthright is different because you had a different father.' She got up from where she had been kneeling. 'Let's light a fire and air the place and whilst we're doing things around *your* house, I'll tell you everything you need to know.' Or almost, she thought, closing her mind on the image of her past, and her fears; for I can't tell her every single

362

thing. Some matters are best not told.

'I was very young when I first met your real father,' Jenny told her as they swept and dusted, and she mused that Christina was going about her tasks with vigour. Was it with anger at what she had discovered or because she now realized that the cottage was hers alone? 'Younger even than you are now. And I loved him right from the start.'

'Did he love you?' Christina stood with her hand to her cheek and it almost broke Jenny's heart when she saw the likeness to Christy in her.

'Yes, he did,' she said, with a catch in her voice.

'But Papa loved you too! He did. I know that he did!'

'Yes,' Jenny agreed. 'But it's possible to love more than one person.' They'd gone upstairs to dust the bedrooms and she looked out of the window and saw the embankment and the railway line, but could no longer see the grave because of it. 'Your papa – Stephen – loved someone else before me.'

'Agnes!' Christina came and stood beside her, putting her arm round her waist. 'Sometimes he took me with him to visit the grave. He told me that it was a lovely lady who had died, and that there was a baby there too, a little Agnes.'

Jenny swallowed as a lump came into her throat at the memory of the child she had lost. 'Yes,' she whispered. 'My baby.' But she couldn't speak of how she had told Stephen that that child was for Agnes. She wasn't, she grieved. She was mine, but my heart told me that to make reparation I must give her up to Agnes.

'So.' Christina swung round to look at the room.

'Papa left this to me in case his father – who isn't my real grandfather – might leave me penniless if he didn't consider me as his own kin? Which I'm not!' She took a deep breath, and Jenny, gazing at her, thought that she was already healing, now that she had something tangible to consider.

'Something of the kind,' Jenny said. 'Though your grandfather does consider you as family. He says that he'll always treat you just 'same as Serena. He took to you straight away.'

'I know!' Christina murmured. 'He does love me.'

'Well, there you are then.' Jenny's voice trembled as she controlled her innermost emotions. 'Love is the thing, after all.'

Christina asked only a few questions about her real father. His name, which Jenny told her knowing that it would mean nothing to her; where he lived, which she said was Beverley. Then, surprisingly, she asked about Jenny's parents, her maternal grandparents, whom she hadn't ever asked about before.

'I haven't seen them in years and years,' Jenny confessed. 'Not since before you were born. I wrote to tell them of your birth, and of Agnes's death; she was my mother's sister,' she added. 'And I told them of my marriage to Stephen.'

'Oh,' Christina breathed. 'So you don't know if they are alive or anything about them since then? But Mama,' she said, as Jenny shook her head at the question. 'I couldn't bear it not knowing about you! And they have all us grandchildren that they don't know about.' She became contemplative. 'They are *our* grandparents, mine and Johnny's and Serena's, and Thomas's and William's.' Her eyes glistened as she realized that she did have something in common after all with her brothers and sister.

'Did they meet my father? Your first husband?' she asked, sitting down on the bed. 'They would have been sad for you when he died. How did he die?' she asked suddenly, as if she had just thought of it. 'He must have been young too?'

Jenny put her hand to her mouth. What now to do or say? 'He was young,' she murmured through her fingers. 'There was a terrible accident. He was shot.' She turned to Christina, her eyes searching hers for any condemnation. 'And – and he wasn't my husband. We were never married.'

It wasn't condemnation that she saw, but dismay; another blow for Christina who was now discovering that she was illegitimate.

'No-one else knows,' Jenny said hastily. 'Except for Grandpappy. I told him.'

'No-one will ever want to marry me!' Christina said tearfully. 'Not when they know that I'm – I'm a–' She couldn't finish. 'I overheard Aunt Laura and Aunt Maud talking once,' she whispered. 'About someone they knew who had a baby out of wedlock, and her father sent her and the child away to an asylum.' She frowned. 'But that didn't happen to you? Or is that why you haven't seen your parents? Did you run away? Were they so shocked that they didn't want to see you ever again?'

In spite of everything, Jenny couldn't help but think wryly that here was the difference between the way she had been brought up and the way

Christina had. Her own parents had only been concerned that the house would be too crowded if she and the baby went to live with them, though her father had said she could if she wanted to.

'They were not shocked,' she said, recalling that her mother had predicted it. 'But I would have been an inconvenience. So I went away to live with Aunt Agnes who was very ill, and Stephen who needed help to look after her.

'Now,' she said, rising to her feet. 'That's enough explanation for today. Let's get on, otherwise we shan't be finished before it's time to go home.'

They drove home in near silence, Jenny trying not to think of her past, but to concentrate on the present, and Christina worrying about her future. They bowled along at a spanking pace along the quiet country lanes, between hedges of blackthorn where yellowhammers and corn bunting flew, where scrubby hawthorn showed the first scattering of white blossom and grassy banks of primroses and cowslips edged the fields of greening swaying corn.

Jenny, keeping her doubts to herself, had tried to reassure Christina that if someone really loved her, then he would want to marry her regardless of her background. 'You are the adopted daughter of Stephen St John Laslett,' she told her. 'He gave you his name. It's legal and binding.' And that is Stephen's true legacy, she thought. Worth even more than the gift of Lavender Cott, comforting though that is.

It was after eight o'clock when they reached the drive of Laslett Hall. They were later than they had intended to be, having spent so much of the day in discussion. 'There's William, Mama. Look, he really is too big for that hack. Will you ask Grandpappy about another horse or will I?' said Christina. 'Goodness! He's riding fast. He's going to come off!'

William was galloping towards them, lashing the horse with his whip to make him move faster.

'Stop, William!' Christina shouted at him. 'Don't work him so.'

'Mama! Mama! I've been waiting and waiting for you. Come quick!' William's face was flushed with exertion and creased with anxiety. He almost fell off the horse as he reached them. 'Hurry!'

'What's happened? Somebody's hurt? Oh, who? William, tell me!'

'No. No! Nobody's hurt or anything, but come quick.' He snuffled back tears. 'Johnny's run away!'

'What! Run away! No. Surely not. You must be mistaken, William.' Jenny stared at her youngest son. 'It's a prank! Johnny wouldn't do that.'

'He has! Grandpa is *furious*. He says he will give him the strap when he finds him!' He pressed his lips together as he stared fearfully at his mother. The boys had never had the strap. Jenny wouldn't allow it and it had caused some dissension between her and John Laslett. 'He's saddled up his horse and gone out to look for him.'

'How do you know he's run away?' Jenny asked. 'He wouldn't have told anyone if he was going to do that!'

'He didn't come in for supper and Grandpa sent Serena upstairs to look for him!' He bit again on his lips, drawing blood. 'He'd left her a letter and another one for you. Only Serena won't let Grandpa read it or tell what it says, except that he's run away! She says she'll only tell you, and Grandpa was really cross with her and you're so late, Mama, and we've been waiting and waiting!'

Christina shook the reins and they continued up the drive with William trotting alongside them, relating snippets of information about how their grandfather wouldn't let any of them have any supper until he had come back with Johnny, and how they all had to go to their rooms.

'Only I saw you coming,' he said. 'I was watching out for you. I'm starving hungry,' he added, 'though Dolly brought us some cake after Grandpa had gone out.'

Jenny wasn't unduly worried. Johnny was such a harum-scarum boy. He's probably gone off with some of the local lads, she thought. Though it was unlike him to leave a note to say where he was going. He didn't usually do that. She sighed. This would again raise the question of his going away to school, which John Laslett was constantly saying was the only way to tame him.

Serena was waiting for her in the hall. Like Johnny she was tall and slender, but her normally calm and untroubled countenance now wore a worried frown. She held an envelope in her hand, which she gave to her mother, and pulled another, opened one from her skirt pocket.

'What's all this about, Serena?' Jenny asked. 'Johnny hasn't really run away, has he? He's just gone off on some prank?'

''Fraid not, Mama.' Serena glanced from her mother to Christina, whose hand rested on

William's shoulder. She looked down at her letter and then handed that too to Jenny. 'He's been talking about it for weeks as a matter of fact, ever since Grandpa said he would send him away to school if he didn't confirm – I mean conform.'

Jenny opened the scrap of paper and saw Johnny's bold hand and poor spelling. 'Dear Serena,' it said. 'Be a good sport and try to keep this secret 'til Mama gets home. I don't want Grandpa to come after me, as I know he will when he hears. I'm off to be a sodger. Much love, your twin, Johnny.'

She breathed hard and, passing the letter to Christina, she opened the one addressed to 'Mama'.

'Dearest Mama,' she read. 'Please don't be angry with me, but I don't want to be a farmer. Thomas or William can have my place instead. I'm going off to be a sodger and fight the Rushans or Afghans or even the French if they like. It's what I want to do. I'll write to you as soon as I'm signed up and in uniform. I shall soon be an officer I expect, so you'll be proud of me. PS. You don't need to worry about me getting shot at as I've been practising with the guns that we use for the rooks, and I've quite a good aim now. Your ever loving son, Johnny.'

Dolly came rushing down the stairs. 'I'm sorry, Mrs Laslett,' she said. 'I didn't know that he'd gone until suppertime. He must have left just after you and Miss Christina went out.'

'Not your fault, Dolly.' Anxiety swept over her. 'But wasn't he missed from his lessons?'

'His tutor didn't come today. He sent a note to

say he was unwell.' A Mr Bradbury from Driffield had coached Johnny for the last year, as the governess had said Johnny was now too old for her to teach.

Jenny nodded. The young varmint must have been waiting for such an opportunity to arise so that he could escape. 'Where do you think he's gone, Serena?'

'To be a soldier, Mama,' she said patiently. 'Like it says on the letter!'

'Yes, I know that! But where would he go first, do you think?'

William was reading the letter over Christina's arm. 'Well, there are no Russians around here!' he said. 'That's a fact. And no Afghans either, so maybe he's gone to Driffield.'

'Don't be so silly, William,' Serena scolded. 'Of course he hasn't gone to Driffield! There are no soldiers there. Except for the militia.'

'He has gone to Driffield.' Thomas's voice came from the doorway. He was windswept and muddy. 'He cadged a lift to Driffield this morning, then he was going to catch a train to York. I saw him go but he said I hadn't to tell anybody 'til later, and then I could be the farmer 'stead of him.'

The door crashed open again and Mr Laslett burst in, almost falling over Thomas. 'Damn and blast it,' he said. 'I've looked all over the area for him and now somebody's just said they saw him this morning in a carrier's cart heading for Driffield!' He sat down heavily in the nearest chair and the children, Serena, Thomas and William, surreptitiously edged their way out of the hall. 'Fetch me a glass of ale,' he bellowed at Dolly.

'I'm parched. Fair worn out. I'm too old to go chasing about the countryside.'

'You shouldn't have gone,' Jenny reprimanded. 'Not on your own. Where's Arabella? She shouldn't have allowed you to go!'

'I'm not some young farm hand you gels can order about,' he roared. 'The boy's run off and I'm intent on finding him! He'll have a taste of the strap before I'm finished with him.'

'Please don't shout,' Jenny implored. 'My son has run away and I need to think. And when we find him, *if* we find him, he will not be strapped! His father wouldn't have strapped him and neither will you!'

He glared at her and then demanded, 'So what did he say in the letter? That young miss wouldn't tell me!'

'She wouldn't tell you because she knew you would be angry,' Jenny said wearily. 'Johnny doesn't want to be a farmer so he's gone to be a soldier.'

CHAPTER THIRTY-SEVEN

They sent a messenger to York, but there was no trace of Johnny. He had simply disappeared. He was under age for the army, but he was tall and had a confident manner belying his thirteen years.

'Once they've got their hands on him, they'll not let him go, even if we could find him,' John Laslett stated gloomily. 'They'll send him off to the ends of the earth. Balkans, Austria, and mark my words the Russians are ready to go to war over Turkey.' He leant his chin in his hands. 'There'll be some bloodshed before the year is out.'

'They'll not send a young boy out there?' Jenny said fearfully. It was three weeks since Johnny had left and there had been no word of him. 'They surely won't!'

'He'll have given a false name and lied about his age. That's what these young lads do.' The old man sighed. 'His father wanted to be a soldier when he was young and I wouldn't let him go. Didn't want him getting killed in some foreign land.'

Jenny left the room. She couldn't bear to think that her son had gone away and that she might never see him again.

'He'll be all right, Ma.' Thomas was standing in front of the hall fire. Like his grandfather he always kept his boots on, though Jenny had banned him from wearing them in the dining or sitting room. 'He'll probably be doing something boring like marching or drilling, and you know Johnny, if he doesn't like it then he'll come home again.'

'But if he's joined the army, he can't just leave,' Jenny said desperately. 'They'll come and get him!'

'Well then, if they find him and he won't go back, then they'll hang him,' Thomas declared. 'He'd have been better staying at home with us. Come on,' he called to the dogs, who got up from the rug to follow him. There were always two dogs, although not the same two that had been there when Jenny had first come here. 'Let's be off.'

She sat down in the old rocking chair that was placed by the fire and gazed into the flames. Thomas was always practical and stated the obvious, but it hadn't helped one little bit.

Arabella, in a caped coat and neat veiled hat and murmuring that she was going visiting, floated past her towards the door, then turned and said, 'Try not to worry, Jenny dear. Johnny can look after himself,' before patting her hat and going out.

Arabella spent a good deal of time visiting. Since Jenny had come to live at Laslett Hall, Arabella had enjoyed socializing. She met friends for luncheon, and went out for afternoon tea and supper. She often invited them back and Jenny was always included, but, trying not to appear rude, she always found some excuse for not joining in the ladies' company or conversation. She knew what gossips they all were, and how they liked to know who was who and what was what, and she had no wish for them to probe into her background.

She thought that Arabella tacitly understood this, for she never made any attempt to persuade Jenny to attend when she obviously didn't want to. 'But you don't mind if I invite them here, do you, Jenny? It's the only pleasure I get,' she had said mournfully. 'I know that I won't find a husband now, I'm too old, so I must make the most of my female companions.'

'It's your home, Arabella,' Jenny had told her. 'If you want to invite your friends then of course you should.' But she had known that what Arabella really meant was would Jenny organize

373

the tea or supper; ask Cook to make cakes or biscuits, and come in at exactly the right time for the ladies to get up and make their departures.

She also gathered that Arabella's friends had initially questioned her about her reclusive sister-in-law who had tragically lost her husband, leaving her with five children. That they knew her background was different from theirs was obvious for she retained her Hull accent, but as they were mostly from farming backgrounds and some had an East Riding accent themselves, that was of no account. She could have been the daughter of a ship's chandler or fish merchant, a shopkeeper or mill owner for all they knew, and that was what made them curious. Arabella simply told them that Stephen had met her when she was very young, but that she knew no more than they. Now, so many years had passed that they no longer showed any interest, and merely passed the time of day with her or discussed the weather.

I was the same age as Johnny when I left home to go to work in Beverley, she mused as she rocked. I too lied about my age. I told Mrs Feather I was fourteen when I was only thirteen. And, she deliberated, if Johnny had been brought up as I was, then he would have been expected to go to work at thirteen or even before. I wonder if Ma and Da worried about me? I rather think they didn't, but then – she gave a sigh – I look at life so differently now.

'Mama!' Serena came to her a few weeks later. 'Can I talk to you please?'

'Now? Don't you see I'm busy?' The furniture in the sitting room had been moved to the centre of

374

the room and was covered in white cloths, and Jenny was in earnest conversation with the painter who had come to start painting and wall-papering. Jenny and Arabella had chosen a dark red flocked wallpaper and velvet curtains to match. This was the first time that any major decorating had been done since Jenny had come to live at Laslett Hall and she counted it a considerable triumph that she had persuaded her father-in-law to agree to it.

'Please, Mama. I need to talk to you whilst it's all in my head and before I change my mind.' Serena looked at her mother appealingly and Jenny gave her a quick smile. She looked so pretty. She was dressed in a white starched cotton blouse and a pale blue ankle-length skirt with a frilled hem, and her hair was tied up with a blue ribbon.

'Where did you get 'skirt?' Jenny asked when she joined Serena in the hall five minutes later. 'Is it one of Christina's?'

'Yes, I've been trying on some of her things. She said that I could. She said I could keep this one, but I need to alter it. Look.' She showed the waistband, which was too big for her. 'I need to take it in.'

Serena did not have her older sister's curves and Jenny thought that she probably wouldn't. Both she and Johnny favoured their father's lean build.

'Mama, you know that Grandpa was always telling Johnny that he should go away to school? He made it sound like a sort of punishment, which was why Johnny didn't want to go.' She sat down on the rug with her skirt draped round her feet, as her mother sat in a chair. 'But if he'd allowed Johnny to go to military school as he wanted to, then he would have gone.'

'Wh-what do you mean? Johnny never told me that he wanted to go to military school!'

'That's because Grandpa told him that it was all nonsense and he hadn't to bother you with such ideas because he was meant to be a farmer.'

Wouldn't you have thought that Mr Laslett would have learned from experience? Jenny fretted. His son wanted to be a soldier and wasn't allowed to and now his grandson wanted the same; and all he has ever achieved is separation from both of them. 'If I'd known, Serena, I would have talked to Johnny about it.' She felt tearful and angry too that her son had been forced to make his own decision without discussing it with his own mother.

'Well, that's what I told him, but he didn't want to upset you, and he knew that Grandpa would make the final decision anyway, seeing as we live here with him. Johnny said we had no money of our own and there would be fees to pay at military school.'

Jenny was silent. So the children had worked it out. At least Johnny, Serena and Christina had. Thomas and William probably hadn't realized yet that their grandfather paid for everything they had or enjoyed: clothing, food, horses, dogs. They had much to be grateful for, of course, and Jenny asked for very little for herself. She had always made her own clothes and those for the children when they were small, buying material and sewing cottons from the packman when he called. Now Serena and Christina did their own sewing.

'So.' Serena glanced at her anxiously. 'I wanted

to discuss something with you. If you say I can't, I promise I won't run away like Johnny did.'

'Oh!' Jenny stroked her daughter's head. 'I hope not. Whatever would I do without you? Bad enough to lose one twin without the other going as well.'

Serena's expression dropped slightly. 'Well, it wouldn't be losing me exactly.'

'What wouldn't?' Jenny frowned. What was Serena going to ask?

'I'd like to go away to school!'

'But you've had an education!' Jenny said. 'You have always done so well. Better than any of the others. Why would you want to go away to school?'

'Not just any school.' Serena took a deep breath. 'Abroad. I'd like to go abroad.'

'But why?' Jenny was flabbergasted. 'You wouldn't understand what they were talking about! Not with 'scrap of French you've been taught.'

'Let me explain, Mama.' Serena gave her mother a very grown-up smile. 'When we were at Aunt Pearl's a few weeks ago – do you remember, we went to tea and all our cousins were there? Well, we – the girls – went off into the garden,' she said, as her mother nodded. 'And Cousin Alice was asking about Johnny and had we heard from him – she's a bit sweet on him, I think – and then she told us that a friend of hers was going away to school in Switzerland. She was going to learn French and German and how to be a lady.'

'Goodness,' Jenny said. 'Can you learn to be a lady? I didn't know that you could.' But why not? She mused. It's possible to learn most things.

'Yes – and?'

'Well, that's what I would like to do,' Serena said earnestly. 'I would like to learn to be a lady. I've got a very ladylike kind of name, haven't I? Serena St John Laslett. It sounds very ladyish, don't you think?' She put her head to one side and lowered her lashes. 'Perhaps that's why you chose it?'

'No,' Jenny said slowly, 'your papa and I chose your name because it suited you. You were a very serene baby, unlike Johnny, who was the opposite! And Mary as your second name after your grandmother.'

'I wish I could remember Papa,' Serena said softly. 'Christina can remember him. She said he was very kind and loving. Not a bit like Grandpa.'

'He was very *much* like your grandfather,' Jenny assured her. 'And your grandfather is also kind and loving! He wouldn't have us all here under his roof if he wasn't,' she said sternly. 'He could lead a much quieter life without us all.'

Serena was chastened. 'Of course he could. I'm sorry. I didn't mean that he *wasn't* kind or loving. So I suppose you'd have to ask him if I could go? Because he would have to pay for it?'

'Yes, that's it exactly,' Jenny said. 'He has never grumbled about the expense of us all, but neither have I ever been extravagant, and I think he appreciates that. I'll ask his opinion. But don't build up your hopes too much.'

'And you haven't enough money then, Mama?' Serena shook her head in anticipation of the answer. 'I suppose if we didn't have Grandpa, then I'd have to go to work as a servant girl like the maids in the kitchen?'

Her mother smiled, and then gave a laugh. 'Indeed you would, Serena. Now wouldn't that be a terrible thing?'

'Dreadful!' Serena exclaimed. 'I couldn't bear it if I had to work all day as they do and have hardly any time off. No, I really must be a lady, Mama, and marry someone rich. Someone even richer than Grandpa so that I can travel to Europe and go to London for the balls and parties and such.'

'You're too young to even think about that,' Jenny admonished her. 'And probably too young to go away to school. I'll talk to Aunt Bella about it, see what she thinks.'

'Aunt Bella! How would she know?' Serena was scornful. 'She hasn't ever been away to school. I don't suppose she's even been to London!'

'She'll know more than I do,' her mother replied. 'She'll know if it's proper for you to go when you're so young – that is if Grandpa agrees.'

'But you wouldn't mind, Mama?' Serena asked anxiously. 'If he says yes?'

Jenny considered. Why not? Serena wants to spread her wings just as I did at her age. It's just that her sights are on bigger and much grander things than mine ever were. Her horizons are wider, and she has greater expectations. I only hope, oh how I do hope, that fate doesn't deal her as hard a blow as it did me.

'Mama? Would you mind? Would you be unhappy if I went away?'

'I should miss you,' Jenny said. 'Just as I miss Johnny. But at least I'd know where you were.' She took a deep breath. 'Not knowing where

379

Johnny is is a terrible worry. But if you really do want to go, then I wouldn't stand in your way.' She smiled at the delight on Serena's face. 'Don't start counting your chickens,' she said. 'Your grandfather will probably say no!'

She discussed it first with Arabella, for it was quite true that Arabella knew more about society's rules than she did. She had been brought up in a household where ladies were expected to marry well. Unfortunately, as her own mother had died before Arabella was of marriageable age, she hadn't been given the opportunity.

'She should certainly go,' Arabella declared. 'It was what I would have liked to do. Pearl never wanted to and Father said that Maud couldn't, because she wouldn't fit in, but Laura went away to school. Though,' she added thoughtfully, 'I'm never quite sure if it did her any good, for she came home and married a farmer anyway.

'Would you be happy about it, Jenny? It's not what you were used to, is it? I suppose all of your brothers and sisters stayed at home until they were married?'

'They all had to work,' Jenny explained. 'The girls as well as the boys, but they lived at home. I left home at 'age Serena is now,' she confided. 'I was 'youngest girl in 'family. I could see which way 'wind was blowing and just like you I thought I'd have to stay at home and look after everybody.'

'So you left!' Arabella breathed. 'How very brave of you, Jenny. But what did your mother say? Did she agree to your leaving?'

'I didn't tell her,' she admitted. 'I found a – a position, and told her afterwards. My father said

I could leave if I wanted to.' This was more information than she had ever given her sister-in-law and she felt she was treading on unstable ground. 'So, yes, I think Serena could go.' She switched the discussion back to Serena. 'But I'd rather she waited a little longer, maybe until the end of 'summer, and maybe', she sighed, 'by then we might have heard from Johnny.'

John Laslett humphed and hawed, grunted and prevaricated as he considered the question. 'Is it what *you* want?' he asked Jenny. 'She'll change. You might lose the daughter you thought you had!'

'It's what she wants,' Jenny said. 'It's her life, not mine. She already has a different life from 'one I knew when I was a child.' Except that I wasn't a child, she thought. I was on my way to being grown up, and maybe Serena is too.

He observed her from where he was sitting by the fire, his booted feet perched on a footstool. 'And does that worry you?' he asked. 'You're not afraid that the gap between you will become too great? You realize that she'll be mixing with people from a different society.'

'You mean am I afraid that she will be shamed or embarrassed by her mother? No, I'm not afraid of that,' she said softly. 'I think I've taught my children to treat all people equally. They say please and thank you to the servants as well as to others.' She said this with a deal of irony, for John Laslett did not always. The servants, in his eyes, were there to work and fetch and carry on his behalf, and rarely were they thanked for it. If they displeased him then they were given notice, which was why his workers didn't stay with him for more than their yearly tenure. 'And if she is, then it will be a loss to both of us.'

He nodded thoughtfully. 'Let's wait a month or two,' he said. 'And if she's still in the same mind, then yes, I think she should go.'

CHAPTER THIRTY-EIGHT

'Gramps! If Serena is going away to Switzerland, could I have some pigs? Please.' William looked up earnestly at his grandfather. 'I don't think they would cost as much, and I could probably pay you back when I've made a profit.'

'What has Serena to do with pigs?' his grandfather objected. 'I don't see how the two go together!'

'Well, it's just that if Serena is going away to learn to be a lady and Thomas is going to be a farmer now that Johnny's not here, then I'd like to keep pigs.'

'We grow crops and keep sheep and cattle. Why should we want pigs?' John Laslett stared quizzically at William.

'No. Not we!' William explained patiently. 'I'd like some of my *own*. I know there's a score over at Mr Dobson's farm and Mr Elliot has half a dozen, but I'd like to breed some myself.'

'Ah!' John Laslett scratched his beard. 'And do you intend selling any of these pigs, or will you be keeping them for home consumption?'

'I thought I'd have two sows for breeding,' William clarified, 'and when they've farrowed I'd keep one piglet for fattening for the kitchen, or maybe two, and sell the others at Driffield market when they were ready. But I intend to start small and build up gradually. I like pork,' he said solemnly, 'but I don't think there's been the flavour lately.'

'I see,' his grandfather said wryly, and raised his eyebrows. 'So what will you feed these pigs on to give flavour? Always supposing I agree!'

'Well.' William put his hands behind his back and expounded. 'Mama said that when she and Papa lived at Lavender Cott, they kept a pig in the orchard. It grubbed about in there and lived mostly on fallen apples, and I thought that was *such* a good idea! But I thought that I'd fatten mine on barley and scraps from the kitchen as well, and we've got *loads* of apples in the orchard, so that would give a really nice taste. Course,' he continued, looking serious, 'there'd be loads of pig shit, but then that could go on the vegetable garden.'

John Laslett put his hand over his mouth, but his eyes twinkled. 'And you'd clear that up, would you? Your aunt Bella wouldn't like walking in the orchard amongst that!'

A crease appeared above William's nose. 'She wouldn't, would she? I hadn't thought of that! Well, I'd have to clean it out and let her go in say just once a week.'

'The sow, you mean?'

'No! Aunt Bella.'

'It seems,' said John Laslett, as he came into the

sitting room later that day, 'that we have a pig breeder on our hands, as well as a farmer and a lady.'

Jenny was sitting with Serena and Christina and looked up with a happy smile on her face. 'And a soldier.' Her voice broke. 'We've just heard that Johnny is safe and well.' She put her hand to her mouth and swallowed and began to explain. 'Johnny wrote to his cousin Alice and enclosed a letter for Serena. He was too nervous to write here in case we tried to fetch him back. Alice kept the letter hidden until today when her mother discovered it and brought her over with it.'

'Cousin Alice didn't think to send it on to me,' Serena said. 'The silly girl is so besotted with Johnny she didn't want to get him into trouble. She was waiting for me to go and visit.'

'Never mind all that!' her grandfather bellowed, making her jump. 'Is the boy all right? Has he signed up for the army?'

Serena nodded. 'I'll read it, shall I, Mama?'

At her mother's assent, she started to read aloud. '"Dear Serena, I'm sorry I've taken so long to write to you, but there's not much time for such pleasures. It's marching and drilling and shooting practice and being sworn at, and all other things that you wouldn't appreciate being a girl, so that all I want to do is sleep at the end of the day. Some of the other fellows go out chasing girls and drinking, but that doesn't interest me greatly at the moment, though I've had to pretend that it does, otherwise they'll cotton on that I'm not as old as I've made out.

'"I've decided that I'm going to work really

hard and stick this out for a twelvemonth, then confess my age and apply for a commission. I've discovered that I'd not be able to go up through the ranks as quickly as I'd thought; but in twelve months I'll be old enough to apply for military school. They select and promote officers on merit now and not on purchase. It's a hard life but I'm determined to see it through. Please give my love to everybody, Christina and Thomas and William, and Aunt Bella, but especially Mama, and Grandpa too and tell them I'm sorry I had to do it this way. Oh, by the way, I miss you too. Your twin, Johnny.''

John Laslett blew hard on his handkerchief and Christina wept into hers. 'Well, he's safe,' he said gruffly. 'Does he say where he is?'

'Y-yes.' Serena glanced at her mother and then down at the letter in her hand.

'It's all right,' her grandfather said. 'I'll not fetch him back. I just thought I'd write to him, tell him how we're getting on, and that if he ever wants to come back, then he can.'

There was a silence whilst they digested this unexpected pronouncement, then Serena said in a quiet voice, 'He's in London, Grandpa, and I thought that when I go away I could call to see him, on my way to Dover, I mean.'

'Yes. Yes, of course. If they allow it,' her grandfather muttered. 'Don't want him breaking any rules.' He sighed, and as he caught sight of Christina wiping her eyes, he turned to her. 'And what about you, young lady? Do you want to go off and leave us too, or are you content with this simple life?'

She shook her head. 'No, thank you, Grandpappy. I'm quite grown up anyway, and although I can't speak French or German, which Serena will learn, I don't think I'll have the need for it. Besides, I'd rather stay here with everyone that I know. I don't really want to live with strangers.'

'Mmm,' he said. 'Good. Because we don't want to lose everybody, do we, Jenny?'

Jenny blinked. She'd been wrapped in a reverie as they were speaking, wondering what life did have in store for her eldest daughter. She had Lavender Cott as her own, and she would be for ever grateful to Stephen for that, but what Christina really needed was a kind and gentle husband who would take care of her. Christina wasn't self-confident or assured like Serena and the boys were, and that's my fault, she mused. I've always been so protective of her, even since before she was born. A sudden flash of recollection seared her mind and she battled to repress it as her father-in-law spoke.

'So, I think you should take her about more,' he was saying. 'Go off to York for a day or two. Bella will go with you. She'd like that. She's a bit of a gadabout. Or take the carriage and go to Beverley. You'd have a nice day out there. Might even come with you myself.'

'Take – Christina, did you say?' Jenny asked. 'Sorry, I didn't quite catch–'

'Yes,' said the old man. 'After Serena has gone off, take Christina out to meet people.' He looked across at Christina and said wryly, 'Your mother must look around to find you a suitable young fellow for a husband. How would that be?'

'Do you want to marry me off, Grandpappy?' Christina said, her voice low. 'Because I don't really belong to you, do I? Not like the others do.'

'What?' John Laslett looked shaken. 'Of course you do! No, not in blood, that's true, but come here.' He put his arms out to her, and with sudden tears springing to her eyes she came towards him. He put his arm about her and kissed her forehead. 'Don't let me hear such nonsense again,' he said gruffly. 'Of course you belong.'

'Mama! What?' Serena looked stunned. 'What does she mean? Not belong!' Her voice dropped. 'Christina! Why do you say that?'

John Laslett turned to Jenny in astonishment. 'Do you mean you haven't told them? Good God, woman! Why ever not?'

Jenny bent her head. 'There never seemed to be a right time. We – Stephen – always treated Christina as if she belonged to him. And because he wasn't here when 'children were growing up, there didn't seem to be any need to say anything. They didn't know him, after all,' she said, raising her head and glancing from Christina to Serena.

'I have a different father from you,' Christina told Serena. Her eyes were moist and a tear trickled down her cheek. 'He died before I was born, so I never knew him. But Papa – Stephen – I do remember him and I know that he loved me.' She put her fingers to still her trembling lips. 'And I loved him and I still miss him.'

Serena gazed at her sister open-mouthed. 'So, does that mean you're not a St John Laslett?' she asked. 'Do you have another name?'

'No,' her mother said firmly. 'Your father

387

adopted Christina, so she has 'same name.' Jenny could almost feel Serena's busy mind working and knew there would be more questions, so she forestalled her. 'So, Serena, you can write and tell Johnny if you wish, and I'll tell Thomas and William, and then it's done with. It was never a big secret,' she said calmly. 'It never seemed anything to make a fuss about.'

But nevertheless she was relieved that it had been told, and in the following two weeks, in the scramble to prepare Serena for her journey abroad, there was no time for chatter or awkward questions. The children had never asked about her own background. She thought they probably assumed that she had been at Laslett Hall for ever, just as they had been, for of course the twins and Thomas couldn't remember living anywhere else, and William had been born here.

Serena was to be accompanied by her grandfather and Arabella on the journey to London. They were driving by carriage to York, where they would catch the railway train to London. Surprisingly, this would be the first time that John Laslett had ever travelled by train, and he would only agree to it if he could travel to the capital directly rather than change trains at various other stations.

Serena was to be met in London by a representative from the Swiss school, along with other young ladies who would travel with them. Jenny had declined the journey. 'I shall be too upset, Serena,' she said to her. 'Bad enough to see you off from here, without watching you disappear with strangers.'

'I expect I shall have to look after Grandpa

anyway.' Serena smiled. 'I think he's quite nervous about the train journey. I can't understand him,' she said. 'It's just the only way to travel.'

'It's strange,' her mother agreed. 'He's agreeable to using up-to-date machinery on the farms, yet he's always refused to travel by railway. But he's getting older, Serena, we must remember that. He thinks 'old ways are best.''

He needs help on the estate, too, she pondered. It's going to be years before Thomas and William can take over from him. He needs somebody he can trust to manage it until the boys are ready, so that he can take life easier. I'll talk to him about it when he returns from London.

After seeing Serena off with her escort, Arabella and her father were going to stay in London for a few days with his sister, which was the real reason why Jenny had decided not to go with them. She knew they would have plenty to discuss, as they hadn't seen each other for many years, and once more she was reluctant to speak of her own background if anyone should enquire.

She bade a tearful farewell to Serena. It was early, only just past seven o'clock, but John Laslett had been jittery and wanted to be off in good time to get to York. 'Damned trains!' he'd snorted. 'You've got to be there by a certain time or you miss them! They won't wait for you, you know. Not like a carriage that's standing by the door until you're ready! Where's my hat?' he demanded. 'And my stick! Come on. Come on. Say goodbye to your mother and let's be off!'

So the goodbyes were hurried and Jenny, Christina, Thomas and William, and Dolly too, stood on the steps waving until the carriage turned out of the long drive and onto the road. Thomas and William looked sideways at each other and nonchalantly started to move away down the steps.

'And where are you two off to?' Dolly asked. Over the years and almost without arrangement, Dolly had slid into the role of housekeeper and nanny to the growing children. Her existence seemed to be wholly for them, for there had never been any sign of her wanting to live another life of her own. 'Breakfast and then upstairs to your lessons! Mr Pearson will be here soon.'

'Oh, but Dolly! He won't be here yet. He never gets here before nine!' William whined. 'I have to go and look at my pigs.' His grandfather had agreed that he could have two sows in litter and he spent all his spare time cosseting them.

'And I've jobs to do before I start on my books,' Thomas complained. 'Ma!' he pleaded. 'Can't we go? Just for half an hour. Then we promise we'll go up.'

Jenny nodded at Dolly. 'Half an hour, then, Dolly.' She didn't like to usurp Dolly's authority. The former nursemaid was so very good, yet firm with them. 'But no longer than that.'

Christina put her arm through her mother's. 'Let's take a walk in the garden,' she said. 'It's such a beautiful morning.'

Jenny agreed that it was. Though there were clouds chasing across the sky, they were lit from behind by the sun's morning brightness, which reflected on the autumn tints of the leaves of elm and oak, still clinging determinedly on to the

390

trees. The summer had been lovely. The flora on the chalk pastureland had flourished, and the air had been filled with birdsong. The weather had been mostly hot with very little rain and although the farmers complained that their crops needed more water, the harvest had been good and the sheep and cattle thrived.

Now they were rewarded by a richness of colour across the land, the pale glow of the harvested fields, the berries on the hawthorn hedges turning to scarlet, the green casing of the horse chestnut spilling out its burnished deep brown nut onto a crisp russet carpet. The fruit trees were heavy with rosy apples and juicy pears, and there was a pungent smoky aroma of bonfires as the workers on the land prepared for the coming winter.

'I'm missing Serena already,' Christina moaned. 'And she's not been gone half an hour. It will be so strange without her. I've only just got used to Johnny not being here.'

'I know,' Jenny said quietly. 'It feels odd that she's not here, that neither of them are. I always felt that while Serena was at home, then Johnny would eventually come back. Now I don't know if either of them will. They'll experience so much more whilst they are away. Life here will seem very dull to them.'

'Oh, don't say that, Mama! Surely they'll come back?' Christina clung to her mother's arm. 'Won't we be a family again?'

'We'll always be that,' her mother assured her. 'But young people grow up and leave home. You'll do that too, Christina. One day you'll perhaps meet someone and want a home of your own.'

'Is that what you wanted, Mama?'

Wanted? Jenny thought. Don't I want that still? For this isn't my true home. It's the place where I live with my children. It's my children's home, but I'm here because of them. If Stephen had lived, would I feel the same way? Would we have made this our home together?

'It was different for me, Christina,' she answered. 'My wants were not 'same when I was young like you. I had no expectations; I handled life as it came.'

'I don't understand,' Christina said, puzzled.

'No,' Jenny murmured. 'I don't suppose you do.'

When John Laslett and Arabella returned home a week later, Arabella burst through the door like a girl, filled with excitement at what she had seen and done, and although her father was tired after the long journey, he admitted that the train ride had been exhilarating, if exhausting. 'It's very noisy and dirty, of course, as I always said it would be,' he said, justifying his previous opinion. 'But my word, the people who travel! Why, every man and his wife were travelling by train, all bustling about. They even had a special van for horses! But, yes, it was an experience, and, I admit, much quicker than by road. Yes,' he mused. 'The last time I went to London in the carriage, one of the wheels cracked and it took us a day to get it fixed. That wouldn't happen on the railways, I don't suppose. But there, I've done it now. No need to do it again.'

'And Serena?' Jenny asked, anxious to know. 'Tell me if she was all right. Not upset at going away?'

'Come here, my dear, and sit by me.' He sat down in his usual chair in the hall, and Arabella, with a quick smile and a nod of agreement, turned to go upstairs to change out of her travelling clothes.

'Serena is fine. She'll do well. We couldn't have managed the journey without her. Bella has no head for timetables, and getting porters and suchlike. I want to tell you something.' He reached for her hand. 'We've seen Johnny! Yes.' He patted her fingers as she drew in a gasping breath. 'Serena had told him where we were meeting her escort, and we arrived early as she requested, and Johnny was there. Came to see her off. I was proud of him.' He dropped his voice, which had become husky. 'Very proud. He looked tremendous. Tall and straight. Good-mannered. He'll do well as an officer. I told him that I would write to his commanding officer when the time was right and give him a personal recommendation.'

'Oh, I wish I'd been there,' Jenny wept. 'I should have gone. I would have so liked to see him. Did he get my letter?'

'He did, and he was sorry that you weren't there. But he said he'll write to you soon. You don't have to worry about him, Jenny,' he soothed her. 'Nor Serena either. They're not children any more. They're out in the world on their own feet.'

Just as I was. Jenny wiped away a tear. Just as I was.

CHAPTER THIRTY-NINE

'How do, Billy!'

'Middlin', Harry!' Billy Brown said. He stood outside his shop window with his arms crossed over his white apron. 'How's thissen?'

'Champion!'

'Family all right? Lad coming along?'

'Aye. Pretty fair.' Harry paused. 'He's a good lad wi' hosses, I'll say that for him.'

Henry Johnson, or Harry as he was always known, had married a widow just a little older than himself. She had brought with her to their marriage two children and a considerable amount of money left to her by her late husband. The new Mrs Johnson had an eye for business and Harry was persuaded to set up on his own as a farrier, rather than work for someone else. During the course of his work he had come across several horses which were for sale at a good price, and being a fine judge of horseflesh he had bought them, shoed them, and brought them up to standard at the stables behind his workshop. His stepson, a lad of fourteen, gave them regular exercise on the Westwood and when they were ready, Harry sold them on.

'He's had a good master,' Billy said. 'You've allus had a way wi' hosses.'

Harry nodded. 'I've just been to Akrill's. I've got a hunter ready to move on. Thought they might know of somebody. Business all right?' He looked through the window and saw Billy's mother. 'Your ma's still here, I see.'

'Aye,' Billy said gloomily. 'She won't trust anybody else in 'shop.' Then he laughed. 'In this one, anyway. I can do as I like in 'others!'

Harry touched his cap to Mrs Brown as he saw her looking towards him, then he glanced down Toll Gavel towards Butcher Row. A woman was walking briskly and determinedly towards them. She was wearing a blue bonnet with a dark blue shawl over her woollen dress and carried a shopping basket over her arm. 'Here's Annie,' he said. 'I'd best be off. Don't want you getting into trouble for jawing when you should be earning brass.'

Billy frowned. 'I'll do as I like,' he said. 'I'm me own master.'

'Aye,' Harry said. 'Course you are. I'll be off anyway. I'm meeting 'Driffield train in. I've some parcels to collect.'

Billy watched him depart, then, giving a deep sigh, he glanced in some trepidation at his mother, raised his eyebrows in concern and waited for Annie.

'Christina asked me the other day if I would ever consider marrying again.' Jenny broke off to turn the lamp up higher, the better to see her writing. 'She remarked that I was young enough to take another husband, which I am, being just under thirty-five years of age. I told her no, but didn't tell her that I had already turned down two suitors. Mr Horsforth was one: the gentleman I

395

met at Pearl's house, when a young Christina announced to everyone that I was expecting a child. I can hardly believe that it was over eleven years ago.

'Mr Horsforth called unexpectedly about six months later. He said that as he was in the district he felt he couldn't pass by without paying his respects to Miss Laslett and myself. Arabella, of course, was thrown into a complete tizzy of confusion, and said afterwards how she wished she had put on her better dress that morning, and worn her new lace cap instead of her old one. It just goes to show, Jenny, she said, one must always be prepared for every eventuality. I assured her that I was sure that Mr Horsforth wouldn't be concerned over such insignificant matters, that he had called out of courtesy to see us and not the latest fashion; for if he had, I had added, he would have been very disappointed. I was wearing my most comfortable day dress and nothing at all on my head, and my hair coiled around my ears.

'That our attire didn't put him off was evident, for he called again, five or six months after that, and I remember the occasion very well. William was just starting to walk and he tottered towards Mr Horsforth with his chubby arms out-stretched. Mr Horsforth obligingly put out his hands to catch him, whereupon William dribbled down the gentleman's coat sleeve. Arabella said later that she had been mortified, but I only recall that Mr Horsforth laughed.

'He called several times after that, and one day, when Arabella was out visiting, I received him alone. He said, without any preamble, on

396

discovering that Arabella was not at home, that he must seize the opportunity to tell me of his regard. I stopped him immediately in his tracks, telling him that I could not consider changing my role as a mother to that of a wife.

'He couldn't possibly have known of my circumstances and I wouldn't have dreamt of disclosing them to him or any other. I am here only because of my children. When they are all grown up and no longer need me, then I will reconsider my life. That I'm useful to my father-in-law I know, for I'm an efficient housekeeper and run the house and servants admirably. I know this because he has told me so. And I am very obliged to him, for I have nothing material of my own.

'My other suitor was, or indeed still is, Stephen's good friend and mine, Dr George Hill. He has been steadfast in his friendship and regard and I have long known that he cares for me. But I could not love him as a husband. He has been a bachelor for far too long and is too set in his ways for marriage or to share his life with anyone else. But he calls regularly to ask about my welfare and I can't help but think that Stephen, during his last hours, must have asked him to be protective of me, to guard me against his father. To be, in effect, my guardian angel. And this amiable trustworthy doctor has been just that, even though he must realize that Stephen's father, with whom he has an uneasy, fraught relationship, does hold me in respect.'

'Shall we have a day out in Beverley tomorrow, Mama?' Christina asked. 'We did say we would go, and the good weather is holding.'

'Your grandfather suggested we should go,' Jenny said. 'I didn't say so.'

'But why not?' Christina asked. 'You haven't been in years and I have never been. Do let's. We always go to Driffield for our shopping, and,' she said eagerly, 'we could go by train from Driffield to Beverley. I have a timetable. It only takes forty minutes.'

'Well, perhaps.' Jenny was reluctant to agree. 'But only for the afternoon, not all day. And besides,' she added, 'you have been! Your papa and I took you when you were a baby. I had to register your birth.'

'Well!' Christina exclaimed. 'I can hardly be expected to remember that, can I? Oh, it will be so nice.' She laughed. 'And just the two of us, not the boys! We can catch the one o'clock train, if you don't want to go in the morning, and come back on the four thirty-one.' She consulted the timetable. 'Or if we went earlier, at say nine twenty, we could have a look round the churches and have coffee and cake, and – isn't there anyone you would like to visit? Any of your old friends?'

'There won't be anyone there who remembers me.' Jenny wavered nervously, wishing she hadn't agreed. 'It's too long ago.' I hope there isn't anyone who remembers me, she thought. Well, only Billy. He'll still be there, I expect. I'd stop and say hello, of course, if I should see him. But I wouldn't embarrass him by reminding him of our friendship. He'll be married with a family now, I expect. He won't want to dwell on the past, any more than I do. And then there's Harry, but he was always so shy, I don't suppose he

398

would speak even if he recognized me.

'I did have two friends,' she told Christina. 'One was a butcher; he used to call on me. The other was an apprentice farrier. He only ever talked about horses. He had no other interests.'

'Like me, then?' Christina said. 'You know I asked Grandpappy if William could have another horse, and he said we'll see! He always says that, and William has grown and grown since that first time I asked him. But,' she frowned, 'they're male. Didn't you have any female friends? Surely you did?'

Jenny thought of the other servants at the Ingram house. Polly, Mary, Tilly and Lillian. They were not friends, they only worked together and occasionally gossiped. Then there was Mrs Judson, who always seemed severe, but who was actually kind to her when she most needed kindness, and Mrs Feather, the cook. But no, they were not friends.

She ran her tongue over dry lips. 'They'll all have left Beverley, I expect,' she suggested. 'They won't be there now. They'll have married and moved away.'

She was persuaded to take the early train and John Laslett drove them to Driffield, as he needed to buy some new boots. 'Here,' he said to Christina as they reached the railway station, and drew out his pocket book, taking out a sovereign. 'Treat yourself, and your mother too. Buy her something nice and have a spot of dinner. She doesn't often have a day out.' He nodded to Jenny, his eyes scrutinizing her. 'Do you good to go out, 'stead of looking after all of us.'

She gave him a nervous smile, sure that anxiety was showing in her face. 'Thank you. Yes, I'm sure we'll enjoy it.'

So many memories came flooding back when they arrived at Beverley railway station. Of the time when Christy had concealed himself in the shadows, waiting for her after she returned from visiting her sick father. Then he'd walked her back to New Walk, where they'd hidden beneath the trees and shared their first kiss. And of when Billy had seen her off on the train to Hull after the hearing, and warned her to be careful not to fall out of the carriage. Dear Billy, she thought with a lump in her throat. What a good friend he was. So patient and caring.

'Mama!' Christina whispered. 'There's a man staring at us.'

'Avert your eyes,' Jenny murmured. 'Don't acknowledge him. Sometimes men will try to attract your attention.' How innocent she is, Jenny thought worriedly, glancing sideways at the man standing by the barrier who was looking their way. She hasn't had enough experience of town life to know when to say hello and when to ignore and walk on.

'Jenny?' The man came over to them and took off his cap. 'Beg your pardon. Am I mistaken?' He looked directly at her. 'Is it really you?'

'Harry!' The name came out on an astonished breath. 'Good gracious! I don't believe it! To see you here after all this time.' She put out her hand in greeting. He looked the same, dressed in his tweed jacket, cord breeches and leather boots, and smelling of horses.

He seemed embarrassed at the gesture and unsure of what to do with his cap as he shook her hand. 'I've not been anywhere,' he murmured. 'So there's nowt surprising about me being here. You're 'one who's been away.' Then he gave a shy grin. 'You look right well. What you doing back in Beverley after all this time? Been far, have you?'

'N-no, not very far,' she admitted. Then she turned to Christina. 'This is my daughter, Christina.'

Harry's eyes lingered over Christina for a moment, and then he put out his hand to her. 'Pleased to meet you, miss – Christina.' He glanced again at Jenny. 'Just been talking to Billy,' he said. 'Billy Brown–'

'Butcher boy,' she added, almost without thinking.

'Aye,' he said wryly. ''Same.'

'What do you do, Harry? Still a farrier? I was telling Christina earlier that I once had a friend in Beverley whose first love was horses.'

'Aye, that's right. Onny don't tell my wife that.' He grinned, and she thought he seemed less shy than he used to be. 'Got my own farrier business now; my wife, well she was a widow, and her son, my stepson, he's good wi' hosses same as I was, so I'm teaching him. And I'm buying and selling hosses as well as shoeing 'em.'

'Oh!' Christina said. 'We need another horse for my brother! Perhaps we should have a look.'

'Not today, Christina,' Jenny said quickly. 'We won't have time, not with shopping and everything.' Her voice trailed away. 'Perhaps another day?'

'Aye, why not?' Harry nodded. 'Got just 'two, have you, same as me? Bairns, I mean?'

'Er, no,' Jenny said. 'I have five children. Three boys and two girls, including twins.'

'Ah!' Harry nodded again, glancing at Christina. 'Keep you busy, then!'

'Yes,' Jenny murmured. 'Christina is 'eldest. William 'youngest at eleven.'

'Ah!' Harry's blue eyes perused her face. 'Call and see Billy if you've time. He's in 'Toll Gavel shop this morning,' he said. 'He'd be pleased to see you. He's doing well, is Billy. Got four shops now. Two in Beverley, two in Hull. Got a nice little house as well.'

'Has he?' Jenny felt her eyes prickle. 'Yes, we'll call. He was a good friend to me.'

'Aye, he was.'

'Goodbye then, Harry,' she said. 'It was nice to meet you again.' She blinked and felt her mouth tremble as she spoke. 'It's so good to come back to Beverley and meet old friends.'

He frowned. 'Have you not been back since—'

'No,' she interrupted. 'Not in a long time.'

She felt shaky as they walked away from the station and down Railway Street towards Wednesday Market. This isn't going to be easy, she thought. I should never have come. She was wearing a grey bonnet with a lace insert and a matching shawl round the neck of her coat. She pulled the shawl up to her chin and lowered her head.

'Are you cold, Mama?' Christina asked. 'You're shivering!'

'Yes. Yes, just a little. Let's go and have a cup of tea. It'll warm me up. I must have caught a chill on the train,' she said nervously.

There was a teashop adjacent to a grocer's in Wednesday Market and Christina ushered Jenny into it. She ordered tea and biscuits for her mother and lemonade for herself. 'It's upset you, hasn't it? Coming back, I mean,' she murmured. 'Were you very happy here? Is this where you met my father?'

Jenny nodded. 'Yes. I was happy for a time. But I was unhappy too.' She looked up as the girl brought their refreshments. She was young, perhaps fourteen, with her hair coiled neatly beneath a white cap and a crisp white apron over her black skirt. She placed the teapot on the table.

'Come to Beverley for shopping, have you, ma'am?' she asked Jenny. 'Don't recall seeing you before, but then we gets lots o' visitors to Beverley. They come to see the Minster and St Mary's. They're worth a look if you've time.'

'Yes,' Jenny murmured. 'We shall try to fit them in.'

Her teeth chattered as she drank her tea, but she felt better for it. How foolish I am, she told herself. Why do I think that people will point a finger at me? Who is going to stare and say there she is, Jenny Graham, she was arrested for murder? No-one. Then a doubt crept in. But suppose I see Mrs Ingram as I did when I came last time? What if she's still living in Beverley? She won't have forgotten, and she would recognize me as I would her. We won't ever forget each other.

'Where shall we go first?' Christina was asking. 'Shall we go to the other market? Aunt Bella says it has some fine shops.'

'Saturday Market it's called,' Jenny told her. 'Yes, it has milliners, haberdashers, booksellers, drapers and dressmakers. Anything anyone could want. At least, it always did have, and I see no reason why it shouldn't have the same now, except maybe run by different shopkeepers.'

'So shall we go?' Christina asked eagerly. 'Are you feeling better?'

'Yes.' Jenny smiled weakly. 'Much better, thank you.'

They paid for their refreshments and continued on down Butcher Row, where some of the ancient timber-framed houses were in a state of dilapidation, yet were still occupied, with scrubbed-clean doorsteps and lacy curtains at their shuttered windows. They stood side by side with thriving fishmongers, barbers and butchers. Laden waggons, traps, donkeys and drays trundled along the cobbled street, people rushed around on their various errands, and Christina exclaimed how very busy it was.

'Now we're in Toll Gavel,' Jenny said. 'This is where my friend Billy Brown had his butcher's shop. His father opened it for him when – oh, many years ago, before you were born.'

'Is this it?' Christina pointed to a bow-fronted shop window. 'It says William Brown's Son. So has he got a son? Your friend Billy?'

'I don't know, he might have, but Billy's father put that sign up. They had another shop in Saturday Market but Billy ran this one.' She glanced in at the window. It was neatly laid out with trays of mutton chops, offal, sausages, ox cheek and tails, pigs' trotters and joints of plum-red beef. Hanging from hooks on a rack inside the window were plucked chickens and pigeons, and rabbits waiting to be skinned.

Behind the counter a lad of about fifteen wearing a long white bloodstained apron was about to slice into a loin of beef; advising him, with his arms folded in front of his clean white apron, was Billy.

Should I go in? Jenny pondered. He's busy. I wonder if that's his son? And there's Billy's mother. Jenny couldn't help but give a little smile as she saw the woman at the back of the shop. She's still keeping an eye on the shop and still stringing sausages.

Billy looked up, seemingly caught by the presence of someone outside the window. He wore a straw boater and in an automatic gesture he touched it with his forefinger. Then he looked again, startled. He spoke to the boy and to his mother, who also glanced at them, then came round the counter and out of the shop.

He took off his hat and stared at her. 'Jenny!' His voice cracked. His mouth opened as he took a breath, and then closed.

'Hello, Billy!' She gazed back at him and her eyes were washed with tears. She swallowed. 'How are you?'

He nodded. 'I'm all right. Wha– I mean, how are you? It's good to see you, Jenny. I thought–' He cleared his throat. 'I thought that I'd never see you again.' His words were halting and strained. He was obviously stunned by her appearance.

'We've come for the day,' Jenny murmured. 'This is Christina.' She drew her daughter towards them; Christina had stood back when Billy came out of the shop.

He gave a bewildered frown as he looked at Christina. 'Not that young babby? Grown into a fine young lady. I saw you when you were in your mother's arms.'

'I'm sixteen,' Christina volunteered.

Billy nodded. 'Aye, I reckon you will be. I remember 'day well when Jenny – your ma – came to Beverley. I've not seen you since. Jenny!' he asked. 'You wouldn't have come without calling?'

'Of course I wouldn't, Billy. This is 'first time I've been back since that day.'

'Why so long?' His forehead wrinkled and he gazed anxiously at her. 'Why didn't you come back? I've wai– well, I thought you'd forgotten all about us here in Beverley.'

'I'd never do that,' she said softly. 'But there have been so many things happening. It would take a month to tell.'

'Will you come in and have a cup of tea?' He nodded over his shoulder to the shop. 'We still live above 'shop. Well, Ma does. I've a place above 'other one in Sat'day Market.'

'We've just had a cup,' Christina broke in. She was fidgeting and Jenny knew she wanted to be off.

'I heard you have four shops,' Jenny said. 'We met Harry at 'railway station and had a chat with him.'

'Did you? Aye, I have.' Billy looked down at her. He was taller and broader than when she had seen him last. A man now, no longer a boy. 'My da died and left me both shops in Beverley and a fair bit o' money. Owd bugger – beggin' your pardon, miss,' he added, glancing at Christina. 'He'd been stashing it away for years. So I took 'chance and bought two more shops in Hull and put managers in. But I go over twice a week to make sure they're doing all right.'

'Well.' Jenny's voice broke as she remembered. 'Didn't I say you'd have a string of shops before I saw you again, Billy?' Jenny glanced towards Christina who had edged away and was looking in a stationer's window. 'I'll have to go,' she said. 'We've only come for the day.'

Harry driving up in a two-wheeled trap hailed them. 'You found each other then?' he called. 'Why don't you come over to my place for a bit o' dinner and you could catch up wi' 'news? 'Young lady could look at my hosses.'

Christina, catching this shouted invitation, came towards them. Her face lit up, shopping forgotten. 'Could we, Mama?'

'I – I don't know. We haven't a great deal of time. The train–'

'Where do you live, Jenny?' Billy asked. 'Did you leave 'district?'

Jenny looked up at him. 'No,' she murmured. 'We live up on 'Wolds. Not far from Driffield.'

'Only up there?' His voice and expression was puzzled. 'You were only as far away as Driffield? Why, I come regular to Driffield!' He shook his head as if bewildered. 'And I've never seen you! I thought – well, I've been about a bit,' he said lamely. 'I've looked for you,' he added quietly. 'Kept an eye out for you, you know. I thought

407

mebbe you'd gone to work in Hull.'

'Are you coming, Mama?' Christina laughingly called from where she was sitting in Harry's trap. 'We can look at the shops later! The train doesn't leave until four thirty.'

'You go,' Billy urged Harry. 'I'll bring Jenny in a bit. I'll just have to change into my coat.' He turned to Jenny. 'She'll be all right with Harry,' he said hastily. 'I want to show you something, Jenny. It's important!'

CHAPTER FORTY

Jenny slowly followed Billy as he dashed into the shop and through another door. She could hear him clattering up the stairs. Mrs Brown looked up and came towards her. 'It's all right, Tom,' she said, in an aside to the apprentice. 'You carry on.

'It's Jenny, isn't it?' she murmured. 'Jenny Graham?' Her sharp eyes seemed to take in her appearance in a second. 'You haven't changed!'

'Nor have you, Mrs Brown,' Jenny said. 'But – I'm not Jenny Graham any more. I'm Jenny Laslett, have been for 'last fourteen years.'

'Oh!' Mrs Brown's face drooped. 'Does Billy know?'

'Not yet, he doesn't. I've barely had a chance to talk to him but he's whisking me off somewhere, I don't know where. And my daughter–' She broke off and looked out of the door but Christina and Harry had driven away.

'Best tell him, then,' Mrs Brown muttered. 'Fourteen years. So long! Have you got other bairns or just the one?'

'Yes.' Jenny didn't know why she felt nervous under Mrs Brown's scrutiny. She wasn't hostile, but she was definitely curious. 'I've five children.'

'Five!' Mrs Brown breathed out the number. 'That's nice; I allus wished I could have had more. They're a comfort to you when you get old. I keep telling Billy–'

What she kept telling Billy she didn't have the chance to say as Billy banged down the stairs again, and Jenny guessed that the treads were uncarpeted. He had removed his apron, washed his hands and brushed his hair, and was wearing a smart black coat with a grey waistcoat beneath it.

'I've just been saying to Mrs Laslett here how I keep nattering on to you to give me grandchildren,' Mrs Brown said pointedly.

'Who?' Billy's blue eyes went from his mother to Jenny. There was no-one else in the shop, so there was no mistaking whom she meant. 'Mrs Laslett? That was– Wasn't that 'fellow you were working for?'

'Yes, but – shall we walk on?' Jenny interrupted. 'I must catch up with Christina. You'll know where Harry lives?'

'Aye.' Billy took her arm and ushered her out. 'I do.' Jenny threw a glancing goodbye to Mrs Brown as Billy told his mother he would be back later.

'I didn't know you'd got married!' Billy muttered. 'I should have guessed! He offered you security, I suppose?'

'How could you have known, Billy? And yes, Stephen did offer security for both of us, me and Christina. That's why I married him. And he gave Christina his name.'

'You didn't love him then?' Billy turned to look down at her as he guided her towards Saturday Market. 'It was for refuge?'

'Not then I didn't. Billy, can we slow down? Where are we going?'

He dropped her arm and put clenched fingers against his mouth. 'Sorry,' he muttered. 'I'm used to dashing between one shop and another. We'll pick 'trap up from 'back of the other shop. It's too far to walk to Harry's if you're in a hurry. But you do now?' He swallowed. 'Love him? I suppose you've got other bairns?'

'Five, including Christina, but Billy–'

They'd come to the front of a butcher's shop, which had a similar sign to the other. At the side of the shop was a narrow passageway and Billy ushered her down it. 'I keep 'trap here,' he explained. 'It's onny a small stable and yard but big enough for one horse.'

'You've done well, Billy,' Jenny said admiringly. 'Four shops *and* a horse and trap!'

'Aye,' he said glumly. 'And a delivery waggon and driver.' He shrugged as if it was of no importance. 'I reckon I have.'

He whistled to a boy who was in the back of the shop and the lad came running, took the stabled horse and hitched it to the smart red and green trap. The yard came out onto Lairgate, one of the ancient streets of Beverley, and Billy, without speaking, helped Jenny into the trap and drove along it before turning up the narrow lane of Newbegin.

'We're going towards 'Westwood,' Jenny remarked. 'Is that where Harry and his family live? Or where his stables are?'

'Both.' Billy nodded. 'Farrier's shop and stables are behind his house, up near 'Westwood. It's a good place to be; his lad exercises 'horses up there. But I wanted to show you something first, before we go to Harry's. Not that it matters now,' he added in a low mutter.

'You've stayed friends a long time, haven't you?' Jenny said, looking about her, as they turned, not onto the Westwood road but in the other direction. 'Since you were boys? I remember when–' She broke off, confronted by memories.

'What?' he asked abruptly. 'What do you remember? When all three of us wanted your attention?'

'Three?' she queried, looking at him.

'Aye. Harry was sweet on you at one time, but he daren't say, and anyway we both saw how Christy would win 'day. We knew he'd more to offer than either of us.'

'It wasn't a matter of having more to offer! It was just–' What was it exactly about Christy? she wondered. He seemed vulnerable then, in spite of his apparent wealth. I wanted to take care of him. But in the end – she gave a deep shuddering sigh. 'I don't know what it was, Billy. He–'

'He sweet-talked you,' Billy interrupted harshly. 'Convinced you that 'fairy story would come true. Rich man and poor girl would live happy ever after! We knew, Harry and me, that it

411

would come to nowt, but we couldn't warn you. Daren't warn you! You were smitten with him. Under his spell.' He shook his head and added softly. 'Not that we ever thought it would end 'way it did.'

Jenny didn't answer. There was nothing to say. No-one could have foreseen what lay in front of them.

They drove past a terrace of three-storeyed brick houses with projecting upper windows. 'I don't remember these,' she said suddenly. 'They're new to me!'

Billy slowed the horse. 'Aye, there's been some changes in Beverley over 'last ten years or so. Some of 'old houses pulled down and new ones put up.'

'This is Union Road. It leads up to 'new workhouse, doesn't it?' she said. She recalled the discussions there had been in the town about a new workhouse's being built near the Westwood to replace the old dilapidated one. 'So where are we going, Billy? This isn't where Harry lives?' She looked up admiringly at the dentilated carving of the fascia above the windows, the freshly painted doors and small neat front gardens. 'These are lovely houses.'

Billy pulled up in front of one of the residences. 'No. Harry lives on 'other road, nearer to 'Westwood.' The middle and top windows of the house in front of them were draped with lace curtains, and blinds covered the lower.

He got out of the trap and came to the other side to hand Jenny down. He looked up at the house for a moment, then, taking a deep breath, he let out a sigh, and said, 'This one is mine.'

He walked up the path in front of her and took a key from his pocket, inserted it into the door and opened it. 'I watched them being built,' he said, as he led her across the hall and into the front sitting room. He drew open the blinds, letting the sunshine flood in. 'I always thought that if I ever made enough money I'd buy one. I didn't use 'money my da left; this came out of my own endeavour.'

Jenny looked round. The room had polished wood floors, but no rug or carpet to soften them, fine furniture but no cushions for comfort, nor antimacassars over the sofas or chairs. A gleaming marble fireplace above the hearth, but no ornaments on the mantel; and flocked wallpaper but not a single picture or painting.

'It's beautiful, Billy,' she said with genuine admiration. 'Really lovely.'

He took her round the rest of the house, showing her the dining room which was panelled in wood and whose window looked out over a long garden; the kitchen and the bedrooms, and all were the same: fitted out with the very best of furniture, but apparently unlived in. No woman's touch of flowers or drapes; no man's pipe, newspapers or slippers.

'But you don't live here, Billy?' she said as they came downstairs, and she ran her hand down the polished mahogany handrail. 'It's all too perfect.'

'No. I don't.'

'Why not?' She turned her eyes away from the ceiling where she had been admiring the carved cornice, towards him as he stood below her in the

413

hall. 'Have you never lived here?'

He shook his head and kept his gaze upon her. 'Too big for just one person.'

'But – why then did you buy it?' she asked. 'I thought that you and Annie Fisher...? You were seeing her.'

'Aye, still do,' he said soberly. Then a ghost of a grin touched his lips. 'She doesn't give up, even though I've told her.'

'Told her what?' she breathed. 'Surely – after all this time?'

He kept his hand on the banister, and looked up at her on the stairs. 'That I wouldn't marry her. I've never – you know. Never given her 'chance to say we had to get married. And she's never been here. Never seen 'inside of 'house, though I expect she's been to have a look from 'outside.'

'I don't understand,' Jenny said. 'Why won't you marry her?'

He shrugged. 'My ma can't stand her for one thing, and for another, I don't love her and never wanted her. I mean, she's all right for a bit o' company. We go for a walk sometimes or to 'music hall in Hull. She likes to do that.' He grinned again. 'She tries to get me drunk so that I'll get amorous. But I'll not fall for that!'

He took his hand off the banister and Jenny continued down the stairs so that her eyes were on a level with his. 'My ma's 'only one who's been here,' he said. 'She helped me with 'curtains at 'upstairs windows, but nothing more. And she suggested I put blinds at 'ground floor if I wasn't going to live here.'

'So it's an investment?' she said hesitatingly.

414

'For 'future?'

'What's the point in that?' he said. 'I've no sons or daughters to leave it to. I allus hoped–' He looked away, across the hall into the sitting room where the sun sent long shimmering stripes across the floor. 'I was stupid,' he muttered. 'Harry allus said so.'

She frowned. 'You're hardly stupid,' she said. 'Four shops and a house! What did you hope for, Billy? That you'd meet someone you'd want to marry? There's still time for that. You're just 'right age for a man to wed.'

'You don't understand, do you, Jenny?' he said softly and turned to her with his frank blue-eyed gaze. 'You've never understood. Or at least you pretended not to.'

'What?' she whispered. 'You're not telling me that after all this time–'

He closed his eyes for a moment as if to concentrate and he clenched his fingers into fists. 'This is yours, Jenny,' he breathed. 'I bought it for you. I thought, fool that I am, that one day you'd come back to Beverley, and – and we could start afresh. Put 'past behind us. I looked for you. I've been all over 'East Riding looking for you. I never asked for you by name, cos I thought, well, that you wouldn't want that. I even went to Hull. But I couldn't find you.' His face was creased as if in pain. 'I never thought that you'd marry him!

'I'm sorry,' he said, bending his head. 'I shouldn't have told you all this, but–' He took a breath. 'I've waited and waited for this day. And when you turned up today, I was staggered. So knocked out at seeing you, when I least expected

415

you.' He gave a lopsided dejected grimace. 'And here you are, a married woman with a husband and five children to take care of you. So you don't need me. I'm too late again.'

She reached to touch his arm. 'No husband, Billy,' she said softly. 'I'm a widow. Have been for eleven years. Stephen never saw our last son. My father-in-law supports my children and me. We live with him and his youngest daughter. I've nothing of my own, apart from my children.'

He lifted his head to gaze at her. 'A widow!' His lips parted and she saw a lightening of expression, a hopeful expectation in his eyes. 'So, would you come back, Jenny? Would I – would I stand a chance, this time?'

CHAPTER FORTY-ONE

He took hold of her hand and led her into the sitting room, where they both sat on the edge of chairs facing each other. 'Would you, Jenny? Consider it, I mean? You'd want for nothing, and – and–' A slight blush suffused his face. 'I do love you. Always have. Always will. Until I die.'

She bent her head. 'I think I always knew that, Billy,' she murmured. 'But I never expected that you'd wait so long. I always imagined that you'd be married by now.'

'But I'm not,' he urged. 'And if you're not...'

'I'm a widow, it's true. But I have to consider my children and their future.' She went on quickly before he could interrupt. 'Two of my sons are going to be farmers; they'll take over their grandfather's estate when they're old enough. Johnny's a soldier and is going to train to be an officer. Then there are my daughters to consider, especially Christina.'

'And you? What about you? Don't you deserve a life?' Billy asked, his face shadowing as if he could foresee what was coming next.

Jenny thought of John Laslett and how he depended upon her. He was getting old and more crotchety as the years went by. She seemed to be the only one who could talk to him. Even the estate manager that he had taken on at her persuasion would sound her out on his employer's temper before approaching John Laslett on a farming issue. 'And 'other thing is, I can't leave my father-in-law at present. He relies on me. I run the household.'

'You said he had a daughter. Why can't she run it?'

She smiled. 'She's not very good at it.'

'So you're a housekeeper, Jenny,' he said brusquely. 'He's taking advantage of you.'

'No. No, he's not! We've been given a home and I'm grateful for that. Goodness knows where we would be if it hadn't been for John Laslett; and he didn't have to take us in,' she said, proceeding to tell him some of the story of the antipathy between Stephen and his father. 'And he's fond of 'children,' she added, realizing that she too had an affection for the old man. 'And we are all fond of him. I can't let him down.'

Billy stood up and wearily leant his hand on the

417

mantelpiece. She saw his look of gloom reflected in the mirror above it. 'Billy!' she said softly and as she too stood up, he turned round and faced her.

'Do I give up?' he muttered. 'Have I been on a fool's errand all these years?'

'I didn't say never, Billy,' she whispered. 'I just meant – not yet!'

He came to her and took both her hands into his. His eyes, intent and appealing, searched hers, then he bent and kissed her lips. 'Does it mean–' he said in a cracked and husky voice. 'Does it mean that I can still hope? That mebbe one day?'

'We need to get to know each other again, Billy,' she whispered, taken aback by his kiss. It had been long years since she had felt the touch of a man's lips on hers. 'We were so young when we knew each other before. We're different people now.'

'I'm not,' he stated quietly. 'I'm just 'same. I've been here in Beverley all this time, just waiting for you to come back.'

She shook her head. 'You are different, Billy. The boy I once knew was shy and tongue-tied and could never say what he meant. You're a man now and able to. You're a man of business too. A householder. Don't say you haven't changed, for you surely have!'

'Well,' he said, still holding her hands, which were lost within his large, firm ones. 'Mebbe a few things have changed, but one thing hasn't, and that's how I've allus felt about you.'

'So are you willing to wait a little longer?' she

asked. 'Until my family are grown up and settled?'

He gazed longingly at her. 'I said, didn't I, that I would love you 'til I die. And I will.'

She reached up to kiss him, stretching up on her toes as he bent his head towards her. 'Then don't die yet, Billy,' she whispered. 'For I have to learn to love you too.'

It was midday when they arrived at Harry Johnson's house, which had a stable and yard at the side of it. In the yard were Christina, Harry, a woman whom Jenny assumed must be Mrs Johnson, and a young man in his twenties who was talking animatedly to Christina.

Harry turned round as the trap approached. He had an anxious frown on his forehead. 'There you are,' he said. 'I'd given you up.' He glanced from Jenny to Billy and his look of wariness communicated itself to Billy.

'Summat up?' he asked quietly.

'Hope not!' Harry answered in an undertone. To Jenny he said, 'Come and meet my wife.'

Harry's wife, Ellen Johnson, dressed in a plain grey gown but wearing a riotously flowered bonnet, was a plump, smiling, bustling woman with a jolly manner and voice, a few years older than Harry, Billy or Jenny. 'I'm so pleased to meet you,' she greeted Jenny. 'Your daughter has been telling us about her horses, and her brothers and her sister who's gone away to Switzerland. What a busy life you do lead. And this,' she turned to the young man who was now standing back from the group, though he kept glancing at Christina, 'is Mr

Esmond, only recently come to live in Beverley. Mr William Brown,' she said, 'and Mrs – er–'

'Laslett,' Jenny said. 'Jenny Laslett.'

Mr Esmond bowed his head to Jenny and shook hands with Billy, who, like Harry, now wore a slight perturbed frown, though he was amiable enough towards Charles Esmond as he introduced himself.

'Mr Esmond is coming to live in New Walk,' Mrs Johnson chatted. 'So we hope to see something of him. He's a keen horseman, are you not, Mr Esmond?'

'I am,' he replied. 'I hope to keep a good stable once I'm settled in.'

'In New Walk?' Jenny asked quietly. 'How very nice.'

'Mama!' Christina broke in. 'Mr Esmond will be looking for new horses and I was telling him about the lady up on the Wolds. You know, the one who is half gypsy, and–'

'I'm sure Mr Johnson will be able to advise him,' Jenny said hurriedly. 'Without Mr Esmond having to travel all that way.'

'Course I can,' Harry declared. 'Though 'gypsies bring their hosses to Beverley anyway.'

Both Christina and Mr Esmond looked disappointed, but Charles Esmond added, 'I would appreciate sound advice, of course, but I don't mind at all about travelling any distance, if I get what I want.'

Jenny thought she caught a cryptic glance between her daughter and Mr Esmond. My goodness, she thought, they've never been plotting for him to call! Christina is growing up. She looked at her daughter with new eyes and thought how pretty she was, with her rounded figure, her sweet smile and glossy dark hair, and saw too how Christina would be perceived by a young man, and how she was being so observed now by an admiring Charles Esmond.

'You're not from this area, Mr Esmond?' she asked.

'No, my family home is in Worcester, though we have had connections with Beverley for many years. My uncle – that is, my mother's brother – inherited a house from *their* uncle, but he never lived in it, and as he didn't have any family, it came to me when he died last year. I was very pleased to have it, I can tell you,' he enthused, spinning his top hat round and round in his hand. 'I used to come to Beverley, for the races, you know.'

Jenny felt a pounding in her ears and her throat was dry as she asked, 'And whereabouts in New Walk is the house? I – used to know a family who lived there.'

'One of the older houses,' he explained. 'Not far out of the town. An imposing dwelling and a lovely garden, though both have been neglected over the last few years.'

'And what name did your relative go by?' Jenny asked weakly. Her heart was hammering, yet she had to know, so that if necessary any friendship between Christina and this personable young man could be nipped in the bud.

'Ingram,' he said brightly. 'I've had to take it as my middle name.'

She felt Billy come up behind her. He put a

421

firm hand on her elbow, and she was glad of the support, for she was light-headed and giddy. The past will *never* go away, she thought wretchedly. It will be there for ever, even affecting my daughter, who doesn't know of it. She glanced at Christina, who in turn was watching Charles Esmond, and as he said his family name she raised her eyebrows and was about to say something when she caught sight of her mother's pale face.

'Are you unwell, Mama?' She rushed towards her in concern. 'You are so white!'

'Good gracious,' Ellen Johnson said. 'So you are, my dear. Come inside. Come, come.' She hurried towards the house with a flurry of her arms and hands. 'You must have something to eat. I declare I often feel faint for want of food. Come along, come along.'

Jenny was taken inside and sat down in a comfortable chair and made to put her feet on a footstool, whilst Mrs Johnson fussed about, calling the maid to make strong sweet tea whilst she herself turned out drawers and cupboards in search of smelling salts. Her parlour was in chaos with chairs and sofas strewn with sewing baskets, magazines, newspapers, coats, bonnets, boots, shawls and other paraphernalia. On the mantelpiece were bottles of horse liniment, cough mixture and tinctures of this and that, as well as face cream, a glass dome containing silk flowers, and, oddly, a ginger hairpiece, which made Jenny look more closely at the fringe of curls beneath Mrs Johnson's bonnet.

'I'm quite all right, Mrs Johnson,' she insisted. 'Really I am. A glass of water is all I need.'

'Oh, but you must stay for dinner. It's almost ready.' Mrs Johnson gave up her search in the cupboards, then suddenly pounced on one of the chairs and withdrew a cushion, which she dropped to the floor. 'There it is,' she cried, fishing down the side of the armchair and bringing out a small dark bottle. 'I remember now, when we had a visitor a fortnight ago, she too felt faint and I gave her this to sniff at.' She held it out to Jenny, who politely declined the offer.

'What a pity that Mr Esmond couldn't stay,' Mrs Johnson prattled as she presided over the midday meal. 'You seemed to be getting on very well,' she added archly to Christina, who blushed. 'Such a nice young man, and wealthy too, I would imagine.'

'Ellen!' Harry warned. 'Don't start match-making. We know nowt of him.'

'Oh, but we can find out,' Mrs Johnson said happily. 'And you probably know of the family, don't you, Harry? I thought you knew everybody in Beverley! I'm not from round here, you see,' she told Jenny and Christina. 'I'm from Wetherby, which is where I met Harry. The races, you know. My father and late husband were keen racegoers.'

It's just as well, Jenny reflected, that we don't have to talk much, for I must plan what to say to Christina, when she asks me what will surely be a vital question. Fortunately, Mrs Johnson didn't require any answers to her monologue as she plied them with mounds of tender beef, Yorkshire pudding, sausages, carrots, cabbage and creamy potatoes. She served up thick onion gravy and red-hot horseradish sauce, which set them on fire.

Jenny noticed that Billy, Harry and his stepson, Ned, didn't listen to her chatter, but ate heartily from their overflowing plates, whilst she and Christina ate little. Mrs Johnson's daughter, Amy, a plump girl like her mother, but very shy, picked at her food and glanced nervously at the visitors.

'We must be off, Mrs Johnson,' Billy said, when they finally rose from the table, the men having partaken of large helpings of apple sponge pudding, which the ladies had refused. 'Mrs Laslett and her daughter have a train to catch.'

'Then you must come again, my dears,' Mrs Johnson said warmly. 'We always have an open door. Any time you are in Beverley, please feel free to call. And if this young lady,' she turned smiling to Christina, 'ever wants to come and ride the horses, I'm sure Harry will be happy for her to do so.'

Harry nodded. 'Aye,' he said. 'Course you can.'

'Mr Esmond said he intends to ride on the Westwood,' Christina said. 'When he gets his stable set up. He said I would be very welcome to – to visit.' Her voice trailed away as she felt all eyes on her. 'Of course, I said that I could only come if Mama accompanied me.' Her cheeks were pink as she added, 'And he understood perfectly.'

Billy drove them back into Saturday Market, for they had time to do some shopping before they returned to the railway station for their train. 'Thank you, Mr Brown,' Christina said charmingly. 'It's been very nice meeting you. Will you excuse me, Mama? I'd just like to dash across to the haberdasher's. I need some more sewing silks. Will you come over?'

'Yes, I'll catch up with you,' Jenny said. 'Wait for me at the Market Cross!' she called after her.

'What will you tell her?' Billy murmured as with a swirl of her skirts Christina hurried away.

'I don't know.' Jenny stared after her. 'She'll ask, that I do know. I told her not long ago that her father's name was Ingram. She picked it up immediately when Mr Esmond said it. What am I to do!' Her words were faint. 'I can't lie to her.'

'She doesn't know how Christy died?' Billy asked quietly.

Jenny shook her head. 'I told her it was an accident. That he was shot. I haven't told her about me.' Her voice trembled and she was close to tears. 'I didn't tell her that I was arrested and accused of shooting him.' She turned towards him. 'What am I going to do, Billy?'

CHAPTER FORTY-TWO

'You don't have to do anything,' Billy said. 'You might never see Charles Esmond again. But would you want Christina to find out from someone else?' Jenny shook her head as he went on. 'Better for you to tell her, explaining in your own words what happened, or–' He hesitated. 'As much as you want her to know. It was a long time ago, Jenny,' he said softly. 'Folks will have forgotten 'details, but they'll remember something and your name will be linked. You have to tell it to those who matter.'

'Yes,' she whispered. 'I know that you're right. But I don't want to hurt her. Everything I've ever done was to protect her.'

'She's almost a woman,' he said. 'Sooner or later, she's going to fly 'nest. You've got to prepare her. She won't forgive you if you don't.'

'I didn't know you were so wise, Billy!' She gave a shaky smile. 'Though I always knew you were a good friend.'

He looked down at her, his eyes warm and tender. 'Aye! You don't know how good, or how much better I can be, given 'chance.'

'I'll tell her,' she said, averting her eyes; now was not the time for making promises. 'But not yet. I need to think about what I'm going to say.'

Christina chatted all the way home on the train, and Jenny was beginning to think her fears were misguided, for Christina was quite childlike in her expressions of delight of the day spent in Beverley. It wasn't until they were driving home from Driffield station in the carriage, which John Laslett had sent to meet them, that she mentioned Charles Esmond.

'Mr Esmond was extremely pleasant, did you not think, Mama?' she said shyly. 'And it was extraordinary how we found we were compatible in so many ways. For instance, he loves his horses and so do I. He was brought up in the country as I was, and he's very taken with Beverley and really looking forward to living there, and I,' she added, 'I said to him that I thought it was a delightful town.'

Jenny restrained a smile. 'You've seen little of it, apart from Saturday Market and Mr and Mrs

Johnson's home and stables!'

'Oh, but Harry – Mr Johnson – took me for a ride when I was in his trap, and pointed out St Mary's church and a strange looking building with an archway beneath it, called North Bar, and the Westwood and the racecourse, so I have seen quite a lot of it!'

'You haven't seen it as I once saw it,' Jenny said softly. 'I'll tell you about it, some time.'

'Of course,' Christina said. 'You lived there. And my father did too. Didn't you think it strange that Mr Esmond's relatives had the same name? Do you think it's the same family, or merely a coincidence?' She paused for a moment and they jolted along in silence, and hung on to the straps as the carriage hit the potholes in the road.

'It might be 'same family,' Jenny murmured. 'Perhaps I'll enquire.'

'I hope it's not,' Christina said in a subdued tone. 'If it is, Mr Esmond might not want to know me.' She glanced at her mother, who had a fixed look on her face. 'As I'm illegitimate, I mean. And anyway,' she added miserably, 'perhaps no-one will ever want to know me.'

'You're the adopted daughter of Stephen St John Laslett,' Jenny said bluntly. 'Don't ever forget that, Christina. That's who you are!' But she could see by Christina's down-turned mouth that the reminder was of no consequence, and she shuddered at the thought that she had even worse to tell her.

'I can't sleep,' she wrote in her notebook. 'It's two o'clock in the morning and I haven't closed

427

my eyes since coming to bed. As I sit here by the window, there's a bright moon shining over the fields and the garden, and everything is lit up as if it is day and I barely need the candle to write by. But even though there is light, I can't see my way out of my dilemma. How do I tell my daughter that I was accused of killing her father? That I was found with the gun in my hand by Christy's father, her grandfather, who was my employer?

'My emotions are very mixed. I felt so happy seeing my dear friends again: Billy, who has been so loyal and loves me still, and Harry who has always been my good friend; yet the happiness I felt was tinged with fear, and my hand shakes as I write, just as it did when I was in prison and afraid for my life, and my biggest worry now is that Christina will turn against me.'

John Laslett was not well the next day. He had a heavy cold yet still went out to oversee some job which the hind could have done. When he came home for supper he was shivering violently. Jenny ordered a hot toddy to be brought immediately and hot bricks to be put into his bed, where she dispatched him straight away, and surprisingly he didn't grumble.

'I'm glad you're here, Jenny,' he said breathlessly, when later she knocked on his bedroom door and went in to see if there was anything he wanted. 'I know that if anything happens to me, you'll see that things are run properly. You know, don't you, that the boys will inherit the estate and the girls will be well cared for? Everything has been put in hand.'

She thought of Johnny, who had given up the

position of heir in order to be a soldier, and John Laslett, as if seeing her disquiet, said gruffly, 'And I haven't forgotten Johnny, if that's what you're thinking.'

Jenny gave a wistful smile. 'I'm also thinking that I hope you're not considering dying yet!'

'No, I'm not, but these colds can turn to something worse in a man of my age. Influenza, bronchitis–'

'All the more reason for you to take things easy,' she chastised him. 'You don't have to do so much. You have men who can do for you.'

'I know,' he sighed, and pulled the sheets up to his reddened nose. 'But I do worry. Two women in the house and no man to take care of them. You should marry again,' he said suddenly. 'A farmer, perhaps – though' – he reached for a large handkerchief and noisily blew his nose – 'I'd have to make sure he didn't get the estate.'

'I've no plans to marry for the moment,' she murmured. 'Perhaps when the children are grown I might consider it.'

'That doctor fellow, I suppose,' he grunted. 'I wouldn't like to think he was living here!'

'Dr Hill is a very kind, considerate man,' she replied. 'But I wouldn't want to marry him. If I should marry anyone–' She hesitated. 'I'd marry someone of my own kind.'

He peered at her through bloodshot eyes. 'Meaning what? Someone from the servant class? Come, come, Jenny! You can do better than that.' He sneezed. 'We'll talk about it tomorrow. I just want to sleep now.'

She closed the door behind her and stood for a

moment with her hand on the doorknob. Should I tell him? she wondered. Would he understand my dilemma? Perhaps I might confide in him.

He was no better the following day and it wasn't until three days later that he sat up in bed and asked for chicken soup. On the same day Jenny received a letter from Mr Esmond saying he was to be in Driffield the next day and would like to call.

'If it is not convenient,' he wrote, 'then please advise your footman or maid to acquaint me at the door and I will go away disappointed, but with the hope that you and Miss Christina will receive me on another occasion.'

Jenny read the letter with misgivings and after some deliberation took it upstairs to show John Laslett. 'He's not coming to see me, of course,' she told him as he read it, 'but Christina.'

'Got an admirer already, has she?' he muttered. 'Where's he from? Who's his family?'

'We met him in Beverley,' Jenny told him. 'He's recently gone to live there. The difficulty is–' She swallowed and licked her lips, which had suddenly become dry. 'He's a distant relative of Christina's father – her real father, I mean,' she stammered.

He frowned. 'How distant?' he growled. 'Got to be careful, you know, breeding and all that!'

'No. No, that's not the difficulty. What I mean is–' She started to grow hot and she ran her hand round the back of her neck. 'It's just that he won't know – I'd have to tell him that Christina is illegitimate and that her father was an Ingram.'

'Do you know that for sure?' he asked. 'That he was her father?'

Jenny flushed and started to protest. He waved aside her objections. 'I have my reasons for asking,' he muttered and remained silent for a few moments.

'Mmm.' His eyes, which were still reddened, glanced around the bedroom, hesitating at the pictures on the wall, gazing out of the window and coming to rest on the flickering fire. He heaved a sigh. 'I've never told this to anyone else,' he said slowly, 'because I never thought it was anyone else's business. But my wife was illegitimate. Her mother, who was from a good family, better than mine, gave birth to her but was never married. Neither did she ever tell anyone who the father was. She was sent away to God knows where. An asylum, I think. My wife was brought up by a tenant farmer and his wife, who received an annuity from the grandparents, whom she never saw.

'When I met her, I knew I wanted to marry her, and I didn't care about her background. Our children never knew, not Stephen nor the girls. We told them that their maternal grandparents were dead.'

'Yet you refused to acknowledge Agnes when Stephen met her!' Jenny was astounded by his double standards. 'How could you do that?'

'That was different,' he said tersely. 'She was a married woman. Another man's wife. Stephen and Agnes should've known better. It wasn't my wife's fault that she was born out of wedlock. That was the fault of her mother, and whoever was her father.'

'I'm Christina's mother,' Jenny said softly. 'And

you accept me – or do you?'

He didn't look directly at her, but again turned his gaze out of the window where the rain was lashing against the pane. His lips pouted. 'I don't know the circumstances of your union with Christina's father,' he grunted. 'But you married Stephen legitimately and you're the mother of his sons and daughter. He saw fit to adopt Christina, therefore she's of our family.'

'But – about me?' she whispered. 'What about me?' and she already knew in her heart that she couldn't confess her past to him, that her predicament was her own and not to be shared.

'You made a mistake,' he acknowledged. 'And I don't hold that against you. You've been an asset to our family,' he added gruffly. 'And I'm fond of you, Jenny. Don't think that I'm not. I couldn't manage without you.'

What was it that Billy said? she thought as she went slowly downstairs. She paused, her hand on the polished handrail, and glanced down at the hall with its gleaming wooden floor and bright fire. The maids were instructed to light the fire early every morning and mop the floor every day. She noticed some finger marks on the wall mirror and made a mental note to tell someone to clean it with vinegar and water. You're a housekeeper, Billy had said, and she'd refuted it. We've been given a home, she'd answered, and so we have, she thought. Perhaps in view of everything, it's as much as I deserve.

CHAPTER FORTY-THREE

Christina brushed her hair until it shone, and fastened a pink ribbon in it. Jenny suspected that she had also applied a little rouge on her cheeks for she looked flushed and pretty when Charles Esmond called. She had dressed simply in a white flowered muslin gown with white suede slippers, and Jenny saw instantly that he was enamoured of her.

They chatted over tea and cake, and Mr Esmond said again how he was looking forward to living in Beverley. 'My mother is coming to visit next week,' he said. 'She is anxious, as you mothers always are,' he glanced at Jenny, 'that I will be unable to manage alone. But I've lived on my own in lodgings whilst I was at university, and am quite capable of arranging help, though Mother insists that she shall choose a housekeeper for me. I have advertised already and received several replies, and conducted some interviews.'

Jenny nodded. He seemed too young and innocent to be at the mercy of servants. 'I think your mother's quite right,' she said. ''Wrong servants might take advantage of you.'

'Because I'm a male?' He laughed. 'Perhaps I should employ a butler, a footman and a boot-black, and then I should be able to shout at them and they wouldn't be offended!'

Jenny couldn't help but think of Christy and

433

how he cajoled the servant girls to do his bidding. 'Yes,' she said. 'Because you're a male. You most definitely need a good housekeeper to keep 'others in order, until,' she added, 'you take a wife.'

'Ah! Yes,' he said softly, his eyes straying towards Christina. 'Yes, indeed.'

I'll say nothing, Jenny decided. Not yet. Not unless he declares himself. Perhaps it's no more than a young man's fancy. Christina is young and so is he. They're not ready for a commitment.

And so she said nothing, not to Christina nor to John Laslett, who when he was up once more seemed to have less energy than he had before.

Billy called unexpectedly. Unlike Charles Esmond, he didn't write first. He told her that he had been to Driffield market, but though she believed that he had been there, she was convinced that he had come specially to visit her. She introduced him to John Laslett as an old friend, and he, on discovering that Billy was a butcher, chatted to him quite amiably on pigs and cattle, and the price they were bringing, and William, coming downstairs from his lessons, joined in the conversation.

'Perhaps when my pigs are ready, Mr Brown, I could interest you in buying them,' the boy said animatedly. 'I'm rearing them myself! They're fed on the finest cereals and apples from our orchard.'

Billy nodded and replied seriously, 'Aye, I'll take a look at 'em. Send me a note when they're ready and I'll come over specially.'

'You can look at them now, if you like,' William said eagerly.

'Not now, William,' his mother admonished. 'Mr Brown won't want to go tramping amongst 'pigs. He'll need to bring his rubber boots.'

'Got those with me,' Billy said. 'I allus bring them in 'trap, just in case I need them.'

William gazed at him and then at his mother. 'You talk just the same as Mama, Mr Brown,' he said. 'You've got the same kind of voice!'

'That's because they're from the same background,' his grandfather interrupted, and Jenny felt his eyes on her. 'Every district has its own voice.'

'Have I?' William asked. 'Some of the lads in the village say that I don't speak the way that they do, and Thomas says that sometimes they talk differently on purpose so that we can't understand them.'

'Then you should see more of them,' Billy said. 'It's important to know where you belong and who your folks are.'

Jenny, not quite knowing why, felt proud of Billy. She had expected him to be reticent or self-conscious in the company of John Laslett. But he wasn't; he was confident and assured and when John Laslett got up to leave the room in order to attend to something, Billy stood up and offered his hand to the older man, and said he was pleased to have met him.

John Laslett grunted in his usual manner, but then said, 'Call again next time you're out this way, Brown. We'll be glad to see you.'

William left the room too and Jenny and Billy were left alone. 'I can see you're settled here, Jenny,' Billy said. 'And I understand that you wouldn't want to leave your bairns.'

'My *bairns!*' she said softly. 'No, I wouldn't, not yet anyway.'

'But one day?' he asked. 'Might you?'

She gave a deep sigh. 'I'm so afraid of my past catching up with my future, Billy, that I can't think forward with any certainty. I don't know what 'future holds for me.'

'I've told Annie Fisher that I'll not be seeing her any more.' Billy clasped his hands tightly together. 'Not for 'music hall or socializing and that. She can come into 'shop for a gossip if she wants to, but I don't think she will, not now she knows there's no hope.'

'Poor Annie,' Jenny murmured. 'She's waited so long.'

Billy stood up from his chair and looked down at her. Then he bent and kissed the top of her head. 'What about poor Billy who's waited even longer?'

'I don't know what to say,' she said. 'I can't give you any hope either.'

'But you're not refusing me or turning me away?'

'No.' She gazed up at him. 'I'm not doing that.'

'Then I'll wait,' he said steadily. 'I'm a patient man. I can wait a bit longer.'

When William came in later after showing Billy his pigs, he was jubilant. 'I've done a deal with Mr Brown.' He beamed. 'We've shaken hands on it, man to man!'

Jenny was sitting by the fireside. She put down her sewing. 'Good.' She smiled. 'Are you both pleased?'

'Yes.' William sat down on the floor by her feet. 'I said to him that I wouldn't expect any favours just because he was your friend, and he said that he wouldn't give any; that he didn't do business that way.' He pressed his lips together and nodded. 'Yes, I'm pleased with my part of the bargain. Mr Brown said he would send his waggon to collect as soon as I wrote to him that the pigs were in prime condition.' He gazed pensively into the fire. 'That's my very first order, Mama! I think that's how I'd like to do business. Selling directly to butchers, I mean. Rather than sending to markets. Shaking hands on a deal!'

He leant his head on her knee and she ruffled her hand through his thick brown hair, thinking how fast her youngest child was growing up. 'I wish I'd known my father,' he murmured. 'Thomas says that he's not all that bothered, but I wish I'd known him, even if only for a short time.'

'He would have been proud of you, William,' she said, and her hand strayed to his rounded cheek and stroked it. 'He would have been proud of all of you.'

'Yes, but–' He looked up at her. 'It's just that – when I was talking to Mr Brown today, he sort of treated me like a grown-up person and asked me questions and my opinion, and Grandfather doesn't do that; and I thought that–' His voice trailed away as he pondered. 'And I thought that if I'd had a father, I would have liked him to be like Mr Brown. Was Papa like him?'

'No, he wasn't,' she answered slowly. 'Not like him at all. He was more like your grandfather;

437

rather impatient, but he was very loving,' she added, anxious not to give the wrong impression of Stephen. 'He would have cared for you and wanted what was best for you.' And if Stephen had still been alive, she thought, perhaps we wouldn't be living here now, for he and John Laslett could not have lived under the same roof.

Charles Esmond called again a month later and so did Billy, though not on the same day. Mr Esmond brought with him an invitation requesting the pleasure of their company at a reception the following week, at which they would meet his mother and he would make the acquaintance of his new neighbours.

'I have a housekeeper now,' he said, 'and she's employed some staff for me. She and my mother are in cahoots, I think, for it has been taken out of my hands.'

Jenny started to shake. Suppose she knew the servants? Suppose the neighbours recognized her? Would she be disgraced? And if she was, then so would Christina be. She started to consider that if they accepted the invitation now, then on the day she could plead that she was unwell. Perhaps Arabella would accompany Christina instead? She looked at her daughter's innocent, smiling face and Charles Esmond gazing back at her, and knew that it was too late. They were in love.

'You should go!' Billy said, when she told him of the invitation. 'Don't hide, Jenny. You were acquitted. Face up to whatever it is you're afraid of.'

'The past has come back to haunt me,' she wrote that night. 'Will I always be retreating from it? Can I go to that house again, where once I was a lowly kitchen maid, and enter through the front door as a guest? What memories, what sp will be waiting there for me?'

She looked in the mirror and tried to see herself as she had been at that time. Have I changed? she wondered. Do I look the same? My mother said that I was a plain girl; perhaps that will be my saving grace. If I had been born beautiful, then I would be remembered and recognized.

On the morning of the reception, she did indeed feel unwell and Christina fussed around her, bringing warm drinks, putting her feet up on a footstool and wrapping a shawl round her shoulders. 'Oh, Mama, please don't be ill! I do so want to meet Charles's mother. Oh,' she said. 'That sounds awful, so selfish, but oh dear.' She clasped her hands to her cheek. 'I do so want to meet her and have her approval. Charles has told her about me, he said.'

'You will meet her,' Jenny said weakly. 'I promise. I just need to rest awhile before we set out.' She swallowed hard and asked, 'Are you fond of him, Christina? You are very young to make a commitment.'

'I love him, Mama. I know that I do.' Christina's skirts billowed as she knelt by her mother. 'I knew that the very first day I met him, even though I do realize that I don't know any other young men with whom I can compare him. But I don't want to. I only want Charles.' She looked so earnest that Jenny's heart went out to her. If only, she thought. If only I could be so sure of her happiness. But what if Charles turns against her, or

439

his mother does, if they should find out about me?

'Leave me for a while,' she said. 'Go and prepare yourself whilst I rest. And Christina–'

'Yes?' Christina turned towards her, her face bright and eager.

'I only want what's good for you,' Jenny said softly. 'I've only ever wanted that: but if it doesn't turn out 'way you expect, remember that life doesn't end because of a broken heart. There'll come another love to live for, another life worth dying for. I know that only too well.'

'Mama!' Christina came back towards her. 'I'm so selfish. I'm thinking only of myself and not how lonely you'll be without me if I should marry and go away.'

'I won't be lonely.' Jenny struggled with her fears. 'Now, off you go and prepare yourself. I shall be rested by noon.'

John Laslett had given in some time ago to Arabella's demands to change their ancient carriage and had bought a single-horse brougham. It was dark navy blue with red trimmings and leather upholstery. The driver, who doubled as a gardener and general maintenance man, wore a matching navy blue cape with red edging, and a top hat.

As they arrived in Beverley and drove along New Walk, Jenny reflected that she would never have thought that she would return in such style. And as they drew up outside Mr Esmond's house, the house she had known so well, she saw that theirs was the finest carriage amongst the dogcarts, gigs and hired vehicles. To her relief, she saw Billy's trap among the rest.

Charles Esmond, who must have been watching

from the window, rushed down the path to greet them. Jenny smiled at his enthusiasm and wondered if his mother would approve of her son's greeting his guests so informally, without waiting for the housekeeper or maid to open the door.

'I'm so glad that you could come, Mrs Laslett,' he said. 'And you too, of course, Miss Laslett.' His eyes became dreamy as he gazed at Christina. 'So very pleased. Come in, come in do, and say that you like my house.'

Jenny took a breath to control her tremors as she entered the front door and saw again the hall with its polished floor, where she had knelt with dustpan and brush, polish and duster. 'It's charming,' she croaked. 'So very nice.' Her heart was hammering, her throat was dry and she closed her eyes for a second as she remembered the last time she was here, the sound of a gunshot, the sudden silence, the blood and then the shouting, the screaming, the heavy tread of boots on the floor, before she was led away.

'May I take your cloak, ma'am?' a voice behind her asked politely, and Jenny turned round, unbuttoning the neck ribbon of her garment. She stopped, her fingers seizing up as if paralysed. Mrs Judson stood before her.

'Perhaps I can help with that, ma'am?' the housekeeper said. 'It seems to have caught in a knot.'

'Yes,' Jenny whispered. 'If you would, please.' She lifted her chin whilst Mrs Judson, without any recognition on her face, unfastened the ribbon, and drew the cloak from round Jenny's shoulders.

'And may I take yours, Miss Laslett?' Christina was unfastening her jacket, which she had painstakingly edged with pale blue ribbon to match her gown. Charles hovered near, looking as if he wanted to help. 'Mr Esmond, perhaps you would like to take your guests through to meet your mother?' Mrs Judson suggested with a little nod, indicating the door to the sitting room.

'Oh, yes, of course.' Charles tore his eyes away from Christina and put out his hand for them to accompany him. 'This way.' Jenny lifted her head to look at Mrs Judson, but the housekeeper simply gave a deferential bob of her knee and backed away with the outdoor clothes.

Did she know me? Jenny felt sick. Was she pretending that she didn't? She hasn't changed very much. Just a little older. Strange, when I was young, I always thought her ancient, and yet she can't have been. It was merely her dour manner, which made her seem old.

Charles led them into the sitting room, which Jenny remembered as always being formal with straight-backed chairs, chaise longues and dark velvet curtains. Now it was transformed by comfortable sofas with flowered shawls thrown over them, and brocade curtains at the window, small tables set with china ornaments and vases full of flowers. I see his mother's hand here, Jenny thought. What kind of woman is she to adopt this style?

She quickly discovered, for a plump smiling woman came bustling towards them, a child in her arms and another clinging to her voluminous skirts. 'So delighted you could come,' she cried out in a merry voice. 'You must be Mrs St John Laslett, and this is Miss Christina? I am so pleased to meet you. Charles has talked of no-one else!'

She gathered them along into a group of people who were sitting or standing by the fire, which was lit and fuelled by blazing logs. 'Come along, my dears,' she carolled, 'and be introduced, for you will know no-one, being from the country.'

She introduced them to Charles's neighbours and Jenny eased out a sigh, for she didn't know them or they her. They smiled politely and engaged in sterile conversation. Then Billy came into the room followed by Harry and his wife. One or two of the guests looked rather coldly at them, and Jenny guessed that they were not in the habit of socializing with tradesmen, but Billy was dressed in narrow grey trousers and waist-coat, with a dark frock coat, and she thought that had these people not already known, then no-one would have guessed that he was a butcher.

Harry too was tidy in brown moleskin breeches and a tweed jacket, whilst his wife was wearing an amazing concoction of flowered muslin and a fruit and feathered bonnet. She greeted her hostess and Jenny with cries of delight and the other guests as effusively as if she had known them for years. She had brought her daughter Amy, who came to stand at Christina's side, and presently the two girls took charge of Mrs Esmond's children and took them away into a corner of the room to play.

'You don't mind the children here, do you, my dears?' Mrs Esmond asked the assembled company. 'You see, childhood is so fleeting that I can't bear to part with them. Why, my goodness, it seems only yesterday that Charles was in nankeen trousers and here he is setting up his own household.'

'We knew the Ingrams when they lived here, years ago,' an elderly gentleman with a fine set of white whiskers remarked. 'Don't think they had any offspring.'

'Yes, they did, dear,' his wife interrupted. 'A son and daughter. The boy died. An accident of some kind. It was in the newspapers at the time.' She put her fingers to her forehead and Jenny held her breath. 'Can't quite remember the details–'

Mrs Judson and a young maid, who was holding a tray with glasses of sherry, appeared at her side, distracting her. 'Would you like to sit down, ma'am?' Mrs Judson asked the elderly lady. 'Perhaps you might be more comfortable?'

'Yes,' said Mrs Esmond, as if concluding the conversation. 'It was a tragedy. Poor young man. We don't talk about it. Would anyone care for a biscuit with their sherry?'

When Jenny looked round again during a break in the chatter, she realized that Christina and Charles had disappeared, and that Amy Johnson was alone with the children. She murmured to Billy that she must go and look for them, for it wasn't seemly that they should go off together. Billy gave her a slight smile and said that he would go and find them and bring them back, which he did a few minutes later.

Mrs Esmond whispered into Jenny's ear, 'I think we have two lovebirds here.' She smiled. 'Charles has spoken of your daughter constantly.'

Jenny bit her lip. 'They are very young, Mrs Esmond. Christina is not yet seventeen.'

'I was not much more when I married,' Mrs Esmond confided. 'And you must have been young too? Charles is my first son. He is twenty-one, and I have a daughter of nineteen, another son of fifteen, a daughter of twelve, and these two young ones.' She gave a beaming smile. 'And I am not finished yet. I love my babies. They give such joy, do you not agree? Oh, but forgive me! I forget. You are a widow. How old is your youngest child?'

'He's now twelve,' Jenny said quietly. 'The youngest of five.'

'You should consider marrying again,' Mrs Esmond proposed. 'You are far too young to live alone without a husband!'

Mrs Johnson caught their conversation and gave Mrs Esmond a knowing look and then, to Jenny's mortification, indicated Billy with a glance. 'Just what I said to Harry,' she said in a loud whisper.

'I think I would like to live in Beverley,' Mrs Esmond said to the assembled throng. 'Everyone is so very pleasant. I will speak to my husband on my return home and ask his opinion on the matter.'

'In what business is your husband, madam?' another elderly gentleman boomed. 'Is he able to choose where he should live?'

'Why indeed yes, sir,' Mrs Esmond answered in a surprised tone. 'He is not in business at all. He is the eldest son of a gentleman and may live wherever he pleases.'

Jenny hid a wry smile at the look of astonishment on the faces of some of the gathering. They assumed, she thought, from Mrs Esmond's free and easy manner that they were tradespeople, and were prepared only to tolerate them. We shall see now if their condescending attitude will change.

As they prepared to leave, Mrs Judson and a young maid appeared in the hall with their outdoor garments, and Jenny remembered how the housekeeper, in the days of the Ingrams, always seemed to know when guests were leaving and bustled the maids to gather together the coats and cloaks, umbrellas and top hats.

Now she stood behind Jenny to help her with her cloak, and almost on a breath Jenny heard the whisper in her ear. 'It's good to see you again, Mrs Laslett.' Jenny turned round, her lips parted in a question, but Mrs Judson's face again was expressionless, though she gave a slight nod of her head. Am I fantasizing? Jenny thought. Is it what I want to hear and therefore I imagined it? But Mrs Judson put her hands beneath Jenny's chin to fasten the neck ribbon, and as she tied the bow, she gently patted her neck with a feather-like motion of her fingers.

CHAPTER FORTY-FOUR

'Christina is to be married. Charles Esmond came to ask my permission which I gave, as there was no reason that I could reveal why they should not be married. He is a pleasant young man, of good connections and prospects, and they are obviously in love.' Jenny pulled her shawl about her ears as she wrote. 'It seems strange to think that had Christina been born a boy, *he* might have inherited the house in New Walk. As it is, she will now marry into it.

'Christmas has gone and January is bitterly cold, but we have April to look forward to, which is when they will be married. My darling daughter, who has shared so much with me, will be seventeen and her husband twenty-two. I am very happy for them both but filled with anxiety and apprehension about the future if my past should be discovered.

'I asked John Laslett for his view of the marriage as a matter of courtesy as he has been very supportive of Christina. He gave his blessing and has promised her a dowry. He appears to have forgotten that Stephen left her Lavender Cott and I chose not to remind him.

'Johnny and Serena both came home for Christmas – *home!* Well, it is the only one they have known or remember, and they seemed pleased to be here, though both are very enthusiastic about their lives elsewhere. Arabella has promised Serena that when she finally comes back after her schooling abroad, she'll take her to London to stay with John Laslett's sister and they will attend the balls and social gatherings as young ladies do. Serena was delighted and although she hugged and kissed me, I knew that her life was going to be quite different from mine, and that one day I would lose her. As I pondered on this, I thought of my own mother and wondered if she had had the same thoughts, when

447

I left for Beverley.

'Johnny is tall and handsome, and much like Stephen in looks and temperament. He brought two friends to spend Christmas with us; they all had time off from the military school – *leave*, they call it, and the two young men spent much of their time making sheep's eyes at Serena, to Johnny's scorn and Serena's amusement. I think they would have done the same with Christina, but Charles Esmond, who had been invited also, stayed steadfastly by her side and they had no eyes but for each other.

'For Christmas dinner we ate a fat goose, and a leg of pork courtesy of William. The salted crackling was crisp and the meat full of flavour. William tasted it thoughtfully and pronounced it good and showed no emotion whatsoever although he had reared it. I looked round the table at the happy smiling faces, and wondered why I felt sad and lonely.

'I had invited Billy to spend Christmas Day with us, but he refused, giving all kinds of excuses. But he came on Boxing Day, bringing a present of embroidered handkerchiefs for me, and a sirloin of beef for the kitchen. It turned out that he had spent Christmas Day alone. His mother had gone to her daughter's house and he had eaten a quiet meal in one of the Beverley inns. Then he said he had gone to his empty house, lit a fire and spent the day reading and thinking of me. That's what he told me as we took an energetic walk around the meadows.

'Thomas and William spend most of their time outdoors as soon as they can escape from the schoolroom. Their grandfather asked them if they'd like to go away to boarding school, but both declined. Thomas, in fact, would like to leave his lessons behind altogether and be a full-time farmer; and so we, his grandfather and I, have said we will consider it in the autumn. Had he been a rural labourer's son, of course, he would have left home by now and be working on another farm, and I don't think he quite understands his very great advantages. But he will, one day.

'As to Christina's marriage to Charles Esmond, she came to me one day and told me that she had confessed to him that she was illegitimate and that she had never known her father as he had died before she was born. Charles had informed his parents and told them that no matter what their opinion might be, he was still going to marry Christina. Mrs Esmond then wrote to me and disclosed that she had had to be married in a hurry, as she had been caught with a child – Charles himself, of course – and that they are looking forward to Christina's joining their family. So that is one worry less.

'I took out Christina's birth certificate in preparation for the wedding ceremony, and I had either forgotten or not previously looked at it properly, but now saw that the registrar had written *Jenny Graham* in the space for the mother of the child, with a U for unmarried at the side of it, and left the space blank where the father's name should be. I have decided, therefore, that I will continue to carry the secret of his death alone.'

Billy visited all through the winter months, sometimes spending more time with Thomas and

William than he did with Jenny. He struck up a relationship with John Laslett too, who now that the cattle and sheep had been brought down from the top meadows stayed indoors, leaving his regular men to the outdoor tasks. He felt the cold more now that he was older and seemed glad of the chance to talk of cattle and markets and the price of corn to Billy, rather than converse with Jenny and Arabella on what he called women's matters.

'You should consider marrying Brown,' John Laslett said one evening after Billy had gone. He stretched his bootless stockinged feet towards the fire. 'You could do worse.'

Jenny put down her book and remembered that the Ingrams' cook had made the same remark to her so many years ago. She had answered at that time that she couldn't stand the smell of blood, but it had been an excuse, for she had loved Christy then.

'Could I do better?' she asked her father-in-law wryly.

He considered. 'No, I don't think so,' he said. 'He's done well for himself. Got a bit of money; he's not afraid to spend some of it, and he seems a decent enough fellow. Not a gentleman, of course,' he declared. 'But I'm not sure that that matters.'

'He *is* a gentleman,' Jenny affirmed quietly. 'He always was, and always will be.'

'Mm,' John Laslett murmured. 'Yes, well, you're probably right there. So what about it? Would he ask, do you think? He seems fond of you.'

'How can I leave my boys?' Jenny prevaricated.

'I'm needed here.'

John Laslett looked askance. 'I wasn't thinking of your leaving here. He could come here to live, or else–' He pondered for some time. 'Some married folks do live separately, you know,' he continued. 'I know of a couple where the wife lived with her parents, and the husband lived elsewhere on account of his business. He came often enough to see her for they had several children.' He pursed his lips as he considered. 'But maybe Brown wouldn't want to leave Beverley. If you leave a business in the hands of others they don't always do right by you. I wouldn't want to risk it. Mm,' he said. 'It needs some thinking about.'

'Mama!' William said the following evening. 'Would you ever consider marrying again?'

'Have you been talking to your grandfather?' she asked severely, prepared to be cross with John Laslett.

'To Grandpa? No. Only to Thomas. We think, Tom and I, that Mr Brown is quite sweet on you. He's always asking us questions about you.'

'Is he?' Jenny raised her eyebrows.

'Yes, and–' William ran his fingers through his tangled hair, pushing it out of his eyes. 'Well, we thought, that when Christina has gone off to be married to Charles, and Thomas starts work properly on the estate, then you really only have me to look after.' He gazed at her anxiously and pressed his lips hard together. 'And I'm quite good at looking after myself, though I would miss you if you weren't here.'

'And what about your grandfather, and Serena when she comes home?'

'Serena won't be home for long,' he stated. 'I expect she'll get married as soon as she finds someone rich enough, and Aunt Arabella can look after Grandpa. She won't be getting married, she's too old.'

Poor Arabella, Jenny thought. She wouldn't like to hear that. I do believe she still lives in hope that someone will ask her.

'So, you think I should marry Billy and go back to live in Beverley?'

'Back to live?' he said in surprise. 'Why? Have you lived there before?'

Jenny could have bitten off her tongue. 'Oh,' she said hurriedly. 'Yes, for a short time, when I was young. That's how I came to know Billy.'

'I see,' William said thoughtfully. Then he looked down at the floor and traced a pattern on the rug with the toe of his boot. 'I don't suppose – well, maybe not.'

'What?' Jenny always knew when something was troubling William; he wore all his emotions on his face.

'I don't suppose – if you did marry Mr Brown, I mean; I don't suppose I could come over sometimes and live with you? Would he mind, do you think?' He gazed at her pleadingly. 'I'd miss you very much if I didn't see you!'

She put out her arms and embraced him. She saw how torn he was by wanting to have a father, yet not wanting to lose her. Then she kissed him on his rosy cheek. 'If I thought that he would mind, then I wouldn't marry him,' she said softly. 'I'd miss you far too much.'

Christina and Charles Esmond were married in

April in the ancient church at Kirkburn. John Laslett gave her away and Serena came home to be her attendant. Johnny was absent as he wasn't granted leave to come. The morning was bright with an occasional sharp shower and John Laslett nodded appreciatively. The spring cornfield had been sown just a couple of weeks before and the rain was a blessing. The cattle were back in the meadows and he agreed with Thomas when he said that the wedding had been timed just right, for the lambing and farrowing was about to start.

'Well, that's one off your hands,' John Laslett said bluntly as they waved the newly-weds off on their honeymoon to Scarborough. 'Serena next.'

'Oh, no! She's far too young to be thinking about marriage,' Jenny objected. 'Not for years. Besides, I don't want to lose another daughter just yet.'

But Serena had ideas of her own. She had one more year of school in Switzerland before returning home, and then, she told her mother, she would like to go and live in London with Great-Aunt Harriet, Arabella's aunt. 'It doesn't mean I wouldn't see you, Mama,' she said as Jenny gave a startled exclamation. They were sitting relaxing after the excitement of Christina's wedding day. 'Of course I would! I'd come back very often.' She lowered her voice. 'But I don't want to stay here in the country. I'd die of boredom! I want to attend theatres and galas, and concerts – and – and visit!'

Jenny sighed. She was sure that Arabella had put these ideas into Serena's head. It was what *she* would have liked to do if she hadn't had to stay at home with her father in the early years.

'And of course,' Serena wheedled, 'Great-Aunt Harriet hasn't any children of her own and she says that she has always *longed* to go to all the parties and balls with young people.'

'So has she said that you may stay with her, Serena?' Jenny asked quietly. 'Have you already arranged it?'

Serena looked embarrassed. 'Not exactly, Mama. I wouldn't without asking you first! But Aunt Harriet has written to me several times and suggested it, and I've replied that I would only go with your blessing.'

'I see.' There was no denying that Jenny felt hurt, even though she understood Serena's desires. 'Well, perhaps it could be arranged. But she's a stranger to me, Serena. I've never met her, though I understand from Arabella that she's very pleasant and kind. Nevertheless, how can I trust a stranger to take care of you?'

Serena's skirts rustled as she rose from her chair and hurried to Jenny's side. 'She's going to write to you, Mama,' she said earnestly. 'She would have done so before, only I asked her to wait until after Christina's wedding. And she also said she would visit you, unless you would like to visit her? Grandpa or Aunt Arabella would take you!'

'No!' Jenny said. 'I wouldn't like to do that!' How nervous and self-conscious I would be, she thought. I'd be out of place, afraid of doing the wrong thing. I know where I belong and it isn't with those grand and influential people. She patted Serena on her cheek. 'We won't plan too far ahead,' she said. 'Let's wait a little while and see what happens.'

But she knew in her heart that the path was laid and Serena would eventually walk upon it, away from her and into another life. Just as I did, she recalled.

A month later, Jenny took the train to Beverley, this time taking William with her, dragging him reluctantly away from his precious pigs. She was anxious to see Christina, to hear how she was coping with married life, and most of all how she was settling into her home in New Walk. It had taken a great deal of effort to convince herself that everything would be all right, but nevertheless as she walked to Christina's front door she felt sick with nerves and her body shook so much that William looked up and asked if she was cold.

Christina opened the door herself and flung her arms round her mother. 'I'm so happy to see you, Mama. Come in, come in, and see the changes I've made. Mrs Esmond – Charles's mother, I mean – hasn't the same taste as I have, although I realize she has more experience, so I'm changing the cushions and the bed hangings, though leaving the curtains, and Mrs Judson is helping me with the measuring and everything.'

Mrs Judson! Jenny held back a gasp. She hadn't expected Mrs Judson to stay on in the household after recognizing her. She had thought that she would leave on hearing of the marriage. I should have asked, she brooded. Why didn't I think to ask?

'Perhaps I might have a word with her?' she said guardedly. 'Just to make sure she understands what's needed,' she added.

'Oh, the poor lady has already had Mrs Esmond telling her what to do!' Christina exclaimed. 'And really, I treat her much the same as I did Dolly when I was at home.'

'Ah!' Jenny's worries over how Christina would cope with a household abated, but she was still nervous about Mrs Judson's being here. 'Well, just to introduce myself,' she prevaricated. 'To make sure all is well.'

Christina darted off to find the housekeeper, calling over her shoulder that she would find Charles to come and say hello. 'Come with me, William.' She stopped in the doorway. 'You don't want to listen to Mama talking about servants' duties! Come and see my little dog.'

Jenny walked up and down the drawing room, waiting apprehensively for the housekeeper to appear. Christina had made changes to the room, getting rid of the fussy covers and ornaments which Mrs Esmond had chosen, putting her own favourite colours and paintings on the walls. There were also souvenirs scattered about, which the young couple had clearly brought back from their holiday in Scarborough. A reminder, Jenny thought, of what I hope was a happy time, and she reflected that she had never had a holiday. I have been closeted away all these years. But it was what I wanted.

'You asked to see me, Mrs Laslett?'

Jenny turned round to confront Mrs Judson. They looked at each other, their eyes meeting. Jenny cleared her throat to speak, but Mrs Judson spoke first.

456

'How are you, Jenny?' she said softly. 'It's nice to see you again.'

Jenny went towards her. 'Mrs Judson,' she began and they both smiled at the role reversal. 'I'm very glad to see you too.'

Mrs Judson nodded and glanced towards the door, which she had firmly closed. 'You don't have to worry,' she said. 'No-one knows that I ever worked here before. All the other servants are new and not from Beverley.' She looked Jenny in the eyes. 'And I'll look after your daughter. She's very young. They both are. She looks like her father,' she added softly. 'And with a merry disposition.'

'But unworldly, Mrs Judson!' Jenny entreated. 'As Christy was, and therefore vulnerable. And—' She hesitated before saying, 'She doesn't know what happened.'

Mrs Judson shook her head. 'No need for her to know. What's past is past. She'll not hear anything from me.'

Jenny felt tears gathering. 'Thank you,' she choked. 'Thank you.'

'I'll take care of her,' Mrs Judson affirmed. 'I'll need to take care of both of them, cos they're just babbies.' Then she gave a rare wide smile. 'But they'll be all right. They'll grow up together.'

They heard the sound of voices in the hall and William, Christina and Charles came into the room.

'Mama!' William exclaimed. 'Christina and Charles have got a dog! And they've got a new horse each!'

'Will that be all, Mrs Laslett?' Mrs Judson

broke in. 'If so I'll just speak to Cook about luncheon.'

'Thank you, Mrs Judson. Yes, everything is most satisfactory,' Jenny said solemnly. 'I'm sure that my daughter and Mr Esmond will have a perfectly run household with you in charge.'

'Oh, Mama,' Christina said as the housekeeper went out of the room. 'I hope you were not too hard on her, for she's such a dear, even though she seems to be so dull.'

Jenny heaved a sigh. 'No,' she said. 'Mrs Judson and I have a perfectly good understanding.' She wiped the corner of her eye. 'I can't think of anyone else I would rather have here to look after you.'

CHAPTER FORTY-FIVE

'Can we go and see Mr Brown?' William asked as they prepared to leave Christina and Charles. 'We've time before the train leaves.'

'He'll be in his shop, I expect, but yes, we'll call and say hello. We'll walk, thank you,' she said to Charles, who was putting on his coat to take them in the trap. 'It's such a lovely day.' She kissed Christina goodbye and promised she would come again soon. She meant it; some of her fears had dissipated, though she had been apprehensive as Christina had shown her over the house, telling her of her plans for each room.

When Christina opened the door to the library

458

Jenny had held her breath. Was there still blood on the carpet? Would there be spectres waiting for her? Was it the same chair where Christy had sat her on his knee and told her that they would die together?

But the furniture was draped in white sheets and a workman's ladder and pots of paint littered the room. 'This will be Charles's study,' Christina had said. 'He said he needs his own room for writing letters and so on, and I quite agree,' she'd laughed, 'for I've discovered that he's most untidy!'

Jenny looked down New Walk. The sun was shining through the chestnut trees, dappling the leaves, and she recalled how on a winter's night she used to open the window in the top attic of the house to hear the hoot of the tawny owls which often roosted within the branches.

The road was still rutted like a country lane as she remembered it, and although there were houses and barns which had remained the same, building work had been started on new houses leading down to North Bar Without. Christina will soon have new neighbours, she thought. The area is changing.

Billy had two assistant butchers in the Saturday Market shop who were busy with customers, but one of them called upstairs to where Billy was working on accounts. He invited them up to his rooms, but William lingered for a while to watch the butchers jointing and boning the meat. There were numerous rooms above the shop, but the one at the front overlooking the Market Cross had been made into a comfortable living room with leather armchairs and a fireplace, which today wasn't lit. 'I've a young lass comes in once a week to do for me,' Billy said bashfully. 'She keeps it tidy. Ma offered to do it, and so did Annie.' He grinned. 'But I was having none of that.' Then he became serious. 'It'll do for 'time being anyway.'

He looked towards the doorway to listen for the sound of William coming up the stairs, and when there was none he said quickly, 'Have you given thought, Jenny? About what I asked you?'

'Yes,' she said softly. 'I think about it often, but I'm still in a dilemma about my children.' She felt morose as she thought that Serena and Johnny had already planned their own lives. There was only Thomas, who was quite independent anyway, and William, who did need her. Yet still she hesitated about her own life.

'Then I'll wait,' he said steadily. 'As long as I've got some hope.'

Going back on the train she pondered the question, and William, who was usually so talkative, was silent, gazing out of the window and not making any conversation. Eventually, when they were almost into Driffield station, he turned towards her and said, 'I wouldn't mind being a butcher.'

'I thought you wanted to rear pigs!'

'Well, yes I do. Would it be possible to do both, do you think?'

Jenny laughed. William had obviously not yet made up his mind about his future. 'I've really no idea,' she said. 'You'll have to ask your grandfather, or Mr Brown.'

During the early summer Jenny spent much of

her time alone. Thomas and William were busy on the land and they were excused their lessons. Young lambs were skipping in the meadows and by the end of June haymaking would be under way. Thomas had boldly asked his grandfather if he and William could have a wage as they were doing almost as much work as the regular labourers. John Laslett was so taken aback that he agreed.

'I'll give you half of what I pay the plough boys,' he said. 'Six pounds each.'

'Josh Smith gets thirteen pounds a year, so half of that's six pounds ten shillings!' Thomas argued and William held his breath, and stared aghast at his brother's effrontery. He wouldn't have argued with his grandfather.

'You young varmint!' John Laslett grunted. But he agreed the amount and said there was to be no slacking or they would be sacked, just like anyone else.

Arabella was out visiting most afternoons, so Jenny walked on her own down the sweet-smelling country lanes, listening to the chorus of birdsong, looking at the wild flowers which grew on the chalk soil; inspecting the ragged hedges for wrens and watching the deer on the high ridges. In the areas which were not cultivated there were masses of cow parsley, and banks of white dead-nettles swarmed with butterflies; rabbits ran unchecked, ox-eye daisies, red and white campion and forget-me-not were scattered everywhere, whilst high above her skylarks with their piping cry flew unseen, and sparrowhawks dipped and dived over hedges. Turtledoves crowed from the tops of young sycamore trees and she knew that she was lonely.

She stood by the window looking out one blustery day, wondering what to do with her time. Everyone was out, the routine of the day was organized, the meals arranged. I'm so efficient, she thought. The house is so well run that I'm almost superfluous. John Laslett's voice boomed behind her. She hadn't heard him come in. 'What's up, Jenny?' he asked. 'Nothing to do?'

She turned to him, her expression set. 'I could find something, I'm sure. But there's nothing that appeals. Too much sewing and planning makes me very dull.'

He looked steadily at her. 'Marry that Brown fellow,' he said. 'He wants you to, doesn't he?'

'Yes, he does,' she admitted.

'Well then!' He leaned heavily on his stick. 'Why not? We'll manage, you know. I'll stop Bella gallivanting about! Come and sit down and talk to me.' He limped across to a chair. 'And tell me why not! You're too young to spend the rest of your life alone.'

How can I tell him? she pondered as she sat across from him. How can I say that I'm afraid? If I stay here then no-one knows me or anything about me. I'm sheltered and safe from pointing fingers and heedless gossip. 'I'm needed here,' she said weakly. 'And I feel that by being here I'm giving something back to you for giving my children and me a home all these years.'

On his face was an expression of astonishment. 'Is that how you feel?' he said bluntly. 'I didn't realize. But your children are my grandchildren,

462

my flesh and blood, and you were Stephen's wife.'

But you disowned your son, she wanted to say, and was startled when he went on. 'Do you not think that I have regrets over Stephen? Do you think that I haven't had sleepless nights repenting of the things I've said? The things I've done or didn't do? No,' he muttered. 'How could you?'

'If I married again, you'd have no obligation to me,' she said. 'And – and I'd be afraid that I'd lose my children.'

'You think that in a fit of pique, I might stop you from seeing your sons? Jenny!' he exclaimed. 'Your boys are almost grown! Soon they'll make their own decisions about what they want to do, just as Johnny and Serena have done. I won't let them down, not the way I let my son down. They'll be safe, no matter what decision you take over your own life. There's something else, isn't there?' he asked astutely. 'Something you don't wish to speak about?'

'Yes,' she admitted in a whisper. 'I can't speak of it and it has blighted my life.'

He looked at her for a moment and then shook his head. 'Then I can't help you.'

She wrote to Billy that afternoon. 'Dearest Billy, I've made a decision regarding marriage, if, that is, you are in the same mind as before and still wish to take me as your wife. I have pondered long on the question and I want to assure you that the delayed answer was not because of any doubts of my feelings towards you, but because of my responsibility towards my children and my father-in-law, John Laslett, who has been most considerate of me since Stephen died.

'I can bring nothing material into our union, for I've no fortune I can call my own, except for my sons and daughters who will, if we should marry, treat you with the respect you deserve. William in particular longs for a father he can talk to and I hope you realize that in taking me as a wife, you'll also become stepfather to my children. If you don't think you can take on this obligation, I'll understand, and because of this I haven't told anyone else of my decision. I realize that this letter may sound dispassionate, but I have held back my emotions for so long that I have difficulty in expressing myself otherwise. I would however assure you that I do and always did hold you in the greatest affection, regard and as my dearest friend. Jenny.'

She sealed the envelope, put on a stamp and called downstairs for one of the maids to take the letter immediately to the post, rather than wait for the following morning. It's done, she thought as she watched the girl scurrying down the long track to the road, her cloak billowing in the gusty breeze. If I'd waited for the morning post I might have changed my mind.

It was late afternoon the following day when she heard the clop of hooves and the rattle of wheels coming towards the house. John Laslett had gone with Thomas and William to the haymaking, and Arabella was out on one of her interminable visits. Jenny rose from her chair and looked out of the window. Billy was jumping down from the trap. He hooked the reins over the foot scraper at the front door and bounded up the steps. She heard the bell peal and the clack of Dolly's heels on the tiled floor as she went to answer it.

Dolly showed Billy in to her and closed the door. His face was flushed and his hair wind-blown, though he brushed his hand over it as he entered. ''Letter came this dinner time,' he said without preamble. 'I came straight away. I can't believe– Jenny, I can't believe that you'll have me! You mean it, don't you?'

She gazed at him and saw in his demeanour the bashful boy she once knew. The boy who had always loved her and yet had been too self-effacing to tell her, because she loved another. She smiled. 'I mean it, Billy. I don't know how it'll work out, because I'll want to see my family – but–'

'It'll work out, Jenny, don't be feared o' that.' He stumbled over his words. 'As long as we can be man and wife.' He took hold of her hands. 'I love you enough for both of us, and maybe one day you'll feel 'same about me.'

He put his finger to her lips as she was about to dispute. 'I know that you once loved Christy,' he said. 'And mebbe you loved your husband. I'd hope that you did. But that's all in 'past now and we can look forward to a future together. It's what I've always wanted, Jenny. I'll look after you and love you and protect you, just as I'll have to promise in church when we wed.'

She felt tears gathering in her eyes and she blinked them away. 'You're a good man, Billy Brown,' she said softly. 'I'll do my best to be deserving of your love.'

CHAPTER FORTY-SIX

Billy thought there was no need for them to wait to be married, but he reluctantly agreed that the end of September, after harvest, would be best for all concerned. Jenny wanted Thomas and William to be at the wedding and they were always busy at harvest time. John Laslett asked if he could escort her to church. She wrote to Serena and Johnny to tell them and although there was no difficulty about Serena's coming back, Johnny wrote that he might not be able to come home as he was due to be posted abroad. 'There is continuing trouble in the Balkans,' he wrote, 'and now that Russia has declared war on Turkey we are on constant alert.'

'There's always trouble in the Balkans,' John Laslett grunted when Jenny read out Johnny's letter. 'And Gladstone and Disraeli are forever at each other's throats. I reckon there'll be trouble in Constantinople before long.'

'But Johnny's so young!' Jenny said fearfully. 'Surely they won't send inexperienced boys?'

'He's a soldier,' her father-in-law barked. 'He wanted excitement and adventure and that's what he'll get.'

'That's of no comfort at all!' Jenny retaliated and stalked out of the room in tears.

I'm so afraid. Afraid for Johnny. Afraid for Christina. Afraid of everything. She sat by the writing table in her room and unlocked the drawer where she kept her pencils and writing pad. She stared down at them. Those notes had been her redemption. All of those years when she had been fearful of confiding in anyone, she had written in her notebooks, dozens of them, which were now hidden away under lock and key. Those secret pages, which contained her innermost thoughts, had been her deliverance, her atonement, somehow setting her free from liability and restoring her to some kind of sanity.

Billy deserves someone better than me, she thought. I know that he loves me and if I ever allowed myself to love anyone again, I could love him. But should I marry him? Is it fair? Will he ever wish that he hadn't married me when fingers are pointed at Billy Brown's wife? Don't I remember her? they'll say. Wasn't there a scandal some years ago? Didn't someone die?

She closed the drawer and locked it as she heard a quiet tap on the door. 'Come in,' she called, and John Laslett turned the brass knob and put his head inside.

'He'll be all right, I expect,' he said apologetically. 'Johnny, I mean,' he added, as a puzzled frown creased her forehead.

'Oh! Yes, I suppose he will.' She was warmed by his unexpected condolence. 'But it's a worry, isn't it?'

He nodded and withdrew. She unlocked the drawer again. I'll write to Billy, she thought. I'll tell him I'm going to stay with Christina for a day or two. I'll see then how I feel when I'm in Beverley again. She shivered. I've Christina's happiness to think of; how will she feel if there is tittle-tattle and gossip about her mother?

When she arrived at Christina's, Charles's mother was visiting along with two of her children. She greeted Jenny gaily and rang the bell for tea. Christina seemed subdued, Jenny thought, and when she enquired after Charles, it was Tilly Esmond who gave her the details of her son's whereabouts, what time he had left and the approximate time of his return.

'I'm pleased to see you, Mrs Esmond,' Jenny said. 'But I hope it isn't inconvenient for you, Christina, to have me here to stay as well?'

'Oh, not at all, Mrs Laslett,' Tilly Esmond broke in. 'The house is very large, too big really for two young people. I love it here, so Christina and Charles can expect me often!' She gave a jolly laugh. 'I've made such friends with Mrs Johnson – Harry Johnson's wife, you know. We have so much in common.'

After they had had tea, Mrs Esmond went off to attend to the children, saying she would be back shortly. 'Christina will look after you,' she said blithely. 'She's such a dear girl. But she's changed all the furniture around!'

Christina gazed at her mother. Her eyes glistened and her mouth trembled. 'She's very nice, Mama, and helpful,' she said in a choked voice. 'And the children are delightful. But–' Her mouth pouted. 'I wish she didn't come quite so often, and Charles thinks the same. He was so pleased to have been given this house because he thought he would have his own life. But his mother has followed him here and is trying to persuade her husband to come and stay too!'

'Mr Esmond may not come. He's probably enjoying the peace of being on his own whilst his wife is here,' Jenny murmured, sympathizing with her daughter. 'Would you like me to say something? Maybe about young married people needing to be on their own?'

'Oh, no!' Christina declared. 'I wouldn't want to upset her; as I say, she is very kind and merry, but, well, I don't feel as if the house is our own.'

'I do know what you mean, Christina,' Jenny said softly. 'We must think of what we can do.'

Billy came for her in the trap the next morning. He was wearing a tweed jacket, cord trousers and a felt hat. 'Where are we going?' she asked, for he was obviously dressed for an outing.

'I thought we'd take a trip into Hull,' he said. 'I'll show you my shops. One of my lads will collect 'trap at 'station and we'll catch 'train. Go and get your hat.' He smiled. 'You never know who we might meet.'

Jenny dressed plainly, as she always did. She spent little money on herself and hoped that if she wore only plain colours, grey or black, then no-one would notice her, or, if they did, wouldn't realize that she was wearing the same gown. But today Christina followed her into the bedroom, bringing with her a colourful silk shawl.

'Wear this, Mama. You need some colour, you're very pale.' She looked anxiously at her mother. 'Are you not well? Is something troubling you?' She put her arms round her. 'I do miss you, Mama. I love Charles, but I do miss you.'

Jenny kissed her cheek. 'I miss you too, but I'm

so glad that you are happy with Charles; and don't worry about Mrs Esmond,' she added. 'She'll tire of the travelling eventually.'

'But that's the worry, don't you see? Perhaps she'll want to come and live here permanently!'

'Then Charles must put his foot down and insist they buy another house. He must speak to his father.'

She tied the shawl round her shoulders and looked in the mirror. Yes, the colour improved her pale complexion and emphasized her dark hair, which she had coiled around her ears. She put on her bonnet, but Christina exclaimed that it was too dull and dashed away to fetch one of her own.

'It's so nice to have some money to spend, Mama,' she whispered on her return. 'Charles said he's going to spoil me! Here, try this one.' She handed Jenny a silver grey pleated silk bonnet. 'Perfect,' she proclaimed.

Billy nodded his approval as Jenny came downstairs to where he was waiting in the hall. As she passed the open door of the library, she glanced in. Her eyes were drawn to the wall where the gun cupboard had formerly been, but it was no longer there and one of Christina's pictures, a hunting scene with dogs, was hanging in its place. She shivered as she stared in and saw Charles's desk in the same place as Mr Ingram's used to be.

She felt pressure on her arm. 'Let's be off, Jenny,' Billy murmured. 'We don't want to miss 'train.'

He chatted of inconsequential things as they drove to the station, gave over the care of the horse and trap to his waiting employee, and escorted her

470

into the concourse where he bought tickets. Jenny thought with nostalgia of the once shy youth who had urged her to hold on tight in the open train carriage, who was now a self-assured successful man of business travelling first class.

They had the carriage to themselves and Billy turned to her. 'You mustn't dwell on 'past, Jenny,' he began, as the engine got up a head of steam. 'Try to put it behind you. I know it can't be easy with Christina living in 'Ingrams' house – it's fate that your daughter should marry into that family. You just wouldn't think something like that could happen, but it has, so you've got to make 'best of it.'

'Christina doesn't know,' she began, but he interrupted her.

'I know she doesn't,' he said. 'And I think you should have told her; but that's your decision and I respect that. Anyway,' he said, taking hold of her hand. 'Let's not talk about such things now. I've got a surprise for you when we get into Hull.'

He wouldn't be drawn on what the surprise was, and she gazed out of the window at the passing view. The day was warm and sunny and she began to relax. She took a breath when they arrived into the Hull Paragon station, and murmured, 'Dear old Hull. A blind man would know when he'd arrived here. There's still the odour of oil mills and fish oil and tallow. It's really quite comforting,' she added. 'As if nothing's changed.'

She felt a lump in her throat as an affecting sensation washed over her. A combination of nostalgia and sadness, which was both touching and poignant. Where are my ma and da? My sisters and brothers? I abandoned them. Never got in touch with them except for that one letter when I wrote to tell Ma that her sister Agnes had died, and that I had married. They know nothing of me, or of my children, or what I've done with my life. They don't know if I'm alive or dead, as indeed they might also be. A sob crept into her chest and she wanted to cry, something she rarely did, so tightly did she keep her emotions in check.

'Billy, I – I'd like to go down Whitefriargate.' Her words were halting, and she looked across from the station concourse towards the town. 'It's where my family live. I've not seen them in a long time. I don't know if they'd welcome me – but I'd like to go.'

Billy looked down at her. 'They're not there any more,' he said quietly. 'They moved. Got a chance of better housing.'

She gazed at him in astonishment. 'How do you know?'

'I told you that I'd looked for you, didn't I?' His neck reddened as he confessed. 'After I'd seen you in Beverley that time, when Christina was just a babby, I went searching in 'villages around Beverley; Cherry Burton, Etton, all the big houses where I thought Stephen Laslett might live. I had it in mind that you'd leave his employ and marry me. But I couldn't find you. Nobody seemed to know you, or if they did they weren't saying. Anyway, then I thought I'd look in Hull. I thought mebbe you'd come back to live with your family.

'Well, I found them after a lot of effort, and just in time, cos they'd been offered a shop with rooms, just out of town on Spring Bank.'

'A shop! They've got a shop?' She gazed incredulously at Billy.

'Aye. Your ma and one of your brothers run it. I've kept in touch with them and they said they'd tell me if ever you turned up. But of course you didn't.' She saw a tenderness in his eyes and realized just how long and faithfully he had cared for her.

'I'm sorry, Billy,' she whispered. 'I didn't know.'

He shook his head. 'How could you?' he said. 'You were making another kind of life, getting married, having bairns. And nobody knew where you were,' he added. 'Nobody at all.'

How well we kept ourselves private, Stephen, Agnes and I, she thought as she walked at Billy's side towards the ranks of horse cabs waiting outside the station. We wanted solitude and shelter from gossip, and even after Stephen's death I was still afraid of being found out; frightened that people might discover who I really was. 'So is that where we're going?' she asked nervously. 'Is that the surprise?'

'Aye. But only if you want to,' he said. 'You don't have to. But it's a start.'

'A start?' She gazed up at him. 'A start to what?'

'To your coming back into the world,' he said. 'To begin living again. To being yourself.'

She gave a weak smile. 'I didn't realize that you knew me so well, Billy.'

'I know you, Jenny!' he said softly. 'Better than you think. Are we going or not? I haven't told them that I've found you, so it's up to you.'

He looked so beseechingly at her that she

wanted to please him and also, yes, she did want to see her parents. 'I found you, Billy,' she reminded him. 'You didn't find me.' She nodded. 'Yes, we'll go and see if they're pleased to see me.' Then she had a sudden thought. 'My da? Is he–'

'He's grand,' he assured her. 'Or he was 'last time I saw him. He's still working down at 'docks.'

She didn't know this part of Hull, and was pleasantly surprised by the new terraced housing and shops that were spread along the tree-lined road which led to the Botanic Gardens. The cab drew up outside a grocer's shop and Billy got out and handed Jenny down. He paid the driver and told him they would walk back into town.

Jenny took hold of Billy's arm. She felt sick and nervous and held back as Billy opened the door, causing the bell to ring. The interior smelled of cheese and paraffin, of yeast and boiled bacon, vinegar, spices and tobacco. On the floor were sacks of potatoes and onions and boxes of sweet biscuits. It seemed to be a shop that sold everything. A man in a white apron was behind the counter, slicing up a large round cheese into portions. He looked up and smiled. 'Morning,' he said. 'Nice morning.' Then he looked again at Billy and his eyes creased in recognition. 'Mr Brown, isn't it?' He grinned, then glanced at Jenny and nodded. 'Morning, ma'am!'

'It's Jenny, Joseph,' she said softly, realizing that her youngest brother, who had been only eight when she had left home, didn't know her. 'Have you forgotten me?'

He looked puzzled for a moment and put his

head on one side, raising his eyebrows as he appraised her. 'Jenny–' Then his eyes widened. 'Not our Jenny?' He took a breath. 'Not our Jenny?'

She nodded. ''Same!'

He came round the counter and stood in front of her. 'I can't – I don't–'

'You don't remember me?' she said sadly.

'I'm – not sure,' he said, glancing again at Billy. 'I still have this picture in my head of how you were! You had long plaits.' He smiled. 'They were thick and shiny and I used to pull them, and you were so bright and clever and–' He put out his hands to her and taking hers he drew her towards him and kissed her cheek. She saw his eyes mist over. 'We've missed you,' he said, and then, as if gathering himself together, he pulled her along with him and went to an inner door. He opened it and yelled up the stairs. 'Ma! Da! Come down here! Our Jenny's come back!'

Jenny's mother hobbled down the stairs and stood in the doorway with her hand on her hip in a familiar position. 'I knew you'd be back sooner or later,' she said in a cracked voice. 'I said to your da, I said, she'll be back when she's good and ready. Didn't think it'd tek so long, though.' She didn't offer to give Jenny a kiss or a hug, but then Jenny would have been surprised if she had. Her mother had never been demonstrative.

But Jenny's father pushed past his wife and wept as he put his arms round her. 'I thought we'd never see you again, lass.' He blew his nose. 'What kept you so long?'

'This young fella's been looking for you for

475

years,' her mother said. 'Shouldn't be surprised if he's not sweet on you. Come on,' she said, turning towards the stairs. 'You'd better come on up and tell us what you've been up to.'

CHAPTER FORTY-SEVEN

Jenny spoke little on the train journey back to Beverley and Billy wisely didn't talk or ask any questions. She felt drained; so much emotion had been expended on the meeting with her family. She had been tense at first, unsure of what to tell them; but then her mother asked about 'the bairn', meaning Christina, and she told her about the other children and that she was a widow. Her father had been very emotional and said that he had worried over her constantly until her letter had arrived, telling of her marriage, and then he had felt relieved, though he was sorry to hear now of her husband's death.

Billy told them that he and Jenny were going to be married and asked them to come to the wedding and there were smiles about that. There was much more that could have been discussed, but they were all hesitant. So many years had passed that it was difficult to know where to begin. But the ice was broken and the next time would be easier.

After they left them to walk back into the town, Billy showed her his two shops. He slipped in to greet his employees and proudly told Jenny they were doing well.

'Are you rich, Billy?' she joked, but he answered in all seriousness that he considered that he was.

The next day in Beverley, Billy collected her from Christina's house to drive her back to the station to catch the Driffield train. What am I to do? Jenny brooded. I was going to discuss my fears with him, and I haven't, nor have I told him that I think he might regret marrying me. It would be surely better for everyone if I stayed where I am, hidden away. I'm thinking of Billy and I'm thinking of Christina. But no, if I'm honest, I'm thinking of myself.

'Stop,' she called suddenly as she saw two people riding on one horse, travelling in the opposite direction. 'Stop a minute. I know them.'

'Gypsies!' Billy said. 'Why do you want to stop?'

She climbed down. 'They stay on Stephen's – Christina's – land.' She hailed the Romanies and went across to them. Floure slipped down from the horse. She was barefoot, her feet brown and muddy beneath her cotton skirt. She wore a shawl round her head and beneath it Jenny saw the glint of gold earrings.

'Hello, lady.' Floure gazed at her.

'Do you still stay at Lavender Cott?' Jenny asked her. 'I haven't been for some time.'

Floure nodded gravely. 'Your *chi*, she said that we could,' she said huskily.

'Oh, yes, I know she did,' Jenny flustered. 'I only wondered if you still did.'

'Tell her to come back,' the Romany muttered. 'Her and her *rom*. The house needs them. It needs *chavvies* there to come alive again.'

'*Chavvies?* What do you mean?' Jenny half understood, and an idea formed in her mind.

Floure smiled. 'Children. Tell her to come.'

'I will.' Jenny smiled back. 'Why are you here in Beverley? Have you come for the horse fairs?'

'No. To sell a horse. Mr Johnson has bought one from us.'

'Oh!' What a coincidence, Jenny thought, and told her, 'Mr Johnson is a friend of mine.'

'Aye, I knows it. We've seen your *chavi* there.' She gazed earnestly at Jenny, her dark eyes probing. 'Tell her to come back. We're moving soon to the country fairs; the house and land will be empty.'

'Yes. I'll tell her.' And what about me, Jenny wanted to say. What shall I do?

'Your life is in your own hands,' the Romany murmured and before turning away, added, 'It always was.'

The summer passed quickly. The weather was hot with light rain during the evenings, which promised an early harvest. Jenny made instinctive arrangements towards her wedding, even though she was still having doubts about it. She shared these doubts with no-one and acted as if all was well. She asked the servants to clean the house from top to bottom so that Arabella didn't have too much to organize after she was married, for Arabella was glum at the prospect of being once more at her father's beck and call.

'I know I'm being selfish, Jenny,' she said. 'But you're so much better at this kind of thing. You've done it yourself, after all.'

Yes, Jenny thought. As if I needed reminding that I was once a kitchen maid. I haven't ever forgotten. But she said nothing and only assured her sister-in-law that the servants knew exactly what to do. 'Dolly will make sure that everything is done properly,' she said. 'And it isn't as if I'm leaving altogether. I'm going to be here often. I must,' she added fervently, 'for I need to see Thomas and William.'

'I don't see how you can split yourself in two,' Arabella grumbled petulantly. '*And* it also means that I shall be tied to the house! Are you sure this is what you want, Jenny?' she implored. 'Perhaps Mr Brown would wait a little longer? Until the boys are older.'

Jenny knew very well that Arabella wasn't thinking of the boys at all, but only of herself, but she held her tongue and promised that she would make sure that Dolly took full responsibility over the servants.

She spoke to Dolly one afternoon as together they were rehanging clean curtains. 'Miss Arabella is worrying over what will happen to 'housekeeping after my marriage,' she told her. 'I'll spend most of my time in Beverley, but I'll come here at least one or two days in the week.'

'Why, you'll wear yourself out, Mrs Laslett!' Dolly said. 'You'll want to see your boys, of course, but you and Miss Arabella don't have to worry about 'housekeeping or 'kitchen.' She gave an apologetic grin. 'Miss Arabella never did have much idea about running a household, begging your pardon, ma'am, but you've got everything organized so we'll just carry on as if you were here.'

'Thank you, Dolly. That will ease my mind. And I'll still arrange 'ordering of groceries with Cook, just as I do at present.'

Dolly looked thoughtful as she arranged the curtains into folds. 'Begging your pardon, Mrs Laslett, but perhaps it'd be as well if Miss Arabella discussed that with Cook as well. Once you're settled back in Beverley again, you might not be inclined to come over just to arrange 'groceries!'

It was a mere slip of the tongue, and Jenny might not have noticed the reference to being settled again in Beverley, but Dolly took in a sudden breath and blushed scarlet.

Jenny swallowed and bent her head. Was it just an error? How could Dolly know? Jenny had come to Laslett Hall from Lavender Cott with her children. Why should Dolly know that she had previously lived in Beverley? Unless – Jenny glanced at the servant. She was plainly embarrassed and biting her lips together, though her blush was fading.

'What I mean is, Mrs Laslett,' Dolly said, 'when you're married to Mr Brown.' She stopped and faced Jenny. 'I'm sorry. It's nothing to do wi' me. I'm speaking out of turn – and,' she took a deep breath, 'I don't usually do that.'

'No, you don't,' Jenny agreed. 'You're always discreet. Have you always been?'

'Yes, ma'am.' Dolly lowered her eyes. 'Always. I'm not one for gossip.'

'And have you heard gossip?' Jenny had to

know. It was vital that she did.

'No, ma'am. I haven't.' Dolly pressed her lips together and paused. 'Not heard. Onny seen for myself.'

Jenny lowered herself into a chair. She could feel a pulse hammering in her temples and she felt suddenly weak and vulnerable. 'What? What have you seen?'

Dolly walked to the door and closed it, then she came back and stood in front of Jenny. 'I once worked as a chambermaid in one of 'old inns in Beverley,' she said quietly. 'We'd heard, 'other servants and me, I mean, about Christopher Ingram's death, and that one of 'servants was being blamed for it.' She put her hand over her mouth and paused as she took a breath.

'We–' She lowered her hand and toyed with the collar of her dress. 'We were right worried that she was being accused of something she mebbe didn't do. Servants get 'blame for all sorts of things – things going missing or getting broken and that, and we said that when it was 'time of 'hearing, whoever had time off would go to 'courtroom and report back to the others. And it was me,' she added in a whisper. 'It was me that was there; and I saw you.' Her last few words were almost inaudible.

Jenny trembled. This was a nightmare that she had always known would come true one day.

'I knew I'd never forget you,' Dolly went on. 'You looked so young and frightened, and I said to 'other maids that I thought mebbe he'd taken advantage of you and that was why you were leaving; though I couldn't work out why he had a gun. We were pleased,' she said, 'when you were acquitted, but we talked of what would become of you, and who would give you another position with that hanging over you.'

She said apologetically, 'I'd forgotten all about you until the day I first saw you at Lavender Cott as Mr Stephen's wife, but I recognized you straight away. You've hardly changed at all. Nobody else knows,' she hastened to add. 'I've never told Cook or anybody.'

Jenny slowly nodded her head. 'Good,' she whispered, her voice suddenly hoarse. 'Good. Because – because not everyone would understand that it was – it was a terrible accident.' She wondered how Dolly could have kept such information to herself. It seemed incredible that she had. But it was a long time ago, and maybe people from the Wolds wouldn't have been interested in old gossip from Beverley. She was also comforted to think that there had been people, servants, who hadn't known her, but had been sympathetic towards her. 'I've tried to make another life, Dolly,' she said. 'I've tried to forget what happened.'

'And now you're going back there, ma'am. I think you're very brave, though mebbe folks won't remember.'

'Let's hope not,' Jenny said huskily, thinking that if Dolly had, then so would others. She rose from her chair and effectively dismissed the subject, though she felt churned up and anxious. 'Let's hope it's been forgotten. Just a seven-day wonder.'

They were to be married in St Mary's church, in Beverley. Billy had asked her if she would, and reluctantly she had agreed. 'It means a lot to me,' he said. 'Folks don't believe that 'bachelor Billy Brown is to be married at last.'

Christina, too, had begged her to leave for the church from her house. 'Please do, Mama,' she wrote. 'I have something important to say to you and I want to tell you before your wedding.'

What? Jenny wondered. What has she to tell me that she can't say in a letter? Has she found out that I once worked in her house as a kitchen maid? Has she discovered how her father died? I should have told her! Should have warned her! Jenny paced to and fro in her room with the letter held in her hand, unheeding of the jobs she needed to organize, unaware of the warm sun shining in at the window, or smell of autumn wood smoke drifting in the light breeze. Will she turn against me? Or is it something else? Has she happy news to impart?

A light knock came on the door and Serena put her head inside. 'I've come to help you, Mama,' she said brightly.

'Help me?' Jenny asked bleakly. 'With what?'

'Your packing, of course.' Serena brought out boxes from behind her back. 'I've bought you something for your trousseau. I went shopping in Geneva. There are some wonderful shops there,' she said dreamily, 'so this is what I bought.'

She opened one of the boxes and unwrapped layers of soft white paper. 'You've never bought anything pretty for yourself, so I asked Grandpa for some extra pocket money. I told him I needed some more books,' she added blithely, and grinned at her mother's shocked expression. 'No, I didn't.' She laughed. 'I told him I wanted to buy you a wedding present. There!' She held up a white silk garment whose hem was edged with lace. 'It's a bed gown,' she said softly. 'Isn't it enchanting?'

Jenny was speechless. The gown was far too lovely to wear in bed.

'And look.' Serena held up another gown in the same white silk, only open at the front with silk ribbons to fasten it. 'It's a *peignoir*,' she explained, seeing the blankness on her mother's face. 'You wear it before dressing. Whilst you're brushing your hair and creaming your face and such,' she added.

'But – Serena!' Jenny found her voice. 'I'm to be a butcher's wife! They're much too grand for me.'

Serena came across to her and kissed her cheek. 'No, they're not,' she whispered. 'You deserve it. And Mr Brown will be delighted, I'm sure.'

'Serena!' Jenny was shocked. What else had her daughter learnt in Switzerland?

There were other treasures in the box. Two pairs of white silk stockings, and lacy under-garments, the like of which Jenny had never seen. Then, carefully opening another box, Serena brought out a delightful concoction of a hat. It was fashioned from grey silk with a silver thread running through it, with a half-veil.

'I – I was going to wear a bonnet,' Jenny stammered. 'I bought a new one.' With a large brim to shield my face, she thought.

'I know.' Serena smiled. 'Christina and I have

been in correspondence about your trousseau and she told me the colour of your gown and so I bought the hat to complement it. Try it on. Oh, Mama! Don't cry. Did I do wrong?'

Jenny shook her head, too overcome to speak, and tears ran down her checks. 'I – I don't deserve this,' she eventually faltered.

'Of course you do!' Serena had somehow become mature and wise. 'We're going to make sure this is the best day of your life.'

Jenny wiped her eyes and blew her nose. 'The best days, my darling,' she mumbled, 'were when I had all of you.'

'And you have given up your days ever since, Mama, to making all of us happy,' Serena said softly. 'Now it's your turn.'

CHAPTER FORTY-EIGHT

Jenny was brought by carriage to Christina and Charles's house in New Walk on the morning before her wedding was due to take place. Serena, Thomas and William were coming with their grandfather and Arabella the next morning. There had been no word yet from Johnny. Jenny had barely slept the night before for worrying as to whether she was doing right by Billy.

Christina looked radiant and ushered her into the sitting room, asking one of the maids to take her mother's luggage upstairs. 'Mr and Mrs Esmond are staying at the Beverley Arms,' she said. 'Charles asked them to as we shall be full up here when everyone arrives. Besides,' she said with a giggle, 'Mrs Esmond would have reorganized the whole wedding if she'd been here.'

'She means well, I expect,' Jenny said nervously.

'Oh, she does!' Christina agreed. 'But Charles and I have hatched a plan.'

Jenny felt a tinge of relief; from Christina's demeanour and chatter, whatever she wanted to tell her wasn't anything she had learnt about Christy.

'We're going to live at Lavender Cott!' she said gleefully. 'That's where Charles is now. He's arranging to have workmen in to paint and do repairs and get it ready for us.'

'But I thought he was looking forward to living in Beverley?' Jenny said. 'For the horse racing and riding on 'Westwood?'

'Well, so he was,' Christina said a trifle ruefully. 'But his mother is always here, so he's told her that she can live in this house until she finds something else to suit her. It's also rather large for us, for the moment,' she added, lowering her eyes. 'And Charles says that his mother won't stay long, anyway, she'll want to be off elsewhere, and so we can come back if we want to. It will be so lovely to go back to Lavender Cott,' she said earnestly. 'And I'll be able to look after Papa's grave. He won't be lonely if I'm living nearby.'

Jenny felt a sudden surge of emotion. It was Stephen, in Christina's eyes, who had always been her beloved father, not the unknown man who had sired her. 'Yes, he'd be happy to know that you're there,' she murmured. 'He loved you very much.'

Christina wiped away a sudden tear. 'Yes, I know.' Then she gave a watery smile. 'But there's something else, Mama. Something I want you to know, though Charles and I agreed we wouldn't tell anyone else just yet.'

A warmth spread through Jenny as she waited for the news that she had already guessed. She smiled at Christina and raised her eyebrows. 'Tell me then. Don't keep me in suspense.'

'I'm going to have a baby,' Christina said softly. 'And I'm going to have it at Lavender Cott. In the same place as I was born!'

Jenny again lay sleepless that night in the first floor guest bedroom. She should have been happy, and she was for Christina, but not for herself on the eve of her wedding. She cast her eyes round the dimly lit bedroom. It looked different from when she knew it, when she used to open the curtains, sweep the hearth or change the bed linen. Christina's taste in furnishing was unlike Mrs Ingram's. It was lighter, more colourful. Where did they go, she wondered, Mr and Mrs Ingram? Did they leave the district? Had Mrs Ingram been back to see who was living in her old home? Suppose she turned up at the church tomorrow and interrupted the proceedings, giving vent to her hatred of the woman she blamed for her son's death?

Wearily Jenny rose from the bed and stood by the window. A full moon, its brightness shrouded by scurrying silver-tipped clouds, showed pockets of mist in the garden below and tinged the trees in New Walk with soft fingers of light.

She took a deep breath. Her heart was hammering and she sat on the edge of the bed. I can't go through with it! But what am I to do? It wouldn't be fair to Billy to leave him standing at the altar. That would be so humiliating for him, and he's a good man, a lovely, kind, faithful man who deserves someone better than me. She got up again and paced the floor; she felt hot and then cold. I do love him. I love him for who he is and because he's waited all these years for me. He's been constant; convinced, I suppose, that one day I would come back to Beverley and we'd be together as man and wife. She gave a little smile. It never crossed his mind that I would ever have married anyone else, or stayed away so long.

She hugged her arms round herself and gave a sigh, then looked at the clock ticking on the side table. Half past one and I haven't slept a wink. Another five hours before the maids go down, unless 'kitchen maid starts earlier as I used to do. She mentally reminisced. Raking 'kitchen range, filling it with coal and putting 'kettle over 'fire ready for Cook when she came down. She'd be fair spitting if it wasn't on 'boil for her first cup of tea.

She shivered. And then there was Christy. He would come in, sneak in more like, wanting a piece of cake or a cup of chocolate. How we all spoiled him. Gave in to his demands. He could be so demanding sometimes and he always got his own way. Well – she took a short gasping breath – not every time. Just that one time when he didn't. She put her head down and wept, her shoulders shaking. I shouldn't – shouldn't have come back here. It's all too painful and I can't go on. God forgive me. Billy forgive me, but I can't do this to you.

She started to dress, her hands shaking violently as she tried to fasten buttons and lace up her boots. She reached for her travelling cloak which was hanging behind the door and put it on, pulling the hood over her head, and then quietly opened the door onto the corridor. The only sound was the tick of the grandfather clock in the hall downstairs. That was a new sound to the house. Charles had brought the clock with him from his family home. She crept silently downstairs and into the hall, glancing towards the darkened servants' stairs.

The door to the library was partly open and she pushed it wider with her foot and gave a nervous glance inside. Charles had made this room his own and lined the walls with bookshelves, which were already overflowing with books. Comfortable old chairs and Charles's new desk replaced Mr Ingram's desk and leather chair, and as she gazed, the moon's light filtering in through the window showed a different room from the one she remembered. But does Christy's shade still sit here in his father's chair? She stood rooted to the spot just as she had all those years ago when Mr Ingram had prised the gun from her fingers.

There was nothing of Christy's clamorous spirit, no sign of his merriment or laughter, nothing of his burning intensity which had almost consumed her. Her eyes searched the shadowed room. 'Do you know, Christy?' she whispered.

'Do you know that the child we created, the child you wanted to destroy, is herself expecting a child?' She listened but heard only a faint echo of his words. *Did you say your prayers, Jenny kitchen-maid?* 'I've prayed since, Christy,' she said hoarsely. 'Time and time again. Asking for forgiveness. Just as we did on that morning.' There was no answering response, only her own remorse hammering in her head.

She backed away and closed the door on the past. Now I must look to the future, Billy's as well as mine, and make amends.

The bolt on the front door creaked slightly as she pulled it back and she stood stock-still, listening; then she turned the iron key and grasping the knob opened the door, stepped outside and closed it behind her. It was quite dark, the moon hidden again behind the cloud, and she was glad of it as she scurried down the path, keeping within the shelter of the laurel hedge, and into the road.

The road surface was rough and she trod carefully so as not to trip or cockle over. The chestnut trees had shed a few crisp leaves which crackled beneath her boots, but their branches hid her from any wide-awake eyes which might be looking out from the windows of the few houses, or, worse, any prison guards who might be taking a night-time stroll in the grounds of the Sessions House across on the other side.

She gathered her cloak about her as she hurried towards the North Bar, through the narrow passageway into the cobbled North Bar Within, past St Mary's where she was due to make her vows the next day, past the shops, the chemist and the glover, and into Saturday Market, breathing a relieved sigh that there were no rowdy revellers departing the many inns and beer houses in the town. Most had closed their doors, although some still had a light in their windows.

Billy will be there, above the shop. She looked up at the dark window above the butcher's. That's where he's living, until– I'll throw a pebble up at the glass. But he'll be asleep; the thought came suddenly to her. Everyone is, except for me. She glanced across to the Market Cross, or that drunken fellow muttering beneath the columns. But maybe Billy can't sleep either, maybe he's thinking of tomorrow.

There was no light above the shop and she remembered that the room at the front was his living room. He'll sleep at the back, she thought, and after a moment's hesitation hurried down the dark passageway between the butcher's and the seed merchant next door. There wasn't a light there either, but she threw a pebble at the window anyway and waited a moment before throwing another one. Still nothing, no face at the window, no lighted candle or lamp from within.

She shuddered, feeling cold and anxious. Is he out enjoying his last night of freedom with his friends? Will he be with Harry and Mrs Johnson? Harry was to stand as Billy's groomsman at the ceremony tomorrow. She took a sudden breath. Will he be at the house? The house he bought for me and has never lived in! Instinctively she knew that that was where he would be, and her cloak swirled as she turned swiftly and cut into

Lairgate, down the long stretch of Newbegin and across in the direction of Union Road.

Her breath caught in her throat as she hurried, conscious of the passing time as she heard the chime of two o'clock as she ran. If he's not there! If he's not there! What will I do? She tripped once, hurting her foot and having to stop a moment until the searing pain subsided, then she made haste once again, turning at last into the lane of terraced houses where she could make her home if she so wished.

'He's still up,' she gasped, her heart hammering. He hasn't gone to bed. Through the window, which was only half covered by the blind, was flickering firelight and as she approached, craning her neck to see within, she saw Billy. He was sitting by the fire, leaning towards it with his elbows on his knees, gazing into the flames.

Jenny glanced around. The windows of the other houses were shrouded in darkness; an owl hooted and a dog barked in response, but there was no other sound in the silent lane. She pulled her hood further over her face and crept towards the door, searching for the bell pull, but finding none gave a soft tap on the wood. She stepped to the side of the doorway to look through the window, but Billy was still sitting there, unaware of her. She tapped on the glass and saw him lift his head. She knocked again on the door, louder this time, and saw him rise from his chair and come to the window.

She kept her back to the street and let Billy see her face, and saw the consternation on his, then he disappeared from her view until he appeared at the door, unfastening the chain, drawing back the bolt and turning the key.

'Jenny! What's up? Come in.' He sounded anxious. 'Has something happened?'

She stood in the hallway. 'Will you close 'blind before I come in, Billy? Anybody can see right in.'

He didn't question why but only nodded and went into the sitting room, then came out again. He put out his hand to draw her into the room. 'There'll be nobody about at this time of night. It's a quiet neighbourhood. And no-one would recognize you dressed like that.' He gazed at her. 'You haven't changed your mind, Jenny?'

'No.' She hesitated for only a second. 'No. But I'm offering you 'chance to change yours.'

'I won't,' he said decisively and took hold of her hands again and led her towards the fire. 'Here, warm yourself. You're cold.'

'I'm not. I'm warm. I've run. I went to Saturday Market. To the shop,' she said needlessly. 'I thought you'd be there.'

'I would have been, but I decided to come here and light a fire, and get it ready for tomorrow. Then it got late and I've just been sitting, thinking.'

Jenny gazed at him. His sleeves were rolled up to his elbows and his shirt was unbuttoned at the neck and she saw the dark wispy curls just below his collarbone. His hair was tousled as if he'd been running his fingers through it. He looked boyish and appealing and a sudden sob shook her as she thought of what she was losing.

'What is it, Jenny?' he said softly. 'What's troubling you?'

'I had to come, Billy,' she began, her voice uncertain. 'I've wanted to tell you before. That day when we went into Hull, I was going to tell you then, but we went to see my ma and da, and there didn't seem to be another opportunity and suddenly–' She glanced around the room; on a small table there were fresh flowers, roses and lilies, in a vase. All this could have been mine. 'Suddenly,' she continued, 'our wedding day was approaching and I seemed to be bowled along in all 'preparation without trying to put a stop to it.' He bought this house for me, she thought. It would have been my very own, to do with what I wished; to put up my own curtains, choose my own chairs and know that they were mine, and hadn't ever belonged to anyone else.

'Why would you put a stop to it?' Billy's quiet voice seemed to come from far away. 'What reason? Unless you don't love me or don't want to spend 'rest of your life with me. I won't ever let you down, Jenny,' he appealed. 'I've loved you since you were a young girl. I'm not going to stop now.'

She sank down into a chair and stared into the embers of the fire. 'It's because I love you,' she said slowly and huskily. 'It's because I now know that I love you, that I have to tell you.'

His face creased into a smile. 'I've waited and waited to hear you say that, Jenny. I can't tell you how happy that makes me, just to hear those words from your own lips.' His eyes searched her face. 'And it doesn't matter what else you tell me, it won't make any difference.' He knelt beside her. 'So tell me. Tell me what brought you out in

494

'middle of 'night. What's so important that it couldn't wait until tomorrow when as man and wife we can disclose our secrets to each other?'

She stroked his cheek and felt the day's bristles beneath her fingers. He would need to use the blade in the morning. 'Dear Billy,' she whispered. 'You deserve a good woman to love you.'

He caught hold of her hand and gently kissed her fingers, and she noticed his short, scrubbed-clean nails. 'And tomorrow I shall have one,' he murmured. 'I've waited so long, and tomorrow, tomorrow...'

She steeled herself. It would be so easy to get swept up by emotion, to forget what it was she had come for.

'Billy,' she whispered. 'I have to tell you.' The words stuck in her throat but she had to say them. 'I killed Christy.'

CHAPTER FORTY-NINE

'You were acquitted,' Billy said calmly. 'The magistrates said there was no case to answer. It was an accident!'

'I know what they said,' she answered mechanically. 'But they were mistaken. I killed him.' She swallowed hard and her eyes glazed as she gazed somewhere beyond Billy's shoulder. Somewhere into the past. 'I pressed the trigger and shot him.'

He heaved a deep breath. 'Tell me then. Tell me what happened.'

'I was always attracted to him,' she said in a low flat voice. 'Right from 'start when I first met him that day when he came through 'kitchen door. He was always lively, merry, full of tricks and excitement. He was like a firefly darting about.'

'Unstable,' Billy groused. 'There was summat not quite right in 'top attic. Harry and me allus said so. But yes, I could see that he mesmerized you. He was always seeking your attention, egging you on.'

'Everybody was fond of him,' she muttered. 'Down in 'kitchen anyway. He could soft-soap any of them, and nobody minded. He seemed happiest when he was there with us, though Cook did once warn me that master and servant shouldn't mix. But we did, and he used to meet you and Harry too.' She lifted her eyes to his. 'Even though he knew that his parents wouldn't approve. They're my friends, he used to say to me.' Her words were indistinct, no more than a whisper. 'But he couldn't take you home and introduce you.'

Billy nodded and sighed. 'No, at least that wasn't his fault. That's how society is. But he should have known better,' he said, with a trace of bitterness, 'than to meet you, a young lass in her first job with no experience of life, and butter you up so that you could feel some hope of how things might be. It'd never have worked, Jenny, not his sort and ours. It never does.'

'Sometimes it does, Billy.' She shook her head in denial, thinking of Stephen and Agnes, and then of Stephen and herself, even though acknowledging that they had been separated from society.

'It depends on 'people involved. But you're right; it wouldn't have worked with Christy. He had his head in the clouds. He was full of dreams and ideas and visions, but no practicalities. I always thought,' she said wearily, 'I always thought that I'd be 'sensible one; that I'd look after him, rather than 'other way round. He'd no idea about money or how we'd live if he lost his inheritance.'

Billy got up and took a turn round the room, his hands thrust into his pockets. 'So what happened?' he asked, coming to an abrupt stop in front of her. 'Would he have lost his inheritance if he'd married you?'

'He told his parents there was a woman he wanted to marry.' Her voice was strained as she recalled the past. 'But he wouldn't say who it was. He never named me. His father was very angry with him; he was worried about losing the house, I think, and they needed Christy's help with money. He'd threatened them that he would run away with this woman and leave Beverley.'

'His father was on 'verge of bankruptcy,' Billy interrupted. 'It was all over 'town.'

'Yes.' She nodded. 'Mr Ingram must have been desperate for he said he would have Christy declared of unsound mind and 'legacy rescinded. I don't know if he could have done that, but it was then that Christy began to change.' Jenny shivered and Billy took the poker and raked the fire, putting on more coal.

'Just odd things at first,' she said, 'and I didn't think about them much, not until later, not until– Well, he used to watch me all 'time to see what I was doing and where I was going, and he was

497

always asking me to be careful and to listen to what 'other servants were saying. He said they were reporting back to his parents, which was nonsense, of course. They'd never have done that.'

Now Jenny got up from her chair and started pacing the floor. 'He told me he had a plan. He'd worked out how we could always be together, but he wouldn't tell me what it was. He said I might confide in one of the other maids and then if it got out we'd both be locked away. I was getting nervous by then. He seemed agitated, his eyes were always darting about as if he was looking in all 'corners of the house, and he was always saying hush and putting his finger to his lips.'

Her pacing increased and Billy put out his hand to slow her down, but she brushed it away and kept on walking. 'Then he locked himself in his room and wouldn't come out or allow anyone in.' She put her hand to her chest and took several deep breaths. 'Down in 'kitchen, Mrs Judson and Cook were always muttering together but they'd stop when any of 'maids came in, except Mrs Judson used to look at me sometimes, almost as if she knew that something was going on between Christy and me.

'Then Mrs Ingram called me and said I had to take some food up to his room. It had to be me, she said, Christy had asked especially. Why you? she said, and had a really suspicious stare. Why has he asked for you? I told her I didn't know, which was my first lie.'

Jenny's face worked in anguish and she pressed her fingers to her lips to stop them trembling. 'When I went up, he was in a dreadful state! His face was white and his eyes were wild. He grabbed hold of me and gabbled that he was almost ready, that he'd worked out what we should do. I said to him that I'd something to tell him.' She ran her tongue round her dry mouth and took another deep breath. 'Something that I was almost sure about, and that it would make a difference to our life together. But he didn't want to know, he wasn't listening.'

She stopped pacing and put her hands over her face. 'It was so important to me.' Her voice broke. 'But he didn't want to know!' She stared at Billy without seeing him. 'He said that whatever it was, it didn't matter, that he had his plan all worked out and he'd tell me what to do in just a few days. I was really frightened! He seemed to be in another world, mumbling to himself, and then – and then he made me promise that I'd love him for ever until death, and it was 'way that he said it that made me wonder if he wasn't going out of his mind. But I did promise,' she sobbed. 'Even though I was having some doubts.'

'Jenny!' Billy implored. 'There's no need for all of this.' He came to her and put his arms round her. 'That's over. You loved him then and now he's gone. It's finished. You've had another life since then!'

She gazed at him, her lips apart. 'I haven't finished,' she whispered, her voice cracking. 'There's more!' She moved his arms and stepped away from him, turning her back. 'The morning when he said we'd be ready to leave, I gathered all my things and went downstairs. I'd already made up my mind that I couldn't stay in 'household any longer, and that I'd write a note to leave on Mr Ingram's desk if I didn't agree with Christy's plan, telling him that I was ill and had to go home. So that part that I told 'magistrates was true. But what happened next, I didn't tell them. Couldn't tell them.'

She started to pace again, her movements becoming faster, her cloak swirling. 'He wanted us to commit suicide.'

'What?' Billy's startled gasp stopped her and she stared at him.

'Christy – he wanted a suicide pact! So that we could always be together in death! I was speechless for a moment, and then I told him. Told him my secret: that I was expecting a baby. His baby. He looked bewildered and frowned as if he didn't understand. I don't want to die, Christy, I said. I have a child inside me. Our child.

'You're ruining my plan, he said, and he was angry with me. We don't want anyone else, he said. Why are you having a child? We don't want a child. It would get in the way. Then he puckered up his face as if he was thinking, his eyebrows beetling together. Will it die if you die? he asked, and I said of course it would, but that I didn't want to die anyway, child or not, and that it would be a sin.

'Well, we're going to, he said. I've planned it and I'm not changing my mind now. And then he took 'gun out of the cabinet.'

Jenny started to breathe fast and she held on to the back of a chair and screwed her eyes up tight. Billy stood motionless, staring at her. 'Then,' she exhaled, her words coming out on a swift breath, 'he said – he said, come here, Jenny, and his voice was really cold and steady. I've told you what we're going to do. He reached out and pulled me onto his knee, and I said that it would be murder if he killed me and my baby.'

As she opened her eyes, tears ran unchecked down her face. 'He seemed startled at that, but then his eyes narrowed and turned cunning and he said that no-one else would know; only we two would know about it. As far as anyone else was concerned it would be considered suicide. I said, but I don't want to die, Christy, I've so much to live for, and I knew as I said it that my life couldn't include Christy any more.'

Her voice dropped. 'I thought that I still loved him until that moment. Then he said, no, I've decided, Jenny. This is what we're going to do. I can't have my plans upset in this way; and he put his head close to mine and lifted the gun and said that 'bullet would go through both of us. I was terrified and I knew that it wouldn't, that one of us would be horribly injured. Wait, I said, I'm not ready, and I jumped off his knee. I pleaded with him that we could have a life together, even though I knew now that we couldn't. But he still wouldn't listen to what I was saying. Finally, he – he grasped my wrist and put the gun in my hand and said – he smiled as he said it – that if it made me feel better I could pull 'trigger to make sure we both died at 'same time.'

Billy breathed in a hard breath and pressed his hand over his mouth.

'So I took it,' she whispered in an anguished voice. 'But instead of putting it against our heads

I pointed it at Christy's heart and fired.'

Her face was wet with tears and her whole body shook. 'I was so frightened! I didn't want to die, Billy! I wanted to live; to hold my baby in my arms, even if it meant living in poverty or 'workhouse. I wanted it!'

'Ssh. Ssh.' In one long stride Billy was by her side, holding her fast as she wept uncontrollably.

'And – and although I've felt s-sorrow for what happened to Christy, I've never regretted what I did, and when I see – when I see Chr-Christina, I know that I did right.' She lifted her head. 'But don't you see, Billy,' she sobbed, 'I've been living a lie all these years; pretending even to myself that I had this great love for Christy, when really I hated him for what he made me do. He turned me into a murderer!'

Billy drew her towards a chair and sat down, cradling her, his arms round her, gently rocking her as if she was a child, dropping soft kisses on the top of her head as he soothed her, murmuring soft words of comfort.

'And so,' she wept, 'that's why I had to tell you, that's why I was racked with guilt, and I couldn't let you go into a marriage with me without telling you.'

'Did you tell Stephen Laslett?' he asked. 'Did he know?'

'No!' she whispered. 'He knew that I'd been accused of murder and had been acquitted, and I told him that Christy wanted us to commit suicide and that his death was an accident. He never really questioned me about it; he was a recluse in a way,

502

not one for gossip, which suited me. But,' she wiped her reddened eyes with her fingers, 'that was a marriage of convenience at first. He wanted children so he could claim his father's estate back.'

'These fathers,' Billy said disapprovingly, 'making stipulations.' He held her at arm's length and gazed at her. 'Will I be 'same, I wonder?'

'And coming back to Beverley,' she continued, as if she didn't hear or understand his comment. 'I couldn't face going into church to say my vows without telling you; knowing what I'd done, and wondering if Christy's parents had heard I was back here, and that their son's daughter was living in their old home.'

'They're dead,' Billy said quietly. 'Didn't you know? Mrs Ingram took her own life and Mr Ingram died a few years later.'

She felt she would collapse at his words. She was washed out with emotion and guilt and clung to him. 'Two deaths, then,' she wept. 'I'm responsible for Christy's mother too. She must have felt so bereft at losing him!'

'No!' Billy said firmly. 'It was 'bankruptcy. She left a letter to her husband saying she couldn't stand 'shame, that she could never hold her head up again. The letter was read out at 'inquest. There was no mention of Christy. And Mr Ingram died of influenza at his daughter's house a couple of years back. She married well after all, in spite of 'gossip, and lives in London.

'It's over, Jenny,' he insisted. 'You can rest your mind. You were protecting yourself and your child. Christy was the murderer, or he would have been if he'd had his way. It's finished. There are no demons chasing you any more. They've gone!'

She looked at him, feeling weak and ill, and put her head on his shoulder. 'I won't hold you to it, Billy,' she muttered, her throat and head aching with crying. 'If you want to change your mind, I'll understand. You've your reputation and your business to consider. And your mother – what would she think if she knew?'

'She's not likely to find out,' he assured her, 'and besides, she likes you. Always did. When you were in prison she was always saying that poor bairn, and asking me if I'd been to see you.'

'Did she?' she breathed in disbelief, and suddenly thought of Dolly and the other servants who had attended the hearing. Perhaps, after all, people made their own judgements on others, rightly or wrongly.

'And as for my business,' he said, 'I'm a good butcher; folks come to me because of that, no other reason. I'm going to shut 'shop in Saturday Market,' he added. 'Ma says she'll retire when we get wed and so I'll just run the one in Toll Gavel and 'two in Hull. Though I've been thinking of opening one in Driffield.' He hugged her closer. 'What do you think?'

She drew away from him and stared disbelievingly at him. 'I don't understand you, Billy.' She gave a dry swallow. 'I've just told you something which has troubled and distressed me for eighteen years. And you ask my opinion on whether you should open another shop!'

'Aye,' he said quietly. 'It might seem trivial and of no consequence after what you've been through; but it's what matters now. What's done is done and we must put all of what you've told me behind us.'

Us, she noticed. He said us. Not just behind *me*, but behind *us*.

'Besides.' Billy drew a deep breath. 'I think I've always known; guessed anyway.'

'Known? Known what?' She was incredulous. 'Not about what happened. You can't have!'

He nodded. 'I know you so well, Jenny! You can't care for somebody as long as I've cared for you, without knowing every single thing about them.' He gently touched her cheek. 'The way you lift your eyebrows, or wrinkle your nose when you're going to sneeze, the way your eyes crinkle at 'corners when you laugh, and 'way your mouth droops when you're unhappy or worried about something.

'I watched you at 'magistrates court when you stood in 'dock and I knew there was something not right; I saw you cross your arms across your belly, like a shield,' he added, 'and – you had a catch in your voice when you were answering questions, and then–' He paused. ''Magistrate asked if you'd had any admirers – followers – and you looked across at me–'

Jenny nodded. She had. She remembered quite clearly.

'You looked at me and said just the one, sir, and – and I felt proud that you trusted me enough to say that, and I knew that what you were saying was important and that it mattered. I would have stood in that dock for you, Jenny,' he said softly, 'if you'd only asked me.'

The town clocks were striking four. Darkness was lifting, the mist drifting away and the light of the moon fading as Billy walked her back to the house in New Walk. She wouldn't let him take the trap, as she didn't want to disturb anyone in the house by the clatter of hooves. Another couple of hours and the servants would be stirring. She had just time to climb back into bed; and she was so tired, so worn out with the telling.

They stood in the shadows and he kissed her, before she slipped along the path to the door. She turned and he was watching and lifted his hand. He could still change his mind, she thought as he left for his walk home. I wouldn't blame him if he did. And I, do I feel confident enough to go through with it? Or more to the point, am I brave enough?

She put her hand on the door and it yielded at her touch. Mrs Judson was there in her night-robe, her greying hair hanging loose beneath her bed cap and a guttering candle in her hand.

'I was worried about you, Mrs Laslett,' she said in a low voice. 'I heard you go out. I hoped you weren't going to do anything foolish.'

'I've been to see Billy,' Jenny answered quietly.

Mrs Judson gave a slight smile, which lifted her gaunt features. 'Mr Brown!' She nodded. 'He was always a nice lad. We always said, Cook and me, that he would do nicely for you if you could only see it.' She held up the candle to light the way to the stairs. 'You'll be all right with him, Jenny,' she murmured. 'He's waited a long time.'

CHAPTER FIFTY

The bells pealed joyously and a large crowd of onlookers were gathered outside the church of St Mary's to watch Billy Brown the butcher arrive for his wedding.

'Never thought he'd get wed!' a woman with two children at her skirts remarked.

'He's Beverley's last eligible bachelor,' a young woman moaned. 'There's not a single other worth having. Course, rumour was put about that he'd marry Annie Fisher eventually.'

'Aye, put about by her,' someone else cackled. 'I'd heard he's been waiting for this young widow for years.'

Across the road at the Beverley Arms, servant girls hung out of the windows, keen to take a look at the woman who had stolen the heart of the butcher, though they'd get a better look at her when the couple and their guests came in for the wedding breakfast. Mrs Esmond, one of their new residents, had told them about her daughter-in-law's widowed mother, who lived on a large country estate somewhere near Driffield. 'She'll be a good catch, I expect!' One of the maids tossed the remark to another leaning out of the next window.

'Of course,' Mrs Esmond had confided to her friend Mrs Johnson on one of their coffee afternoons, 'I know that Mr Brown is trade, but I told dear Christina that it shouldn't matter to her

507

at all; her mother is old enough to make her own decisions about that. My own grandfather was a tea merchant,' she confessed. 'But he only sold quality tea.'

The carriage pulled through the archway of North Bar and a ripple of excitement ran through the expectant crowd. 'She's coming! She's coming!'

Harry Johnson, waiting in the porch, dashed to the gate, saw the approaching beribboned carriage and ran back inside, returning a moment later with Billy.

Jenny looked out as the horses drew to a halt; she saw Billy and her eyes became moist. He looked so splendid, dressed in grey morning suit with a white cravat, a grey top hat, and a white rose in his buttonhole. She saw him take a deep breath and exhale, a wide smile on his face.

'Well, Ma!' Johnny, handsome in his scarlet tunic, sat opposite her in the carriage, next to his grandfather, so as not to crush her gown. He leant towards her. 'Are we going in or do we drive on?'

Johnny had been given special leave of absence from military school and had arrived at Laslett Hall late the previous evening. Although he was too young to give his mother away, she'd insisted that he accompanied her to church in the carriage with John Laslett. The rest of her family had gone on ahead in the carriage in front, with Christina and Charles leading the way in their own conveyance.

She gazed at Johnny now and thought again how much he looked like Stephen. Whatever reason she and Stephen had had for marrying, she had no regrets, none at all, when she looked at all of their children and thought how lucky she was. And they were glad for her, happy that she was making a new life; and she had overheard William telling Dolly that he was very excited about going on holiday with his mother and new father.

Jenny lifted the short veil and drew it back over her hat, revealing her face. Just as well to start now, right from the beginning, she decided; no hiding away any longer.

Johnny smiled at her. 'You're beautiful, Ma,' he said softly. 'Isn't she, Grandpa?'

John Laslett nodded and she was surprised to see tears in his eyes. I do believe he's fond of me after all, she thought.

Johnny sprang down as the groom opened the door and put down the step. He helped his grandfather out and then turned to his mother. Jenny was looking into the crowd who were gathered by the gate. Christina was holding her husband's arm and talking animatedly to Jenny's mother and father and Billy's mother and sister. Thomas and William were gazing wide-eyed at their newly discovered relatives. Serena, elegant and lovely in rose silk, was standing with Pearl and Arabella and some of her cousins. Dr Hill smiled and lifted his top hat when he saw her looking towards him.

Billy's done this, she thought. He's arranged it all, especially for me. She shook out the folds of her silver-threaded gown and stepped out and Billy, disregarding convention, came towards her and took her hand.

'Shall we go to church, Jenny?' he murmured.

She smiled, joy rushing through her. 'Yes, Billy. I think perhaps we should.'

Late that night, wearing her silk peignoir, Jenny sat at the writing table in her bedroom. She had brushed her hair, letting it hang loosely down her back. Billy had gone into the guest room to check that William was asleep, for he was to accompany them to Whitby the next day. It had been Billy's idea to take him. She took out her notebook and picking up a pencil she wrote down the events of the day and her feelings about it.

'What are you doing?' Billy, coming back in, stroked her long dark hair, running his fingers through it. He had undressed and put on a maroon dressing robe.

She looked up at him through the mirror on the wall above her and smiled. 'I've just finished writing about the end of one life.' She glanced down at the words she had written. *I have married Billy, the butcher boy, who has always loved me.*

She turned towards him and put her hands out to him. He drew her up and kissed her tenderly. 'Tomorrow,' she whispered, 'I will write 'beginning of another.'

The publishers hope that this book has given you enjoyable reading. Large Print Books are especially designed to be as easy to see and hold as possible. If you wish a complete list of our books please ask at your local library or write directly to:

Magna Large Print Books
Magna House, Long Preston,
Skipton, North Yorkshire.
BD23 4ND

This Large Print Book for the partially sighted, who cannot read normal print, is published under the auspices of

THE ULVERSCROFT FOUNDATION